FREE MEN and DREAMERS

TWILIGHT'S LAST GLEAMING

OTHER BOOKS AND AUDIO BOOKS
BY L. C. LEWIS:

Unspoken

Free Men and Dreamers, Vol. 1: Dark Sky at Dawn

FREE MEN and DREAMERS

TWILIGHT'S LAST GLEAMING

a novel

L. C. LEWIS

Covenant Communications, Inc.

Covenant.

Cover image: A Frigate off the Eddystone Lighthouse by Henry A. Luscombe.
Private Collection/ © Royal Exchange Art Gallery at Cork Street, London/ The Bridgeman Art Library.

Cover design copyrighted 2008 by Covenant Communications, Inc.

Published by Covenant Communications, Inc.
American Fork, Utah

Printed in Canada
First Printing: May 2008

15 14 13 12 11 10 09 08   10 9 8 7 6 5 4 3 2 1

ISBN 13: 978-1-59811-379-2
ISBN 10: 1-59811-379-8

To my father,
Allen K. Chilcoat,
and his patriot ancestors who
defended America in the War of 1812.

And to my mother,
Bernice G. Freitas Chilcoat,
whose immigrant ancestors
arrived generations later
and served this land with equal valor.

ACKNOWLEDGMENTS

I first have to acknowledge the support of my husband Tom, my patient travel agent and navigator. His investment of love and resources turned a mother with a hobby into an author. Always gentle and encouraging, he takes the stress out of leaving our empty nest to venture on research excursions. We have thoroughly enjoyed discovering America's heritage together.

Thanks to my mom, Bernice Freitas Chilcoat, for becoming an unexpected but able research assistant on this book. Abundant thanks to my children, those by birth and by marriage—Amanda, Nick, Adam, Josh, Tom, and Krista—caring, solid people who make our family a refuge of strength and humor. The courage you have shown in making your own dreams come true has encouraged me immensely. Added thanks go to our Utah children, Tom and Krista, and to Krista's parents, Don and Judy Ekker, for their love and support during the long marketing trips and for making their homes and cars my own whenever I head west. To my grandchildren, Tommy and Keira, you two are my motivation. You and the other little boys and girls are the hope of our nation and world.

I have been blessed with great friends who've added to the accuracy of this book. Dr. Jeffrey L. Fillmore, an excellent ER physician and Renaissance man, was an invaluable resource in helping me keep the medical elements of the book true to the period. Sigrid Rodgers is my Washington, D.C., touring buddy. It is a privilege to explore the nation's capital through her patriotic eyes. Once again, Kay Curtiss has been an invaluable resource, sharing from her own noteworthy library and lending me her expertise into the LDS fiction market. Thanks go to Stephanie Quinn for leading me to the wonderful information on Columbus. I owe special appreciation to Melinda Grenier for proofreading and editing the rough manuscript and to Judi Stull for proofing and hand-holding during editing and cutting pages. Thanks for letting me bounce storylines off you,

Melinda and Judi. To Wally and Kathy Brant I extend my gratitude for making our Virginia research trip such a memorable pleasure.

Many park service people have been instrumental in the writing of this book. My gratitude goes first to Mr. Scott Sheads, curator of Fort McHenry and the Star-Spangled Banner exhibit at the Smithsonian Museum, for sitting down with me and personalizing the people and events of Fort McHenry's history, and for separating the history from the folk stories regarding the real Star Spangled Banner story. I hope I will do the truth justice as I illustrate those events in the next volume. Thank you also to the kind docents at the Hampton Visitors' Center for helping me locate such important sites as the British landing point at Celey's Plantation and Little England Farm, and to the lovely docents at the Mount Vernon Ladies Association for providing data on the father of our country from their new facility, the Donald W. Reynolds Museum and Education Center. Lastly, my sincere appreciation goes to the National Park Service Library in Denver, Colorado, and their patient specialists who replied to an e-mailed request, supplying me with access to historical documents that were invaluable in corroborating my facts.

Continued thanks to Angela Eschler, my brilliant first editor at Covenant, who signed on to help with this project as well. She has been my cheerleader (or psychological counselor), and friend. Thanks also to Robby in marketing for his continued and caring support, and to Melissa Dalton, April Hiatt, and Rachel Langlois, who patiently held my hand and nudged me forward as I promoted *Dark Sky at Dawn*. Thanks also to my current editor, Kirk Shaw, for his generosity and confidence while preparing *Twilight's Last Gleaming*, and Kathy Jenkins, managing editor, who continues to carry the banner. Great thanks are owed to Heather Wiscombe for both the gorgeous cover design and for her detailed work on the historical maps; as well as to Ryan Browning, a good friend who developed my beautiful website, www.laurielclewis.com. I hope you'll visit it and see his work.

To you, the reader, thank you for trusting me on this journey to the past.

THE AMERICANS

Residing at the Willows Plantation along the Patuxent River in Maryland
JONATHAN EDWARD PEARSON III, or Jed, the twenty-two-year-old owner of
the plantation and lieutenant in the Maryland Militia.
FRANNIE PEARSON, his twenty-year-old sister and a musical entertainer.
MARKUS O'MALLEY, the twenty-four-year-old Irish foreman of the Willows.
BITTY, the former slave, age thirty-six, who raised Jed and Frannie.
JACK, age forty, Bitty's freed brother and Jed's best friend.
ABEL, late thirties, Bitty's husband and a man set free by Jed.
JEROME and SARAH, Abel's parents.
CALEB, ELI, GRANDY, and HELEN are Abel's children and Bitty's stepchildren.
ROYAL and MERCY, married slave couple.
CAPTAIN ANDREW ROBERTSON, twenty-four-year-old career officer in the
military, currently engaged to Hannah Stansbury.
SAMUEL RENFRO, Baltimore medical student and friend of Jed Pearson and
Timothy Shepard.
TIMOTHY SHEPARD, college chum of Jed Pearson and former beau of
Frannie, currently on loan from his position in Senator Gregg's office
so he can serve as Mrs. Madison's aide.

Residing at White Oak Plantation, the neighboring farm
STEWART STRINGHAM, the master of the plantation.
MRS. STRINGHAM, Stewart's wife.
FREDERICK STRINGHAM, Stewart's recently crippled son and former beau of
Frannie Pearson.
PENELOPE STRINGHAM, Frederick's wife.
PRISCILLA, White Oak slave and sister to Bitty and Jack.
SEBASTIAN DUPREE, Creole freedman and former pawn of a British entre-
preneur who was sent to conquer the Willows. He is now a British spy
and guide.

The Stansbury Family of Coolfont Manor
BERNARD AND SUSANNAH, parents of Beatrice Snowden, Myrna
Baumgardner, and Hannah.
BEATRICE STANSBURY SNOWDEN, oldest Stansbury daughter and wife of
Captain Dudley Snowden, prisoner of war.
MYRNA STANSBURY BAUMGARDNER, middle Stansbury daughter and wife of
Harvey Baumgardner.

HANNAH STANSBURY, eighteen, in love with Jed Pearson but engaged to Captain Andrew Robertson.

CAPTAIN DUDLEY SNOWDEN, husband of Beatrice Stansbury Snowden, American military officer captured at the surrender of Fort Detroit and currently imprisoned in Lachine, Quebec.

The O'Malleys of Hampton, Virginia

RYAN, uncle to Markus and father of Patrick.

PATRICK, Markus's cousin.

DRUSILLA, Patrick's wife

LYRA HARKIN, blind friend of Drusilla who has come to help out during her pregnancy.

THE BRITISH

The household of the Earl of Whittington
LORD EVERETT, the Earl of Whittington and member of the House of Lords.
VISCOUNT DANIEL WHITTINGTON, eleven-year-old son of the earl.
CLARISSA, Daniel's nanny and a commoner.

The Ramseys of London, England
STEPHEN RAMSEY, wealthy entrepreneur.
ARTHUR RAMSEY, Stephen's son, a former divinity student who enlisted in the British Army.
FELICITY RAMSEY, estranged wife of Stephen.

The McGowans of London
TREVOR MCGOWAN, an ex-con who once served time in a Barbados prison with Sebastian Dupree.
MRS. MCGOWAN, wife of Trevor.

Note: Please see the end of the book to review the significance of the historical persons that are discussed or with whom characters interact.

PROLOGUE

November 1812
White Oak Plantation, Maryland

Just as he did every day, Stewart Stringham glanced at the threshold of his front door for the sign. Today a charred willow branch lay there, and he knew the time had arrived.

"It pleases me to know that you've suffered while waiting for my return . . ."

Stringham's eyes darted left in the direction of Dupree's elegant Creole lilt as the maddening cramp of disgust returned to his gut. A moment later, the chiseled leer of his tormentor appeared around the corner of Stewart's grand White Oak mansion.

"In fact, knowing that the master and ruler of White Oak Plantation cowers before me is sweet indeed. And how is that sniveling son of yours?"

His jaw clamped in fury, Stringham longed to feel Dupree's throat crushed between his hands, but he held his control and looked away. His gaze fell on the dimly lit room of the nearby house that his son Frederick shared with his unloved wife. Stringham growled a reply. "He's still a cripple. Is that what you wanted to hear?"

Dupree shrugged nonchalantly. "The penalty for violating our arrangement."

Without thinking, Stringham took a rage-filled step toward Dupree, and, in an instant, five armed slaves stepped from the bushes, rifles raised at Stewart's head.

"Tell me, Mr. Stringham. How does it feel to be the master of some men of color while having to beg me, a former slave, for your very life?"

At the suggestion that he do so now, Stringham's hands clenched in defiance, and a flash of fury ignited Dupree's face as the ex-slave came close. Stringham could feel the heat of his enemy's breath and smell his expensive aftershave as he jutted his lips near Stringham's ear and snarled in a slow, menacing growl. "Oh, you'll beg me. You'll beg me now . . . or you'll beg me later when I lead the British Navy up this river to your front door—right up to your bed to stand beside you as they torch every blade of grass and every building on White Oak. You'll beg me for mercy as they drag your wife and son out of their beds and—"

"Stop!" Stringham cried out mournfully. "Stop. All right! I beg you! I beg you . . ." he pleaded as he fell to his knees, clamping his hands over his ears.

Dupree grabbed the lapels of Stringham's jacket and jerked him to his feet. "Do not defy me again! Your son is proof of how intolerant I am when crossed, and tonight the Pearsons and their uppity maid will know as well. They too will beg me for mercy! And then they'll die . . . while White Oak and your family will be spared to watch America smolder."

"Tonight . . . ?"

"Yes. If all goes as planned, tonight is the night."

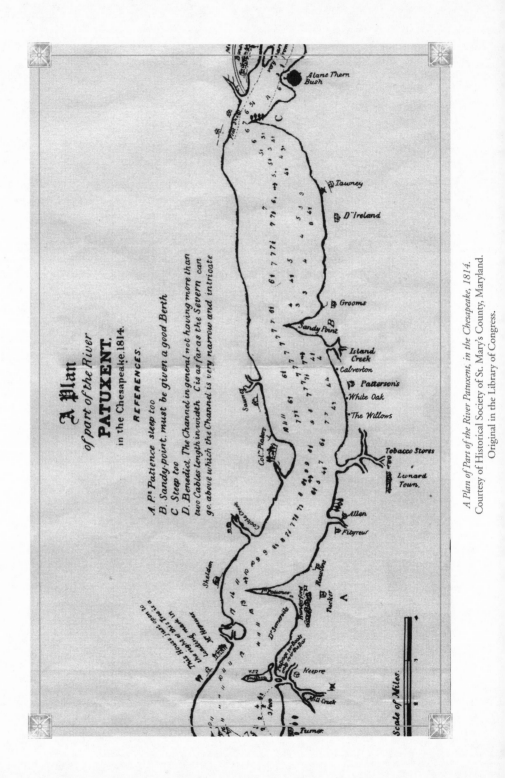

A Plan of Part of the River Patuxent, in the Chesapeake, 1814.
Courtesy of Historical Society of St. Mary's County, Maryland.
Original in the Library of Congress.

CHAPTER 1

November 1812
The Winding Willows Plantation, Maryland

Jonathan Edward Pearson III closed his eyes and drew in the smells of autumn along the Patuxent River. He smiled at the sight of amber light glowing through the trees lining the meadow to the rear of his manor house. Cocking his head, he listened until he could hear the sound of singing drifting along with the campfire smoke.

The families are settling in for the night . . .

A flood of peace ran down his spine, and for a moment he allowed himself to relax his vigil, to simply be a young man, unburdened by the hefty responsibility that weighed upon his young shoulders. At only twenty-two, he again felt the weight of being the owner of the mammoth Winding Willows estate, willed to him at birth by the grandfather whose name he bore.

Making a last scan of the thickets that bordered the river, searching for a flash of British color, he set his rifle down and rolled his neck, releasing the tension that seemed to rise with him each morning and follow him to bed each night.

A second later, a blinding flash of light and the acrid smoke of sulfur burned his eyes, sending him scrambling for cover down the riverbank. His arms thrashed about, searching for the steel barrel of his rifle as he focused to determine the direction of the assault.

"The meadow!" he screamed as he frantically tried to get his footing to reach Bitty, Jack, Jerome, and the others. His fingers clawed the earthen slope that barricaded his progress, and his feet dug deeply to get a foothold. He heard another cannon blast and looked up in time to see his home splinter before his eyes. "Frannie!" he screamed as he gathered every ounce of strength in his muscled body to thrust his tall frame upward. A sting bit his calf and he moaned in pain, clamping his hand over his bloody leg. He tried again to stand as another bullet hit his shoulder, throwing him backwards and leaving him unable to force his limbs to work in concert.

The cannon blasts increased, burying his home—his memories— beneath an ugly layer of debris and rubble. Searing blazes, intended to devour flesh as well as wood, now burned in every corner of the Willows as screams rang out. He cried helplessly as his beautiful world and the people he loved were obliterated before him. He raised his face to the blackness and wailed at the uniformed devils whose red forms began to break across the rise, and then he saw him—Dupree—leading the assault.

In futility, Jed cast a handful of dirt at the red-blazoned hordes running in his direction, and as a musket muzzle bore down upon him, he mournfully cried out to the woman whose absent face haunted every second of his thoughts, filling his final moments. "Hannah!"

His door flew open and the soft scent of a woman pulled him from his nightmare, guiding his sweat-soaked head to a white, silk-covered shoulder. A voice, love-filled and worried, cooed to him.

"Shhh," she whispered. "It's all right now, Jed. It was just a dream. A terrible dream . . ."

The voice was immediately comforting, but it was not the voice he longed for.

"Oh, Frannie," he moaned, concealing his disappointment. "I'm sorry I woke you." He released her and sat upright, combing his trembling hands through his dark, disheveled locks.

Frannie quickly stood, worry evident on her face. "Was it the same dream?"

"The same." Jed grimaced as he stood and pulled his robe on to curb the discussion.

"You can't go on like this . . . you're exhausted, Jed. The Willows spreads too far for you, Markus, and Jack to protect her alone."

He knew she was right, but in his frustration he snapped his reply. "It's not your concern, Francis! I'd prefer you return to Philadelphia to . . . 'Le Jardin de whatever it's called.'"

"You'd like that, wouldn't you?" she said, cinching the tie on her silk wrapper and stomping her foot. "Then you'd have no one to cross you when you become obstinate."

Jed laughed derisively. "I'm sure Bitty would say differently."

"But with a baby of her own on the way, Bitty's attentions have been focused elsewhere. Henri understands my absence, so if and when I return to sing at *Le Jardin des Chanteuses,*" she emphasized, "be assured, brother, it will be on my own terms."

Jed smiled at her arrogance. Surrendering, he squeezed her hands and, letting them fall, turned and walked to the French doors that led to a steep veranda overlooking the moonless lawn. The landscape was dotted with oaks that spread two hundred rods from the Willows' porch to the thickets that marked the river's edge. The horseshoe-shaped lane ran from the river road to the porch and back again and was lined on each side with more oaks, but the view of the river remained unobstructed.

Frannie came and stood beside him, her shorter frame barely reaching his shoulder. She looked up at his piercing dark eyes. "Rich, handsome, kind . . . you should be the most sought-after bachelor in the state. And you could leave us briefly to find a wife, you know."

"Frannie," he scolded softly as he laid his arm across her shoulders. "You're all I have in this world right now."

"We're a tragic pair, aren't we? Do you realize that your sleep has been disturbed ever since the night you gave Bitty and her family their freedom papers?"

"That was also the night our fears about Dupree were confirmed," he reminded her.

"True. But you always suspected that our neighbors would reject our warnings that Admiral Cockburn had hired a mercenary to incite slave revolts and guide the British fleet down the Patuxent. No . . . this unsettledness is different."

"Since you have obviously invested so much thought on the subject, why don't you simply hurry on to the answer and spare us both the agony of argument."

"Fine. Instead of finding joy from presenting Bitty and her family their freedom papers, I think you actually feel more concerned for some reason. I can't explain it, but I've sensed it. You've been particularly concerned since Bitty announced that she and Abel were expecting a child. Am I right?"

Jed drew in a deep breath, and as it escaped him, he seemed to shrink. "She now holds those papers as if they alone change the world, when in fact, nothing is better and perhaps is even worse. Now she has a hope of something so grand I doubt any happiness can possibly meet her expectations." He turned to face his sister, whose worry made her appear older than her own twenty years. "But worse, she sings lullabies about freedom to the babe inside her, and I cringe because his world may be no better than the one that enslaved his parents."

"All the slaves you released understand how precarious our freedoms are right now. They are well educated, Jed. Abel was tutored by his father from birth, and slave or not, we both know Jerome is more educated than most whites. And don't discount Bitty and Jack either. They know the danger, but they also know that today they are free. And Bitty knows that her and Abel's child will be the first free-born American in her line. You gave that to them, Jed, and they are pledged to stand beside you in this fight. So will the others—for the dream of freedom. Don't coddle them like children. You made them equals when you placed the dream within their grasp and solicited their help. Now you must begin to treat them as such."

"You're right," he conceded humbly. "I'll call for a meeting tomorrow, and we'll make new assignments and share the duties more equally."

Frannie moved to secure a quilt, which she laid across her shoulders before returning to the windowed doors. She turned the handle and walked onto the veranda, sitting in one of two chairs there. Jed rolled his eyes, realizing that his sister had not yet finished all she had to say.

"Have you not pried my soul sufficiently for one night? Do you intend to freeze the truth out of me?" He drew his own wrapper more tightly around him and stepped to the railing. When she spoke, the sorrow-filled tone of her voice made the hair rise on his neck.

"You called for her, Jed. That's why I rushed to your side. Your cries broke my heart."

Jed gripped the rail until his hands turned white, avoiding Frannie's eyes as he barked sharply, "Leave it alone, Frannie! Not even you may mention Hannah to me."

Gasping from his rebuke, she muttered, "Forgive me, Jed," as she rose and headed across his room and out the door.

Jed hung his head as fury and sadness swept over him. He would fix things with Frannie in the morning. *How could she possibly understand when he barely did?* He knew he had made the same mistakes with Hannah that he had begun to make with Bitty and the other Willows' slaves, hovering and fretting over her as if she were a child, awakening to the truth when it was nearly too late. He opened and closed his scarred hands, muttering, "Perhaps it already is." After all, he had received but one brief note from Hannah, postmarked in Baltimore just before she and Beatrice had caught a ship north. It had been less a *profession* than a *confession* of love.

He had committed it completely to memory—her admission that circumstances had not allowed her the privacy to end things properly with her fiancé, Lieutenant Robertson, requiring that she sail to New England, still engaged to Jed's rival. Jed's heart sank despite Hannah's assurance that her declaration of love for him had not been made casually. She'd encouraged him to do all in his power to settle the issues that prevented their union, and though she had closed with another assurance of her affection, it was the last word he'd received in two months.

It frustrated him, even angered him at times, that every imaginable requirement of a man should befall him at once—love, honor, conscience, duty, patriotism, family. Each was good, each essential. He knew that, but wished he could divide himself, devoting all that he was to each cause singularly for a time, setting that one thing in its proper order before being called on to devote his limited and precious reserves to another.

Jed rose to stand at the rail again, making one last survey of the land. The November air had chilled him so deeply that his bed again seemed inviting, but as he turned to leave the veranda he heard voices drifting from the river. Glad for the cover of darkness, he stood as still as stone, his every sense heightened and every nerve on alert. As he strained to decode what was being said, a blazing arrow pierced the night sky, rising from the river's edge and landing in one of the oaks on the front lawn. It immediately hit its combustible mark, a dangling mass. Fire quickly engulfed the form, illuminating it, and defining its shape.

Jed squinted in disbelief, unwilling or unable to accept the conclusion his mind had reached. "No!" he screamed.

He ran for his pistol on the nightstand and, taking careful aim, pierced the rope that held the form in midair, dropping it to the ground. "Help!" he wailed from the veranda as the blessed sound of the Willows' bell began pealing from the meadow. *Bless Jerome . . .*

He quickly scrambled down the veranda's railing and dropped heavily to the ground. A searing pain radiated through his ankles and into his shins, momentarily disabling him as he scrambled to reach the burning form lying in the grass fifteen rods in front of him. He was grateful to see Abel appear over the rise from the meadow with Jack following quickly behind.

"Water! Get water!" Jed yelled.

Frannie flew through the front door with a blanket, speeding past Jed's hobbling form to the flames, beating at them while sparks singed her gown and hair. Jed reached her and pushed her aside, attempting to spare her the sight he feared would be revealed when the flames on the ground were extinguished and the human form was illuminated by the flaming tree.

Soon Markus came, hollering in his Irish lilt while throwing a shirt over his muscled shoulders. Bitty, Jerome, and several others who'd appeared wailed pleas to God as Jack and Abel doused the flames that danced upon the body. Once Jed's trembling hands lifted the edge of the charred blanket to identify the remains, he fell back hard against the earth and gasped. "It's an effigy."

"A prank?" asked Jack nervously.

"More likely a warnin'," grunted Markus as he revealed the charred remnants, dressed in a white shirt and blue trousers, with a head made from a stuffed pillow case. Markus's short, strong frame sagged as he raked a trembling hand through his thick, red hair. "Blast the vermin that did this."

Adrenaline drained, Frannie slumped to the ground beside her brother. "Look, Jed," she whispered eerily as she pointed to the charred remains. Pinned to the shoulder, blackened and burned but still identifiable, was the unmistakable shape of a heart. "It's a tin heart, on the same spot where your own heart-shaped birthmark lies. This figure was meant to be you!"

As the crowd gathered around to stare at the heart, Jed pulled Frannie's shaking form close, stealing a nervous glance at Markus and Jack. "It's time for you to return to Philadelphia, Frannie."

"You're not running me off," she argued.

Jed offered her no chance for rebuttal. Leaping to his feet, he pointed at Markus as he stormed toward the house. "I don't care if you have to tie her to a horse. Just get her there!"

"Mr. Jed!" hollered Caleb. Bitty and Abel's oldest was pointing to a figure rapidly exiting the trees.

"It's Royal!" said Bitty, who knew each Willows resident like a hen her chicks.

"Royal?" called Jed as he began running in the direction of the trusted slave. A memory of that now-strange day in the summer of his sixteenth year when he'd purchased Royal, his wife Mercy, and their three children filled Jed's mind. Three more children had since been born on the farm, further endearing the family to Jed.

The entire crowd followed close behind as Jed questioned the man excitedly. "Did you see him, Royal . . . the man who shot the arrow toward the house?"

Royal bent over, presumably to catch his breath. "Yes, suh, Mr. Jed. I seen 'im."

"Did you see his face? Could you identify him if you saw him again?"

"Mebbe . . ." Royal stammered. "I caught sight of 'im in the brush, lightin' up his arrah, and then I followed 'im. He jumped in a boat and rowed . . . up riva' I think. It was so dark."

"Was he wearing a uniform? . . . Was he? For heaven's sake, Royal, give me something!" Jed grilled the shorter man, grabbing him by the shoulders until fear made the Willows resident tremble. "Could you at least tell me if he was white or Negro?"

"Jed," cautioned Jack as he placed a dark, calming hand on his friend and former master's shoulder. "I think he's done told you all he can."

Shrinking in humiliation, Jed released Royal with an apologetic nod and reassuring pat as he turned for the house. "Of course you have, Royal. I'm sorry . . . so sorry . . ."

Bitty caught the look in her surrogate son's eyes. "Where you goin', Jed?" she pressed as she followed him, her soft tufts of black, cottony hair bobbing around the edges of her nightcap.

"I'm going after him, Bitty. I've got to stop him. It's the only way we'll have any peace."

Bitty rose on her tiptoes, placing her hands upon his chest. "And how do you suppose *I'll* have any peace knowin' my boy is headin' into harm's way?"

Jed smiled at the reference. In the past two years she had gained a real family—a husband, stepchildren, and soon, a child of her own. Glancing cautiously at Abel, Jed was relieved to find him more accepting of the special relationship he and Bitty shared. It had not always been so, and Jed was pleased at the budding trust growing between himself and Bitty's husband. He took her hands to comfort her just as Jack made an offer that granted his sister the needed assurance.

"I'll go with him," the forty-year-old freed slave declared matter-of-factly.

"Thank you, Jack," replied Bitty.

Markus wedged his hands on his hips. "Francis, tell Jed you'll get yourself on that coach. He needs me in the brush with him, not as a wet nurse to you," he snorted.

Frannie glared at him, her eyes finally flitting away in resolution. "All right . . ." she conceded. "All right. I'll put myself on a coach." She shifted her attention from Markus to Jed. "But understand this, brother. I'm not going because you command it. I'm choosing to go."

Jed shook his head in frustration. "No. I want Markus to see to you." To Jack, he added, "Pack rations for a few days, then meet me back here in an hour."

As Jack turned to make preparations, Abel, who had previously remained silent, spoke up. "What if we're playing right into his hands?"

All three men turned to face the giant man whose diction did not betray his slave heritage. "What are you saying?" Jed asked.

Jerome, the wise old sage, smiled at Abel. Still prone to dipping his aged head in the deference taught him through decades of slavery, he added his own cautious wisdom to his son's as he answered Jed. "This could be a

Trojan horse. Remember how the Greeks created a diversion to sneak inside Troy and plunder the city? What if your enemy is trying to lure you away so he can do the same here?"

"Is there reason to suspect such a thing?" Jed asked.

In defiance of the required obsequiousness that had long muted his father's brilliant mind, Abel raised himself to his full six-foot-four frame and—as his recent emancipation dictated—freely spoke his mind. "He showed his location with that flaming arrow. He could have set that fire in a less conspicuous way. You have to ask yourself why he set such a clear trail for us."

"He's got a good point," advised Markus, grabbing his chin in thought. "Perhaps everyone ought to just stay put and concentrate on guardin' the farm for now."

Jed blew out an exasperated rush of air and kicked at the ground. "I'll not sit here and wait for him to terrorize us night after night, Markus."

"Of course not. None of us are sayin' that, Jed, but if those of us most handy with a gun leave, who'll protect the others?" The larger group murmured in agreement.

"All right," Jed conceded. "You tend to Frannie, Markus. Jack, you stay and help Abel. Royal and Sooky, guard the farm. Use the older boys as well." Again, he began to head for the house.

"Where are you going now?" called Frannie.

"I'm going search along the shore and see if his boat pulled out farther upriver."

Markus spoke up. "Don't be foolish, Jed. You won't be able to see anythin' unless you carry a lantern, and then you'll just be makin' yourself an easy target. Did you think that maybe the person who hung the effigy used that tin heart to bait you, to draw *you* out?"

Jed hated the indecision he felt. He wanted to hunt down the swine who dared to terrorize his home and loved ones, but he couldn't let pride and impetuousness rule his judgment. He had to be wise. He thought of the conversation he'd had with Frannie earlier about relying on the others. The point she'd made seemed almost prophetic now, and he hung his head as the weight of his situation bore down upon him. "Let's go inside. Give me your suggestions on how best to secure the Willows. Then, at first light, I'm going after him alone."

* * *

Jerome slowly lifted his own, aged body from his chair, concealing a wince as he straightened and headed for the bread table where Bitty was furiously working biscuit dough into small, round forms. Noticing his discomfort, and without saying a word, she grabbed a glass jar and filled it with hot water from a steaming kettle. Wrapping a thick, muslin towel around it, she handed it to her father-in-law, placing a kiss on his cheek as she said, "Set this across your knees for a spell. It'll take the stiffness out."

"Ahhh . . ." He smiled, receiving her offering. "'Who can find a virtuous woman? For her price is far above rubies. Many daughters have done virtuously, but thou excellest them all.'"

"Aesop?" Bitty asked, her round, dark eyes twinkling with pleasure.

"Psalms," Jerome answered, patting her cheek lovingly. He glanced at her belly and smiled sweetly at her. "You should rest, Bitty. Leave us men to tend to ourselves."

Bitty noticed the same look of concern on the other men's faces and she scolded them affectionately with a deliberate wag of her finger. "You just save your worryin' for when I really need the help—don't make yourselves scarce the first time he needs a changin'."

Markus laughed and rubbed his fingers deep into his eyes, the act bringing the discussion back on topic. His Irish lilt grew more evident with fatigue, frustration, or inebriation, and it was the former that now increased his brogue. "As I see it, tonight's little spectacle could 'ave been courtesy o' Dupree—a callin' card so to speak—or it could 'ave been from the British themselves, but my money's on a local. That heart . . . that's more likely a local lettin' us know they're unhappy about somethin' here on the Willows. They were none too happy in September to hear that we were armin' the slaves. Now, if they've heard you've freed some, or that they're bein' taught to read, well, that'd likely stir them up enough to try and put a scare in us."

Jed scanned the dark faces. "Did you tell anyone about getting your freedom papers? The children, perhaps . . . or . . . Bitty, did you mention it to your sister Priscilla at White Oak?"

Hurt washed across Bitty's face. "I made you a promise, Jed. I'd never break my word."

Jed nodded silently. "What about the children? If they can read, then they could . . ."

Jerome jumped in. "I have been teaching the older children to read, Jed, but they know they must hide their ability. They understand the dangerous consequences. And as for them seeing the papers, Bitty has all our papers rolled up in a linen towel and buried in her trunk. Those children know better than to even peek in that trunk, let alone to take something from it."

Another idea crossed Jed's mind. "No one else knew about your emancipation but my attorney. After I track our intruder, I'll think I'll head to Baltimore to see Mr. Ridgely."

Jed stood and leaned over the table. "Meanwhile, we must tighten the perimeter from the meadow to the stockyards. Markus, you and Jack will take shifts patrolling the riverbank. Abel, I'd like you to drill the men and the older boys, assigning them shifts to guard these areas." He drew circles on the map, and Abel nodded his agreement. Jed next looked to Jerome. "I'd like you to get bells hung on the corners of the property so we can alert everyone of an attack from any direction." He smiled at the graying man. "Now's the time we can most use your wisdom, old friend. If you think of anything else we can do to protect our people, I'd be glad to hear it."

"I think I should remain at the Willows," interjected a firm, feminine voice. Frannie entered the room and continued. "My trunks are packed and I'm prepared to leave if that is what you still think best, but you know I'm as sure a shot as any of you, and right now you need me."

"You gave your word, Francis," Jed reminded her as he moved to place his hand on the small of her back. He escorted her out through the kitchen doors and into the privacy of the hall.

"Yes, I gave my word." She bit off each word bitterly. "You were furious with me a few hours ago for daring to mention Hannah, and I fear it has overruled your judgment."

"Frannie," Jed muttered, "I assure you, the one thing has nothing to do with the other."

"Doesn't it?" she argued as her voice broke. "Jed, I can't get on a coach to Philadelphia believing you denied my help because the last words spoken between us were voiced in anger."

Jed drew her close. "Then let me say that you were right, sister, on all counts, and that I'm no longer ruffled. I'm sending you away because I love you, and because, unlike Markus, I think Dupree is behind last night's attack. If I fail to stop him, I mean to be sure that at least one Pearson lives to bring him to justice."

Frannie looked in his serious eyes and nodded. "Philadelphia, then." She sighed.

CHAPTER 2

The Same Night
White Oak Plantation, Maryland

Penelope Stringham stared off into the dark distance through the window of her mangled husband's sickroom. Many weeks had passed with as many agonizing surgeries to rebreak and reset his shattered bones. For three months she had listened to his groaning pleas for the welcome release of death until his moans became barely more than the normal din of her loveless, monotonous life. The last resetting had finally taken, and the infections were clearing, allowing the man occasional periods of rest and lucidity, as was the case on this night. Earlier that day, he had offered her release of her marriage vow. But she had remained, thinking over his words.

"Penelope? It's the middle of the night. Why are you still here?" he asked suddenly from the shadow of his bed.

"Except for light and darkness, my nights and days differ little. Every hour is the same."

Frederick groaned as he struggled to raise himself. "I meant, why are you still with me at all? You know that I would have betrayed our marriage if Francis Pearson hadn't refused me. And had Dupree not broken both my legs, I likely would have chased after her regardless."

Penelope's plump face was silhouetted in the muted glow of the bedside lamp. "I accept that you don't love me, Frederick, but whom else do either of us have? We know too much for Dupree to allow us to leave here. And though your father's treachery is now concealed, it will one day be revealed. Then my family will disown me, and you and your mother will become pariahs. If this is our situation, if we cannot be as husband and wife, let us at least be friends to each other."

Frederick pressed his eyes shut, and his voice came out broken and graveled. "I would think death more desirable for you than to stand by the side of such a pitiable scoundrel as I."

Her quiet voice was emotionless. "I pray you always remember what you have just said."

Penelope turned away to again stare out into the darkness. As she did, she caught him staring at her, but his gaze no longer carried its previous sting of disinterest.

"You really are a lovely woman, Penny. I'm sorry I never noticed it or told you before."

His use of the nickname was unexpected, as was his compliment, but she remained unmoved. "You don't need to say such things, Frederick. I don't expect flattery from you."

"It was not intended as flattery. You've cared for me and stood by me, attending to my every need. Such kindness changes a man—opens his eyes."

Penelope tried to deny the feelings his words stirred in her love-parched soul, but she felt herself wavering. "My loyalty is sure, Frederick, offered with only two conditions."

"If it is within my power, I would do my best to make it so."

"First, I ask for your kindness and respect. If you must philander, please do not flaunt your doings before me or others. Can you promise me this?"

Her dismissal of his fidelity wounded him. "I am a broken man, Penny. No other woman would want me. Regardless, I vow my fidelity to you forever. It is all I have to offer in exchange for your willingness to stand by me." He cleared his throat. "Tell me your second condition."

Feeling a chill course through her, she turned to him, her former gentle countenance replacing the uncharacteristic firmness that had set into her narrow brow and small, full mouth in the months since their marriage. Hope and wonder sparkled in her brown eyes, and a blush rose to her cheeks. Her voice was soft and encouraging, and he hung on her every hopeful word.

"We both know our marriage was a charade, an arrangement made by two disappointed fathers, desperate to make quick matches for their inadequate offspring. Still, I did come to love you, Frederick, and I was faithful both in deed and thought. You were not, and though I have grounds to end our marriage, yet I have pledged myself to you again. In return, I ask you to grant me one grand request—redeemable at the time of my choosing."

Frederick cocked his head. "If that is your desire, then I agree."

"And you will never renege on this promise?"

"I swear it, but . . . will you not give me some idea of what request you desire?"

"Not until our fates are clear. Then I will call for you to redeem this promise." She smiled and turned back to the window, relishing the moment and the happiness this request would portend for the future. Her reverie was broken by the sight of smoke rising above the tree line.

"There'a a fire at the Willows!" She spun on Frederick. "Do you think it's beginning?"

Panic washed over Frederick's face. "I . . . I don't know! Call for Rosie! Have her send someone to my father's house!"

Penelope did so, and in mere minutes, Stewart Stringham crossed the threshold to Frederick's bedside. "You asked to see me?" he inquired as matter-of-factly as he could.

Penelope ran to him, pointing out the window. "There's a fire at the Willows!"

Stewart strode to the window and peered out. "So there is," he muttered as he turned to face his daughter-in-law. "Penny, would you leave me alone with Frederick for a few minutes?"

Her eyes darted nervously between the two men, but she knew enough not to question Stewart Stringham, and she hurriedly left father and son alone.

Exhausted, Frederick fell back hard against the pillow before sparring with his father. "You've arrived fully dressed and across the grounds in record time. You knew that something was going to happen at the Willows tonight, didn't you?"

"It's none of your concern," Stewart Stringham snarled in return. "Your warning to Francis Pearson already got your legs broken! Do you now want Dupree to murder us all? It's out of our hands, beyond our control. What will happen will happen, and no one can stop it!"

Frederick threw his arm across his eyes and moaned. "Even in my broken state, I would still try!"

"You are only alive because I bartered for your life! Open your mouth again and I will not be able to spare you *or* your loyal wife!"

Frederick sat up again, grimacing in pain, and sneered in reply. "It was not I who disclosed Dupree's plans, though I wish to the Almighty that I had. Frannie already knew everything. Your informant is still out there, Father, and soon others will know as well."

Stewart stared into Frederick's eyes, trying to intimidate his battered son, but Frederick remained resolute and embittered. "So there is a spy amongst us, you say? Well, we shall see who it is. If it is one of Dupree's people, he will deal with them in his own way, but if it is one of White Oak's own . . ." His face paled momentarily. "Well . . . I will close their mouths myself."

CHAPTER 3

The Next Morning
The Willows

After packing his haversack, Jed laid down to reread Hannah's letter, feeling the anxious knot return as it did each time he noted the delay since her last posting. He had written her five letters, but having no address to dispatch them to, he had piled his notes in a drawer, vowing not to write another until he had heard from her again. He now reconsidered his position, aware as he was of the possibility of his demise if he should fail this day. That thought made him relent, realizing that he must actually write four letters before departing, to be delivered in the event of his death. The first was addressed to his attorney, authorizing the rapid enactment of the plans they had previously discussed. The next two letters were loving notes written to Frannie and Bitty, thanking them for their unfailing affections throughout his life and urging them to offer the same to one another. Lastly, he began a final note to Hannah.

> *Dearest Hannah,*
> *If you are reading this, then surely you realize that short indeed was the time apportioned to us to love on this earth. My heart aches from the cruelty of circumstances that prevented us from ever knowing the fruit such love could have yielded. How sweet indeed to have received even one more note from your hands, attesting to me your love, freed and unfettered from any other. But I do not say this to injure you, merely to attest that you were my one hope and desire to my last breath.*
> *And if it so be that we are separated by death, be comforted that I leave this earth with glad expectations, recalling the*

*sweetest words of hope muttered from your lips during one of
your fevered conversations when you took sick on our travels
last August. You said they were your sister Beatrice's musings
on the subject of death and love. Do you recollect these? I
remember them clearly, for as you hovered so near the edge of
life and death, I clung to every word, praying that what you
uttered could be so.*

*I feel a similar desperation today, hoping that God, in whom
you so wholly place your trust, has a plan for His children that
is as loving and merciful as the one Beatrice imagined, and I
pray that surely such a Being as you call Father, being greater
than mortals, would offer mercy beyond that which mortal
man or woman could hunger. And if love can indeed tran-
scend death, then I shall spend my eternal days waiting and
watching for you to cross over and into my embrace, to warm
my cold soul once more.*

*In death as in life, I am always,
Your dearest Jed*

He folded all four letters and tenderly placed them in the pouch of his
haversack. A shiver ran up his spine at the notion that events could provide
occasion for them to be read, and then, steeling himself against that very
eventuality, he set about to complete his preparations.

He caressed his rifle and set about to clean its specially made sight.
Muskets were still the principal firearm, but the tedium of loading them and
their rate of misfire were factors he could not afford now. His very life might
rest in the reliability of his weapon. For these reasons, he had never felt
gladder to have the treasured, more modern firearm. First designed for the
expedition of Lewis and Clark, only a few thousand of the Harper's Ferry
1803 rifles had been manufactured, and he had been fortunate indeed to
have obtained one.

He laid his pack and rifle by the door and tried again to rest, but he felt
as jittery as a racehorse, ready to get on with it but confined by the darkness.
Sleep finally came, and the first streaks of light were breaking through the
trees when he awoke. He pulled on his boots and grabbed his gear before
quietly making his way down the stairs. He found Bitty in the kitchen,
tying up a parcel of food in a linen square. Her elbows rested flat on the
shortened work table Jack had built her to lessen her back strain during

pregnancy. Most days she still moved around the room like a ballerina, but Jed noted her lagging pace this morning.

"Bitty? You look exhausted. What are you doing up?" he scolded lovingly.

"The same thing I always do when you're gettin' ready to leave here," she answered, glancing down at the parcel.

"You need your rest now," Jed argued as he rounded the table and came to her side.

Bitty was uncharacteristically flustered as she fussed with the knot. Gently lifting her hands from the parcel, Jed pressed them together, causing Bitty's eyes to mist.

"I need you to tell me somethin', and I need you to be honest with me," she began.

"I'm always honest with you, Bitty," Jed answered as he carried the bundle to his pack. "I've got enough people who want to kill me. I surely wouldn't want to place my name on your list as well." When he looked up, he saw tears welling in her eyes, and her head slowly shook.

She raised her gaze, staring at him across the room. "Don't joke about such things. I pressed you about those freedom papers and pestered you to take care of yourself 'cause our fates rode on your back. Then you said you had made all those pervasions . . ."

"Provisions?" he corrected as he moved to the table and leaned down on his forearms.

She nodded, embarrassed, and went on. "Yes. You said you did that so we'd be taken care of if somethin' ever happened to you."

Jed's heart sank that this concern remained paramount to her. "It's all taken care of. If anything happens to me, the remaining residents will be freed and deeded five acres of land."

"See?" she said angrily as she pushed away from the table and clasped her hands together. "That's what I've been worried about!" She came back to the table and leaned toward him. "I don't ever want you believing we love the gift more'n the giver. You don't, do you?"

A lump formed in his throat as he asked, "Is that what worries you, Bitty?"

She met his eyes and nodded tentatively. "I'm afraid you'll take chances now since you made these pro . . . visions. Tell me you won't be foolhardy out there, Jed."

His jaw tightened to check his emotions, Jed pledged, "I won't. I promise."

Bitty framed his face with her hands and said, "In every way that matters, you're my child. If not by blood, then by love."

Blinking against the sting in his eyes, he nodded, and she beamed back at him.

"I love this free-born baby, Jed, and I love Abel and his children as if they were my own. I love all of them, but you and Frannie have been mine since the day you were born, and nothin's ever gonna change that. Don't ever think that a freedom paper can replace either of you."

He squeezed her hand and pressed his eyes shut, placing a kiss upon her head. She untied the red-checked cloth that bound her short, curly hair and pressed it into his hand.

"Now, you take this to remember what I said."

Struggling to swallow, he tucked the kerchief into his pocket, then he grabbed his things and headed out to the porch where Jack was waiting with Tildie saddled and tied to the rail. Jack reached for Jed's bedroll and haversack, tying them to the saddle while Jed secured his rifle.

"I'd feel better about this if I were goin' along," said Jack.

"We've each got jobs to do, Jack," Jed replied. After patting Jack's back reassuringly, he mounted Tildie and headed down the lane. Several minutes later, after disappearing into the trees, a rustling sound in the thicket sent his heart racing. Instinctively, he dismounted and hid behind Tildie while reaching for his rifle.

"Jed? Come here and take a look!" The quiet but excited voice bore Markus's Irish lilt.

Awash with relief, Jed moved to the voice. "Markus! What are you doing out here?"

"Me and Abel decided to scout ahead a bit. What we found is pretty interestin'."

Jed followed his voice through the darkness to a lump in the tall grass. "What is it?"

"A dead man. He was stabbed and tossed over here." He lifted a small, charred iron pot containing dead coals. "I think the archer used the coals in this pot to light his arrow. And looky here," Markus directed as he walked a few paces into a clearing and pointed to a boot-shaped depression. "There are several sets of tracks, each of them made by boots bigger than those on the body. Didn't Royal say the archer jumped in a boat and rowed upriver?"

Jed nodded, adding, "Don't the tracks bear that theory up?" He noticed a menacing form approaching from the river bed and tensed until he was certain the hulking figure was Abel. "Don't they lead to the river and a boat?" Jed finished.

Markus shook his head as he rose and turned to Abel. "Did you see any sign of a boat puttin' in or pushin' off up there?"

Abel looked at Markus and shook his head. "And I walked at least fifty rods up the bank. There're plenty of footprints around here, but as far as I can see, none headed into a boat."

Jed placed his hands on his hips and thought. "Royal was shaken last night. I must have pressed him to give answers he didn't have."

Abel grunted at Markus, who raised an eyebrow.

"What are you thinking, Abel?" Jed inquired.

Abel glanced back and forth between the two men. "Counting those of the dead man, we've got tracks for two, maybe three other men here. Someone may still be nearby."

"I agree with Abel," chimed Markus. "If someone pushed off in a boat, he had a partner who stayed behind and covered his tracks to the water. It's hard to say, but if it went like that, he did a fine job. I'm more inclined to say that our culprits hiked out of here."

Jed felt the skin on the back of his neck prickle as his jaw tightened. He looked up at the rising sun and then back into the two men's faces. "Then I suppose it's time I head out."

Markus and Abel glanced warily at one another and then at Jed. "Perhaps we should speak with Royal again . . . now that he's calmer. Maybe he can think more clearly now."

"You two do that," Jed said as he moved toward his horse. "I need to get started."

"This might be a trap, you know. It may be that our archer set himself up to follow *you*."

Jed grabbed Tildie's reins as he glanced at the men. "Keep in mind that he could just as easily be planning another attack on the Willows, so maintain the guard as we've discussed."

Jed saw Markus kick at the ground in frustration. "I'd love to have you with me, but getting Frannie in a carriage to Philadelphia is the greatest help you can give me right now."

Markus nodded his understanding as he watched Jed mount and pass through the thicket. "I've dreamed of bein' alone with Francis Pearson a time or two, but I'd rather be protectin' my friend than nannyin' her." He closed his eyes in frustration and grumbled under his breath, "Let's go Abel. I've got an errand to keep, and I believe you've got some questions to ask."

* * *

Jed moved slowly along the jagged bank of the Patuxent, which flowed to his right, as he followed the assailant's tracks south. Signs of deer and rabbit soon distracted Jed's youthful mind as he began peering into the brush for motion. He spotted a small deer herd and a family of rabbits. Among the calls of wild turkeys and pheasants sounding from the underbrush, he heard the snap of a twig, instantly reminding him of the dangerous reason for his ride.

His heart pounded as he slid to the ground and withdrew his rifle in one motion. Using his loyal Tildie as a shield, he laid the gun across her haunches to steady his aim, then peered through his prized sight. A large buck appeared in the crosshairs, and he scolded himself for failed vigilance while breathing a grateful sigh of relief. Remounting, and now fully focused, he meticulously scanned his surroundings, measuring the natural cacophony of calls and cries that filled the morning air in order to note any change in the mix that could signal a warning.

As the trail wound south, the bank rose, forming cliffs that fell off to Jed's right while the path turned sharply east, following a smaller tributary instead of continuing south along the Patuxent. Several times, Jed criss-crossed the creek, scouting his assailant's tracks as they became masked among the tracks of the animals sprawled out over the expansive Shipley family acreage. Plumes of smoke indicated a few homes obscured behind the cedars and thick, defoliated oaks and maples along the creek, though not a person was visible, due in part to the hour, and Jed found himself feeling surrounded by life yet utterly alone.

When the sun had fully risen, Jed urged Tildie to a clearing to address his hunger. Untying the parcel of victuals, he removed a biscuit and a boiled egg from the bundle before replacing it in his pack. He went upstream from where Tildie was drinking and drew a cup of icy water from the stream, downing it quickly. Bending to draw a second cup, he heard another snap from behind him. Turning cautiously, Jed expected to see another buck or member of its herd, but none could be seen. After gulping the second cup of water down, he wiped his arm across his mouth and rose slowly, his ears tuned to every sound as he moved to Tildie's side, keeping the horse between him and the water. There were loud squawks and then an eerie reduction in the birds' cries and he again pulled the gun from its sheath, supporting it on Tildie's haunches as he slowly scanned the woods. Back and forth, his eyes bore deep into the foliage, scanning left to right across his field of vision. Content that he was alone, he relaxed his finger from the trigger and stepped aside as a loud "crack" pierced the morning air. His reaction was too slow.

The hot sear of a bullet bit his right shoulder, wrenching him sideways and to the ground. He was now facing the direction from which the shot came. Scrambling low in the grass, he reached his rifle when the glint of metal in the tree line on the opposite shore revealed that a gun was again bearing down on him. The urgency of the moment dispelled his pain as he rolled onto his back to take cover in the long grass. Positioning the gun against his body, he rolled back to his stomach and sighted his enemy as another gun blast sounded. Determined not to die without at least firing at his unknown assailant, he cursed the fiend while quickly squeezing the trigger.

He waited an eternity for the enemy bullet's entry, but no burn or sting came, and neither did he hear the whistle of a shot passing near. Confused, he again raised his gun and sighted the location of the gun's gleam, but found only a writhing lump there. While scrambling to his feet, he became acutely aware of the burn in his shoulder and the approach of feet to his left.

"Jed! Jed!" came a voice to the left.

The figure appeared male, but the voice was a woman's. A sickening mixture of gratitude and panic flooded over him. "Frannie?" he hollered. "Get down! Get down!"

He watched her instantly drop and crawl as they had as children when pretending to be attacking natives. Jed held his left hand up to stall her as he scanned the area for other attackers, and deeming it safe, he waved her on. When she drew near enough for him to see her wide eyes filled with a mixture of fear and relief, he grabbed her outstretched hand and pulled her to him. As she clutched him close, he closed his eyes, grateful the assailant had not shot Frannie first, and then, as his senses restored, his fear turned to frustration.

"What are you doing here?" he spat angrily. "Did you not hear a word I said?"

Shocked by his failure to appreciate her timely shot, she pushed away from Jed, barking back in an angry whisper. "I did but I didn't much care for it!"

"I was trying to protect you!" he argued.

"And I was trying to protect you!" she pointed out with raised eyebrows. "You're bleeding!" she added in a voice filled with composed concern.

Jed opened his shirt and found no exit wound. "The bullet's still inside, but that's the least of our worries. Markus and Abel felt there may be two attackers. We may be pinned down."

"I don't think so. I agree that there were at least two men, but only one came ashore."

Jed scowled dubiously at his sister's assessment. "But Royal said . . ."

"He was wrong. The boat headed *south,* back the way it came. There's a rocky spot two hundred rods or so downriver with a gouge in the shore. That's where the footprints begin."

"It was still dark when they went out. How did you see what Markus and Abel couldn't?"

"Jack would have found it. Remember, we've been crawling along that stretch of river since we could walk. There are overhangs all along the shoreline. I tucked myself under the abutment where my lantern wouldn't be seen and followed the path south until I found it."

"And you've been following me all along?"

"Just like Jack taught us."

Jed glanced at the modified Springfield musket still clenched in her hand, unable to repress his admiration. "Nice shot," he relented humbly.

Smiling wryly, Frannie raised an eyebrow and said, "You're welcome. Now what about the shooter? Do you think I killed him? He's not moving."

"He's either dying or lying in wait, so reload and cover me."

Frannie nodded as she pulled a cartridge from her knapsack and proceeded to reload while Jed divided his attentions between reloading his rifle and marking the position of the enemy. In less than thirty seconds the siblings looked at one another and nodded again.

"We aren't playing 'Indians and Settlers,'" Jed warned. "These men will shoot back. And I swear to you, Francis . . . if you get hurt, I don't know with whom I will be more vexed."

She smiled lovingly at him. "Now you know exactly how I felt this morning."

He tried to smile, but the gravity of his concern for her overwhelmed him. "You scan left, and I'll take the right. Are you ready?" he asked. She drew her knees near her elbows and gave him one determined bob of her head. "Now," he whispered, and the pair shot to their feet.

Jed scanned left and right, then slowly crossed the creek, nosing over to his attacker. He was stunned to find that the brazen shooter was a slave, which he determined from the despicable brand on the man's arm. "He's alive, but he's bleeding badly. He's a slave, Frannie."

"Dupree threatened to turn the slaves against whites. I suppose it's already begun," she replied soberly as she arrived on the scene. "He's just a boy. He can't be more than seventeen."

Jed used Bitty's bandana to secure the man's hands behind his back before turning him face up. Pointing to the branded mark on the young man's forearm, Jed growled, "*B.H.* . . . I've seen that mark before . . . Broadhurst Manor. He's bleeding badly, but I need answers."

Jed groaned in pain as he hoisted the young man's body against the tree. "Who sent you after me? Was it Dupree?" The young man's eyes fluttered open and closed, and Jed shook him to bring him around. "Tell me!" he screamed in the slave's face in the hopes of intimidating him. "Why would a slave from Broadhurst come to my house to stalk me?"

The young man leaned his head against the tree and smirked. "I ain't a slave no mo'."

Jed drew within an inch of the boy's face and growled in a voice so menacing it even frightened Frannie. Biting off each word with deliberateness, he asked, "Did Dupree offer you freedom in exchange for killing me?"

The slave spat into Jed's face, and Jed reacted by pinning the young man's throat to the tree with his right forearm. Then he wiped the spittle from his face with his left coat sleeve.

"That there's a dyin' man's dream. 'Sides . . . whad you gonna do to me dat my massuh ain't already done?" the Negro asked as he glanced down at his chest.

Jed noticed the discoloration peeking above the first button on his coarsely woven shirt, and opening a few of the scant buttons, he revealed the scarified flesh that covered the young man's chest. Frannie gasped and hid her face while Jed winced back stinging tears. He closed the man's shirt and leaned against the tree, bringing his face near the dying slave's ear. "I am sorry for what has been done to you," Jed groaned. "Such things are forbidden on the Willows. Surely you've heard this from our people. Dupree has sent you after the wrong man."

The young man's smile faded and sorrow filled his eyes. "Colored or white, we is bof marked. Good or bad don't mattuh ta dem dat jes sees our mark."

"Who marked *me?* Dupree?"

"Dupree is marked hisself. You is his way free."

Before the comment registered, Jed saw the glints of guns across the creek. Throwing himself at Frannie, the pair crashed to the ground as two shots rang out. Stunned by the fall, Jed also felt additional weight drop upon him, and he cried out for his sister as he turned to investigate.

"I'm all right, Jed. I'm all right," she groaned.

"They killed him . . ." Jed muttered as he discovered the slave's body slumped upon him. In disbelief, he scrambled to his feet in time to see a boat disappearing around a bend in the creek. Scooping up his rifle, he took a step and declared, "I'm going after them."

Frannie quickly grabbed the hem of his coat, weakly pleading, "Stop, Jed. Just stop."

"I can't let them get away, Frannie! They're Dupree's men! They can lead me to him!"

"Jed!" she hollered as she rose on wobbling legs. "They've planned this too well. They've likely got horses waiting nearby. Besides, you need to be seen by a doctor."

Adrenaline drained, Jed slumped over, looking down on the body of the young man. "They've made their point. They know they can get to us at their will."

Frannie shuddered, and Jed extended an arm around her to draw her near.

"It's like some dreadful nightmare," she groaned. "Why has Dupree singled you out?"

"Our attacker said Dupree and I are both marked. Supposedly, I am Dupree's way free . . . but Frederick said you're in danger as well. I need to determine who has marked us and why."

"At least we can prove that one of Broadhurst's slaves attacked you. Perhaps it's enough to convince the militia to listen to us now."

"Perhaps, but it's still not enough to implicate Stewart Stringham." He sighed and leaned back against the tree, momentarily giving in to the pain.

"We've got to get you home." Frannie's face twisted in worry as she called to Tildie, who was again drinking lazily from the creek. "I rode Figaro. He's tied a few hundred yards downstream. We'll put the boy on my gelding, and I'll ride double with you on Tildie."

"Frannie," Jed muttered through the pain as he took her sleeve. "I am grateful you were here today, but you must go back to Philadelphia now. You can see that, can't you?"

She dipped her head. "I know."

Breaking the tension, he tugged playfully at her chin. "Now it's my turn to protect you."

"Protect me? From whom?"

"From Markus," Jed chuckled. "He must be beside himself with worry. I'm sure he and his hot Irish temper are out looking for you right now."

* * *

Markus leapt from the porch as the wagon pulled up. Jack and Jed had been gone for days. "So . . . how'd Jed make out?"

Jack pointed to the wagon bed. "He's propped up in back. It's been a slow, hard trip."

The pair carefully eased Jed from the wagon and helped him up the steps of the porch.

"You say you put Frannie on a boat two days ago—are you sure she's not hiding out in the woods?" Jack teased Markus.

Markus shot Jack a resentful glare as he slowly lowered Jed into an Adirondack chair, guarding his swathed chest and shoulder. "I pity the man who tries to tame her, but I do dread what might've happened had she not followed Jed last week."

Jack winced and turned to lead the team toward the barn. "Have Jed tell you what the sheriff in St. Leonard's said. Seems that Broadhurst reported four runaways two weeks ago."

"It's true," groaned Jed as he adjusted his position. "A boy of sixteen and three others, right after a stranger came to their property . . . a *Frenchman* buying slaves, or so he claimed . . ."

"Dupree," snarled Markus. "His skin's so light he can assume any identity."

"This *Frenchman* asked to examine the men himself before deciding whom to purchase. It must have been then that Dupree laid out his plan for helping the group escape," added Jed.

"Does the sheriff believe our warnin's now?"

"He's more inclined to, but to avoid looking like a fool, Mr. Broadhurst insisted that the visit from the Frenchman and the slave escapes are coincidental, but there have been too many peculiarities lately. Escapes are up, strange boats have been spotted. Everyone's on edge."

Markus noticed Abel, Jerome, and Royal heading up the path from the meadows. Wondering how his friend would handle the next bit of news, he added, "There's more, Jed."

Noting the ominous tone in Markus's voice, Jed leaned forward curiously. "Such as?"

Billy walked out to the porch then, but Markus didn't pause. "Royal's story seemed odd, so Abel checked up on it. You won't like what he found out."

Royal edged to the front of the group and climbed the four porch steps, all the while fumbling with the bow clenched in his hand. Jed turned and grunted from the pain, drawing a worried Bitty to his side, but her concern for Jed shifted as soon as she saw Royal standing there.

"Have you something to tell me, Royal?" Jed asked.

"Mistuh Jed, I should've just come to you, but I thought I could handle it."

"Handle what, Royal?" There was an edge to Jed's voice, and Bitty squeezed his shoulder.

"A slave from Broadhurst was snoopin' 'round here a few weeks back. Me and Mercy had the babies out by the river, swimmin', and he pulled me aside . . . said he could set us free if we could get the others to revolt. I refused him but he said iffen we didn't, he would come and burn us out whilst we slept." A wave of shaking hit him so hard he could scarcely continue. "He told me to use the next three days to get the slaves ready. I was to build that effigy and hang it in the tree on the third night, when he'd be back to start that fire. During the panic we was all supposed to turn on you. Then some man named Dupree would lead us all to freedom."

An eerie sickness, like the one he'd felt when he'd heard Hannah was engaged to be married, crept into Jed's heart, and his entire body went slack. "*You* made the effigy, Royal?"

With a barely noticeably bob of his head, Royal indicated that he had, and Jed groaned in disbelief, wondering what value any of them placed on his life at that moment.

It was Bitty who saw the look of defeat and betrayal in his eyes. "There's more to the story, Jed," she pled softly. "Let Royal tell you the rest."

Jed wouldn't even look in the slave's eyes, and it was clear by the expression on Royal's face that Jed's disillusionment had wounded the lanky man more deeply than a whip.

"Tell him, Royal," Bitty urged as her hand continued to squeeze Jed's shoulder.

Royal tried twice to swallow past the lump in his throat. "Me and Mercy never said nothin' to nobody. You know how we feel about you . . . about the Willows. This here is our home, and we'd never do anythin' to bring harm to none we love . . . but fearing what he'd do, I made a plan. I hung that effigy so he'd think I was agreed, then I hid in the thicket by the river and met him . . . just like we'd planned. I wasn't even goin' to let him get a shot off, but whilst I checked to be sure he didn't have another man hid, he shot that arrow. Soon as he let it fly, I killed him and drug his body into the thicket. Here's his bow."

His voice wavered and he clamped his eyes closed as if the memory of the vile deed still haunted him. When he continued, his voice was thready and frail. "I was goin' to bury him that night but you all was up so late patrollin' and talkin' that I put it off 'til daybreak, but then Abel and Markus found him first. That's it. I swear. I didn't know there was other men waitin' up the river. I swear I didn't. I never meant any harm to come to you. I thought I handled it like a man."

As silent seconds passed, Royal's frame began to quake again. Sliding to his knees he cried out, "I know it's your right to do whatever you please with me. Sell me or beat me or hang me if you want, but please, please don't take no offense against Mercy or my babies! Please, Mistuh Jed!"

It was as if Jed's neck could no longer bear up the weight of his increasingly burdened mind. Leaning his head back, he brought his arm over his face to shield the pained expressions of the pleading man from his view. "Why didn't you just come to me or Jerome?" Jed implored. He removed his arm and glared at the man. "I could be dead . . . and so could all of you! There were three more armed men out there. Three! And all you had to do was tell me the truth!"

Jerome hung his head and inched closer to Jed. "Most men would never believe a slave."

"Am *I* such a man?" Jed bellowed, a new hurt overwhelming him. "Have I ever been such a man to any of you?"

Royal and the others shrank in response to Jed's rebuke. Hanging his head and speaking small and childlike, Royal nearly broke into a fragment of himself. "Mercy begged me talk to you, but with all this talk of freedom comin' to the Willows someday, I thought I could be a man . . . protect my own," he groaned, his voice echoing the futility of his expectation. "I swear to you on my baby's brow, I wasn't in cahoots with them."

Jack arrived, his breaths quick and short. His eyes met Jed's as he assessed the mood of the group. "Sooky just told me Dupree wanted more than to scare us. So the weasel thought he could divide us. Royal sure showed him, huh Jed?"

Jack's simple view of the conundrum was like soap in a bowl of greasy water, pushing the muck to the sides and restoring clarity. "Is that how you see it, Jack?"

Jack stalled and tilted his head slightly, questioning how it could be viewed any other way. "Of course. Now he knows the Willows isn't just a farm. He knows we can't be turned in on ourselves. He won't try that game again. Not on us."

Jed leaned his head forward and laid it into his hands, pausing to rub his fingers over his brow as his thinking cleared and his mood softened. "Royal, freedom alone doesn't make a man invincible." He touched his chest to make his point. "Even free men need help. They need to depend on the loyalty of their friends and family. Remember that next time. All right?"

"Yes, suh?" it was more of a question, portending what was to follow.

"Go home to your family, Royal."

"Suh? Yes, suh! Yes, suh, Mr. Jed! Yes, suh, and thank you. Thank you!" He nearly shook Jed's hand off and then ran to the meadow at top speed, allowing no time for Jed to change his mind.

"That was a good thing you just did," beamed Bitty.

"It was Jack," Jed stated as he turned to his friend. "I'm glad you came when you did."

"Nah," Jack replied modestly. "You'd've figured it out. You'da hollered first and said a slew of things you'd regret, and then you'd stew a few days until you couldn't stand it any longer, but sure as shootin', you'd have eventually said the same things."

Even the normally quiet and unreadable Abel laughed along. He was as opposing a figure as any Jed had ever seen, but a light was coming into his eyes that cast away the mistrust that once ruled them. "And thank you, Abel," Jed said. "What made you question Royal's story?"

"The timing of his arrival . . . his story about the boat's direction. Nothing added up."

Jed extended his hand, and Abel's giant one wrapped around it. Jed turned his attentions to Abel's aged father. "Jerome, your son's as wise as his father. You should be very proud."

"I am," Jerome preened. "Always have been."

As the father and son turned to leave, Bitty wrapped her arms around Jed's neck. "Supper'll be extra fine tonight, but we need to get you upstairs and into bed, mister!"

"I'll have Markus and Jack help me up in a few minutes," Jed replied with a pat to her arm.

She tapped his head in mock frustration, wagged her finger at the other men, and went inside, leaving Jed, Markus, and Jack alone.

Jed became pensive again. "It galls me to think that Stringham likely knew the whole thing. Dupree may have been waiting on his front porch for word that we were all dead."

Jack pushed his hat back and wrinkled his brow. "Could be, but Priscilla would have sent word. Stringham owns her, but her loyalties are here, to the Willows, where she was born."

"Someday I'll find a way to repay your sister, Jack. If it weren't for her son overhearing Dupree's plans and her message to Bitty, we would have been even more unprepared."

Markus nodded his agreement. "Whether Stringham knew about the attack or not, this has still been a pivotal day, Jed. You realize that, don't you?"

Jed nodded as he stared off into the meadows where Royal and the other workers lived. "I do," he said with a thoughtful nod. "I heard men discussing the war while we were in St. Leonard's. America has enjoyed some decisive victories lately, and it's given us new courage. As undersupplied as we are, we're finally giving the British a fight at sea, and we cannot doubt but that they will soon come our way." He turned to Jack. "When that happens, Markus and I will head to war, Jack, and you and the others will have to protect the Willows alone, but now I know it will be all right. You and Bitty won't have to stand alone to protect her."

Jack comprehended the trust implied by Jed's words, and his eyes conveyed his commitment.

Markus pulled a weed and pointed it as he spoke. "You know that General Hull who surrendered at Fort Detroit? Well, the papers say Commodore Isaac Hull is his nephew. It seems the Hull what took to sailin' instead of soldierin' is the family's hero in this war. He and his ship, the USS *Constitution*, destroyed Britain's *Guerrierre*, and the old girl shows nary a mark. They're callin' her 'Old Ironsides.' And our Captain Barney and the *Rossie* have bested eighteen of Her Majesty's finest ships including the *Princess Amelia*," he scoffed. "We began this war with only seventeen vessels in our navy, but privateers have increased that number by sixty-five ships. They're not much to look at, leastwise some of them aren't, but they could be our best hope in this war. All are manned by trained seamen who know their own waters well."

"Are you hinting at something?" Jed asked soberly.

Markus placed the grass between his teeth. "I've been givin' some thought to headin' south to Virginia . . . after the first of the year. I've still got a few people there . . . and my father's ship, the *Irish Lass,* is in dry dock in Hampton, near the James River. I thought I'd get her seaworthy again." He spat out the grass. "I'm best suited to do my fightin' on the water, Jed."

Jed nodded. "I anticipated that." He scanned the farm, adding, "You can feel change in the air, can't you?"

Markus glanced at the bandages. "And we'd best get you fit. What'd the doctor say?"

The very mention of the doctor made Jed scowl. "He said the bullet lodged near my lung. From the looks of the incision I think he used a coal shovel to extract it. In any case, he said I'd be meeting my Maker sooner than I expect if I don't lie still and let it heal, so I'm laid up for a few weeks at least. As soon as I'm fit to ride again I plan to head to Baltimore and meet with my attorney. Dupree is obviously able to move where he chooses, and with his sly tongue, he can weave a rather convincing tale. I don't want him to gain access to Willows files and accounts."

"And then what?"

"And then I plan to share these recent events with the commander at Fort McHenry."

"And find out if a certain lieutenant has received word from a certain young woman?"

Jed's shoulders slumped in defeat. "Yes. I'm so hungry for some word from her, to simply know that she's well . . . that I'm willing to debase myself and ask Robertson if he's heard from her. But there is more. Unlike you, I'm a better shot than sailor. If my militia company isn't called up soon, I may enlist in the Dragoons. I'd rather be busily engaged in preparing for this fight than sitting idle—waiting for Washington to move while watching for the postman to bring me word from Hannah."

CHAPTER 4

Late November 1812
Boston, Massachusetts

Hannah Stansbury tightened her wrap and leaned into the howling Boston wind as she trudged to the Castleburys' home where she and her sister Beatrice had taken refuge for the past three weeks. Her mind was troubled as she mounted the steps leading to their rooms, filled with worries the eighteen-year-old could not dispel. She and Beatrice had begun their journey the twenty-second of August by ship from Baltimore to Boston harbor, but the pitch and roll of the vessel had rendered Beatrice so deathly sick that the ship's captain changed course and put in unexpectedly at Long Island. Beatrice was carried off the ship and to a rooming house where the women remained for nearly a month. It was only then that she'd revealed her secret.

"I'm expecting a child, Hannah . . ."

The loving timbre of Beatrice's words had pierced Hannah's own aching heart, and then her sensibilities were raised. "Beatrice!" she'd said in shock as her fingers counted the passing time. "It was barely June when Dudley took his leave. That would mean . . ."

"Yes, Hannah," Beatrice had confessed. "I'm nearing my sixth month. I suppose my weak constitution has kept the baby small so far."

Chills ran down Hannah's extremities. "Do Mother and Father know?"

"Aside from God and me, no one knows but you, and so it must remain."

Hannah had experienced mixed feelings of joy, pride, and worry over the revelation. "You should return home where we can care for you and this child safely!"

Beatrice bolted upright in her sickbed. "All the more reason I must free my husband from that British prison, Hannah. Please tell me you're still agreed to stay and help me."

Hannah's loyalty had never wavered. "Of course I am, Beatrice. Now more than ever . . ." she'd said.

But the weight of the new worries made Hannah sink upon the ninth step. Slipping her bonnet from her dark, pinned hair, she leaned against the rail, replaying their frightful journeys. By the time they had reached Long Island, Beatrice's weight had been so reduced that she required a month of bed rest to restore her stamina and color. As soon as she was fit to travel she insisted they set out again by ship to Boston, but the result was the same. So limp and lethargic was she upon arrival that two sailors carried her to the Boston dock. Luckily, Mr. Castlebury had been there awaiting a shipment of goods when he heard Hannah inquiring after the name of a boarding house and physician. He immediately intervened and ferried the women to his own home where he and his wife waited upon them as if they had been their own daughters.

The Castleburys' kindness had been as a balm to the two heartsick souls, and Hannah wished that she could remain there indefinitely where past complications and obligations could not reach her until she was ready and able to deal with them. But keeping her promise now, she rose, moved to her sister's door, and tapped, calling out, "Beatrice? Are you up, dearest?"

When the door opened, Hannah was relieved to see the faint glow of health upon her sister's lean face once more. Her brown hair was twisted and pinned to the back of her head, and her gray eyes sparkled slightly. "You look like my dear sister again! Do you feel as well as you appear?"

Beatrice took Hannah's hands, replying, "I feel strong enough for a walk, but since the air is frigid I'll settle for a chat. Come, sit with me," she coaxed as she patted a spot beside her on her bed. Worry clouded her face as she leaned in close to Hannah. "First . . . how are you?"

The question was not anticipated or immediately understood. "How am *I*? I'm . . . fine."

Beatrice brushed a wisp of dark hair from her sister's cheek and studied her green eyes. "I know you are well of health and that you have served me with the utmost tenderness since we left Baltimore, but Andrew and I abruptly plucked you away from Jed Pearson's care, and then, in our hurry to pack and depart on the next ship, you and the good lieutenant were allowed neither privacy nor time for a proper farewell. Then we had barely settled into our cabin on the ship and made our plans when I took ill. Since my health has consumed us ever since, we have all but avoided the subject of your month-long journey with Jed and Doctor Renfro."

Hannah stalled, fumbling nervously with her hands. "Other things were more pressing."

Beatrice laid her quiet hand over Hannah's busy ones. "Yes, they were. But now we have a moment of peace, and I want to know how you are."

Hannah paced to the window that overlooked the harbor. "I'm fine," she muttered softly.

"I saw your faces, Hannah, yours and Jed's, the day Andrew and I arrived at the inn . . . and I'm sure Andrew saw it as well. What transpired between you and Jed Pearson?"

"It is as I have said before . . ." She stalled, trying to focus only on the major details of the events. "The wounds General Lee and Mr. Thomson received in the Baltimore riot were so severe that it required two weeks at a snail's pace to reach York Town, Pennsylvania. During that time, Jed all but lived in the driver's box while Dr. Renfro and I rode in the carriage attending to our patients. When we reached our destination, Jed read reports in the paper of vigilantes seeking the men who had taken their stand with Hanson against the war. He feared that having secreted two of those men away, he may have made targets of anyone associated with him, and our attentions were next turned to warning all of you."

Beatrice listened thoughtfully, adding, "When we were staying at Jed's Baltimore home, a courier came with a letter from him warning us to leave the city. I sent word to Andrew asking for his help, and the good lieutenant came to my rescue and helped move Jed's servants to the Willows."

Hannah nodded, expecting nothing less from Andrew. She then filled in more details of her journey. "We raced from York to Philadelphia, and on the way home the weather became severe. I fell sick, and Renfro and Jed nursed me back to health. Once I was well, we dashed back to Maryland to honor Jed's promise to Andrew, arriving at that inn the very night before you two arrived to meet us. As you already know the rest of the harried tale, there is little more to say."

Beatrice dipped her head and winced. "I awoke with nothing but a note to tell me you had fled with Jed Pearson in a carriage filled with men being hunted by a mob! You can imagine what worries went through my mind. Andrew threatened to detach a regiment to intercept your carriage until I convinced him that doing so would likely lead the mob right to you. You can imagine the self-restraint it required of him, knowing that you were not only in harm's way, but that you were alone with Jed Pearson. What prompted you to leave as you did, dearest?"

Hannah had not considered the impact her impulsiveness had had on anyone else. All she knew was that she had needed to press Jed to speak to her, and she saw her opportunity slipping away the morning he and Renfro were preparing to remove Lee and Thomson from the city.

She leaned against the window glass, grateful for even a few inches of distance between herself and Beatrice. "I don't know what you told Mother and Father, but I am grateful for your efforts to shield me from their inquisition." No longer able to hold back the flood of emotions her sister's prodding had begun, Hannah wrapped her arms around herself and revealed the truth. "As to my reasons for going? I needed answers, Beatrice. As soon as he rescued us from the fire set by those rioters, as soon as I looked into his eyes, I couldn't accept that Jed had coldly ignored my letter. I became so tormented with questions that I became suspicious of everyone. I was willing to risk anything to finally know the truth, so I coerced him into taking me along."

Beatrice swallowed hard. "And did you get your answers, Hannah?"

Hannah closed her eyes against the sting of tears welling there. "Not until that last morning did he finally reply to my earlier declaration of love." The tears began to spill down her cheeks, but as Beatrice moved to draw nearer, Hannah raised her hand, bidding her to stop.

"He confessed that his love for me was in every manner equal to that which I had professed for him, having begun before he felt it proper to express it, and he explained the complications that prevented his reply to my letter . . . and then . . . he kissed me, Beatrice."

Hannah watched as her sister rubbed the prickled skin of her arms, and she saw tears well in her sibling's eyes as well. "You don't condemn the love I feel, do you?" Hannah implored with amazement. "You recognize that it is akin to the love that compels you on your current quest."

"I cannot—would not—ever deny the love you feel for Jed," Beatrice replied hoarsely.

"Oh, Beatrice! He stirred passions in me I never felt with Andrew. At that moment I believed that our previous concerns would melt away, but it was not to be so. It was as if a wall went up between us. He confessed that he could not offer me the full expression of his love in a proposal of marriage while the stains upon his family name rendered him unworthy in Mother's eyes. I was willing to throw caution to the wind . . . to marry him without regard for the cost, but he would not allow it. Someone had called his love selfish, convincing him that no happiness we could find would ever compensate me for the coldness of Mother's contempt, and our moment was over," she choked, "stolen from us by someone else who dared to interpret *my* heart!" She pounded her clenched fist against her breast as anger etched its way across her tear-streaked face.

Beatrice did not rush to her side. She simply slumped against the bed poster and hung her head as Hannah crossed the room to rest her forehead against the far wall.

"We were wrestling with our dilemma when you arrived in Andrew's care, ending our talk. I dared believe that while I was away with you Jed might find a way to win Mother's favor. I believed everything was happening in accordance with the dream that had haunted me all summer, but each day my hope wanes. Mother will never relent, and Jed's honor will not allow him to marry me if the cost will be the forfeiture of Mother and Father's association."

Beatrice shuddered when she breathed. "And where have you and Jed left things?"

Hannah felt hollow and empty, as if the question had drawn her soul dry. "Knowing that Jed has always loved me and that petty circumstance alone keeps us apart, and having felt the power of his love, even if only for a moment, I can no longer marry Andrew. I could never be happy with less, and Andrew deserves to marry a woman who reserves no part of her heart for another."

"If you can't resolve things with Jed, will you also refuse Andrew?" gasped Beatrice.

"How can I do otherwise? I have written a dozen letters explaining these things to him, but I have posted none since Baltimore. I don't want to resolve such tender things in a letter."

Beatrice's head crumpled into her hands with a groan. "How can you justify leaving two devoted men to suffer over their futures while worrying if you are alive or dead, Hannah?"

Hannah closed her eyes and faced the real reason she had not mailed the letters. "Because of the dream that plagued me last summer! Each event proceeded as Divine Providence showed me in my dreams—the fire, that Jed would come for me, even that he and I would have to be apart for a time—so I've dared hope that Providence will again intervene so I don't have to injure either man. I am trusting that God's plan for me will make everything right."

As Beatrice sank onto the bed, Hannah felt her sister's skepticism and sat beside her to issue her plea. "Please, Beatrice, at least consider the possibility. Couldn't God soothe Andrew's heart? And if Jed and I are meant to be together, couldn't He clear the obstacles from before us?"

"You mentioned having had . . . suspicions earlier," Beatrice nervously pointed out while stroking her sister's hair. "What suspicions could have persuaded you to run off as you did?"

"Please don't ask me to repeat them. The very mention of them would break your heart."

Beatrice swallowed again. "I promise not to take offense. Please, Hannah. Tell me." Hannah drew a slow breath and buried her face in

Beatrice's shoulder. "I am ashamed to say I feared that you and Myrna had broken your promise and withheld my letter from Jed."

Hannah noticed her sister blinking rapidly to stave her tears. "See? I've wounded you."

"No . . . no," Beatrice muttered, taking her sister's hands in hers. "I'm . . . I'm crying for your pain, not mine. My dear sweet Hannah . . . I didn't understand how tormented you have been. Promise me you'll write to Jed and Andrew while you await God's intervention, and I promise you that the opportunities that should have been yours will indeed come to pass."

"I wish the person who cautioned Jed had loved me as deeply as you do. Why would anyone try to convince Jed that Mother's approval would be more important to me than he is?"

Beatrice was slow to respond, and Hannah looked at her. "Beatrice? Did you hear me?"

"Yes, dearest. I was just considering your question. Could you entertain the possibility that as wrong as it was for them to meddle, perhaps it was because they loved you very much?"

"What are you saying?"

"*Could* you be happy with Jed if you could never see our parents or Coolfont again?"

"I could never count anyone's devotion true if securing it required me to forfeit the affection of the only man I have ever loved. I pity any person who could."

The color drained from Beatrice's face, and Hannah asked worriedly, "Are you all right?"

Beatrice nodded slowly as a flutter of life moved within her. Grateful for the diversion, she moved Hannah's hand to her protruding belly, refocusing her attention to the spot.

"Was that the baby?" exclaimed Hannah. "You've a very robust little babe!"

Beatrice smiled wistfully. "That's why I feel safe in pressing on."

"Mr. Castlebury thinks we are too late. He also says there is typhoid in the area."

"Then we'll only stay in reputable places. I have sufficient funds to get us there comfortably. Please understand that Captain Mack believes he knows to what camp Dudley has been taken, but if we delay, the British may move him again. If they do, we'll be following a cold trail with the concerns of a fragile infant to consider."

Hannah was still wary, but Beatrice's confidence caused her to reconsider their situation. "If you feel it is best for you and the baby to press on for Tunbridge now, then I am agreed."

"Thank you, Hannah," Beatrice whispered huskily. "And promise me you'll post letters to Jed and Andrew before we leave, assuring them, at the very least, that we are well."

CHAPTER 5

Late November 1812
The Prison Camp at Lachine, Quebec

Major Dudley Snowden drew the heavy Iroquois blanket more tightly around him. He traced the elaborate markings of turtles and suns painstakingly woven into the fabric and brought to mind the face of Red Jacket, the giver, and of the circumstances that had introduced the two men.

It had been more than midway through the humiliating trek along the Canadian border to the prison at Lachine, near Montreal. The group was a mix of several conquered companies, his men from the fallen Fort Detroit having been joined by prisoners from the defeated Fort Michilimackinac, some of them the former heroes of Tippecanoe. Britain's Eighth Regiment Band mocked their American prisoners by playing "Yankee Doodle" as they publicly paraded them through countless towns along the trail. General Hull was accorded certain privileges, being ferried in front in a horse-drawn, four-person calash while lesser officers and their men followed on foot, flanked on either side by armed British soldiers. The most onerous stretch of travel took them along the Niagara in view of the bedraggled troops of their compatriots on the other bank—on American soil—who stared anxiously at them as they marched past their view like cattle, being incapacitated by the armistice agreement and therefore as powerless as ghosts.

Some Canadians cheered their misery while others were stilled by the pitiful spectacle the Americans presented, bearing countenances of defeat and exhaustion. They were forced from Detroit to Montreal by foot and ferry, arriving in Montreal September sixth, but dysentery and all manner of ailments plagued the defeated Americans along the way. Dudley had tried to alleviate his men's suffering and to rally them where he could. When one rail-thin corporal was shivering so badly he could hardly keep pace, Dudley forfeited his only blanket to warm him. He had dreaded the coming night when the temperature would dip, huddling as near the fire as his tethers would allow and certain that morning would dawn to find him dead. It was then that the Iroquois chief had approached him and handed him the turtle blanket.

Dudley had spotted the older native a few times before. Possessed of a lined face that radiated a quiet reverence, he was dressed in fringed leather leggings and wore a breechcloth beneath a tattered British red coat from the Revolution—the source of his name. He was not a member of the British battalion. Rather, he appeared sporadically, stealthily moving through the camp, speaking with members of his Seneca brothers whose loyalties lay with the British, managing to convince a few to defect to the Americans' service. When he spoke, his English was clear and strong.

He'd handed the heavy blanket to Dudley and gestured for him to put it on, which the shivering man did gratefully. "I Red Jacket . . . and you?"

Dudley tapped his hand to his chest and replied, "I am Captain Dudley Snowden."

"Snow-den," Red Jacket repeated as a pleased smile stole across his face. "Snow-den is a good man. I watch you many days, helping others, sharing food, healing wounds. You . . . must not die, Snow-den. You . . . must live." He'd circled his arms over his head and brought his mournful eyes to meet Dudley's. "The great Turtle, Mother Earth, struggles. The Seneca made a seat for the white man. Now we barely have room to spread our blankets. The white missionaries tell us we must worship the Great Spirit as you do or we are lost. How do we know this to be true? We understand that your religion is written in a book. If it was intended for us, as well as you, why has the Great Spirit not given it to us, and not only to us, but why did He not give to our forefathers the knowledge of that book? How shall we know when to believe, being so often deceived by the white people?" He stood abruptly and brought his fists together. "There is no trust, Snow-den. You must help make peace."

"But how?" Dudley had asked tentatively. "I am but one man . . . and a prisoner."

Red Jacket had thumped his chest. "The Great Spirit speaks to you. Listen. You will hear what to do."

Dudley's momentary reverie brought a contemplative expression to his pale, lean face. He looked up then to examine his fellow captives clustered around the snowy parade ground for their hour of "exercise." He now ranked among the senior officers remaining since General Hull and his eight highest-ranking officers had been paroled back to the States. It had been a hard enough blow for the men to see their faulted general residing and dining with the commander in chief of the Montreal forces, but it had been a far more bitter day when they had watched their commanders extend field promotions to a few of their underlings before they departed for home. Dudley had received the rank of major along with the duties and moral obligations that accompanied it.

He wrestled within himself. Red Jacket had called him a good man. There was a time when he'd believed that about himself, when his heart was tender and filled with hope and optimism, but he fought daily to repel the feelings his current circumstances set churning in him. He looked at his shivering, shriveled hands. His hair was thinner too now, as was his torso. He had his belt cinched tightly, but the trousers of his ragged uniform hung as if on a scarecrow.

What would Beatrice think if she saw me now?

He bore the signs of war, but the worst scars were on the inside, the ones that would not heal or be concealed beneath finery. It was what he had witnessed among the British. Such a well-trained army was as much the result of sharp discipline as it was excellent training and materiel—discipline that was enforced with stern, at times brutal, punishments. A defector had been caught. Stripped bare to the waist and tied with his arms wrapped around a whipping post, he had been lashed to his death while all his comrades were compelled to look on and listen in horror. Dudley knew the sound of the man's cries would never be erased from his memory.

He noticed the return of a young woman whose sad eyes always acknowledged the suffering of the imprisoned men. Today she carried a basket, approaching the officers' quarters nervously, but upon exiting, she smiled as the British guards peeked inside her basket, gluttonously plopping some of the contents into their mouths.

Dudley's eyes met hers and she moved toward him, drawing him as near the fence line as it was safe to do without reprimand. She was completely covered by her blue, hooded cloak, except for the oval of her face and her slim hands, which lifted the linen napkin from the basket.

"Quickly, before they change their minds . . . take these and share them with the others."

Her dark eyes implored him with kindness and urgency, but Dudley stood frozen, staring at the basket of little cakes. Their warmth, and the sweet, spicy, pumpkin aroma wafted up to his nostrils, filling them with memories of another place, another life, and tears came to his eyes.

"Please, hurry. They may change their minds," she again warned as she hefted the basket.

Dudley wrapped the parcel in his blanket, hoping the layers would keep it warm.

"Happy Thanksgiving!" she whispered as she turned to leave.

"Thanksgiving?" he returned with melancholy.

She turned warily and smiled sadly. "Yes, at least it would be if I were still in New Hampshire. I just wanted to . . . to do something. It's not much when there's so many of you."

Dudley reached a quaking hand to her and touched her arm. "No, no. It's wonderful. If each man gets but a morsel, it will be glorious. Are you American?" he asked with awed hope.

She shook her head nervously. "We were . . . before. My father fought in the Revolution, but we lost all we had and moved north where land was more affordable. He is a colonel here."

Dudley's heart ached at the changes that turned allies into enemies. "Thank you . . . Miss . . ."

She paused before answering. "Peddicord . . . Laura Peddicord," she whispered.

"Thank you, Miss Peddicord," he said gratefully, and then a notion struck him. His earnestness was increased by the approach of the guards who were gathering the men to return inside the compound. "Miss Peddicord, could you get a message to my wife for me?"

"No!" she gasped, taking a nervous step backwards. She turned her back and whispered, "Such an attempt could be construed as treason, and you have seen what happens to traitors."

He scolded himself for hastening her departure, knowing how he hungered for the normalcies of life, the pleasure of human kindness, and any other shred of gentility.

"My name is Dudley Snowden. Miss Peddicord, will you come by again? Just to visit?"

"I must go now," she said as she began to stride away.

Dudley's hopeless eyes followed her every step and then he saw it—the slightest turn of her head followed by the slightest of nods, a simple gesture that effused renewed hope in him.

A young corporal separated himself from the bulk of the group and lingered nearby, tightly wrapped in a ragged blanket. Dudley knew he was trying to make eye contact to initiate a conversation, but Dudley tried to ignore him in order to have an additional moment of solitude to savor the sweetness of the previous exchange. But as he turned his head to avoid the young man's gaze, he caught sight of his officer's epaulets riding upon his now-narrowed shoulders. He straightened, reminding himself that, free or captive, he was an officer—a man who lived by the call to duty and service. He closed his eyes in disgust at himself and drew near the soldier.

"How are you holding up, Corporal Lutz?"

The lanky scrap of youth shrugged his shoulders. "At least it's not snowin', sir."

Dudley patted the lad's shoulder, touched that the boy chose to find something in their circumstance for which to be grateful. "Have your feet healed?"

"Nearly, sir. They're still tender but leastways they're scabbed over now." The boy's eyes began to shine, and he blinked rapidly. "I'm sorry, Captain. I suppose I'm being a coward."

"No . . . no, son, you're not. You just seem like a boy who misses his home and family."

The boy lifted his face to fully meet his officer's. "Yes, sir." He blushed with a dip of his head. "Does that make me weak, sir? I s'pose you're missing someone too, aren't you sir?"

Dudley wished he could express to the boy the number of times he thought of his dear wife, Beatrice, or the regret that filled him every day at their separation. Life was so much more precious to him now. Perhaps that's why he ached so deeply for the hurt heaped upon Hannah, Jed, and Lieutenant Robertson. By his silence, he too became part of the meddling that had wrenched hearts and orchestrated lives, a heinous thing when love was such a rare and precious treasure, a thing for which he hungered more deeply than food or drink.

"Yes, Corporal, I am missing someone . . . a wife and her sister whom I love as my own."

Corporal Lutz straightened his shoulders. "I left a widowed mother with four little ones so I could fight, sir. I can endure prison. Why, I'd even gladly die, so long as I knew my cause was just."

It required less than a momentary search of Dudley's soul to retrieve his answer. Leaving for war was harder now; the cost more onerous since other lives depended on him. But his commitment to America's cause was more cemented in him than ever, because now it was more personal. He was no longer fighting only for the futures of other families. Now he was fighting for his own, and God willing, the hope of children was now a dream he might still see realized.

Dudley cradled the treasured bundle while looking deeply into the corporal's expectant eyes. "Yes, son. We were right in our cause. Every person has a right to choose their freedoms and how they will be governed. No one has the right to curtail that choice. Sadly, freedom's cause is inconvenient, pulling men from the bedsides of sick loved ones and fields that need planting. Homes will lie unfinished until our return, causing us to mourn for the shoulders of the women and children upon whom all that burden and anguish falls. We will lose some battles, and we may trip over our own pride or folly at times, but never doubt that our cause is just."

The boy nodded and choked out, "Yes, sir."

Dudley's heart broke for the lad. He understood the loneliness that set in when the glory was thin and the monotony unending, two conditions in abundance in the prison. He finger-combed the lad's dirty hair and pulled at his collar to straighten it as best he could. "Let's make you look like an American soldier again, son," he said with a wink. "Now, Corporal, take this bundle of cakes and distribute morsels to the men so far as they will go— enlisted men first. Then take a message to the other officers. Tell them that in view of General Hull's departure, I request to meet with them at eighteen hundred hours. It is time we reorganize our companies."

Lutz pulled his shoulders straight and stood as if on duty once more. "Yes, sir."

As he watched the corporal stride away, Dudley saw the soldiers gather toward him, anxious to know what had transpired between the two men, and as the morsels of sweets were shared, he saw more than a few tears in eyes that were coming back to life.

CHAPTER 6

Mid December 1812
White Oak

He remembered so clearly the last day the servant had entered the room carrying the wash basin. He was sick of being an invalid, sick of the bedpans and of being dressed and washed by others, and in defeat he had shrunk into the quilt and waved the servant off, preferring to rot in his bed than to endure another day of being coddled like an infant. A few seconds later Penelope had silently entered the room carrying the same basin. Sitting tentatively at his side, she gently lifted his nightshirt from his thin torso and pressed the sweet, steaming cloth to his brow, barely glancing at him. He was the unaccustomed recipient of such kindness. Knowing not what to make of it, and unsure how to respond, he had trembled like a frightened child. When she had finished dressing him she placed a hand on his chest, gazing into his eyes, and something changed in him. He had determined that day that he would not allow the pain to deter his progress, and he began the grueling work required to strengthen his legs so he could walk again.

A few days later he dared to reach for the crutches. It was a shaky effort, with teeth gritted and eyes pressed shut against the tears, but moment by moment he was able to shift more weight onto his legs until he was standing—trembling and bent—but standing. He'd caught a glimpse of himself in the mirror and cringed at the frail spectacle he made, but then he saw another image in the reflection. Penelope was standing in the doorway, her face taut with worry. She laid an encouraging hand on his back and another on his hand as it rested in the hold of the crutch, and with her support, he began the trek back to regaining his independence.

After weeks of practice, Frederick mastered the stairs, reopening his world to him. As he sat on the porch, he watched Dupree come and go as if he owned White Oak. One day the slaves gathered in the meadow. Minutes later the air carried the relentless slap of the whip and cries that surrendered into groans and then silence. Three times he heard the ritual repeated. He wanted to retreat into the house where he could hide from the misery, but something inside him would not allow him to withdraw. Penelope came out and sat beside him, cringing as he did with every crack of the lash. They looked at one another, accepting that, so long as Dupree remained, they had more in common with the bound souls of the slaves than they did with other whites. An hour later, Frederick saw his father in the yard, watching as the tortured, lifeless bodies of Priscilla, her son, and her husband, were dragged across the yard and tossed into wagons. Stewart Stringham's head turned twice toward the porch, receiving contemptuous glares from his son but offering no explanation as he ordered the wagons to roll before hastening back into his own house.

Frederick again sat on the porch this December day, wrapped in a quilt to ward off the winter chill, when his father stopped by on his horse to visit his recuperating son.

"It's good to see you finally up and on the mend," Stewart began awkwardly.

Making every attempt to disregard his father, Frederick responded dryly. "Dupree must be in quite a snit. I heard his efforts to take the Willows failed. I, for one, am delighted."

His father leapt from his horse and stood before him, glaring into his face. "Do you never learn?" he spat incredulously. "The man comes and goes as he chooses. He could hear you!"

Shocked by his father's fearful response, Frederick shot back, "So *he's* the master of White Oak now? *He* owns *you,* and *you* are *his* slave!"

Stewart's face registered shame, which quickly turned to fury. "*I* am the master of White Oak! And I recently proved it. Priscilla, her husband, and their oldest son were the traitors who betrayed my business to the Pearsons, and I dealt with them. No one else will dare defy my trust."

"Won't they?" Frederick laughed. "Your world is crumbling and you don't even see it."

Stewart pulled his hand back to strike his son, but Frederick did not flinch. Instead, he seemed emboldened by his father's desperation.

"Don't you think Jed Pearson already suspects your role in the attack on the Willows? Bitty will soon realize that her sister's family is missing. They may be just slaves to you, Father, but their deaths will not be ignored by Jed

Pearson. Face it, Father. Dupree's taint is fully on you now. You are just as much his pawn as Penny and I, except we have already made peace with our fate. How will you face it, Father? Where will you find peace?"

CHAPTER 7

Mid December 1812
London, England

The young viscount's nanny heard the muffled, loving voices of father and son from behind the heavy door. She regretted her errand as she rapped upon the old wood. "Lord Whittington? Your carriage is ready." She heard the heavy sigh in his voice before he answered.

"Thank you, Clarissa. Please, come in."

She found the handsome pair as she always did, delightfully engaged in play, and the tender sight caused another episode of the blushing that overtook her each time her eyes met the dark gray eyes of the earl. She saw the shy smiles he strained to suppress each time the crimson tones tinted her porcelain face. Though she could not deny the many times his gentle face appeared in her dreams, Clarissa never allowed herself to forget that while a few members of the aristocracy had reached outside their circle for marriage, she knew that this widower loved only two things—his son and England.

At this moment the Earl of Whittington was standing beside eleven-year-old Daniel, both of them poised behind the boy's puppet screen and leading their clown-painted marionettes through the final moves of an erratic dance until the two toys became desperately entangled in the pair's unskilled hands. The earl grimaced at the knotted mess, then quickly calmed his son's concerns, promising, "I'll work on this when I return tonight, all right?"

Daniel nodded grudgingly. "I wish you could stay home with me."

Lord Whittington kissed his son's head and answered, "So do I. Perhaps if you ask her nicely, Clarissa will challenge you to a game of chess."

Clarissa smiled encouragingly at Daniel, her blue eyes crinkling at the corners as she turned to the earl. "Shall I fetch your coat to allow you a few more moments with Daniel, sir?"

Lord Whittington nodded gratefully. "That's very thoughtful of you, Clarissa," he said as she scurried out, her yellow, twisted hair providing the last glimpse of her.

"Are you going to the palace, Father?" Daniel asked with sudden enthusiasm.

"Yes. The Prince Regent is hosting a holiday ball tonight for all the ministers and Parliament. Even the officers of the military will be attending."

"Will Arthur be there?"

The earl tensed at the mention of the young man. "I suppose he might. You've missed him since he left to visit his mother, haven't you?" Noticing the sudden furrow in his son's brow, he gestured for Daniel to join him. "Oh, dear. Something's the matter. Tell Papa."

Daniel's slight frame scooted near as he peered deeply into his father's eyes. "Arthur and his father had an argument, and now they don't speak. That's why he came to live here, isn't it?"

"Yes . . ."

"You're all I have, Papa." His voice was waiflike and timorous. "What happened to Arthur and his family will never happen to us, will it?"

The earl's throat became tight. "No, son. Never." He scooped the eleven year old onto his lap, wishing he could strap the child to his very chest. "Nothing could ever separate us."

"Good." The boy smiled and hugged his father, and then his face clouded again. "Father, I can't picture Arthur as a soldier. It's not that I don't think he is brave . . ."

The earl's voice was heavy with worry over mention of the post Arthur had begged the earl to secure for him. "Perhaps they use his training in the clergy to bring comfort to the men."

Daniel considered that option and nodded his approval of the idea. "I'd like that."

Clarissa returned with the earl's coat and white woolen scarf over her right arm while her left hand clutched his top hat. Keeping her eyes fixed on his shoes, she handed him each piece.

"Will you check in on me when you get home?" Daniel petitioned his father.

The earl's throat tightened as he considered how many times he checked on his boy's safety each night. "I promise. Now change for bed while I give Clarissa some final instructions."

Daniel went to his dresser to comply as the earl gestured for Clarissa to follow him out the door. "You understand that you are to remain by his side at all times?"

"Yes, sir," she answered quickly.

"And Mason and Robert are positioned at the doors?"

"Yes . . . yes they are, sir."

"Promise me that you will call for them if anything seems awry."

The twenty-four year old's resoluteness wavered as she looked into the earl's worried eyes. "Is there something in particular I should be aware of, sir?" she queried nervously.

The earl looked back at Daniel's door and then returned to meet her gaze. "He's all I have, Clarissa. Please . . . please keep him safe."

* * *

Lord Whittington dreaded attending this pompous affair. The monarchy was in crisis since madness had forced King George III to resign the throne the previous year. The heir, his son, George, was himself an enigma. Blessed with natural intellect and wit, he dishonored himself and the throne in the scandalous pursuit of extravagance, lewd women, and drink, becoming a mere caricature of what he might have been. Such weakness on the throne added to the tensions tearing at Parliament as the prince vacillated between political parties, throwing his support first to the Whigs and then to the Tories, creating partisanship at a time when the British economy was in tatters from funding multiple wars on a variety of fronts. *Social upheaval seems a breath away and the prince wants to throw a party!*

The earl loved England and her good people, and despite the flaws of her monarchs, he believed in her traditions and history, for which he was committed to fight.

The carriage neared the sprawling brick castle, its three stories of windows afire with light, illuminating the winter skyline. When the carriage stopped, two footmen saw to the earl's exit while red-and-gold festooned guards framed the threshold that led to the grand hall. Inside, a similarly dressed man with a white wig took the earl's invitation and announced, in a voice that bordered on a bellow, "The Right Honorable Earl of Whittington, Lord Everett Spencer!"

The earl nodded and bowed as he passed the silk- and brocade-clad gentlemen and ladies of court who lined the opulent hall. He bowed deferentially to Prince George, whose attention was so riveted upon the woman who had passed prior to the earl that he broke the line to pursue her, leading her up the curved grand staircase with a portion of his entourage following close behind.

"Good grief," Lord Everett muttered to himself as he passed through the gauntlet of nobility. He felt a hand on his back as a familiar voice whispered, "Tall of stature, regal . . . You're turning heads, Whit. Now keep smiling and meet me under the tapestry of King George."

Knowing that only those closest to him ever used the endearment "Whit," Lord Whittington nodded and smiled until he reached the corner, whereupon he turned and met the strained visage of his cousin and dearest friend, Marshall Northrup, the earl of Norwich.

"Your expression does not portend good news."

"It seems your fears are well founded. I've been making inquiries, and it appears your Mr. Ramsey has been seen in the company of a ne'er-do-well named McGowan whose reputation for larceny and violence precedes him. He has two brothers with equally sordid reputations. All three fit the descriptions of the men you've seen following you and Daniel. One of them has a cleft lip and a strange marking on his neck, like an eye. I think these are your men."

Whit's head fell back against the wall. "Ramsey as much as threatened me last summer. He believes I turned his son against him, and in return he now menaces Daniel."

"Sadly, until these men cross the law, you've nothing to charge against them."

"Have they no outstanding warrants? No prior debts or crimes left unanswered?"

"None that can be found. The marked one was sent to the sugar-cane plantations in Barbados for ten years for assaulting a man, but he was released early. A generous restitution was made in full to the victim, who in turn petitioned the court for the man's reprieve."

"Who made the restitution?"

"It's untraceable. A bondsman presented the cash to the victim and the court, saying that he received his instructions in a letter." Marshall placed a compassionate hand on his cousin's shoulder. "You've no recourse other than to continue on as you're doing. You've hired two guards? Hire more. It's your only option right now, Whit."

Lord Whittington angrily pushed away from the wall, challenging his cousin. "What kind of life will Daniel have, being followed and accompanied every moment?"

"Be prudent, Whit. Better this course than for you to confront these men and leave your son an orphan."

A group of guests began approaching, and the two men abruptly ended their conversation.

"My lords," one of the men began, bowing slightly before offering his hand. "I don't believe I have had the pleasure of introducing myself. I'm Nelson Mitchell. I've assumed my brother Edward's seat in the House of Commons. And this lovely woman is my wife, Caroline."

"Ahhh," Lord Norwich responded carefully. "It's always a pleasure to meet a new member of Parliament, isn't it, Lord Whittington?"

Lord Whittington extended an obviously reluctant and limp hand to the man and his wife.

"Well . . ." stammered Mr. Mitchell. "I just wanted to tell you what an honor it is for me to serve in my good brother's stead. Be assured that I shall avail myself of every opportunity to familiarize myself with the pending legislation so that I may honorably fill my brother's seat."

"And how is your brother, Mr. Mitchell?" Lord Whittington probed derisively. "What a shame that his retreat from Parliament and his medical pilgrimage place his burden on you."

Flustered by the earl's sarcasm, the man replied purposefully, "From all reports, his health is improving quite nicely, thank you."

"How splendid," Lord Norwich quickly interjected to deescalate the conversation. "Do tell your brother we inquired after him, Mr. Mitchell. Mrs. Mitchell . . . lovely to meet you."

The pair sensed the conversation had concluded and exited hastily, as visibly pleased to leave the interrogation as the two cousins were to see them go.

"What was that about, Whit? I've never seen you behave so brusquely. It was bad form."

"Mitchell was never ill. He was involved with Ramsey who began bearing down upon him, making his life miserable. That's why he forfeited his seat and fled England."

"Mitchell and Ramsey?" Marshall was stunned by the revelation. "I always found Mitchell to be an honorable sort."

Whit leaned back against the wall and closed his eyes, the rudeness of his behavior finally sinking in. "He was . . . once, until Ramsey corrupted him. In any event, I had no cause to treat his brother and Mrs. Mitchell as I did."

"Don't look now, Whit, but the devil himself is approaching."

Whit caught the approach of Stephen Ramsey and steeled himself as the man bullied his way across the crowded floor.

"Steady ole man," warned Marshall. "You'll accomplish nothing by creating a rabble."

Decorum shattered as Ramsey affronted Lord Whittington from the first word. "Wasn't it enough that you poisoned my son against me? Will you not be content until he is dead?!"

Lord Whittington felt the pounding of his heart. "I am very fond of your son, Ramsey! Any so-called 'poison' you refer to was administered by you, not by me!"

"So you continue to deny that you arranged for Arthur to arrive at the exact moment of our confrontation where you slandered me? Do you now also deny that you have arranged a post for him in the military? And not just a military post but a post in the very thick of the conflict!"

The earl rose on his toes and pressed forward until his nose nearly met Ramsey's. The two bit their words to keep the volume low, but their eyes flashed with visible fury.

"I'll not discuss this with you, Ramsey. Go speak to your son!"

"Thanks to you, I have no son!" Ramsey bellowed out, drawing curious looks. "You've taken the only thing that ever mattered in this world to me. Pray that you never know such pain."

Feeling the hint of a threat, Whit menacingly jutted his finger in Ramsey's face. "I've seen the vermin you've recently hired to follow me and my son. Know this. If Daniel gets so much as a splinter that I cannot explain, I will come for you."

The two men faced off as a crowd settled around them. There was a slight recognition of movement in the assembly, and then Arthur Ramsey burst through.

"Please tell me I am not the object of this clash!" Arthur snapped, but getting no reply he turned to Lord Northrup and asked, "Is this about my enlistment?"

"That was the beginning of it, but it encompasses so much more now."

Arthur shook his head and stepped in between the warring parties. "*I* asked Lord Whittington to arrange a post in Maryland for me, Father! I felt it only right that one of us should witness the horrors you and your mercenary Dupree have planned. The earl only agreed to assist me because he felt his influence could afford me an assignment with a manner of protection, though I do not feel entitled to be spared from what is planned for others."

Ramsey's face went slack. "Do you really hate me that much? I did it for you, Arthur." He raised his hands to circle the grand hall. "Look at us . . . a merchant and his vicar son . . . guests of the Prince Regent. The Admiralty applauds my efforts. They know Dupree can infiltrate the enemy, in turn saving British lives. Can't you see? I am a hero here."

Arthur's mouth twitched slightly. "A hero? Throughout the war with Napoleon we have condemned the French for their rapacious actions. Are we now justified in doing the same or worse to the Americans? I know that's why you selected Dupree. I also know you plan to profit heavily from the spoils of his talents. Is this the heroism I am to applaud, Father?"

Ramsey's face flushed red. "This is war, Arthur! This is how war is won . . . and the spoils? Admiral Cockburn is pleased to reward those who assist him in protecting England."

"You dare call lining your pockets at the expense of young British blood '*protecting England*'? I'll fight and die by their sides for the honor of reuniting Britain if that is how it is to be, but I want none of your spoils of war. All I ever wanted was to bear a name that I could proudly pass to my own children. In these regards, you have left me nothing."

Arthur was shaking by the time he finished. He drew two heaving breaths and stormed out, his father's devastated eyes following each step as if watching him for the last time. Ramsey spun on Lord Whittington, and, with an icy coldness that chilled the noble, he growled, "You!"

"Your choices alone caused this," Lord Whittington seethed in reply.

"No. You disclosed things the boy was unprepared for. There is a truth you've yet to understand, my lord," he sneered. "There are things men must do that cannot be shared betwixt father and son. You violated that law, my friend. You betrayed my privacy. I told you then you would rue that day, and so you shall."

CHAPTER 8

Late December 1812
Hanover, New Hampshire

It was twilight when the carriage lurched to a halt. Hannah opened the door against the bitter wind and called to the driver. "Have we arrived, sir?"

"Sorry, little lady. We'd have reached Tunbridge if we hadn't thrown that shoe. We're in Hanover, New Hampshire, just a few miles from the Vermont line."

Hannah was exasperated. Beatrice had been a valiant traveler but her fatigue was apparent, and the younger woman had become her fierce protector. "And how long will we be delayed *now,* sir? We were hoping to be settled with our hosts before Christmas Eve."

The driver pointed to the inn situated near the road. "Perhaps you shall, but you'd best get a room for this night. I doubt I'll find a blacksmith at this hour."

Beatrice smiled reassuringly at her vexed sister. "It appears to be a satisfactory place. Besides, I'm rather tired . . . and I'd hate to arrive at the Macks' home bedraggled."

A sense of foreboding warned Hannah that they should flee away. "But Beatrice . . ."

"You're exhausted too. Let's find the proprietor and see if he has any rooms available."

Uneasiness filled Hannah as the pair entered the inn and found the proprietor, a brash man named Mr. Pickett, waiting by the door. After registering the women he called for a porter at the top of his lungs. "Mister Harden!" he shouted before muttering under his breath, "I told the wife not to hire that lazy deserter. Mister Harden!" He began to storm out of the room when a man entered wearing a white linen rag tied around his slim waist. He was pale and sweat-soaked though the day's temperature was cold enough to put a heavy layer of ice on the outside trough.

"Did you call for me, Mr. Pickett?" He lifted the corner of the apron and mopped sweaty hair away from his ashen face. "I was helpin' your missus in the kitchen."

"Clean yourself up," Pickett barked, "and carry these ladies' bags to room five!"

Harden's eyes seemed to roll farther back into their sockets with each step as he struggled to manage the women's luggage. Hannah put her hand on his arm to stop him and felt the warmth there. "I think this man is sick, Mr. Pickett. He has a fever and he's as wet as a rag."

"I'm fine," Harden protested, making a heartier effort. "Just been cookin' all afternoon." Suddenly he dropped the bags, clutched his midsection, and leaned against the wall. "I'll get them bags to your room real quick. I promise." And then he shuffled to the doorway and into the yard.

A wary look crossed Mr. Pickett's face as several other guests who were seated in the parlor began to whisper worriedly amongst themselves. "He just has the grippe is all," assured Pickett. "I'll help you myself, ladies. Dinner has already been served, but you just head to your rooms. I'll have my missus rustle up some leftovers and I'll bring them to you there."

* * *

A ruckus awoke the women before dawn. Hannah tucked an extra quilt around her sister and added a log to the fire before dressing and heading outside to seek their carriage and team. It was nowhere to be found and, curiously, neither were any others, except one private rig, though numerous tracks in the snow leading onto the road explained the early disruption she had heard.

Beatrice had fallen back to sleep by the time she returned. Growing increasingly uneasy, Hannah reminded herself of Captain Stephen Mack's invitation, requesting that they consider themselves as family and stay as long as they desired. The terms of the invitation had melted Beatrice's heart, but it was Dudley's letter, written on his last night of freedom, affirming his love for her and describing the pact he and Captain Mack had entered into the night before the fall of Fort Detroit, that had brought Beatrice to tears. Both officers had assured the other that whoever survived would look after the other's family. That blessing had fallen to Captain Mack. After signing pledges that they would not raise arms during the remainder of the conflict, Mack and the other members of the militia had been paroled and escorted out of Fort Detroit, while Dudley and the regulars had been marched away to prison in Quebec.

Knowing that she had been Dudley's constant thought had steeled Beatrice's determination to reach him, and Hannah chided herself for worrying and strolled to the parlor for a book to entertain herself. She found the finely-appointed room empty and in disarray. She also noticed that there were no inviting aromas wafting in from the kitchen as she stuck her head in the back to inquire about breakfast. Bowls filled with cracked eggs and muffin batter sat unattended while two men in heavy overcoats grilled the Picketts. One was an older man, short and gray, while the younger, a tall man with dark hair and a moustache that constantly moved side to side as he gritted his teeth, stood nose to nose with Mr. Pickett.

"A sick soldier named Peter Harden left his fort while under quarantine. Three persons attested to having seen him at this very inn two days ago, and you say he was never here?"

Hannah listened intently by the doorway, remembering the sickly appearance of the man.

Another heavily attired, fair-haired young man entered through the outer doorway and dusted snow from his coat, and Hannah pulled back out of view before he spoke.

"He's dead, Dr. Morgan. Frozen like a log out back by the outhouse—under a canvas."

Hannah covered her mouth to stifle a gasp as she heard a scuffle and then the sound of the first man's angry voice again.

"So you never saw Harden? Liar!" Dr. Morgan accused in a disgusted voice.

She heard another scuffle, and then Mr. Pickett offered a haughty reply. "A bunch of doctors . . . You've no legal authority here! A sick vagrant came looking for work and died here! So what? He had no money to call for the undertaker, and the ground was too frozen to bury him. What of it? Now get out of my establishment. We've got to feed what few guests we have left, or will you not be content until your ranting has scared off the remainder of our clientele?"

Hannah peered back into the room. She saw Dr. Morgan turn to his older colleague and nod, signaling him to action. Bringing his young companion along, the man headed in Hannah's direction, but she pushed flat against the wall and watched as they retrieved signs which they then nailed to the doors while Mr. Pickett cursed at the doctors. When she presumed Dr. Morgan had had enough, he drew in a long, angry breath and offered his devastating explanation.

"Allow me to explain our *legal* authority," he growled. "We are trying to abate an epidemic of typhoid fever, sir, and under the authority of the governor we're shutting you down and quarantining this inn until we are certain none of your remaining guests are symptomatic."

The news made Hannah quake as she heard Pickett's reply. "Quarantining my inn?"

"That's right. You should have received notice of the disease. Broadsheets describing its symptoms and prevention were distributed, and the papers have issued warnings to the public." He thrust his finger into Pickett's face. "You had an obligation to protect your clientele! Instead, you allowed a man who displayed obvious typhoid symptoms to serve in the kitchen—of all places—exposing more people to the disease and sending more carriers out into the populace!"

Hannah felt her knees go weak as she thought about Beatrice and her baby.

"For how long?" Pickett grumbled angrily. "This kind of setback could ruin me!"

"As long as it requires," Morgan shot back. "If any of your departed guests were infected, they are carriers, and one in five of them, and all those they infect, may die," Morgan barked angrily. "Now get me a list of who is still registered and their room numbers."

Hannah leaned her head against the wall as if having heard a death sentence pronounced on her and Beatrice. She saw the young, blond doctor returning from his errands. As soon as he crossed the threshold, she pounced on him. "Typhoid fever? Is it true?"

The young man returned her question with a compassionate nod. "I'm afraid so, miss, but don't panic unnecessarily. There's no guarantee that everyone here was infected, and the medical school of Dartmouth College is right here in Hanover. We'll do our best to care for everyone."

Hannah's eyes began to well. "My sister and I are traveling alone from Maryland. She's expecting, and she hasn't felt well the entire trip, Dr . . ."

"Dr. Butler," he said, extending his hand. "My colleague and I will be making rounds to each room shortly, Miss . . ."

"Hannah Stansbury. I'm grateful for you're help, but what do we do if we prove to be infected? We've no family in the area and our ready resources are limited."

The angry exchange occurring between Mr. Pickett and Dr. Morgan suddenly intensified.

"If Mr. Pickett has even the slightest shred of decency, he won't charge you for your rooms while you recover. Ethically, the boarding costs should be free as well, since . . ."

"Free?" bellowed Pickett in response to Butler's comments. "Are you mad? First your snooping around scares off the majority of my guests, then you quarantine me, cutting off any new revenue, and now you want me to board my current guests gratis? I absolutely will not!"

Hannah's first response was shock, and then anger overtook her. Her green eyes narrowed as she charged toward Pickett. "You were notified of the disease, yet seeing Mr. Harden's condition you didn't have the decency to warn us, knowing my sister's condition?"

Dr. Butler pulled her away and turned her to face him. "Let Dr. Morgan handle Pickett. Your health and well being, and that of your expectant sister, must be your only concern now."

Hannah's head dropped into her hands. "That's exactly why we can't stay here. I can't leave our fate in the hands of such a man. Surely there is another place where we can stay. We have ample financial resources back in Maryland to pay for our care. Please help us."

Dr. Butler's face melted with empathy. "Money is not the issue. Typhoid spreads easiest in crowds where sanitation cannot be assured. The hospital staff is already overly taxed, and you'll fare better in a more controlled environment. Is there someone I can notify for you? Your sister's husband . . . or your own, perhaps?"

Hannah's face fell. "My sister's husband is a British prisoner who was marched to the prison at Quebec. We're here because a local man who served with him, a Captain Stephen Mack of Tunbridge, offered to help us contact him."

"Oh, yes. The entrepreneur. Perhaps he would arrange for your private care."

"Oh, no! You mustn't!" Hannah implored. "Please. We have not even made their acquaintance yet. I'm sure Beatrice would prefer to remain here before thrusting this upon our benefactors. Hopefully we'll prove to be uninfected and free to travel soon, correct?"

"Perhaps," the good doctor replied guardedly.

Hannah was too wrung out with worry to argue, and Dr. Butler seemed determined not to offer her false hope, so an awkward silence ensued until Mr. Pickett stormed off and Dr. Morgan addressed his colleagues. "Mr. Pickett is getting the guest registry, and I need to find those who've already checked out. I trust that your Dartmouth colleagues can manage things here?"

Butler and the gray-haired doctor looked at one another and nodded.

"Very well. Keep me apprised these next few weeks."

From then on Dr. Butler and Dr. Perkins returned daily, and on Christmas Day the first of Mister Harden's confirmed victims were the

Picketts themselves. It boded poorly for the other residents of the inn, as each of the doctor's subsequent visits identified more guests who were becoming symptomatic. Explicit directions were given regarding hygiene and the safe handling of food. These directions were posted on the privies as well as in the kitchen, since the task of food preparation fell to those who were still well. Hannah volunteered as a cook and maid.

Dr. Butler arrived one day to find her squinting and squealing while a dead chicken dangled from her hands. "I take it this is a recently acquired talent?" he teased.

"Ugghhhh!" Hannah groaned with a rapid shudder, brushing her disheveled black locks away from her face with her wrist. "I doubt if I shall ever be able to eat chicken soup again."

Dr. Butler laid his overcoat aside and removed his derby, displaying a hearty head of straight blond hair which he combed back, revealing inquisitive brown eyes that radiated from his light complexion. "Here," he said, as he stretched out his hands. "Let me have a go at it."

Hannah gladly passed the poultry, watching inquisitively as he dipped the bird into a pot of boiling water before deftly clearing a patch of feathers, exposing pale, yellow flesh.

"Was chicken plucking part of Dartmouth Medical School's study of anatomy?"

He gazed at her and then roared with laughter. "That's very good! Actually, my grandfather was a preacher at a small church here in Hanover. He bought a little farm near Lebanon so he wouldn't be a burden on his parishioners," he said affectionately. "I spent summers there and visited as often as I could during medical school."

"Is he still living on the farm?" Hannah asked as another patch of clean chicken emerged.

"Yes, but my grandmother died recently after a long illness, and he's nearly blind now."

"So he's more a preacher than a farmer?"

"He doesn't have a congregation of his own anymore. The parish became so large it required a second preacher. The new clergyman was a real showman, getting the congregation all fired up, then scaring them into repentance with his predictions of hellfire. My grandfather disapproved of the fear mongering, but the congregation seemed to respond better to sermons about an angry God than to those about His love. That's when my grandfather decided to retire. He said he couldn't preach doctrine he didn't believe in."

"He must be a man of great integrity to stand alone in matters of faith."

Butler paused his plucking to search her face. "Have you some experience in the matter?"

Hannah considered the question, then changed the subject. "You say he's nearly blind?"

Dr. Butler smiled wryly. "He's a proud, stubborn cuss . . . won't take a penny from me. When I can, I take some groceries along and cook a good meal for him. Members of his old congregation still call on him to perform a baptism or a funeral service here and there, for which they pay him in goods or services, and he sells his hens' eggs. He says his needs are few now that Grandmother is gone. I think he's anxious to be done with this life and to cross over to her."

After a long pause, Dr. Butler stood and set the pot of water aside so he could carefully pass the bird over the flames, singeing off any remaining feather traces. "There you go," he said as he dangled the clean bird in her direction. "Do you know what to do with it now?"

"If a person can read a book they can learn to do most anything." She rose with attitude and carried the bird to the preparation area with the doctor close behind her. He quickly commenced pulling ingredients from the shelves.

"Salt, sugar, bicarbonate of soda . . ." he muttered as he gathered his ingredients.

"Are you planning on making a cake?" probed Hannah.

"No . . . a tonic." He took a pitcher of water and began dropping measures of each ingredient into it, then stirred it all together. "In the first phase of typhoid, patients' fevers may rise as high as 104 degrees. Their situation will deteriorate as their symptoms increase—dramatic sweats, failing appetite, and coughing spasms."

Hannah's expression became grave as she considered Beatrice.

Dr. Butler continued. "They become listless and constipated, but as the disease progresses, diarrhea will commence and fluid loss will become a critical issue. This tonic should help keep their body fluids balanced. I am leaving a copy of the recipe for you to mix additional batches. From here on out, administer this in place of all other fluids to anyone who is symptomatic."

Hannah nodded as her eyes began to well. "What if Beatrice gets sick? Her health is already poor. Do you think she and the baby could survive it?"

He kicked idly at the floor, attempting to avoid her gaze. "Dr. Perkins is the partner of Dr. Nathan Smith, my professor. Dr. Smith has done extensive research on typhoid. If Beatrice does show signs of the disease, I'll consult with him on her care. He will be her best hope."

Hannah slowly sank into a chair. "Every time she coughs or shows a hint of a fever I panic. People's symptoms seem to present so differently. When will we know?"

Dr. Butler blew out a long breath and furrowed his brow. "The incubation period is from ten to twenty days. We won't know for sure until then, but let's not forget that you are also one of my patients, little miss. I'm delighted you are feeling so well, but you are not out of the woods either. And since the number of sick increases with each visit, I'm arranging for some medical students to come and relieve some of the workload. They won't be much help in the kitchen, but they are trained to attend to the next phase of the illness when the patient care and the sanitation will become more critical and difficult."

Hannah nodded soberly before taking the recipe from him. Images of Beatrice, sick and fevered, gnawed at her peace, and she ached over her failure to heed the warnings the night they had arrived at the inn.

CHAPTER 9

December 26, 1812
Baltimore, Maryland

Christmas at the Willows overflowed with people, yet it had still seemed lonely to Jed. His college friend, Timothy Shepard, had stopped by a week earlier to make another attempt at winning Frannie's heart, but in an interesting twist of fate, a sullen note arrived from Jed's musically-inclined sibling informing him she would not be home for Christmas. The owner of *Le Jardin* had begged her to remain in Philadelphia through the season to entertain the seamen filtering in from the ships patrolling the Delaware Bay. Timothy was ready to head to the City of Brotherly Love when a winter snowstorm arrived, stranding the young lawyer at the Willows through Christmas. Jed noted the amusement the situation offered Markus, who had once been smitten with Frannie himself.

The only word Jed had received from Hannah, however, had been a terse note from Boston dated November 25:

Dearest Jed,

Please forgive me for not writing sooner. Contrary to the worries my silence may have planted in your mind, Beatrice and I are well. Our journey has been riddled with complications that have greatly hindered our progress. Despite our difficulties, she is determined in her quest, and I remain to support her; I must allow that she feels guided by that same Spirit that I trusted in, that I still trust in.

*I pray all is well with you and that we are each allowing that
same spirit to guide us to the end Providence desires for us.*

Your dearest Hannah

He had mentally dissected the note, conversely feeling hopeful and then
morose about the meaning of its cryptic reference to Providence's will. In the
end, he dwelt on the conspicuous absence of any clear disclosure of her feelings, aside from her closing, and so the abundant joy he had felt when the
letter had arrived quickly faded into worry, further dulling his happiness.

So the lonely bachelor's only comfort lay in the festivities planned by
Jerome and Bitty. Jerome had planned a beautiful Christmas Eve service by
firelight in the frosty meadows. The children had acted out the tender tale
of Joseph and Mary's journey to Bethlehem and their rejection at the inn.
Royal and Mercy's wriggling infant played the baby Jesus, and Jed found
himself deeply moved by the play. He wasn't sure if it was the earnestness of
the children—enslaved, yet fully invested in the story of the child who was
sent to free all from the bondage of sin and death—or if it was the thought
of the Child himself, of whom Jerome constantly testified, whose love for
mankind required His very life to provide a way to that freedom. Perchance
it was the sight of Royal's baby son, the child of a man who himself had
been willing to offer his life to protect his family. Perhaps it was all of it, but
for whatever reason, the story became real to him, not merely a fable or tale
like Aesop's; yet he was glad when Sooky's music began the triumphant,
rhythmic singing that indicated the play's finale, ending the harrowing of
his aching heart.

On Christmas Day, presents lay under the tree for each resident, and
Bitty and the ladies prepared a feast for everyone using game the men had
shot on the previous day's hunting trip. The only thing that marred the day
was the recent dearth of communication from Bitty and Jack's sister's family
on White Oak. Nonetheless, after warning everyone to be especially vigilant, Jed, Markus, and Timothy each followed through with their respective
plans, leaving the Willows at first light on Saturday December 26.

Markus and Timothy took the ferry across the Patuxent. Timothy
picked up the Washington Road while Markus headed south for Hampton,
Virginia, where his father's relatives resided. Jed, however, turned Tildie
north for Baltimore, attempting to seek for answers regarding Hannah, in
the hopes that next Christmas might be a happier one.

He knew his doctor would share Bitty's dim view of his plan to ride into
Baltimore. The incision had healed over but the area was still tender, and

three weeks of limited mobility had left him stiff and weak. His body jostled in the saddle, causing him to wince from time to time, but to him, the pleasure of the ride and the freedom it afforded him was well worth his discomfort.

He had a full agenda planned, and first on the list was the best of the items. Jed rode Tildie to the corner of Eutaw and Biddle Streets where the city's workhouse sat. Its infirmary provided a facility for the poor's ill to receive medical attention from the faculty and medical students of Maryland's College of Medicine, one of whom was Jed's dear friend, Dr. Samuel Renfro, who, to Jed's delight, was walking his way as Jed rode up.

Upon seeing Jed, the fatigue instantly lifted from the portly medical student's gentle face, and his blue eyes crinkled with delight. In minutes the pair were sitting at Samuel's table, his light brown hair noticeably molded in the shape of his hat, right down to the end curls which had been molded by the brim.

"You're lucky you caught me. I've been traveling all fall, visiting various hospitals and medical schools. I'm off to New England next—to Dartmouth. My professor, Dr. Davidge, sees a surgeon in me, and he is set on having me observe the country's finest."

"A surgeon?" Jed drew out with great admiration.

Samuel waved his hands before him to subdue Jed's praise. "It's more a matter of need than gift, I'm afraid. It's the war. Though the War Department still denies the fight is coming to Washington and Maryland, the physicians want to have more surgeons ready beforehand." He bowed his head and shook it. "It's a grisly thing we're facing . . . as well you know. I received your letter. So Dupree is back, eh? Shall I have a look at your shoulder?"

"It's mending fine." Jed shook him off with a smile. "I saw Timothy over the holidays."

"Timothy? Is such familiarity still appropriate when speaking of the assistant to the president's wife? I had supposed we'd have to call our old chum 'Mr. Shepard' from now on."

Jed chuckled. "Mrs. Madison's personal assistant . . . What an opportunity!"

"What would either of us give to enjoy the liberties he does over at the Congressional Library? I heard how Mrs. Madison arranged permission for him to borrow whatever he wants. Just think of it," said Samuel, practically salivating, "having access to the Congress's private collection of books, sitting and sharing ideas with those great political minds. President Jefferson personally selected a great many of the volumes included in the collection, you know. Imagine . . ."

"Yes," Jed replied wistfully. "I'm ashamed to admit how jealous I was when I heard. But what about you? So you're off to New England, are you? Is Vermont on your schedule?"

Samuel pulled out his pocket watch as a smile crossed his face. "Twelve minutes . . . I daresay I never thought you'd hold out that long before bringing her up. And how is Hannah?"

"I've hardly had a word from her since she left," said Jed, trying to appear unflustered.

Samuel's brow furrowed. "Didn't you part with an agreement between you?"

"In a manner of speaking." Jed looked at the table and tapped nervously on it. "She felt she owed the lieutenant the courtesy of a personal explanation, which circumstances did not permit, but she assured me that her affections were mine." He abruptly stood and paced across the tiny apartment. "Oh, who am I fooling, Samuel? It's apparent that Robertson used his final hours with her to play on her heartstrings until her honor and loyalty shifted back to him."

"Do you really believe her to be that fickle?"

"She's made little effort to contact me! What other explanation could there be?"

There was a conspicuous pause before Samuel answered. "She loves you. I saw you both that morning. No one could dissuade a woman who is that enamored from loving you."

"Except me." He saw the confusion on Samuel Renfro's face, grasped the chair back, and slumped. "I told her I could not marry her while her mother hates me so. I hoped to win her mother's favor so she wouldn't have to choose between a husband and her family. But perhaps she decided to choose the man her parents already find acceptable."

"Why didn't you simply tell her that you loved her and that you couldn't wait to marry her? *Then* you could've spent the rest of your life endeavoring to win her parents' approval!"

"Out of fear that they never would," he answered weakly.

"And what if they hadn't? Would that outcome have been worse than being apart?" Seeing the pain in Jed's face, he softened. "What was Hannah's position on the matter?"

Jed was stilled by the recollection of her words, and his breathing nearly halted. "She chose me . . . so long as I could promise that I would not be driven by the voices of our critics."

"But your pride would not allow you to make such a promise . . ." Samuel groaned.

Jed felt as limp as a rag doll. His slipped into his chair, allowing his head to fall. Samuel patted his friend's good shoulder as his own head continued to shake over the situation.

"I admire you greatly, Jed, but you have one annoying inclination. For some reason you believe that you must fix everything . . . that you are somehow responsible for every injustice you see. I have news for you. The Willows is not a sovereign nation and you are just one man. You do not have armies to fight for you nor diplomats to dispatch, yet you adopt responsibility as if you did. Hannah's a good woman . . . capable of making her own choices. If you truly see her as such and not as a child, you must accord her your respect by honoring those choices."

Jed raised his heavy head. "You're right. Even I can see what a prideful fool I was. She bravely offered to be mine despite every obstacle, and I treated her gift of love as if it were of less value than my family honor. I've lost her. Why else would she remain nearly silent?" he moaned.

A pause ensued, and then Samuel muttered, "I pray there is not another explanation . . ."

Jed raised an eyebrow.

"I'm sorry. I was just thinking aloud." Samuel stared at Jed as a look of resolution crossed his face. "Jed, I must tell you, I'd almost prefer the reason for her silence to be her anger with you."

Jed leaned forward upon hearing Samuel's ominous response. "And why is that?"

His friend drew a heavy breath. "You recall that I am headed to New England? Well, my reasons for going there are twofold. Initially I was being sent there to observe a brilliant surgeon, Doctor Nathan Smith, the Professor of Medicine at Dartmouth, but my departure has been hastened because there is an outbreak of typhoid in the Connecticut Valley, Jed."

Jed's jaw dropped. "That's Hannah's destination."

Samuel stood and flapped his hands in a call for calmness. "She's probably absolutely fine, taking time to settle in with her hosts." He wagged a finger, underscoring his next point. "We both know she has ample reason to withhold her letters. More likely than not, she is torturing you, hoping you will come to your senses and beg her to marry you."

With sagging shoulders, Jed stood to study Samuel's eyes. "How bad might it become?"

Samuel couldn't meet Jed's eyes as he delivered the sobering news. "They believe that upwards of six thousand may die. I know how that sounds," he rushed in, "but she may be absolutely fine. Is there someone else she may have written? Her other sister perhaps?"

Jed, eyes lit up and he rose abruptly, gathering his hat and woolen coat. "Perhaps . . . I must go. Once I have some idea where to begin, I'll head north to search for her."

Samuel leapt to his feet to get the door. "I leave in two days for New England, Jed. Let me know if you want to travel with me."

"I will. In either case, you'll keep an eye out . . . ask about her as you make rounds?"

"Of course."

Jed felt as if his already-threatened world had shifted cataclysmically in an hour. The concerns of war that previously pressed so severely upon him were suddenly made irrelevant by his worry over Hannah, and he knew there were only two places where he might find answers.

Thus he rode to the court house in the hopes of discovering where Mister Harvey Baumgardner lived. Though it was a Saturday, and the day after Christmas, several local officials were conducting business in the building boasting a portrait of Mayor Johnson, the man Jed held account-able for the August riot in Baltimore when a publisher's rights had been trampled and his attackers supported by bayonet and gun. Jed now wondered if Mr. Baumgardner, the mayor's counsel, deserved his equal contempt.

Jed found the door that bore Mr. Baumgardner's placard and rapped loudly upon it, whereupon a short, rumpled man, wrought with fatigue, answered.

"Mr. Baumgardner?" Jed inquired dubiously to the plain, mousey man, who bore no resemblance to the gregarious, merry style-setter Hannah had described in her letter.

"Yes?" the man replied rapidly, as if awaiting bad news.

"Are you the Mr. Baumgardner who is married to the former Miss Myrna Stansbury?"

Mr. Baumgardner's short, round body bent as he returned to his desk to grab his quill. "What has she stirred up now? Are reparations in order or will a simple apology suffice?"

Knowing Hannah's older sister, Jed now understood. "I've no complaint, sir. My name is Jed Pearson. I've come to inquire after your sister-in-law, Miss Hannah Stansbury."

Baumgardner stood and pulled his spectacles down his nose. "Did you say Pearson? Jed Pearson?" He immediately began moving in Jed's direction with his hand extended. "Please, Mr. Pearson, have a seat," he said, vigor-ously pumping Jed's hand. "It is a pleasure to meet you, sir!"

Jed eyed the man curiously as he sat. "You have the advantage over me, sir."

Baumgardner sat on the front edge of his desk, animatedly dangling one of his short legs back and forth. Moment by moment the reported twinkle returned to the man's eyes. "We've not met in person, Jed . . . may I call you Jed? However, I feel as if I know you already." He chuckled.

Slightly overwhelmed by the man's conviviality, Jed remarked, "I didn't expect to find you here on a Saturday, sir. I was prepared to track you down at your home if need be."

"Oh . . . I feel more at home here than in my own house, but I have no doubt you would have found me were I at home. I know you are a very determined man. You see, Jed, your reputation precedes you. Last August, when news of the riot broke out, my wife and I hurried to ferry her sisters out of the city, but when we arrived at the Snowden's home . . ." he threw his hands into the air, "well, you can imagine what we thought when we saw the house ablaze and firemen scrambling everywhere. Myrna nearly collapsed with fright as did I. Hours later we received a note from Beatrice describing how you rescued her entire household and our dear Hannah! My wife was reluctant in her praise of your deeds but I, sir, was most impressed!"

Jed was cheered by the prospect of having an ally in the Stansbury circle. "Thank you, Mr.—"

"Call me Harvey," Mr. Baumgardner corrected with a smile and a wag of his finger, "but I know your audacity saved more than the Snowden household. That Mr. Thomson you secreted out of the city to safety along with General Lee? He is a dear friend. Let me say that while I did not favor Mr. Hanson's editorials, I was appalled by the city's violent response to them."

"Would that include your superior, the mayor?" Jed asked pointedly.

Harvey's head seemed to slide into his neck and shoulder. "The citizenry reelected our mayor, you know. People want decisive leadership in such times as these. Mayor Johnson, as imperfect as he may be, is such a man." He sighed, adding, "I do not have to always agree with the man to serve him. At times, our situation becomes muddled, but duty drives us to honorably serve those to whom we've pledged ourselves. I know this is a principle you already understand. And how do I know that? Because a man tends to overhear things when two regretful sisters converse. I know Myrna and Beatrice have suffered greatly over a certain ruse they committed."

Harvey raised an encouraging eyebrow, and Jed felt a lump form in his throat over the reference to the women's efforts to deprive him of Hannah's first letter declaring her love. The air rushed out of him as he wondered if Baumgardner's favor could possibly trickle down to the rest of Hannah's family.

"Let there be no mistake," Harvey continued cautiously. "Robertson's a fine chap—as good as they come—but no one should have tampered with fate. They should have allowed the chips to fall where they may. But I cannot tell you how highly I esteem you for setting your own desires aside and doing what you thought was best for Hannah, and in that spirit, I offer you my help. I'd be delighted to answer your inquiries regarding my sister-in-law, though to my knowledge, my wife has received but a single, terse note, saying they were detained by weather."

Jed uncrossed his legs and leaned forward. "Doesn't that alarm you?"

Harvey Baumgardner folded his hands into his lap and sighed. "I don't know how well you know my wife, Jed. It came as a complete surprise to me to discover that the agreeable lady I courted is in fact a very *rigid* woman. When things are not to her liking she tends to voice her displeasure boldly. She was opposed to Beatrice's plan to seek her husband and furious over Hannah's journey with you, so it does not surprise me that her sisters would withhold the details of this trip from her."

Jed moved to the very edge of his seat. "But just one letter in four months? Not a memo assuring you of their safe arrival . . . or a Christmas note?"

Mr. Baumgardner, ever the barrister, tapped his pencil on the table and smiled. "Was it not you who spirited Hannah out of Baltimore for an entire month with no word beforehand and only one during, which itself was only written to warn Beatrice of possible danger? At least we clearly know these ladies' destinations and travel plans."

"But did you know, sir, that there is an outbreak of typhoid in that region?"

Baumgardner sobered. "Yes . . . but I can assure you that despite the ladies' differences of opinion, they are devoted to one another, a result of their gloomy upbringing, I suppose. If Beatrice and Hannah were in need of help, the first person they'd contact would be my wife."

Jed's momentary peace quickly faded as the only other reason for Hannah's silence settled in. "Have you had word from Lieutenant Robertson regarding Hannah?"

Mr. Baumgardner smiled sympathetically, "I have not . . . but I can't speak for my wife."

Renewed determination flooded Jed as he stood and offered his hand. "Then I'll need to ask the good lieutenant myself, Harvey. Thank you for your kindness to me."

"My pleasure, Jed. But don't fret. I'm sure all is well with the ladies."

Nodding and then exiting the courthouse, Jed rode along the street to a large, two-story brick building bearing a painted placard indicating the residence and office of *Mr. John Ridgely, Esq.* He tied Tildie and knocked on the door, which was answered by Mr. Ridgely himself.

"Forgive me for coming without an appointment, John, but may I come in?"

"Of course!" his lawyer replied with concern. "Follow me into my office and tell me what is so important as to drag you into town during the holidays."

"I have a rather unorthodox request. I'd like to see all my files."

John led Jed to a tall vertical file cabinet, pulled out the middle drawer, and removed a packet of papers bound in a leather tie. Obviously unsettled by the request, he gingerly slid the packet across the table to Jed, who untied the strap and riffled through the documents one by one. Satisfied that everything was accounted for, he retied the packet and tucked it under his arm.

"Are you ending our business association, Jed?"

"No, John, but did you know that someone orchestrated an attack on the Willows a few weeks ago? The man behind the attacks is determined to ruin me, and he'll use whatever means possible to succeed. I can't afford to have these papers fall into his hands."

"I understand, but I can assure you I've never lost a document before. Still, if you're that concerned, I could keep your files in my personal safe rather than in the cabinet."

Jed's eyes widened and his head nodded. "That would put my mind at ease."

"Fine. We'll do it right now." Ridgely took the packet and headed for the door, then stalled, straightened, and looked back at Jed. "There are . . . *other* files, Jed, files my father drew up for your grandfather years ago. They're purely personal documents, bundled up and sealed on condition that they were to remain so unless circumstances required your knowledge of them."

Now Jed straightened. "And who was designated to make that determination?"

"I was. By your father."

More secrets . . . Jed hated their constant appearance. "I came to you asking for information about my grandfather. Why did you not mention them before?" he challenged.

"As I said, I was bound by your father. He kept these files at his office, but a few weeks before he died he brought them to me and directed that you not be made aware of them unless circumstances required it. I'm not completely certain what they contain, but in view of your recent concerns, perhaps the time has come."

Jed tightened his jaw in frustration, directing, "I'll take them now,"

Ridgely heard his irritation and nodded. "As you wish. I'll be back presently with them."

Pacing around the room, Jed wondered what information was so sensitive that his father's dying thought had been to shield it from him. It annoyed him that at one moment people looked at him as if he were Solomon, and the next he seemed regarded as a child to be coddled and protected. Worse yet, in either moment, he felt like Atlas, sentenced by his predecessors to bear the weight of their world upon his young shoulders. *Well, if that is my lot, then at least let me fully know my burdens!*

Ridgely returned carrying Jonathan Edward Pearson's old leather valise. Jed took his father's documents gingerly. "Are there any others," he snapped, "or do I now know as much about my business as you?"

"There are no other documents, Jed." He sighed. "And please understand my position . . . trying to honor old promises made to the grandfather, the father, and now to the son. Sit down and read what's inside, and then I'll answer what questions I can."

"I've got something more pressing to attend to now," Jed said as he stood and headed out.

"Return soon then," offered John as he opened the door. "We need to talk further, my friend."

Jed looked back over his shoulder at the man as he mounted Tildie and headed off into the dusky street. Then he turned toward the stronghold of Fort McHenry for his final errand of the day.

The original earthen fort had been strategically placed during the Revolutionary War, forcing enemy ships to pass by it on their way to the city, and whether by luck or strategy, the war had ended with no attacks on Baltimore. The brick, star-shaped fortress which now occupied the site was undergoing months of vigorous preparations to assure that the stronghold's previous record of protection was matched during this conflict.

Jed marveled over the change in mood that had obviously overtaken the fort since his previous visit. After crossing the bridge that joined the Baltimore Road to the fort's acreage, two very young sentries raised their rifles directly at him, demanding to know his business.

"I've come to see Lieutenant Robertson. I'm a . . . a friend, here on a personal matter."

"*Captain* Robertson has not left word that he is expecting you, sir."

Jed noted his rival's promotion as he looked down the unyielding gun barrel. Sighing, he asked, "Then would one of you at least carry a message to him for me?"

While the younger-looking of the two left to inform the captain, his companion dutifully held Jed at bay. Awed by the defensive preparations underway, Jed studied the fort's arrowhead-shaped initial defensive mound, called a ravelin, which boasted cannon and other artillery with trained artillerymen who stood at rigid, wary attention. He noted the harried activity of men repairing and building gun platforms near the shoreline while the sounds of drilling soldiers arose from behind the twelve-foot-high walls of the actual fort.

The soldier returned, escorting Jed over a footbridge which led to the sally port. This main entrance was centered in one of five twelve-foot-tall brick walls, which Jed had heard were called curtains. Each curtain was then anchored between high battle stations. These bastions formed the arrowhead-like points of the star and the entire pattern rose from a dry moat which placed attackers in a direct line of fire upon their approach. All in all, it was a spectacular structure, and on this day, with soldiers poised for battle on every side, Jed felt the reality of the war rush over him.

He and his escort stopped in front of a building where a throng of soldiers were beleaguering a second lieutenant granting access to the building on an exceedingly limited basis. Finally, Captain Robertson strode through the door and over to the pair. As the men's eyes met, both were transported back to that miserable August day, four months previous, when circumstances forced Jed to deliver Hannah over to her fair-haired intended, First Lieutenant Andrew Robertson. Both men knew their situations had been altered by Jed's and Hannah's month-long journey, but on that day, affections and loyalties were weighed, and neither man knew where the balance would tip. It was clear that neither still did.

The captain quickly dismissed the young soldier, then took Jed by the arm and pulled him aside. "Have you heard from Hannah?"

Jed's stomach tightened and a nervous quiver traversed to each of his limbs. "Only a brief November note," he stated incredulously, too sick to gloat. "And you?"

"Nothing since I put her on the ship," said Robertson as his complexion paled. "And her sister, Mrs. Baumgardner, received only a brief note from Boston saying that they were leaving soon for Tunbridge. I keep in contact with Hannah's sister, Myrna. It comforts her to know I've ordered the riders carrying dispatches north to make inquiries about the women along the way. So far, they've uncovered nothing more. She and I agreed to notify one another if either of us received further word, but I've heard nothing from her since. I had hoped that you . . ."

Robertson's report reminded Jed that he was still the outsider in the family's eyes. Adding insult to injury, he recalled Samuel's comment that he was only one man, without armies to deploy or diplomats to dispatch, yet here was Robertson with both at his disposal.

Robertson continued, seeing that Jed had nothing to add. "Beatrice was determined to reach the Mack family before the holidays. I wrote to Captain Mack, but he has received only a brief note apologizing for their delay. I'm becoming worried."

"Then I'm going north to Boston," Jed blurted out impetuously.

"To accomplish what?" Robertson spat back. "My men . . ."

"Your men are not me!" Jed argued. "Your men are not invested in her discovery. I have spoken with my friend, Dr. Renfro, and there are other dangers there."

"The typhoid?" Robertson guessed, his cobalt-blue eyes blazing. "Yes, I know about the epidemic, and I assure you, Pearson," he sneered, "I am equally invested."

Jed felt impotent and useless. His only resources were himself and his love for Hannah, which, when weighed against Robertson's hefty connections, seemed paltry and juvenile, like a child throwing rocks at a giant. The two men glared at one another as several nervous soldiers carrying documents began to gather, seeking their superior. One dared a timid approach.

"Captain," he called out weakly. "The major wants to see you right away, sir."

"Tell him I'll be there straightway," Robertson replied, his eyes never leaving Jed's face.

Disgusted by their impasse, Jed offered Robertson a proposition. "Perhaps we should combine resources. You tell me where your men have been and I'll search elsewhere."

Robertson stared at the ground as the group of soldiers approached, shoving a memorandum before him. His jaw became taut and his normally flushed face became remarkably so as he read on. Then, after stepping aside to speak to the soldiers, he turned back to Jed with futility etched on his unlined face. "Neither of us can do anything for Hannah right now."

Jed moved to argue, but Robertson shoved the memo in his face, explaining, "It's from an American sympathizer imbedded with Cockburn's troops. Because of our current success along the Canadian border, we anticipated that they might attempt to divert our attentions by opening up a new theater of attack elsewhere, and we have to suspect that the Chesapeake will be one target. If they cut off the bay and march inland, they could effectively sever our nation in half. Dissatisfied New Englanders are already talking secession over the loss of trade revenues, and the southern agricultural states are hotly divided over the same. If Britain can split us further, we may see an abrupt and perilous end . . . not just to the war, but to the democracy itself."

"Do you think they'll attempt to take Washington?" Jed pressed.

Robertson looked away and stalled. "The War Department does not think so."

"I'm asking what *you* think!"

The captain closed his eyes and sighed. "Carry word along your route that the British are coming. Warn them that the first rotation of the militias are being called up, including your unit."

* * *

Hungry to turn Tildie north toward Hannah and Frannie, Jed nonetheless headed south, pounding on doors from Baltimore to Calverton, spreading the word and distributing orders to militia captains until first light when he finally reached the Willows. He rushed upstairs to pack his bag, placing his previously prepared letters inside, and then he wrestled over whether or not to spend his last hours at home delving into his grandfather's papers when so many other worries pressed on his mind. Years of second-guessing himself and his family convinced him that any truth was better than conjecture, and he opened the packet and spilled out the contents.

There were six documents in the packet—four were primarily financial documents that were altered and amended in subsequent letters, but one was a letter from his grandfather written to the reverend, and the last item was a letter addressed in a delicate, decidedly feminine hand and folded to enclose something. When Jed opened it, a locket was revealed on which the letters *SAB* were engraved with an *M* added to the end in a different hand. Jed remembered the locket in his grandfather's portrait and the initials carved into the casket he had uncovered; the pieces began to make sick sense. He looked at the heading of the letter. It was dated November 12, 1781, and when he turned the letter over the signature simply read, *"Sarah."*

His body chilled at the sight of the name that had been at the clouded center of his troubles with Hannah, and whose body lay mysteriously buried by the Willows' dock. He suddenly realized that the date also matched that which was etched into the coffin and he knew this was likely that last note written by Sarah Benson McClintock before she'd died. Resigned that he could no longer deny there had been a connection . . . perhaps even the rumored romantic relationship between his grandfather and Hannah's grandmother, he now hoped that the documents would vindicate his grandfather from the innuendoes that had poisoned Hannah's mother against him—his complicity in Sarah's demise.

With the hour of his own fate so close at hand, Jed dared believe that Providence or Sarah herself had directed the packet to him at this pivotal hour. He felt the need to touch the letters of her name, as if the very paper itself had come from some mystifying, ethereal plane. The reading of the letter did not dispel that feeling.

Dearest Jonathan,
You will never forgive me. I know that now. I dared hope what the Bard said was true . . .

". . . Love is not love,
Which alters when it alteration finds,
Or bends with the remover to remove:
O, no! it is an ever fixed mark . . ."

Where is that mark, Jonathan? Does it exist here? Is it in the dominion of God?

Why did they soil such sweetness, calling good evil, and love mere lust? I faltered Jonathan, allowing others to corrupt my conscience with what was never in our hearts.

He said our souls were in jeopardy, and that he could lead me to forgiveness, but a penance was required. Your salvation was within my grasp. How could I not submit what was required to secure your eternal reward?

My penance required my greatest sacrifice. I thought in time an angel would come and tell me my test was passed, my reward secured, awarding me that which I had forfeited for our salvation, but none such came, nor do I now think you would answer if He called you back to me.

And so I go to heaven to plead my cause, girded in the vestments of my fidelity . . . dressed in blue, the color of my maidenhood, and wearing the locket you gave me, bearing my childhood initials with a "M" added—proof of my marital faithfulness.

Fault the hand and not the ax, for my actions were not of my choosing.

I was true to two, in love with one, apparently loved by none . . .

Sarah

Jed read the puzzling note three times, unsure what the confusing imagery meant. He laid it aside and picked up his grandfather's note, and then the picture cleared somewhat.

> *McClintock,*
>
> *I dare not call you reverend and honor you with a title undeserved. What evil courses through men, entitling them to hew their fellowmen down with the sword of righteousness selfishly wielded? I know your sin and count you a ruined soul. You deceived both your Father and His daughter and took what was to be mine . . .*
>
> *Spurned once before, in my youth, I should have easily borne another refusal of my affections, but in truth, I inflicted hurt for hurt, heaped upon your own deception, and twixt these wicked crosshairs, sweet Sarah was destroyed. We are both damned men.*
>
> *My only relief is that you have restored to me my faith in the God I falsely cursed for my fate, and if I have any favor remaining with Him, I shall not squander it petitioning God for vengeance upon your soul. In view of all Sarah endured for love, forgiveness is the right course; since I have not sufficient measure of such at this time, I leave you to your own fate, asking only to allow me to render to those children who should have been mine, some minuscule relief for what has been lost them.*

Jed's mind reeled as the details of his grandfather's financial plan for the care of Sarah's children followed the letter. He thought back on the preceding summer's conversation he'd had with Ichabod Pratt, the bank manager, whose previously obscure clues shed light on the cryptic letters he now held. Jed recalled his mention of the prejudice the gentry held against his indentured grandfather, finding him unfit for one of their own debutantes. He confessed that the gentry had poisoned Sarah's parents toward such a pairing, and in turn urged her on to the young Reverend McClintock. While answering some questions, the letters served to raise even more, and there was no one left to consult. Cursing his situation, Jed considered that perhaps that was precisely his grandfather's plan—to draw out the date of disclosure until the only recourse was to let it go.

He considered the irony of finding himself in a similar circumstance of love. What had Sarah said? "I *was true to two, in love with one, apparently loved by none* . . ." Three lives were once ruined by jealousy and blame. He thought of himself, Hannah, and Robertson, and vowed to do what he could to avoid making the same devastating mistakes.

* * *

In the morning he heard a gentle tap on his door. Jerome had come to his room clutching his favorite hat in his hands. "Are you packed?" he began awkwardly. "I thought . . . I mean . . . I wondered if you might have some last-minute items you'd want to . . . discuss before you leave."

The somberness of the situation stunned the pair, but Jed finally said, "You must have read my mind, Jerome. Please, come in. I have some personal documents here. I want you to take them. If there's a chance anyone could get them, I want them destroyed."

Jerome nodded uncomfortably. Then the two spent a few minutes reiterating old plans, putting off the inevitable moment of Jed's departure. Finally, knowing the moment had come, Jerome laid his withered brown hand on Jed's arm.

"Jed?" he said through trembling lips, "if you'd allow me, I'd like to pray with you."

Jed pursed his lips tightly and nodded. As the older man struggled to his knees, Jed slid down, facing Jerome's weathered face. The former seminarian, abducted and enslaved over fifty years previous, laid his hands on Jed's shoulders, asking a blessing upon the young man. When the words ended, they remained in that modified embrace for some time.

Jed quietly placed his scarred hand over Jerome's aged one and pressed it to his face. Bitty appeared and disappeared behind the door, while Abel approached to comfort her. Jed overheard Bitty's anguished exchange behind the door, and again he felt the awkwardness their unique situation created.

"I've been dreadin' this terrible day for months . . . imaginin' him goin' off to fight, and no words can make it better, Abel. I just want my boy back home safe!"

When Jed and Jerome exited the room, Abel's towering frame was bent and rounded. Jed moved tentatively to Bitty, sweeping her against him with one arm while placing the other on Abel's massive shoulder. When Abel looked at Jed, his face was a wave of emotion.

"I'm a free American now." His face was a wave of emotions. "I should be going too."

Understanding the man's frustration, Jed squeezed Abel's shoulder. "I'd be honored to fight by your side, Abel, because I know you understand what's at stake, but the fight might come to this very house, and if it does, you'll be needed here." Each step down the staircase echoed a somber farewell. Jed found Jack standing on the porch, staring out at the yard. He went to the railing and stood beside him.

"Don't you worry about a thing. We'll take good care of her," Jack pledged in a broken voice, his face turned away from Jed. "Each time you come home from one of your rotations she'll look better'n better." He swept his hands toward the tobacco fields. "We'll be sweetenin' the fields soon and startin' to germinate the seeds. You'll see. Everythin's goin' to be just fine . . . yes . . . just fine . . ." His voice trailed off in broken tones.

Jed patted his back and choked out a reply. "I'm looking forward to it."

Jack followed Jed down the steps to where he had Tildie saddled and ready. Jack secured Jed's haversack and rifle while Jed tied his pack on the horse's back.

"After you send those Redcoats home we'll head off to the cabin and hunt for a spell."

Jed nodded and hurriedly mounted Tildie, unable to bear another minute of farewells. He looked back over his shoulder at the Willows and saw his beloved little group of freed slaves huddled together on the porch. Resigned to the labors that lay ahead, he turned Tildie north and headed away in defense of all he knew.

CHAPTER 10

December 28, 1812
London, England

As Trevor McGowan waited on the bridge overlooking the River Thames, he opened and closed his hand, remembering the dull thud it had made when it hit his poor wife. The sound still haunted him. After his release from prison, she'd been the only person who'd made him feel worth anything. Today, all she'd done was ask for food to feed the two boys, but having not even a shilling for a soup bone, his frustration had gotten the best of him, and he'd gone and hit her.

He saw the wealthy people walking in and out of the pricey London shops and wondered what it would be like to just see something in a store window and have the means to buy it on the spot. He wanted that for his family . . . wanted to put food in the cupboards and hang a ham in the larder. He longed to fill his pockets with treats for his babies like the rich folks did.

The bells at St. Paul's signaled the five o'clock hour, and he craned his neck until he saw the grand carriage coming his way with its curtains drawn. It slowed down and one black shade lifted slightly, from which a low whisper commanded, "Get in." Once McGowan was seated, Stephen Ramsey quickly pulled the shade and settled back against the seat, his menacing face illuminated by the eerie glow of a single candle's light.

"What have you to report?" he demanded.

McGowan squirmed as he began. "Me an' me brothers 'ave been followin' that boy an 'is nanny ev'ry bloomin' place they've gone, we 'ave. An' we made sure she sees us. Now she don't 'ardly ever take 'im out wifout the earl. I think we put the fright in 'em real good."

Ramsey snickered with pleasure. "Good, and how is Lord Whittington?"

"'E's doubled the guards at the doors and now 'e's got a man patrollin' the yard. The place is a fortress, it is."

Ramsey handed a packet of money over. "Excellent. Maintain your surveillance. I don't want that man to draw a breath without worry. I want him to cringe over every creak of the floorboards and to tremble in fear that someone will steal his son as he stole mine."

CHAPTER 11

January 4, 1813
Hanover, New Hampshire

At Hannah's insistence, Beatrice spent the next ten days resting in her room, sequestered from everyone but Hannah and the doctors while she read and stitched things for the baby. Hannah noticed that each day her resting periods grew longer and more frequent, and on the twelfth day, when Hannah entered the room with a breakfast tray at eight, Beatrice lay on her side, fast asleep. She closed the door softly, persuading herself that the fatigue was simply a result of the pregnancy, and returned to the kitchen to help divide up the day's chores.

The doctors often remained through the night now, doling out medicinals to some patients and issuing water therapy to others. After breakfast was cleared, Dr. Butler began making rounds. Hannah followed along, administering tonic to each person on the "sick list," advising him of each patient's fluid intake during the day. The putrid odor of vomit and fetid linen now permeated every inch of the inn. Even with a mask on, Hannah could hardly bear the smell, and she frequently fled to the outside to vomit, then return to carry on. It was so on this morning.

When she fled the room this time, Dr. Butler followed, finding her leaning over a fence rail heaving so forcefully that her hair shook loose from its twist. He gathered her hair up in his hands and held it clear until she was able to stand. Eyeing him curiously, she took his proffered handkerchief and wiped her mouth, becoming withdrawn when he reached to run his hand along her moist brow. She warily studied his face, and then she abruptly turned away from him.

"I was only checking to see if you were fevered, Hannah."

"I'm fine," she replied bluntly. "My stomach turns, but it always settles back down."

He retreated a step and nodded cautiously. "So far, but we are at the peak of your incubation period, and for the sake of the patients as well as yourself, I need to know if your nausea becomes triggered by the onset of the disease instead of the odor."

Hannah knew his explanation made sense, but she'd also seen something else in his expression. "I'll inform you of any changes, Dr. Butler. You can trust me to be honest with you."

"I have no doubt," he replied as he turned to walk back to the inn. Hannah fell in step beside him, and the tension began to ebb between them. "May I ask you a personal question?" he began.

"As long as you understand that asking does not guarantee a reply."

"Fair enough," he replied as he clasped his hands behind his back, restoring her sense of separateness. "The way you recoiled at my touch . . . Are you pledged to someone, Hannah, or are you mistrustful because someone has hurt you?"

Hannah's green eyes blazed as she stormed past Butler. Spinning around to face him, the hurt and anguish of childhood torments and Jed's image rushed in on her. She blinked rapidly and held her hand up to hold the doctor at bay, then speaking through quivering lips she said, "You have no right to diagnose out of curiosity what you can neither understand nor heal."

Her harrowed hurt seared him, and he remained still, absorbing her glare, willingly receiving his lashing. "Forgive me . . ." he muttered as he hung his head and walked past her.

A medical student met him by the kitchen and grabbed his arm. "Mrs. Pickett's fever is 104 degrees now, and her husband is hallucinating. We can't keep up with his fluid loss."

Butler winced at the report. "Send for Dr. Smith and increase the paregoric for the pain, then commence rubbing Mrs. Pickett down with alcohol to lower her fever. Is there anything else?"

"Yes. It's Mrs. Snowden. She has a rash, a fever, all of it . . . every symptom."

Dr. Butler careened down the dank, malodorous hall to Beatrice's room with the medical student close behind. Beatrice lay on her back, as white as death and drenched in sweat, her brown hair matted against her rash-mottled cheeks as an unnerving cough rushed through her dry, cracked lips, rattling her frame and rendering her unable or unwilling to remain lucid.

Dr. Butler quickly examined her. "Has she taken fluids today?"

"You'd have to ask Miss Stansbury," the student replied.

Dr. Butler dismissed the idea. "Her stomach is distended . . . beyond the pregnancy . . ." he mumbled to himself before barking, "Get my bag, and when Dr. Smith arrives, bring him here straightway!"

As soon as Hannah saw the commotion, she pushed past the exiting medical student, flinging herself by her sister's bedside. She buried her face in her sister's sweat-matted hair, repeatedly castigating herself. "Forgive me! I should have listened. I should have listened . . ."

Butler tried to comfort her. "There's no call to blame yourself. You did all you could."

"No . . . there was more. You wouldn't understand, but I *knew* . . . and I failed her."

Dr. Butler didn't pursue it further. "Her pregnancy complicates her situation. We must address her fever. Bring some tonic and spoon as much into her as you can."

She fetched the pitcher, and drop by drop, Hannah spooned tonic through Beatrice's trembling lips until Dr. Nathan Smith, the founder and head professor of medicine at Dartmouth, was ushered into Beatrice's room. Hannah was, at first inspection, disappointed in the highly esteemed man from whom her miracle was expected. He was large with a bumbling gait, boasting no outward signs of aptitude or brilliance. Still, she noted how his colleagues hung on his every word and how he showed the same deference to the questions of the students as he did to his partner, Dr. Perkins. After soliciting the opinions of his colleagues, he cupped his chin in his hand and pondered his treatment plan. Once he offered his instructions, he came face-to-face with Hannah. "You are Mrs. Snowden's sister?" he asked in measured tones.

"I am, sir. What will you do for Beatrice?"

"We'll simply continue the sound treatment plan Dr. Butler has outlined." His manner was matter-of-fact, and as he began to move on to another room, Hannah started after him.

"Dr. Smith!" she called out boldly.

The men turned and Dr. Butler rushed to her, his eyes wide. "I'll answer your questions, Hannah. You needn't bother Dr. Smith."

"Nonsense," Smith replied as he shuffled back to her. "I'm always willing to entertain a question. Forgive me, my dear. What did you want to ask me?"

"Couldn't we give some tartrite of antimony to Beatrice? Others have received it."

Her voice trembled and Dr. Smith took her hands. "The form of the disease your sister contracted has two primary stages. In my experience, the wisest course of treatment is to allow it to run its course through the first stage, offering as little of remedies as possible, as they often create new problems. We'll use all that is at our disposal as it is necessary, but for now, addressing the fever and keeping her hydrated seems to me to be the most prudent course."

Nodding apprehensively, Hannah returned to Beatrice's bedside to spoon more tonic into her. Numb to the inn's chaos, Hannah tried to block out the needs of the others, dedicating herself solely to her sister. She cringed with each of Beatrice's coughs, spooning broth and tonic down between spasms, until she could no longer raise her arm. At some point she laid her head down on the bed beside Beatrice's, and, in the fog of night, she vaguely recognized the feeling of being hefted and carried to her own bed, though she was too exhausted to acknowledge the kindness. She awoke two days later to find Dr. Butler seated by her side.

"How long have I been asleep?" she asked groggily, straining to rise and then flopping back against the pillow.

"Two and a half days," Butler replied. "You've contracted the fever, Hannah, a very mild case. Had you not pushed yourself to the point of collapse you might have passed through it with little notice. Still, I want you to remain in bed a few more days."

Fighting against the confusion swirling in her mind, a single thought brought her to instant lucidity. "How is Beatrice?" she asked, bolting upright and straining to see her sister.

Butler hushed her and gently pressed her back down. "She's resting."

The madness of it all made her head spin. "Please . . . help me sit up for a few minutes." Dr. Butler scowled, then gently slipped his arm behind her back and lifted her forward, putting pillows in place around her. "Thank you," she replied sleepily. She leaned her head back and looked into Butler's weary eyes, strained and ringed with dark circles. "You need to rest."

He simply smiled and shrugged. "First I'm arranging to move you and Beatrice to my grandfather's farm as soon as you're back on your feet. Beatrice has stabilized, but her symptoms are progressing so quickly that I fear she might go into premature labor, and with so many sick here and the lack of sanitation, her baby won't have a fair chance of survival."

It was all too surreal for Hannah to grasp. "But what if she goes into labor there?"

"If there's time, come for me, and if there isn't, my grandfather will talk you through it. He delivered my mother and my uncle and a few other babies as well."

Her mind was numb. "If you think that's best . . ."

"I do." His voice was firm and final. He ran his hand through his long, blond hair. "Mr. Pickett passed away today. He was our first casualty. I want him to be the last."

Hannah's hand instinctively went over her mouth. "I can't believe he's dead . . ."

"Dr. Morgan stopped by yesterday. The epidemic is spreading throughout the entire valley. Thousands of people are sick already, and hundreds have died." He shook his weary head. "Our medical resources aren't adequate. Luckily, doctors headed to Princeton for a surgical conference on the war are coming here to study the disease under Dr. Smith."

"It seems as though we need a miracle." Sarcasm permeated her tone.

Butler cocked his head curiously. "According to Dr. Stone, we may have had one." Hannah's eyes widened, and Dr. Butler explained. "My colleague was called to attend to a young lad from West Lebanon with a different strain of the disease which settled into his shoulder. All eight children of this family suffered through the disease, and all were recovering, except for this lad and his nine-year-old sister. Their previous physician had attended to her for eighty-nine days, but despite his best efforts, on the ninetieth day her condition had so deteriorated that he discontinued treatment and left her to her family and God. Family witnesses attest that she neared death when the parents began to pray by her bedside. When they opened their eyes she appeared to have stopped breathing, but believing that death was not the promise given them in their prayer, the mother wrapped the child in a blanket and gathered her in her arms, pacing and petitioning God to restore her. Witnesses testify that the child began to breathe again."

"Are you saying that she was brought back from the dead?"

He shrugged his shoulders. "Some think the gift of medicine is miraculous, but this report is beyond the limits of any medicine or treatment of which I am aware. All Dr. Stone told me was that her former doctor did indeed consign her to death, and family at the home attest that she stopped breathing for a time, though she is now well. The family is named Smith. Interestingly enough, Mrs. Smith is the sister of your friend, Stephen Mack."

* * *

For the next three days Hannah attended to Beatrice as wretched abdominal pains seized her sister. On the third day, Dr. Butler insisted the move had to be made. The snail's pace trip to his grandfather's little farm took nearly an hour, with Beatrice lying prone in the back of the wagon, completely swathed in blankets and quilts and with Hannah seated by her side, holding her hand.

Dr. Butler called back, inquiring about her condition, then adding, "Hannah . . . I want to apologize for the other day. Remember when you told me that I had no right to harrow up what I could neither understand nor heal? You were right. I had no cause to delve into your personal affairs. The first principle we're taught is to do no harm. I suppose that should apply to injuring a person's feelings as well as their body. It's clear that you love someone dearly, Hannah. It must indeed be a pleasure to be that man, but I'll willingly offer you my friendship if you'll have it."

"I don't even know your first name."

"Zachary," he replied, looking over his shoulder before turning back to guide the team.

Once they crossed the bridge that spanned a briskly moving stream, a rustic frame house and farm appeared. A broad porch set with rocking chairs stretched along the house's front, while a small barn and pasture broke off to the right with a rope that stretched between the two buildings. Before the wagon stopped, a tall, lean man wearing black trousers and a gray, plaid coat appeared on the front porch, waving with delight and smiling like a jack-o-lantern.

"I heard you coming!" he called out in a voice laced with a German accent.

"Hello, Grandfather," Zachary Butler greeted as he jumped down from the wagon seat. The two men immediately embraced and thumped one another on their backs. "Let me introduce you to your two guests." He reached for Hannah's hand and helped her down. "This feisty one is Miss Hannah Stansbury. Hannah, this is my grandfather, Emmett Schultz."

Hannah stretched out her hand, and the large man encased it in both of his as the huge grin returned. "Thank you, sir, for having us. I don't know what we would have done."

"You're so welcome. Hannah, heh? That's a good bible name. Are you a believer?"

Hannah stammered from shock at the blunt inquiry. "Uhhh, yes, sir . . . Reverend . . ."

"Just call me Em, dear. Oh, we'll have some fine conversations. It gets lonely living all alone, especially in the winter. I'm so glad for the company."

Zachary smiled apologetically at Hannah and shrugged. "Grandfather, I need to get Mrs. Snowden right into bed. Which one is hers?"

"I've set the two women up on the main floor to make caring for the sister easier. Got a fire going in the stove already. Knew she'd need warming after that ride."

Zachary gently lifted Beatrice and carried her into the house. Once Beatrice was settled, he prepared to leave Hannah to tend to her. "Grandfather moved upstairs so you two could have the downstairs to yourselves at night."

Hannah's eyes were moist with gratitude as she drew in a deep breath of the clean, pine-scented air. "Thank you for . . . for arranging all this, Dr. . . . Zachary. I can't thank you enough."

He lowered his eyes. "Grandfather insisted, and knowing he has company eases my mind."

Hannah stepped closer. "And I'll be a help to him. I'll cook and clean and—"

Zachary pointed a cautionary finger at her. "Try and remember that you aren't completely out of the woods yet yourself. Now come to the kitchen for supper. Doctor's orders."

The three dined together on a delicious pork stew which Hannah later ground and thinned to make a nourishing gruel for Beatrice. After feeding her sister, she returned to the kitchen to find the men finishing up the dishes. "I'm sorry. I meant to do those after Beatrice fell back asleep."

"Never you mind about the dishes," Emmett argued. "You've got your priorities right. Any two loons can wash up the dishes, but no one can care for a person like the one that loves them."

Hannah beamed at the dear older man as an immediate affinity warmed her. She loved the way he still dressed like a preacher, with his black pants and white shirt, with a tall black hat and coat, which he kept at the ready by the door. He was slightly taller than his grandson, with larger features and brown eyes dulled by blindness. And his face was clean shaven except for a nub of beard at his chin. All in all, he was someone she knew she could come to love as family.

"All right," Hannah agreed, "but tomorrow is my turn. And I want to pay you for our room and board and do some cooking."

Emmett smiled at Zachary. "If it's all the same, missy, I'll do the cooking. I heard about that poor chicken you were plucking a while back."

CHAPTER 12

January 12, 1813
London, England

Lord Whittington was in his study reading the latest military reports. President Madison's reelection in December meant the United States' position on the war was unchanged, forcing Britain to proceed with the next phase of her battle plan. He dropped his head into his hands, lamenting how many young British lives had been cut short over the long campaign with Napoleon, and now they were at war with America. They could not afford to be wrong again about the infant nation's resolve, since the original loss had been damaging to the British economy as well as to her world standing and to the monarchy.

He wanted a united Britain, believing as he did in her system of life and government. There was much to be proud of in her noble traditions, proven over centuries, as opposed to the chaos of "government by the voice of the people." He believed that bringing the Americans back to the womb of their beginning would be better for them, and Britain needed America's resources to maintain her position in the world.

A soft knock sounded at the door. Checking his pocket watch, he scolded himself and called out, "Come in." Clarissa coyly entered, offering an apologetic smile. She seemed like a yellow wisp of wheat among the heavy, leather furnishings and mahogany-paneled walls.

"I'm so sorry to disturb you, Lord Whittington, but it's four o'clock."

Rising to meet her, he smiled and briefly laid his hand on her arm, adding an affectionate squeeze which caused her to shiver. Quickly releasing her he said, "No need to apologize. I simply lost track of time again." As she turned to leave, the earl caught a soft floral scent. "Are you wearing the rose water Daniel gave you for your birthday?"

Her cheeks flushed crimson against her pale skin, and her head dropped in embarrassment. "He kept asking me why I never wear it, so . . ."

"Shhh. I think it's lovely on you."

"Thank you," she uttered, making the briefest eye contact before turning to get Daniel.

The earl closed his eyes and savored the sweet, lingering scent that made both Whittington Castle and his London house feel like home, reminding him of his departed Severina who had worn the similar soft scents of lilac and rose water appropriate for her tender age and bearing.

He grabbed a gray woolen coat and, hoping the gesture would please her, the red scarf Clarissa had knitted for his birthday. As he entered the foyer he found her negotiating with Daniel over a hat, and when the negotiations failed, she playfully tugged his hat over his eyes anyway.

"Daniel!" Lord Whittington scolded playfully. "Are you being rebellious today?"

Clarissa stood quickly to defend her young charge, and when she caught sight of the red scarf, a look of pleasure passed over her face that delighted the earl. He playfully tossed the longer length over his shoulder and winked at the pair, causing Daniel to giggle.

"Can't Clarissa come with us today, Father?"

Clarissa began to sputter, but the earl piped up. "You must ask Clarissa, Daniel."

"Yes! Come with us!" pleaded Daniel as he hurried off to fetch her cloak.

She smiled and diverted her eyes, but a moment later the earl glanced up and caught her staring and smiling at him in a way that made him feel like a boy again. Chiding himself for the silly nostalgia, he wondered how this commoner girl *really* saw him . . . simply as a man with a title, or as a relic, perhaps not unlike a weathered old statue? When Daniel arrived, she reached for the sack of toys at the same moment as the earl. Their eyes met as their hands brushed. She responded by quickly retracting her hand while Lord Whittington surrendered to the blush that warmed his own cheeks. A notion hit him.

"Clarissa . . ." he began with a nervous clearing of his throat. "I've been thinking that . . . I'd be pleased if you'd call me Whit when we're here in the castle or out alone with Daniel."

The earl wouldn't have believed it possible for the young woman to change color so quickly, but the last trace of blush drained from her face at the suggestion.

"Oh, no sir! I could never! It . . . it . . . it wouldn't be proper!"

His effort to narrow the societal divide had apparently only increased the distance, but he tried again. "Would you at least consent to use my given name? It would . . . mean a great deal to . . . to . . . to Daniel. Wouldn't it, son?"

"Oh, yes! Please, Clarissa! It will be like a secret club between you, me, and Father!"

Clarissa's eyes remained unsure, but something reflected there made the earl believe she was considering the notion. "You do *know* my first name, don't you?" the earl teased.

Her head remained dipped as she swallowed and asked, "It would only be when the three of us are alone?"

He laughed softly and shook his head. "And anytime we're at home."

"But the rest of the staff!" she exclaimed.

"It's my household," he replied with a raised eyebrow. "I set the rules."

A tug of a smile began to play on her lips until it stole across her face, breaking into a large grin. The usual crimson blush followed, which relieved the earl. "All right then," she replied.

"Very good! Now let me hear you say it," he cajoled, anxious to hear the expression of familiarity that would ease the disparity in their stations.

"Very well," Clarissa replied nervously, dipping her head. "Lord . . . Everett . . ."

"L—?" he began to contest, disappointed that she had insisted on adding the title 'Lord' to formalize his name. Then chuckling softly, he nodded. "Lord Everett it is."

They walked past the two armed doormen, past the bull mastiffs that roamed the fenced yard, and through the gate where another armed guard patrolled. Crossing Highland Street, they entered the park, all the while scanning for signs of the men who seemed to appear wherever Daniel was. Upon seeing the pond, Daniel requested his sailboat and hurried to the water's edge to launch the little craft. His nanny and father followed close behind.

"Do you see them today?" whispered Clarissa nervously.

"There's one on the bench . . . by the fountain," the earl whispered angrily, "and one on the back of the chimney sweep's cart."

Clarissa quickened her step to stand a yard behind the spot where Daniel was kneeling.

With her eyes darting from one intruder to the other, Clarissa became emboldened. "Let's just walk up to them and confront them! Let us rattle *them* for a change!"

Lord Everett delighted in the timid woman's uncharacteristic defiance, a reaction he knew was motivated by her own love for his son. But the gravity of the situation pressed upon him. "The guards have confronted them. They've even dragged them to the police station, but they were out in hours. No . . . they will not be dissuaded by a mere warning."

"What do they hope to accomplish by following us wherever we take him?"

The earl looked up and squinted against the bright sun. He looked left and right, noticing children running carefree and adults whose own burdens seemed lighter once they'd crossed into the park. He then measured his own tense form and the apprehension in Daniel's eyes, and he knew the answer. "To take away our peace." He glanced at the rough, unshaven perpetrator on the bench and growled under his breath, "Well, not today, you devils. Not today!"

He threw off his heavy coat and grabbed a ball from the bag before hurrying off to lure Daniel into a game of football. Clarissa watched the handsome pair kick the ball past one another and race away as they shuffled it from foot to foot. Two young men joined the game, and father and son became a team, passing and kicking the leather sphere until an hour had passed. Dusk was settling when the pair finally ended the game and returned to the blanket where Clarissa sat.

Daniel flopped down beside her, laying his tousled head in her lap and gazing proudly into her eyes. "Did you see me, Clarissa? I kicked it right past the biggest boy! Right past him!"

Clarissa smiled down lovingly at him and finger-combed his unruly brown locks. "It was a grand kick, Daniel. I believe you could keep up with the blokes at those Rugby schools."

He sat up abruptly. "Do you really, Clarissa? Do you really think I'm that good?"

Clarissa's face clouded as she noted the somber face of the earl, realizing the impossibility of her words. There would be no enrollment at a school in Rugby or any other town beyond his father's gaze. Not for now at least, and she quickly hurried to cover her error. "You know, my brother once played a game of football against some Rugby lads, and his team beat them two goals to one. No . . . on second thought, I think we should keep you close to home in the fall and use your talents to help the Whittington lads beat those Rugby boys instead."

"Yah!" Daniel agreed as he bolted up and began practicing to prepare for that great day.

The earl peered down at his son's nanny with awe. "You're a wonder, Clarissa. You take his tiny, restricted world and make him see it as limitless." Offering his hand to lift her up, he came so near to her that she trembled as he said, "I don't know what we'd do without you."

They hovered, inches apart for several seconds, and then a loud voice called out a greeting across the park. "Lord Whittington! Daniel!" It was Arthur Ramsey, and like the wave of a vocal magic wand, the moment changed instantly, reopening the social chasm between the noble and the commoner as she dropped her eyes again and bent to gather up the blanket.

The earl coughed to clear his throat as Arthur ran over, his brown, curly hair billowing with each footfall and his square jaw appearing all the more so. Smiling brightly, he headed straight for Daniel. Shuffling his feet rapidly, he taunted the boy to dribble past him, and the lad joyfully took the bait. Arthur managed a convincing defense before purposely stumbling, and Daniel gladly took the advantage and ran away with the ball, leaving Clarissa to hurry after him.

Arthur gently caught her arm before she escaped. "You look lovely today, Clarissa."

Before exiting she quickly glanced at the earl, who noted Arthur's gaze following her. "What brings you here, Arthur?" he asked abruptly as he started walking in the direction Clarissa and Daniel had headed.

"I've been wasting my time, serving fat, lazy generals and ferrying documents all over London for weeks now, awaiting the day when I would receive my orders to sail for America. I've read the reports. I know that Admiral Cockburn plans to blockade the Delaware and Chesapeake bays prior to attacking inland. What is the delay? Why am I still here?"

"I'm looking for the proper post for you," Lord Whittington replied. "We agreed that you would be assigned to General Ross, but he is currently tying up details in France. Until he is sent to America, the ground operations will be minimal and your services are not needed."

Arthur stepped in front of the earl and stopped him. "With all due respect, sir, if other men are fighting and dying, why am I to be spared?"

"With all due respect, Arthur," he snapped in reply, "you desired to serve in Maryland. That theater of operations has not commenced yet. Besides, why are you so anxious to head into battle? Are you looking to serve your country or merely to punish your parents?"

Arthur hung his head and breathed a long, despondent breath. "My mother sent me a letter. She is as opposed to my military service as she is to me remaining here in London. She will only be content when I have joined her in Ireland, beyond my father's influence and infamy, and because that is her position, I don't know if I can trust the foul things she reports as truth."

"What has she told you?"

"She says she had a meeting with Mr. Mitchell, just before he forfeited his seat in Parliament. During this meeting they supposedly exchanged information. The picture the amalgamation of facts conjures about my father is uglier than I dare believe."

"And what is in that picture, Arthur?" Lord Whittington questioned.

"My mother says Father is not merely looking for his share of profit from Cockburn's plundering of Maryland's tobacco coasts. He is particularly targeting one man's family. He wants to destroy them . . . out of . . ."—he struggled to find suitable words to express his vehemence—". . . out of some twisted sense of injustice he imagines done him."

Lord Whittington cocked his head and furrowed his brow questioningly as Arthur began pacing in a tight circle, rambling out facts.

"His mother was supposedly engaged to a Liverpool man named Pearson before she met my grandfather. This Pearson evidently wronged grandmother somehow, requiring her to call off their engagement. Soon thereafter, Mitchell's grandfather took Pearson under wing, indenturing him to America where this indentured teacher became a very wealthy landowner. According to my mother and Mitchell, Father has pledged to take from this man's family what Providence denied him when, by Pearson's wronging of his mother, she refused his hand. As preposterous as it sounds, Mother and Mitchell attest that it is why he 'acquired' Dupree's services and 'loaned' him to Cockburn. Dupree is not in America to simply help win the war. Dupree is there to destroy this man's family and steal his home."

"And what is the name of this family your father has targeted?"

"Pearson. The family of Jonathan Edward Pearson."

Talk of Ramsey's hunger for vengeance reminded the earl that he too was in Stephen Ramsey's crosshairs, prompting him to begin a frenzied search for Clarissa and Daniel. He saw them near the park entrance. Daniel was pressed against Clarissa with her arms wrapped tightly around him while an old man dressed in tatters approached them, reaching out to touch the lad.

As the earl rushed to their side, he saw Clarissa move Daniel behind her, demanding that the man depart. Catching snippets of the conversation, the earl realized the effect Ramsey's stalkers were having on his household. Placing himself between Clarissa and the man, he offered the poor fellow his outstretched hand. "Forgive us, sir. My son is exhausted from playing so hard, and his nanny is understandably protective of him."

The man withdrew a step. "I didn't mean no harm. I'm from here, Lord Whittington. I just wanted to say hello to the lad. Me wife and me hung a banner in honor of his birth, we did. We walked in Lady Severina's funeral procession and put flowers on her grave, every year since. I've fallen on hard times, but when I saw that you was here, I just wanted to see the boy."

Clarissa shrank in shame at the sight of Daniel's fearful reaction. Only after extensive fatherly cajoling did he consent to meet the man whose hand was offered in such loyalty. When they were safely back in the earl's London town-house, Lord Whittington sent Daniel upstairs to change and asked Arthur to wait for him in the study while he spoke with Clarissa.

"I'm so sorry, Lord Whittington," she cried as soon as they were alone.

"It's all right, Clarissa." He took out his handkerchief and gently wiped the welling tears from her eyes, a kindness which only served to release the floodgates all the more. "We're all on edge, but we *must* find a way to return to some sense of normalcy, or the fear we instill in Daniel will be as damaging as anything those men can do to him." She closed her eyes and hung her head, but the earl lifted her chin to entreat her. "And what of our agreement? Our secret club?"

"I can't," she replied with a sob. "I don't deserve it! I don't deserve to be here at all!"

She ran from the room, and in frustration the earl slapped his fist on top of his desk.

"What is happening to cause such distress in your household?" inquired Arthur.

The earl spun to voice his anger, but as soon as he looked into the gentle brown of Arthur's young eyes, his fury abated to a groan. "You have burdens enough to bear. I will not add mine to your load."

"You offered me a sanctuary when I needed one and made me as a member of your family. You have met my every need, and I have repaid you with impatience and ingratitude. Please, my lord, if there is any service I can render, allow me that pleasure."

Lord Whittington studied Arthur's face, looking deeply into eyes that seemed a conduit to the young man's very heart and soul. "I appreciate your offer, Arthur. It makes what I am about to confess much easier to divulge." Arthur's trust in the earl was so great that even such an ominous start did not affect him.

"The truth is, I have not merely refrained from requesting your transfer, I have fought against it. I have purposely detained you to keep you close at hand for selfish reasons."

Arthur eyed the earl with curiosity, and then peace returned to his face. "What do you need from me?" was his loyal reply.

"God willing . . . nothing. But if my current troubles persist, I will ask a great favor of you . . . one I can only commend to someone with whom I could entrust my very life."

Arthur's expression grew grave. "Speak it, and I shall pledge my very life to fulfilling it."

Lord Whittington clasped his shoulder. "Not today . . . but soon, I fear."

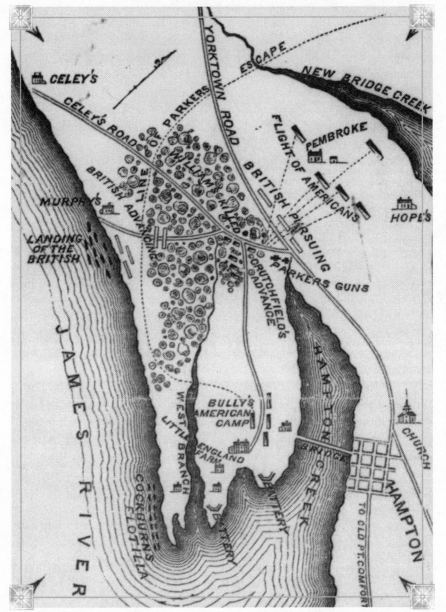

From B. J. Lossing, *Pictorial Field Book of the War of 1812*, published 1868.
Courtesy of *Images of America: Hampton's Old Wythe*.

CHAPTER 13

January 15, 1813
Hampton, Virginia

Markus relished the salty Atlantic air blowing across the narrow peninsula that created the grand Chesapeake Bay. Eventually, stands of Virginia's green magnolias, scrub firs, and wisteria appeared as the James River led to Hampton Creek and the sign for "Hampton" at the edge of town. He cut his horse to his right, and there, tucked into a clearing, he saw his first glimpse of a familiar, gray clapboard house from which an Irish voice bellowed, "What misfortune would bring an ugly cuss like Markus O'Malley back ta these parts?"

Markus's green eyes stared into the similarly colored ones of the sturdy, russet-haired man seated in a rocker who chewed on a corncob pipe. Riding his Morgan right onto the man's porch, he leaned forward and scratched his chin. "Well, you see," he began with a highly exaggerated brogue, "I was ridin' me fine New England Morgan horse, drawin' down a bottle of Maryland's best rye, and I started missin' an ornery cuss I once knew who had more kick 'an either of them!"

"Ha!" roared the squatty man, rising with a hearty laugh. "Well why'd it take ya six years ta find 'im? Now come on down here, boy, and give your old uncle Ryan a hug!"

Markus jumped from Donavan, sending him down the steps, then opened his arms wide to receive his uncle. "I've been away a long time, uncle. I'm sorry."

"Too long, son, but I understand. 'Tis a hard thing for a young man ta see 'is father cut down before 'is very eyes, and by renegade British pirates no less. I suppose you've heard the rumors that them Redcoats are said ta be gearin' up for some foul play along the coast now."

"Aye," Markus barked. "But I can't make a lick of difference without a ship."

"So that's why you're here, is it? Ta resurrect the *Irish Lass* and go after them British!"

"That's right," Markus admitted as he sat down. "They're headin' ta Baltimore and Washington, Uncle Ryan. The government won't admit it, but Jed and I know it."

"Jed? Is that the young buck you've been workin' for these past six years?"

"Only five." He shook his head apologetically. "I spent that first year sailin' the rivers and buyin' tobacco, but betwixt the loneliness and my anger, I started to lose myself. Jed was just a lad, two years younger than me that summer we met, but he offered me a home and steady work and a hundred acres of prime land with a parcel on the water. I love him like a brother now."

Ryan O'Malley laid his hand across his nephew's shoulders. "Just don't forget that you've still got blood what loves you plenty right 'ere."

"I've never forgotten that, Uncle Ryan. It's true that I want ta shore up the *Lass* and outfit her, but I also came home ta be with my family for a time before I head off into this fray."

"That's good, Markus, real good. Rememberin' where 'e comes from helps a man see where 'e's goin'." He crooked his finger, saying, "We O'Malleys think alike. Come with me."

Markus smiled curiously. "Have you already started workin' on her?"

It was only a few hundred yards' walk to the tributary called Hampton Creek, which bordered the western shore where Little England Farm and the local batteries were located. There, on a secluded dock, the crippled *Irish Lass* was moored. Blackened and charred, she looked worse than Markus knew she was. Some refitting had been done, but her burned mast still lay in what was left of her damaged rigging, and what threads remained of her tattered sails were also blackened, testifying to his father's dreadful demise.

Ryan stepped near his nephew and laid a hand on his shoulder. "Your da loved this ship, son, and though he was in no hurry ta leave this earth, 'e died where 'e lived the best adventures of 'is life . . . on the sea, and with 'is son by 'is side."

Markus tensed at his uncle's words. "I don't remember it being so glorious, Uncle."

"No . . . I don't suppose you do at that," Ryan sighed as he let his arm slip. "You've faced some hard things in your young years, son. Let them make you wise, Markus . . . not foolhardy . . . nor turn you into a filthy pirate like them what shot your da and set 'is ship ablaze. You were saved for a purpose. It were your father what pushed you overboard, away from those renegades' guns, but remember that it were the good Lord what spared you that day whilst you was treadin' water. Least 'til another ship plucked you out from the deep."

Markus swallowed hard and longed to change the topic. He stared at the work that lay ahead and asked, "So, how long do you think it'll take to outfit her?"

"Depends on how many men we gather. Your cousin Patrick and me did what you see."

Markus smiled at the mention of his cousin. "And how is Patrick?"

"Fine. Drusilla's expectin' her third. Remember Lyra Harkin, the blind child the Harkin's adopted? Well, Patrick brought her up 'ere from Norfolk ta help Dru with the other children."

"Lyra Harkin . . ." Markus mused as he imagined what the scrawny girl looked like now.

"You'd never recognize Lyra now. She's become a real beaut, and you'd be hard pressed to convince anyone that she's blind, what with the way she moves around a kitchen. She can identify anyone who comes round before they get a chance ta tell her, too. It's eerie the gifts God's given her ta compensate for her eyes. Come along. I'll take you by Patrick's."

It was a quick stroll to Patrick O'Malley's two-story house. His large yard boasted a garden with a swing that hung from a magnolia branch. Chickens scratched in a yard shared by sheep, two dairy cows, and a horse. As soon as Ryan was sighted, two small boys scurried outside crying, "Grandpa!" followed by a pregnant woman with a towel slung over her shoulder.

"You boys be gentle with Papa O'Malley," the woman scolded lovingly. "And who's this you have with you, Ryan?"

"Shhh, Drusilla," the squarely built man scolded with an exaggerated wince. As Markus extended his hand to her, Ryan explained, "I want to test Lyra . . . ta see if she remembers him."

At that moment a tall, slim woman with loosely piled brick-red hair came to the doorway. Her eyes were a soft blue against a pale palette, and they shifted back and forth with every sound. Her long, oval face boasted lips and freckles that matched her hair, and her bearing was calm and sure. One look at her stole Markus's breath away.

Placing her hands on her hips, she challenged in her Irish lilt, "So what will you be wagerin', bein's that you already owe me a pound of tea, an hour of wood choppin', and a pup?"

Markus raised a captivated eyebrow. "This can't be that scrawny, shy child I recall."

Ryan's face contorted, and his fingers fluttered rapidly, urging Markus to silence. "It is, but shhh, lad, or you'll give yourself away." He turned back to goad Lyra. "I'll stump you this time, child. In fact, I'll bet you double or nothin' that you can't name this lad."

Lyra turned to the mistress of the house. "Hmmm. Do you remember the man, Drusilla?"

The woman smiled wryly. "I do believe I recall him from when Patty and I first met."

"So, Mr. O'Malley. You're takin' me back a few years, are you? And double or nothing? Well . . . all right then." Lyra's head turned slightly and cocked in Markus's direction. Pausing for a moment, a smile soon stole across her face. "So . . . you think you remember me, do you?"

"I believe I do," Markus replied as his uncle restrained him from taking another step.

"Your voice tells me you're Irish, but you've been away from your people for a time."

"And how is it that an Irish waif raised by English parents has such a brogue as you?" Her smile broadened and then tightened. "Tell me about your hair. Has it grown back?"

He looked quizzically at his uncle, whose face fell flat in resignation. "Grown back?"

"Yes. As I recall, you nearly burned it all off one night when you were eleven. On one of my visits you and Patrick were showin' off and you wrestled right into the fire."

Markus broke free of his uncle's grip and walked toward her. "How did . . . ?"

"You used ta go off and whistle 'Shule Agra' when you thought no one was listenin'."

"Shule Agra?" Markus repeated in melancholy wonder. "I had completely forgotten . . ."

"Oh, not I, Markus O'Malley. I can still hear your soft, sad tones. I always wondered how someone barely a year older than I could've felt so deeply about life and love at eleven."

Markus laughed softly. "I'm sad to report that I know little more about them now than I did then."

"Dear me," she hooted. "Well . . . your uncle owes me greatly this time. Perhaps we'll let you take a turn at repayin' his debt, and maybe we'll have a go at teachin' ya a thing or two."

* * *

"Give me an hour with them and I'll change their minds," argued Markus O'Malley to his cousin as they approached Patrick's house where Lyra was feeding the chickens.

Shaking the remaining corn from her apron, she listened to Patrick's feisty reply.

"I'm tellin' you, the area is hotly divided. Many of the locals lost fortunes on account of Jefferson's embargo, and now they're none too happy about Madison's war, either!"

"Madison's war?!" she heard Markus shoot back. "Are you sayin' you don't have a stake in it?"

"No . . . 'e's not sayin' that," Ryan cut in with a conciliatory tone as they neared the doorway. "'E's just sayin' . . ."

"He's just sayin' he's mad because his tea costs twice as much now. Isn't that right, Mr. O'Malley?" Lyra called out as she approached the trio, taking Ryan's arm. "And bein' that you now owe me *two* pounds of the stuff, Ryan O'Malley, I'd say that's a particularly sensitive O'Malley topic."

"Ahhh, Lyra," chuckled Ryan innocently. "And how might you be this fine mornin'?"

"Well, my mornin's peace's been disturbed by you three, and I'm callin' in me marker."

"Ahhh," groaned Ryan. "I'm down ta me last pound. I doubt it will last until we can get a ship back ta Europe. Please darlin'. You're too good a woman ta take a man's last bit o' tea."

She cocked her head and arched a brow. "You owe me dearly, Ryan O'Malley, and that's a fact, so tell me what you'll offer me in exchange—and you'd best make it good." She winked.

Ryan gave her shoulder a squeeze before taking her hand and turning toward Markus.

"Markus, I'm in need of a favor." He threaded her arm through Markus's and turned back to Lyra. "Will you accept an hour of my handsome nephew's attentions in partial payment?"

Patrick laughed and smacked Markus on the back. "Good luck ta you, cousin. If you survive Lyra's tongue waggin', I'll introduce you 'round ta the boys."

Father and son moved off along the street leaving Lyra in Markus's unexpected care.

"Well, get on with it," she ordered with a nudge. "It's an hour I'm owed, and I won't take less or Ryan'll hear about it."

Markus scowled at the woman and muttered under his breath.

"What's that?" she asked as she began strolling, dragging Markus along.

Markus stopped cold and spun to face her. "You're a lovely enough woman. You don't need to behave so uppity and ornery. I've had my fill of such as that."

Lyra's eyebrows arched with interest. "So I'm uppity and ornery am I? And lovely ta boot, you said, but I suppose that isn't enough to make you fancy me now, is it?"

Markus clasped his hands around her arms to still her arguing. "What's this really about, Lyra? You were once such a shy young lass. Is bein' this way so much better?"

She dropped her head slightly, then raised it back up and tipped it, indicating her desire to walk. Markus complied. "A shy girl gets coaxed and encouraged while a shy *blind* girl gets coddled and hovered over. But I discovered something interestin' over time . . . that when I was feisty and tough, people thought less about my blindness and focused their attentions on my words instead. I finally feel like I'm equal in everyone else's eyes."

"But are you happier, lass? It would seem to me that actin' brassy all the time would tire a body out. Sooner or later, it won't be an act anymore. You'll just become as hard as you've pretended, and what a waste that would be."

Lyra drew in a deep breath of the river air and stood still and tall as the breeze tousled her hair. "Aye. You're right," she sighed. "You're also the first ta have the vinegar ta tell me so."

He led her to a bench by the dock, and they sat in awkward silence for a time. Eventually, Lyra laid her head on Markus's shoulder and said, "Your accent's back as strong as ever. Now you sound like that Irish lad I remember so dearly."

Markus stared out at the river as it lapped against the pier. "I hardly remember 'im."

"You left here so angry after you buried your father. I thought I'd never see you again, and that you'd never be yourself again . . . that dear, haunted boy who whistled 'Shule Agra.'"

Markus chuckled softly. "I took more than one lickin' from my mates for that tune. It's a woman's song, you know, about her Johnny goin' off to be a soldier. My mother used to sing me to sleep with that ditty, and I never forgot it after she was gone."

"Hearin' ya sing that song is what made me realize you were more important to me than just as a friend. I knew I was in love with ya."

Markus turned abruptly, glaring at her. "What are you sayin'? Don't toy with me, woman! You can't spout such things to a man you barely know as if they had no consequence!"

Lyra's expression was filled with immovable reassurance. "But I do know you, Markus, as you helped me know myself. You were the first person ta see past my blindness and notice the rest of me. It was only on those trips when the Harkins brought me up here, ta know my own kind, that I felt whole. You brought me a stack of leaves one day so I could learn the names of the trees by their shapes and smells. And then you did the same thing for me with bugs and seashells and the like. You were patient and kind with me and helped open the world up to me."

"We were children then, Lyra . . ."

"There's more. I know you stayed ashore ta care for your mother when she was sick, and that you cried openly for her when she passed. I remember hearin' you pray by her graveside, too, and I thought how I'd give anything ta have you love me enough to miss me that much."

Markus stood and moved away from her.

"I wrote letters in my mind and daydreamed about you comin' home as if wishin' it would make it so." His silence brought a blush to her cheeks. "You think I'm brazen for speakin' my mind so openly, but I determined a long time ago that if I ever got the chance ta tell you, I wouldn't let it pass again. And it's not for lack of suitors. I've had my share of men who fancied me, but they either coddled or provoked me. No one else ever made me long for their company. No one but you, Markus. I believe my prayin' and wishin' drew ya here . . . ta me."

He didn't know how to respond to such a profession of affection. He marveled how what would have made most men roar with bravado made him all the more unsure and uncertain.

"I'm not much to look at," he confessed soberly.

"Come here ta me," Lyra called huskily as she patted the space on the bench beside her. He sat tentatively and flinched as she gingerly placed her hands on his face. He chuckled nervously as she moved from feature to feature, but then he began to relax as her hands slipped to his shoulders and along his arms to his hands.

"You've got a fine pair of shoulders and strong 'ands, made rough from 'ard work." Her voice became soft and tender. "It's as I always knew . . . You're a glory of a man, Markus."

A glory of a man . . . The words echoed in his head until he could grasp the sincerity of them. He closed his eyes and leaned in close. His voice was raw with want and emotion. "Please don't toy with me, Lyra. My heart is parched for want of love."

"'Tis not a game for me, Markus."

"Then what?" he uttered as he nuzzled her brow.

"'Tis a dream . . . 'tis a sweet dream come true."

CHAPTER 14

February 2, 1813
Baltimore, Maryland

"Lieutenant Pearson!" the young corporal called out. "Mail call!"

This new moniker didn't immediately register with the young dragoon of Maryland's Third Regimental Cavalry, so he stalled before raising his hand. Breathless for word from Hannah, he was disappointed as soon as he saw the penmanship, knowing it was Jerome's weekly report on the farm. Nonetheless, he smiled whimsically as he read it. They were on their own, and though Jack and Bitty once ran the Willows with only occasional input from his father, they all realized that the plantation had since become a much more complex operation.

Bored and restless, the soldiers drilled again in the afternoon while Captain Blunt called the officers together to review the latest reconnaissance information. The fiftyish man was a farmer by trade who owned a sizeable spread purchased after serving in the Great Revolution. His thick hands shook a dispatch at his officers as his face flushed bright crimson.

"A British flotilla was sighted sailing south past Assateague Island two days ago. They had four ships with seventy or so guns each and some smaller armed vessels. We assume the Chesapeake is their aim, so Major General Samuel Smith has ordered us to Baltimore to assist in the defensive preparations of Fort McHenry. Be ready to ride in an hour. It's our time, men!"

It's our time . . . Jed felt the same rush of emotion that had propelled him into the fray of the riot five months earlier, and he saw equal passion rise in the other men as well. He buttoned his blue coatee and looked at his black shako hat. After staring at the heavy battle headpiece for a few seconds, he pulled it proudly over his dark curls. Fingering the plume, he realized that for the first time he felt like a soldier, and he hurried off excitedly to aid others in his company.

His was a standard company, consisting of one captain, three lieutenants, four sergeants, and four corporals who led sixty-four privates, a drummer, and a fife player. Community standing influenced rank, and factoring in his months of militia training, Jed was granted the rank of second lieutenant, a responsibility he had neither sought nor enjoyed—until today. Finally, neighbors regarded one another as comrades in arms, and though battle was not imminent, they were brothers in war, looking to him for leadership; he was determined to rise to the call.

They ate and drank in their saddles, riding at a staggering pace. The first light of dawn began to break over the horizon before Jed entered Fort McHenry. His company set up their tents around the fort's earthen and wood-flanked perimeter while their captain met with the fort's commander, Captain Beall. As he leaned against the enlisted men's barracks, Jed's patience was eventually rewarded when Captain Andrew Robertson exited with the other officers.

Militia duty had taught Jed military protocol. He could no longer rush over to Robertson as he had previously done. He was a soldier now, and Robertson was his superior, a status change that completely altered the previous balance in their already tenuous relationship.

"Captain Robertson," Jed choked out respectfully. "May I have a word with you?"

The young first lieutenant who always hung near his captain stepped toward Jed. "May I have a word with you, *sir!*" he corrected with exaggerated smugness as he sneered at Jed.

Jed towered over the short regular who so deliciously enjoyed the authority his rank and assignment offered him. "May I have a word, *sir?*" Jed repeated snidely.

Captain Robertson stepped in to calm the snit. "That will be all, Lieutenant."

The young man saluted and exited, casting malicious glances at Jed with each step.

"I don't have time for this," spat Robertson. "As long as your company assists in readying this fort, you'll address me with the respect accorded me. It brings me no pleasure to require it of you, but in battle men's lives depend on obedience and order, and that begins here."

His voice was heavy with fatigue, and for the first time Jed noticed the lines of stress across the young captain's brow and surrounding his tired, blue eyes.

Ashamed, Jed responded, "I apologize. I was . . . wrong."

Robertson appeared skeptical. "Do you have military business with me, Lieutenant Pearson?" He began walking away with Jed on his heels. "As worried as I am about Hannah, I cannot dwell on my personal concerns while the British move a fleet of guns into range of us."

Jed stopped cold. "So you've still received no further word?"

Robertson's shoulders slumped, reminding Jed that though he had loved Hannah longest, Robertson loved her as well. "No," he uttered, his sorrow evident. "Mrs. Baumgardner is sure they're purposely keeping her in the dark. I wish I could . . ."

Jed brought his hand up. "I know . . . I know . . ." he moaned as he turned away.

Several agonizing seconds passed, and then Jed heard, "There is one possibility . . ." Jed turned to stare dubiously at the captain. "Dispatches need to be sent north regarding the movements of the British. We have men who serve as couriers . . . but perhaps I could . . ."

Jed immediately sprang on the idea. "Send me! Give me a map and send me north. I'll convey your information and make some inquiries about Hannah along the way."

Robertson immediately regretted having made the offer. "Why do I feel this is akin to sending a fox to rescue my hen? She is still *my* betrothed, you know."

Jed's face grew somber. "Does that status afford you any peace when you don't know what her current situation is? First and foremost, I need to know that she is well and safe, and I know you feel the same way."

The two men stared at one another, each assessing his rival. After a silent standoff, Robertson began nodding his head reluctantly. "A courier is to be sent out in a few days. I'll see what I can do."

CHAPTER 15

February 4, 1813
Hanover, New Hampshire

The symptoms of the disease had racked Beatrice Snowden's constitution, leaving her in a listless state. Frenzied with worry, Hannah leapt upon each short period of lucidity to beg her for permission to send for Myrna, but Beatrice refused, and Hannah would not betray her trust.

"We need her here with us, Beatrice," Hannah pled. "*I* need her."

"No!" Beatrice retorted, her resolve firmly set. "I'll hire a nurse first."

"Then let me send for Jed. He'll come and help us! Please, I'm frightened, Beatrice."

"Have you decided to choose Jed, or do you simply believe he can succeed in coercing me to return to Baltimore? Go home and settle *your* business, Hannah, but swear to me that you will leave mine to me. I am already racked with guilt for having pressed us to leave Boston against all warnings, knowing that I have now endangered my baby." Her voice broke, and she laid a shaky arm across her eyes. "I could not bear Mother's or Myrna's rebuke as well."

Hannah knelt beside her sister's bed. "Surely Myrna already suspects that something is awry since what few letters we've sent have been filled with nothing but drivel. I can't continue this way, Beatrice. What if something else happens to you? I would gladly endure Myrna's chastisement in return for her support."

Beatrice turned her face to the wall. "I've put you through so much. Go home, Hannah. You deserve to have your peace of mind."

"I will not leave you!"

"Then choose what you will for yourself, but grant me the same privilege! If you stay, these are my terms, as selfish as they may seem." Her resolute tone and expression softened as she took her sister's hand. "I will understand if you decide to return to Maryland. You've problems of your own, and I will not count you fickle or negligent for seeing to them. Go."

Hannah's head fell onto her sister's pillow. "No . . . I'll stay with you."

And thus it had been. Day by day, the strain of worry took its toll on Hannah. Emmett became her sole consolation, attending to her needs while she attended to Beatrice's. While she dealt with the tedious duty of laundry, he would entertain her with stories or by playing his mandolin, a sound she came to cherish each day. She marveled at his caring as he seemed to antici-pate her every concern, and for the first time in her life, Hannah enjoyed the full, fatherly association of a man.

She marveled at how he managed the farm as if he were fully sighted, relying on the ropes and other aids positioned around the farm to guide him through the snow and wind as he performed his chores. Zachary came by regularly with groceries and sundries, which Emmett now accepted "for the women's sake." The doctor checked on Beatrice, refilling the bottles of remedies and prescribing treatments and dietary changes, proving how like his grandfather he was.

Hannah rarely left Beatrice's side, but on those rare occasions when her sister was resting peacefully, Emmett would lure her outside into the brisk, clean air, and they would talk until her heart was calmed and her hope refreshed. But it was his prayers that lifted her, returning her to spiritual places she had forgotten and filling her empty heart. Hannah was certain Emmett *knew* God.

She fell asleep in the chair by Beatrice's sickbed while pondering these things. Emmett's tentative tap on the door was answered by Beatrice. "Come in, Em," she called softly.

"Things got real quiet, so I thought I'd better check in on you little ladies."

"We're both so exhausted. Poor Hannah just fell asleep, right there in the chair."

"She's a good one, that little lady there. You both are. Here you are, trying to get to your husband, and Hannah leaves her own love behind to help you. You're both marvels to me."

Beatrice was surprised by his comment. "Has Hannah told you she's in love, Em?"

"Oh, no. But I told Zachary he should pursue her. He told me her heart already belongs to someone, but that she doesn't talk about it because it appears to cause her great pain."

Beatrice was glad Emmett couldn't see her face at that moment. "Em, may I ask one more favor of you? Would you take Hannah out for a walk this afternoon? She's suffered so much, and I've hauled her so far away from our family and home. I can't do much for her."

"Do what?" asked Hannah as she stretched and yawned.

Another coughing spasm gripped Beatrice, but masking the severity of her symptoms, she said, "I asked Em take you out for a walk while I sleep. I just need to rest now, dearest."

"Are you certain?" replied Hannah. "But your cough . . . you shouldn't be alone."

"I'll rest easier knowing you're entertained."

Hannah attempted to argue, but Beatrice offered her such a convincing smile that Hannah took Emmett's proffered arm. The pair walked along the snow-crusted lane to the bridge and then back toward the barn where they took to oiling harnesses. "You're awfully quiet, little one," prodded Emmett.

"Does anything frighten you, Em? I can't imagine you being afraid of anything."

"Everyone's afraid at one time or another. I was afraid when my wife took sick, and when my eyes dimmed. It's all right to be afraid, Hannah, so long as we share our fear with God."

Hannah kept polishing her harness without replying, and Emmett nudged the conversation along with his comforting German baritone. "I like to make sure He knows I need Him. Then soon enough, I feel Him wrap His arms around me. I talk candidly to Him in my prayers, too," he continued. "He already knows what's in my heart, so I figure saying the words just makes me honest."

"I never thought of it that way before," she finally replied.

"Why, sure, it's really that simple. Then afterwards, I try to be very still and push the world away. I figure heaven must be a quiet place, so to make God comfortable in my world, I need to invite Him into a place where the peace makes Him feel welcome."

Hannah took Emmett's wrinkled hand in hers. "I can feel how much you love Him, Em."

"Of course I do, and you do too, Hannah. You just need to believe that He loves you back. And He does, you know. Trouble doesn't mean He's left you."

He couldn't see the moisture welling in Hannah's clamped eyes.

"Haven't you felt Him speak to you, Hannah? Haven't you ever felt an idea rush into your mind when you needed it, or felt your heart burn or the hair rise on your arm when you've heard a beautiful violin or seen the first light break across the morning sky? These are among the many voices of God, Hannah, reminding us that He loves us and that He is aware of us."

"I've searched for such a God, Em. But I couldn't find a religion that believes as you do."

Emmett leaned against a stall. "I hope to find it myself," he confessed thoughtfully. "My parents emigrated from Germany as newlyweds, with only the Bible to guide them to God. I spent four years in theology school memorizing scriptures and biblical history, but the passion and peace of Christ's teachings became lost in the confusing debates over His word. The university had a copy of the Gutenberg Bible . . . nearly three hundred years old back then. I spent hours admiring the red-painted rubrication of the first lines of each section and the tiny works of art painted on sheets of gold—it made the pages appear as if heavenly light shone from the book. It was beautiful, and I felt the testimonies of those who created that volume with their heavenly gifts. I discovered that the truths of Christ's gospel would not be unfolded to me in a classroom. They too were gifts that would require my equal dedication, so I asked *Him* to reveal His word to me . . . and He did, though the answers I received caused me to fall out of line with my church's doctrine. You see, I truly believed that the church Jesus established and its practices were to be the model for the Christian church forever. I see some of it in every Christian church, but where it is in completeness, I cannot say."

Her shoulders slumped in hopelessness. "It sounds like a cruel puzzle."

"No, Hannah, it's a wondrous puzzle, and He gave us the clues to solve it. Listen."

"'And he shall send Jesus Christ, which before was preached unto you, Whom the heaven must receive until the times of restitution of all things, which God hath spoken by the mouth of all his holy prophets since the world began.'"

"I know that passage, Em! I've read it a hundred times."

"You understand that Peter was speaking of Christ's *return* in that scripture?"

"Yes. My pastor preached of a Second Coming as well, but this '*restitution of all things*'— I can't get anyone to agree on it. What do you think that means?"

He leaned forward thoughtfully. "I believe we must be faithful to His established word and Christ will again reestablish His church in the manner and time of His choosing."

Dead hopes began to stir within Hannah. She'd once prayed for a miracle to heal her mother's mental illness, but the rigid pastor with whom she had confided her prayers had assured her that the power Jesus and His Apostles held no longer existed on the earth. "And what of Jesus' authority and the healings and the miracles He performed? Do you believe these will return also?"

"I do, Hannah. Perhaps not in my day, but I have asked God, and I have felt Him confirm these feelings in me. I don't believe He would whisper an untruth to one of His children who came to Him in prayer, seeking an answer."

Hannah remained conspicuously silent on that topic.

"Hannah, haven't you ever had a time when you felt as if He was right with you? As if He was holding your hand in His?"

A deep melancholy overwhelmed her. "I had that when I was a child, and then again a year ago . . . but I've lost it, Em. And I need answers so badly."

Emmett dropped the harness and stretched his hand out to her. "Don't lose faith, child. Even His choicest children have trials. Do you remember to pray, and do you still read your bible?"

She hung her head. "I've been less inclined these last months."

"He can make water come from a rock, but He most likely won't when He knows you have a perfectly good well to draw from. The same holds true for communicating with Him. He *can* reveal Himself to His children when He chooses, but for the most part, if you want to talk to God, you must pray. If you want Him to speak to you, you must read His word."

The sound of an approaching carriage broke the stillness, and Emmett rose to meet the rig. "I think Zachary is here," he said, laying a hand on Hannah's shoulder. "Are you coming?"

"In a minute," she replied, to which Emmett nodded and left. As soon as she heard the door close, she knelt by a bale of hay and folded her hands. She began simply, raising her voice heavenward to God's ear, speaking to Him as if He were the gentle father Emmett knew. Minutes passed until she felt those very feelings Emmett described and which she had longed to feel again—the burning in her chest and the prickle on her arms. As she closed, she felt a lump come to her throat, and she rested her head on the hay crying, "Thank you. Thank you."

After a time she stood and brushed her coat clean. A disturbing chill ran up her neck, but she hunched her shoulders to dispel it. As she did so, the door opened revealing Emmett and Zachary, who was impeccably dressed with his woolen overcoat topping his best Sunday suit. "Hannah!" he called out. "Dartmouth provided me a first-class rig to ferry my colleague around. Come see!"

She approached him with a smile. "Surely this proves that you are Dr. Smith's favorite protégé."

"Ha! I believe it has more to do with my esteemed guest from Baltimore."

"Baltimore?" She quickly exited the barn and caught her first glimpse of Dr. Butler's visiting colleague. "Samuel?"

It took a second for Samuel Renfro to believe his eyes. "Hannah?" he exclaimed. "I've been searching for you!" With outstretched arms he ran to her, easily sweeping up her lean frame and focusing on the fatigue so present in her once-bright green eyes. "Are you well? I heard we were here to visit some women afflicted with typhoid."

She began to weep with release, realizing that, like an answer to her prayers, someone from home was now here. Clinging to him she cried, "It's Beatrice. She's been so very sick." Again, Hannah felt the unusual chill go up her neck, but she was distracted from it by Samuel's next question.

"Dr. Butler claimed that . . . What I mean to ask is . . . is Beatrice with child?"

Hannah's eyes grew as large as saucers at the question. "No one knows but me, Samuel . . . not even our mother or sister, and Beatrice insists it must remain so."

"*No one* knows *anything* about your situation." His arched brow drove his point home. "It has been cruel of you to leave them fearing you were dead, Hannah."

"Please," she entreated as the strange chill returned. "I'll explain everything. I promise."

Evidencing his discomfiture over the private dialogue, Zachary loudly cleared his throat, and Hannah blushed with embarrassment. "Please forgive us. Dr. Renfro and I are dear friends. Samuel, Dr. Butler and his grandfather have been our angels of mercy. Beatrice and I are only alive because of Dr. Butler's skills as a physician and his grandfather's kindness in taking us in."

Scoffing at the compliment, Emmett extended his hand. "Just call me Em, Dr. Renfro, as I am not a licensed reverend any longer, but be assured that any friend of Hannah's is welcome here."

All eyes were fixed on Hannah, whose own expression grew more curious each minute. She no longer heard the conversation the men were engaged in but gazed worriedly at the house as the furrows of her forehead increased. "Something's wrong with Beatrice . . ." she murmured.

"What did you say?" asked Zachary as he caught hold of her arm.

"Something's wrong with Beatrice," she repeated, taking another step.

Catching hold of the conversation, Samuel asked, "What is it Hannah? Are you sure?"

Hannah's head swung in the direction of the one who believed in her promptings. "Beatrice is in trouble, Samuel!"

She broke for the house in a full run, leaving the men behind. Samuel ran to the carriage for his bag while Zachary followed, calling after him. "What's happening?"

Samuel took only a moment to convey the urgency. "Experience has taught me that if Hannah says something is so, it likely is. Hurry Dr. Butler."

The men careened into the house to find Hannah standing over her ashen sister. Beatrice's cheeks were flushed and fevered, and her mouth was twisted in pain as she writhed in discomfort, swathed in sheets now red with blood-tinged wetness.

"What's wrong with her?" Hannah cried out to both doctors.

Zachary touched Beatrice's abdomen and felt the rigidness there. His face tightened as he looked at Samuel and frowned. "She's in labor."

Before Hannah could react, Zachary began barking orders to her, keeping her too busy to dwell on her sister's peril. After an hour Samuel entered the kitchen, his face drawn and sober. Looking at him, Hannah felt her spine weaken as she mumbled the words, "Is she . . . ?"

"Beatrice is alive," Samuel assured as he moved toward her.

Hannah felt a momentary relief which was undone by his pervading sorrow. "The baby?"

"He was too tiny, Hannah. Beatrice was so ill for so long, and he came so early . . ."

"He?" Hannah choked out. "Beatrice and Dudley lost a little son?"

Zachary now entered and his face also bore that same incredible sorrow. "I'm sorry, Hannah. My grandfather is with Beatrice, but you should be there when she wakes up."

Hannah felt her shoulders slump. "So . . . she doesn't know she lost him?"

"No . . . not yet, but I think the news would be easier coming from you."

Another chill ran down her spine, and she shivered to shake the feeling off, declaring soberly, "I should have been there with her. I should never have left her side."

Samuel braced her shoulders. "Listen to me, Hannah. You could have done nothing to change today's outcome. Not for Beatrice or for the child. But I do agree about your importance now," he continued. "Do you think you can bear telling her when she comes to?"

Swallowing hard, she nodded. "When will that be? Doesn't she need to see her son?"

"Of course she does," answered Emmett as he entered. "If she cannot raise the child in this life, then give her the chance to know him for these few seconds." He turned toward Hannah. "Do you think you could wash and dress the baby for her? Did she pack things for her new son to wear?"

Hannah's eyes welled at the request. She thought of the baby clothes Beatrice had made in loving anticipation of this day. There were smocked gowns and crocheted caps and booties, all wrapped in a beautiful knitted blanket that Hannah had worked on by her sister's side. Now there would be only a moment to see the child for whom the sweet things had been created.

"Will you draw water for the tub?" she asked Zachary. "And Samuel? Will you light a fire to warm a kettleful for his bath?"

"Warm . . . the . . . kettle?" Samuel stammered. "But Hannah . . . the baby is . . ."

Emmett placed his hand on his arm and shushed him. "Of course he will, Hannah."

As the men moved numbly through their chores, Emmett followed Hannah into Beatrice's room, laying a hand on her shoulder for comfort. She laid her own hand on top of his and then bent her head until her cheek rested there as well. "I don't know if I can do this, Em."

He squeezed her shoulder gently. "Of course you can, Hannah. Remember, God chose good women to prepare His own child for burial."

She swallowed hard and moved closer to the bed where her sister now slept so serenely. Beatrice's face was still flushed with fever, but her countenance was no longer contorted in pain, and the tiny bundle rested, wrapped in a birth-soiled towel, by her side.

Hannah reached to touch the baby, but recoiled, and then a warm sadness swept over her, replacing the earlier feelings, and she prayed with all her might for a miracle like the one given to the Smith mother who had prayed life back into her breathless babe. She held the tiny bundle to her chest and cried, cradling its tiny head in the crook of her neck, but no miracle happened other than the change in Hannah's heart as she unwrapped the infant form, knowing instantly that she would know the child again someday.

She tenderly washed him and cooed to him, introducing herself as if he could hear her. Zachary and Samuel became dismayed by the scene, but Emmett simply replied, "She knows she is washing a dead babe, but she is speaking to his spirit, which she believes is very much alive."

The two men of science watched Hannah swaddle the bathed child and carry him to his mother's room. She opened the bundle of clothing, and then she heard a frail voice behind her.

"He's beautiful, isn't he?"

"Beatrice?" Hannah replied in a startled voice. "Have you . . . seen your son?"

She nodded weakly. "Many times . . . lying in his cradle looking up at me, toddling about the house . . ." Her voice broke and she buried her face in the coverlet. "What have I done?" she wailed. "What will Dudley think of his reckless wife? I killed our baby, Hannah!"

Hannah moved to Beatrice's side but had only weak words to offer the grieving woman. "It wasn't your fault, Beatrice."

"Whose was it then?" she implored. "Who do I blame? Dudley, for volunteering to go to Detroit? Or General Hull for surrendering? Perhaps I should simply blame the entire British army . . . or war in general. Where does it stop, if not with me?"

Hannah placed the baby by Beatrice's side. "It must stop here and now, Beatrice."

Beatrice turned her face from the child. "It's easy for you to say." Her tears began anew. "I had so clearly seen him. Even this very morning. Why did I see that, Hannah? Why?"

Hannah combed her fingers through Beatrice's damp hair. "I believe this child will be part of our family, somehow." She saw Beatrice's doubt. "And there will be . . . other children."

Beatrice slowly gathered the tiny bundle against her and began kissing her son's head. "I'm going to name him Bernard, after Father." And then she began to cry again.

Hannah closed the door, leaving the mother alone to grieve her child, and found Samuel and Zachary hovering nearby, awaiting her exit. Desperate to be comforted, she knew whose arms she desired, and in Jed's absence, their common friend offered her her best compromise. Though she dreaded the conversation she knew she'd have to have with Samuel, she walked straight to him and melted into his arms. "Would you walk with me, Samuel?"

They grabbed their coats and headed out into the star-filled dusk, Samuel's arm enfolding Hannah against his corpulent frame. She led him to the stream in silence, but when they reached the bridge, she left the safety of his arm and faced him. "How is he?"

"Which of the two broken men are you referring to, or shall I say which of the three, assuming you realize that you've now added Dr. Butler to your list of admirers."

She hung her head. "It's not that way, Samuel." She walked to the rail and stared into the frigid water, racking her heart for the words to explain her silence. "Please tell me. How is Jed?"

Samuel joined her by the rail and sighed. "He came to me a few weeks ago, as sorry a sight as I've ever seen. He told me how he answered amiss when you two parted last September. Surely you don't hold that against him, knowing how desperately he loves you."

"I offered to surrender all—my family, my home . . . even my reputation if our critics were to slander me for marrying him—but he refused me, Samuel."

"He *delayed* . . . to provide time to right the situation with your parents."

"Things may never be right between Jed and my parents. It is folly to expect they will."

"It is equal folly to expect Jed to make plans for a future with you whilst you maintain your engagement to Lieutenant Robertson. Two men's happiness hangs in the balance. A single letter to either, sorting out your affections, will at least settle things for one, but you leave both dangling."

"I cannot discuss this tonight," she moaned as she turned to leave the bridge.

"Answer this for me. Do you love Jed?"

Hannah stopped in her tracks. "What does it matter if the fates are aligned against us?"

"Ultimately, Hannah, we each decide our own fates by the choices we make."

Disconsolate, she met Samuel's eyes for a moment. "I wish I could believe that."

Samuel stepped toward her, but she began walking away again. "Hannah . . ." he called after her as she broke into a run heading into the barn.

Flustered and knowing it would be fruitless to pursue the topic, Samuel headed into the house to prepare for his own exit, saying, "I think I should be going, Dr. Butler. I'd be happy to drive myself and return for you in the morning."

"Nonsense," replied Emmett. "Stay here. There's plenty of room for both of you."

"No, I really must leave, but thank you."

Minutes later, intent on securing the animals, Samuel entered the barn and noticed Hannah off in a corner by a moonlit window. Focusing his frustrations on the task at hand, he led the horses into the yard where Zachary was waiting to help him harness the team. The pair was silent until Samuel climbed into the carriage driver's box. "I'll return by nine so we can keep our appointments," he stated.

"Where is Hannah?"

Looking sadly over his shoulder, Samuel muttered, "In the barn."

"Is she all right?" It was more of an accusation than a question.

"She is beset by woes you cannot mend."

"The man she loves . . . Are you a friend of his?"

"Has she admitted to being in love?"

Zachary shook his head. "But the truth of the matter is apparent. Is he a good man?"

The young Baltimore physician looked down the road and sighed. "He is perhaps a fool . . . but he is also among the finest men I have ever known."

Dr. Butler's jaw tightened at the news. "He should be here. She needs him."

"Pride and circumstance keep them apart. Neither can heal, neither can let go, and all their friends can do is watch and suffer." With that he clicked the reins and drove on.

Fighting the urge to find her, Zachary went inside to tend to Beatrice, passing his grandfather on the way. Emmett strolled out to the barn and found Hannah crying where he had left her hours earlier, sitting in a ball on the barn floor.

"All our chats and you never revealed your experiences in hearing God's voice?"

Hannah faced forward, away from where Emmett sat. "When I was small it was as if I could speak to Him like a father, but I have felt estranged from Him lately. Then, two years ago, I began having vivid, frightening dreams. I didn't understand them—in fact, I was terrified by them. But I came to see that they were given to prepare me to face a future challenge that came with near exactness. Faith in the dreams gave me the courage to hold on, and because I trusted in the images, my life and Beatrice's were spared, as well as three others'." Hannah lifted her head and saw Emmett staring blindly forward, his face taut with concern.

"And yet you lost faith in this guidance."

"Em, I thought if I followed the promptings, they would lead me to answers and happiness, but they didn't! Things are worse now than ever."

"Because He stopped speaking or because you stopped listening?"

Hannah paused as she considered how to answer. "I suppose I stopped trusting." Defeat underscored the melancholy of her reply.

"Hannah, Hannah, Hannah . . ." he groaned as his head shook slowly back and forth. "Did you think that because a certain path was right, it would be easy?"

"Yes!" she replied defensively to his somber tone. "Yes I did! And why not? Shouldn't there be a reward for heeding His voice?" Hannah's lips began to quiver. "The truth is I'm not sure about any of it anymore. I did what I thought God wanted . . . I went where I thought He was leading me, but then I couldn't feel Him prompting me any longer." She rose to her knees, facing Emmett. "What if God wasn't really speaking to me? Or worse yet, what if He was and I lost the privilege? I should have been with Beatrice today, Em. I should have known not to leave her. Don't you see? If my judgment is so wrong about this, maybe I was also wrong about . . ."

Her voice broke, and Emmett laid his large, rough hands on her head. "About leaving the young man? Samuel's friend?"

Hannah brought her heavy head up to fall against the old man's chest, and Emmett's arms slid up to encircle her as she cried. "Beatrice's baby is dead, and Beatrice is nearly so. I have sorely wounded two men because I thought God loved me so much that . . ."

". . . That He would work out all your problems."

Hannah lifted her head to look into his wise face. "As selfish as it sounds . . . yes. I love them both, but I am only *in* love with one. I just couldn't bear hurting someone who has been so dear to me. I had hoped that one of the Lord's purposes in bringing me here was so He could fix things, that perhaps, in my absence, He would incline the one man's heart toward another love."

Emmett stroked her hair. "The good Lord does have the power to do all things, but He won't always intervene. Messy though it might become, He leaves the living of our lives to us, and sometimes that means that even the best people have cause to mourn."

"Like Beatrice . . ."

"And like these men who are so smitten with you. Who we marry and raise a family with is one of life's most important choices. Choosing one may hurt another, but running from the decision will cut a far broader swath of pain. Little one, faith is a noble virtue because of the courage it requires. One cannot win the prize without first paying the price."

"You're disappointed in me . . ." she muttered sadly.

"No. Not in you, Hannah." His large, weathered hands lifted her face to see the admiration reflected in his own. "After what I witnessed tonight I can assure you that God loves you very much. Trust me, if He elects to speak to you as clearly as He did tonight, then you are a worthy instrument in His hands. Not perfect . . . but worthy."

Hannah wiped her eyes and looked into Emmett's deeply lined face. She saw sadness etched there, and it dimmed her welling peace. "Then why are you so melancholy?"

Raising his head to the rafters, he sighed. "Because I'm an old, blind man who will not live long enough to see all that is about to unfold here."

"What do you mean, Em? The war?" she scowled with a shake of her head. "In this case your blindness may be a blessing."

Emmett's dull eyes sparkled anew as he spoke to her. "You cannot yet see the things God may do with you, can you, child? Use those gifts God has given you. Look beyond the conflicts to the purposes they uphold. Not just political ends, but divine ones as well."

"How can you see divinity in war?"

"Not in war itself, but in those principles for which we struggle. When I was a young lad I heard the Reverend Jonathan Edwards speak from his Northampton pulpit. He implied that it was not coincidence that this land was discovered in the midst of the religious reformation. He claimed that the reformation was the first step in renovating the world, saying that when God undertakes a glorious work, He accomplishes that work in a new world, like America, free of previous foundations so its manifestations are conspicuously attributable to God."

He gently tipped Hannah's chin. "I joined in the revolution to create that new world, and I saw some deplorable things, but every time I read the printed accounts of George Washington's speeches, calling religion and morality 'the great pillars of human happiness,' I was renewed. He rarely spoke of this government without tying political prosperity to godliness." His face brightened as he savored the memory. "You can't imagine the feelings of pride that swelled in my bosom each time I was reminded of the privilege it is to be in this place of heavenly expectation."

Emmett then sighed. "God has great plans for this nation, but first He must prepare a generation to receive what He will bring forth. I regret that I will miss those events, but today, seeing how God speaks to you and how you have learned to listen . . . Perhaps you, Hannah, are part of that generation."

CHAPTER 16

February 4, 1813
Hampton, Virginia

"Markus O'Malley!" Lyra called out whimsically from the dock. "Three of my finest hens surrendered their all to the fryer, and if you're not down here off that ship in three shakes to escort me to the dance, someone else'll be eatin' 'em."

"Ahhh, Markus!" hooted Patrick and three others working on the *Irish Lass*. "Take it from the voice of experience. If you give her the upper hand now, there'll be no goin' back."

Just then, Drusilla O' Malley's voice chimed in, "Is that a fact, Patrick O'Malley?"

And laughter erupted again.

Tuning out the playful banter of the group, Markus paused to steal a long look at the object of his happiness. Lyra Harkin stood poised against the first streaks of evening light that shone as red as her hair. Her blindness denied them the pleasure of exchanging long, loving glances, but he relished the secrecy her blindness afforded him, allowing him to stare at her for however long he liked without her blushing or turning away. And he never tired of that delight.

Astonished by her early profession of love, he was no less astounded by how easily he'd surrendered his own heart to her; though fear had commanded him to deny the attraction he'd felt the first time her slim arm lay in the crook of his own, it had been the tender exchange of childhood memories—with someone who could recall firsthand the gentle touch of his mother and the rumble of his father's laugh—that had completely disarmed his every apprehension.

"Hurry it up, Mr. O'Malley! Don't be thinkin' that just because I've spent every wakin' minute fawnin' o'er ya, nor because you're present in me every sleep-eyed dream, that I won't give my heart *and* my fried chicken to another, more punctual, suitor!"

He jumped to the dock and ran up to her, stealing a kiss as he hurried to the bar of soap. "Sorry darlin'. We just got so caught up in the work today, but she's comin' along just fine."

"I'm sure she is," Lyra offered proudly. "You can tell me all about her on the way."

He was shaved, scrubbed, and dressed in clean clothes before the other men had finished shaving. "You'll be the prettiest girl at the dance," he cooed as he wrapped Lyra's arm over his.

She smiled broadly and placed a soft kiss on his cheek, stalling there a moment to rest her brow against the softness of his smooth and scented cheek. They loaded into the back of Patrick's wagon along with his and Drusilla's rambunctious little ones and made the short trip north from Hampton Creek along Celey's Road, leading to Celey's Plantation.

"I missed you," she whispered in his ear, and I've somethin' for ya." From her pocket she withdrew a watch fob made of her braided hair. "Now you'll have a bit of me with you always."

A lump formed in his throat as it did each time she offered him such assurances of her love. "My sweet Irish sprite," he muttered as he nuzzled her ear. "How I do love you, Lyra."

She noted the husky tone to his voice that attested to their rising affections and advised, "You're makin' my heart race. You'd best tell me about the *Irish Lass* for a spell."

Markus cleared the emotion from his own throat with a cough. "She's goin' to be a beaut, Lyra. Once we repair the riggin' and sew a new sail, we'll be ready to mount the guns. Patrick and I are headin' to Norfolk next week to buy them. She'll be fightin' ready by March."

Lyra turned to hide her worry, but Markus caught her expression and tipped her chin back toward him. "Don't worry, darlin'. Nothin's goin' to happen to me. I'm charmed, don't you know? Got my own little sprite to bring me luck. Besides, The USS *Constellation* is fresh from being outfitted in Baltimore and is sailing round the mouth of the Chesapeake as we speak."

Drawing him close, she laid her head on his shoulder. As they passed through the woods into the clearing, they again faced the waters of the James River off to their left. The first wafts of smoke from a huge bonfire blew their way, and the children began squealing with excitement. Candles flickered from lanterns, and fiddle tunes filled the air accompanying the laughter of children playing Blind Man's Bluff and Red Rover in the ebbing twilight.

The men helped the women and children from the wagon, and Markus proudly led Lyra into the barn on his arm. Despite weeks of courting, this was their first public outing together, and all conversation stopped as they crossed the entrance. Markus squeezed Lyra's hand to calm her, but she needed no assurance as she led out boldly then stopped a few steps inside.

"All right now," she called out audaciously. "I know I'm blind, but don't make me think I'm deaf as well. Surely you've seen a man courtin' a woman before."

A loud laugh broke loose from one of the corners, and the happy chatter resumed as well wishers crushed in upon the beaming pair. Markus was finally able to break free from the throng to add Lyra's chicken to tables heaping with Hampton's finest southern cuisine. Platters of roasted duck, turkey, and pig were added to dishes of oyster stew, meat pies, and steaming bowls of squash, potato balls, and corn bread. Puddings spotted with currants and raisins sat beside bowls of boiled custard and cakes and pies of every variety, but the crowning glory was Drusilla's pecan pies, made from the nuts grown on trees given to her as a wedding gift from her Georgian kin.

There was no time to eat as affectionate, prattling women swarmed Lyra. Markus felt as if the room were closing in on him, so with Lyra's blessing he pulled away from the throng to a corner where a gaggle of mesmerized children sat listening to Ryan O'Malley's storytelling.

"There's no such thing as pirates," a doubtful lad challenged.

Markus O'Malley shifted his weight and eyed the dubious scamp as Ryan replied, "Ta be sure, pirates are real! Why, the murderin' dog Blackbeard scoured this very area, robbin' and plunderin' ships that were comin' or leavin' our very James River! If the ship's crew surrendered, 'e would strip them of their cargo and let them go, but if they put up any fight at all . . . well, then 'e would set 'is crew of mad dogs on 'em with orders ta murder every one!"

Squeals of horror erupted from the children, and Markus wanted in on the fun.

"Did you ever meet him, Uncle?" Markus asked with feigned fear in his voice.

"No, son. I did not have the opportunity." He leaned in close to add to the suspense. "You see, by the time I was old enough ta go ta sea . . . 'e was already dead, beheaded by a captain named Maynard. The people of Bath, in the Carolinas, were so glad to be rid of old Blackbeard that they took 'is 'ead and hung it from a pike."

One youngster grabbed his throat comically and pretended to die on top of several of his companions. Ryan began to rise, marking the end of the tale, but another imp grabbed his leg.

"But what about his treasure? Was there ever any pirate's treasure, Mr. O'Malley?"

Ryan sat back down, pulled his pipe from his coat pocket, and began to chew on it. "Aye, there was . . . lots of it, especially up north. For instance, the dreaded Pirate Bellamy's ship, the *Whidah,* wrecked off the coast of Massachusetts carryin' millions in gold, and another of his comrades is said to have hid a fortune in the same area. But there's more'n just *pirate* treasure! Captains of warships and merchant vessels that got in ta trouble had the ship's treasury rowed ashore and buried or hid away with plans ta come back for it another day. I did see some of that with my very own eyes, off the New Jersey coast."

"Did *you* get some buried treasure, Uncle?" teased Markus.

"All right, you Doubting Thomas, you. As a matter of fact, a terrible storm hit the Jersey coast soon after a British payroll ship went down. My good friend Ian Rollins went walkin' along the shore and found enough gold doubloons awash in the surf that 'e was able to buy himself a fine farm on Gardner's Island, and that's the gospel truth! And there'll be others who'll benefit from lost treasure. Some pirates and British soldiers left money in towns in the care of sympathizers 'til they could return. Wait and see. As they die and their property turns hands, some chap will likely go inta his yard ta dig a garden and find gold doubloons in his spade."

The music struck up and Markus stood and slapped an appreciative hand on his uncle's back. "Thanks for the tale, Uncle Ryan. I've got a treasure of my own to claim now."

Upon seeing Lyra, he was again struck by the presence she embodied, unlike any other woman he'd known. By the cock of her head he knew she was listening for him, and the instant flood of warmth that enveloped him each time he saw her rushed over him again.

"May I have this dance?' he whispered in her ear.

"Are you askin' because you miss me or because your uncle has run out of blarney?"

Drawing close enough to her to warm her neck with the heat of his breath, Markus caused Lyra to shudder. "What do *you* think?" he asked.

Lyra's eyes nearly closed, and Markus could feel the hair rise on her arms. "I think we need a turn on the floor," she sighed.

He swept her away, and all eyes were on them as he stumbled through a country dance, paying little mind to his performance or the audience until a waltz began. "I suddenly like dancing very much," he taunted as he rubbed his thumb along Lyra's porcelain wrist.

She kept dipping her head to keep her hungry lips from their desired target, but once, as she brought her face up for a moment, Markus allowed his own mouth to brush hers so lightly only they could tell they had met. He heard her sigh, and in response, he tightened his embrace.

"You're makin' my heart race again," she said breathlessly.

"That was my intention," he muttered as he pressed his cheek to hers.

They were moving as one now, in tune with each other's bodies, oblivious to the instruments or the other dancers until titters began to sound.

"The music's stopped," Lyra whispered, burying her grin in his shoulder.

Markus halted and then picked right back up again, drawing gentle laughter from the barn's perimeter. "I'm not ever lettin' go of you," he whispered in her ear.

Lyra buried her face more deeply into his shirt.

". . . Not until you confess that you love me."

She lifted her face to his, kissed his chin, and uttered, "I love you, Markus O'Malley."

Brushing his lips along her neck, he entreated her, "Now tell me that I'm a glory of man."

Lyra blushed again and pulled away enough for him to see the joy on her face. "Indeed you are, a glory of a man," she confessed tenderly.

"Now, agree to be my wife."

Lyra suddenly stopped cold. Markus's feet halted as well while the rest of his body swayed back and forth, holding her, awaiting her response.

"What did you say?" she asked shakily.

He buried his face in her scarlet hair and muttered, "I'm never lettin' go of you, Lyra Harkin, until you pledge to be my wife."

He heard no sound, save for Lyra's shuddering breaths. When he pulled away to judge her response to his proposal, he found tears filling her eyes.

"Is that a yes?" he asked in a broken voice.

For once, Lyra Harkin was speechless, simply offering her reply with a nod of her head. Markus clutched her to him as the host and owner of Celey's Plantation climbed onto a barrel and called out. "I believe our Irish neighbors have an announcement to make! Mr. O'Malley?"

Markus laughed loudly and swung Lyra under his arm. "We're gettin' married! Lyra's consented to be my wife!"

A loud whoop went up from the small band of musicians. They struck up the band and began to play a merry little tune as the crowd rushed in to congratulate the pair. Markus waited for Patrick and Ryan to add their congratulations to the mix, but when neither man appeared, he kissed Lyra and told her he was going to find them, leaving her in Drusilla's able care. After scouring the barn, he headed outside where he saw three forms standing in the shadows of the firelight, each of them peering earnestly in the direction of the moonlit water of the James. Recognizing Patrick's crossed-arm stance and his uncle's short, stout build, he hurried down to the water to share his news. "Uncle Ryan! Patrick! I have wonderful news!" he called happily, but the men remained fixed on the water.

"Wish we could say the same," said Ryan ominously.

Patrick finally turned, and the look of worry on his face stilled Markus's heart. "Part of the British fleet just dropped anchor off the point at the mouth of the bay."

Markus's face went slack. "Are you sure? How do you know?"

The third man stepped forward. "I saw it myself. There're four big seventy-four-gun ships and several smaller ones. I got close enough to read the name of the flagship. It's the *Marlboro*."

"Cockburn's flagship," groaned Markus. "So he's come to our waters now."

"Aye. It gets worse," the man added. "The *Constellation* was just off the coast when his fleet arrived. She sailed up the Elizabeth River to hide until they passed. Now she's hemmed in with no option to escape other than to fight the entire fleet, which is hopeless."

"The devils," growled Ryan. "So a new wave of pirates has come to wreak havoc on us, have they? Well, lads, we'll give 'em a fight they won't soon forget."

CHAPTER 17

February 10, 1813
Fort McHenry, Baltimore, Maryland

"Lieutenant Pearson!" a soldier called through chattering teeth, going from tent to tent in the frozen night. "Captain Robertson wants to see you right away, sir. In his barracks."

Jed pulled on his trousers and boots and stoked the fire pit before heading into the eerily quiet fort. A fine snow had fallen after midnight, its pristine appearance still intact except for the messenger's footsteps. A lone lamp drew Jed to the door of the junior officers' barracks. His three brisk raps sent sharp pain shooting into his stiff hand. Recoiling, he attempted to massage the circulation back into his fingers, but when Robertson opened the door, Jed snapped his salute.

Their eyes met in a tense gaze before the captain said, "Come in, Lieutenant Pearson."

Four other officers exited as Robertson pointed to a chair in the corner of the room. "Please sit, Lieutenant," he ordered tersely, as a sense of foreboding washed over Jed.

"It's imperative that a dispatch head north as soon as possible," Robertson began. "I've asked Captain Beall if I can send you, assuring him you are a crack shot and an able rider."

Jed was conversely elated and wary. "What's happened?"

Robertson stared at the floor for a second. "Are you agreeing to go? I should tell you . . . I received another vague note from Hannah yesterday. I'm convinced that something is awry, but you'd need to put this duty first before making any effort to locate her. Are you agreed?"

Jed wondered if he too had a note waiting for him at the Willows, but spurred on by the urgency of both situations, he answered, "If you think I am suited, I'll deliver your dispatch."

A look of respect crossed Robertson's face as he handed a packet of materials to Jed. "There are maps marked with the forts you need to reach and a list of the officers you're to speak with. Have them each sign the dispatch to attest that they've received the information. When you reach Boston, the trail will divide north and west. Give the commander at Fort Winthrop this second pouch. Have him direct one of his men to take one of the legs so you can take the other. I'll leave it to you to choose which route you take."

Jed knew what he learned about Hannah would determine that. Leafing through the items, he pulled out a sealed document. He looked at Robertson, asking, "Is this the dispatch?"

"Yes. Go ahead. Open it."

Jed read the news and he shivered. "Norfolk? My friend Markus is nearby in Hampton."

"Can you put duty above personal concerns?" Captain Robertson implored. "All our outposts need to know of the British incursions near Norfolk. Cockburn's and Warren's ships have blocked the Chesapeake, including the USS *Constellation* which is locked in the Elizabeth River. If they block the Delaware, our navy will be all but eliminated from this war."

Jed's hand clenched tighter around the packet. "I'll pack and leave by dawn."

"Delay until morning," Robertson corrected. "I know there's no love lost between you and the mayor, but we need the cooperation of the citizenry. Get a letter of support from him, and then ride north." Robertson paused and then began again. "If anything prevents you from finishing the route, assign the duty to a soldier at the last fort you reach, and send me word. This assignment will likely take longer than your duty rotation calls for. Are you still agreed?"

"Of course."

Robertson's face clouded. "There've been atrocities committed on the western frontier. Soldiers, residents . . . even women and children have been murdered." His eyes pressed shut at the very mention of it. "Last month, in a little village called Frenchtown along the River Raisin, the British unleashed the Indians against an army of a thousand men, mostly Kentuckians, who were protecting the town. Only thirty-three escaped. The rest were either killed or taken prisoner. The wounded were slaughtered . . . some were burned alive in their sickbeds. I hear the Kentuckians have assumed the words 'Remember the River Raisin!' as their motto."

"The British sanctioned this attack?" Jed gasped.

"The British general left a token force of three British regulars to enforce his oath to protect the wounded prisoners from hundreds of riled Indians."

"Was this Tecumseh's work?" Jed groaned.

"No. He was off in Ohio. He holds no love for us, but from the reports I've read of him, I think things would have been different had he been there. We'll never know. I just want you to know what you may be facing."

* * *

The mayor needed a moment to compose his thoughts. Unable to abide the man, Jed warned that he'd return in thirty minutes, and upon exiting the building he saw his attorney, John Ridgely. Jed walked over to meet him. "I have only a few minutes before I must leave, John."

Leading Jed to an alley beside the grocery where several barrels sat, Ridgely began. "What I need to say will take but a minute, but it will ease my conscience considerably. When I handed you that packet I told you to return with your questions, but you never did, so I'm ready to tell you about the disparaging gossip that was circulated in this city. However unseemly, it may be the very piece of information you've been seeking."

"This just occurred to you?"

"You asked if I had any more *documents,* which I do not. All I have is the very gossip my father spent his life deflecting out of loyalty to your grandfather's memory. Trust me, it affords me no pleasure to dredge it up, but I feel I should."

Jed leaned against the barrels, bracing himself for what revelations were about to come.

"Did you understand the file's contents? Did they help you comprehend enough about this messy triangle to understand the positions the principles were in?"

"I understand that all parties were guilty of misunderstandings. What I don't understand is how my grandfather came to be blamed for the mess, and why he continued payments to St. James after the reverend died."

John nodded. "The townspeople disparaged Sarah Benson for encouraging the interest of a philanderer, as your grandfather was deemed to be. McClintock—the new, unmarried reverend in town, informed her and her parents that regardless of what indiscretions had been committed in deed, the town prattle assured him that indiscretions had been sufficiently committed in spirit to require a penance. The reverend issued his own proposal of marriage, offering to guide her soul back to purity and to absolve your grandfather. As a result, the Bensons forbade Sarah from accepting your grandfather's proposal and coerced her to accept the Reverend McClintock's on the same day. Your grandfather never understood that Sarah had no voice in the matter. She supposedly tried to speak to him on multiple occasions, to offer an explanation, but he, believing her attempts to contact him were efforts to cause him further injury, blatantly snubbed her.

"For the next ten years, as he married and amassed his wealth and standing, he flaunted it before her, taking occasion to drive his fancy carriage past her modest home with his wife aboard, dressed in all her finery, making Sarah's misery complete. The reverend loved her dearly, and she was faithful to the last degree, but her heart could never accept what the rector tried to give her, and in time, his own heart became as hardened to her as your grandfather's had. She was pressed by bitterness on every hand, and in time, something in her snapped.

"She cared little for her own appearance or the appearance and welfare of her own children. It was rumored that she sent hateful notes to your grandfather by courier and that he sent acrid replies to her in return. The townspeople made sport, prattling about their little war until, finding his personal business on such display, the reverend entered the fray.

"His previous scriptural discourses became angry condemnations, decrying his parishioners' sins. My father said he made such a spectacle of himself that crowds flocked to his church simply for the performance. Then, after Sarah's public display in the streets, following madly after your grandfather's carriage in the parade feting him after Yorktown, McClintock accused her of infidelity, nearly flogging her right there in front of everyone. My father said he was so mad with rage that he nearly ripped that blue dress off of her right in the street.

"The dress, you see, was a symbol. Sarah had asked Pratt's wife for a dress patterned exactly like the one she'd worn when your grandfather courted her. Mrs. Pratt knew she'd lost her mind, but unable to dissuade Sarah, she stupidly spread the news until everyone, including the reverend, knew the significance of the dress. As soon as Sarah recovered from his throttling, she washed and mended the dress and then she went straightway to the jewelers to have the 'M' added to her locket. He was the last person to see her before she jumped off the Willows' dock, ending her miserable life."

Jed reeled from the details. "Did you know the locket was in the parcel?"

Ridgely shook his head. "As I said, I had suspicions of what was in there, but I wasn't certain. I suppose your grandfather took it off her body."

"The tale is deplorable," anguished Jed, "but why was Grandfather dealt all the blame?"

"Sympathies ran to those most damaged. Sarah's family had already suffered greatly, and then the reverend suffered a breakdown. So few people came to services that he could barely support himself or his family, and the synod threatened to close his parish. When your grandfather saw how the sins and foolishness of a few had destroyed an entire congregation . . ."

"He arranged to have stipends paid to support the family and the church," Jed finished.

"Exactly," nodded Ridgely. "But his generosity was misunderstood, sparking rumors that it was his penance for sins committed with Sarah. You can imagine the distorted stories they wove to explain her disappearance, but your grandfather never defended himself. He bore the gossip to protect Sarah's children from the truth. I assume you know about Sarah's grave."

"Not until we stumbled upon it over a year ago."

"Charles Kittamoqund found her body washed up down river. The two of them stood alone at her grave. Was the note she left prior to the suicide in the packet?"

Jed nodded soberly and muttered, "What a miserable waste."

"You now know the entire story, Jed. I hope it brings you some peace. Your grandfather's only crime was his pride. He allowed his hurt to shut his ears to the truth, and who knows how understanding Sarah's position could have changed the outcome for everyone."

Jed ached again over another, similar triangle. "Thank you, John," he mumbled. "I've . . . got to go now, but thank you for filling in the details, and . . . for protecting my grandfather's name."

Taking his leave, Jed crossed the street to the mayor's office. The letter was still being edited by the mayor's aid, but desperate to get away from the city and from his thoughts, his temper flared. "I'll take it now or not at all!" he blared to the aide, who handed it over promptly.

With the letter in tow, he stormed away, heading Tildie toward the first fort noted on the map—Lewes Battery at the mouth of the Delaware Bay. As he entered the town preceding the fort, he enjoyed the pristine clapboard houses with their shaker roofs and widow's walks. Passing storefronts and a school for young ladies, he counted the steeples of three churches in the town, at once feeling welcomed by the peaceful waterfront village. Upon reaching the battery, Jed explained to the two sentries that he needed to see their superior. A few seconds later, the commander hurried out, his concern evident. "How bad is it?" he inquired as he took the dispatch and began scanning the documents.

"The ships in the Delaware are the last hope of the navy."

The man shook his head angrily. "We're no match for Cockburn's armada, but they'll not sashay up our river unmolested! We'll knock the air from their sails, Lieutenant, and they'll be sure to remember their visit to Lewes! You have my word on that!"

"I wish you well, Colonel," Jed assured him as he shook his hand.

A snowstorm slowed his progress north to Fort Delaware, then to the New Castle Battery, and Fort Union near Wilmington, where news of the British incursions had not been unexpected. As he saw each facility being fortified with supplies and arms, he couldn't prevent the worry that kept creeping into his thoughts as he pressed on. *Is Markus already engaging the enemy?*

Six arduous days passed, and Tildie's right front fetlock became swollen from lack of rest. He cursed himself and turned back for Philadelphia where he could leave her in Frannie's care while he headed north on another mount. Arriving in the city barely past nine, he headed straight for *Le Jardin,* hurrying on to the address of Frannie's apartment. The building was already dark except for the glow of one lamp in an upstairs window, but Jed knocked nonetheless, raising an older woman who scolded him soundly before she finally relented and fetched Frannie.

"Jed!" Frannie squealed excitedly as she ran to him. "What are you doing here?"

"I'm on military business, but Tildie can't go on, so I thought I'd stop here for a visit."

"I'm so glad to see you," she confessed, wrapping her arms tightly around his neck. "I need to talk to you, Jed. Let me try to convince Mrs. Burrows to allow you in."

After enduring the matron's scrutiny, Jed was allowed to follow his sister into the parlor where they settled into a settee. Jed took her hands in his and asked, "What is your news?"

"*Le Jardin* is closing, Jed. Henri heard the British may sail up the Delaware and take the city. He's so afraid that his French ancestry and ties to L'Enfant will make him a British target that he plans to close the theater and head to Washington, then west. He advises us to leave also."

Jed felt the familiar weight of worry settle over him. "The British have already blockaded the lower Chesapeake. The Delaware may very well be next." His head dropped to stare at the floor. "You were the one person I felt was safe, and now . . ."

"I will be safe, Jed. I'll head to the Willows."

"No! Have you forgotten Dupree's threat? I don't think it's safe for Bitty or Jack or the others, but they won't budge."

"Then what would you have me do? I can't go to Father's and Mother's relatives. They treat us like pariahs. Henri is taking the majority of the company to Washington to perform at President Madison's inaugural in March. Once that obligation is met I'll head home. I have no where else to go, Jed."

"Are you still corresponding with Timothy Shepard?"

"Some, but with the new duties he performs for Mrs. Madison, he has little time to write." She eyed him curiously. "Why do you ask? I've written to tell him that I'll be in town for the inauguration, but you're certainly not thinking of asking *him* to take me in?"

"No . . . of course not. I just thought he might know of someone . . . It was a foolish idea. His contacts would be too close to the federal city anyway." He bit his lip as he pondered the situation. Suddenly, his face relaxed as an idea came to mind. "Uncle Will! Father's old hunting companion from Upper Marlboro! Doctor William Beanes!" he exclaimed.

"Uncle Will? . . . The Scotsman with the accent? I haven't seen him in years!"

"I came across some recent correspondence between him and Father when I went through Father's things. Besides his farm and his medicine, he's also in politics now, but he and Father remained the best of friends until the end. Promise me you'll at least contact him."

Frannie looked dubiously at her brother. "What makes you think I'd be safer there? Upper Marlboro sits on the road to Washington City."

"If the British decide to march to Washington, we'd at least have some warning. Promise me, Frannie. Promise me you'll contact Dr. Beanes."

"All right. I'll send him a letter, but I need to go home at least for a visit."

Jed knew there was no point in arguing further. "A short visit then."

"Very well. Have you had any word from Markus?"

Jed's face clouded. "None. His family lives in the very area where the British have anchored. He may be caught up in the fray if a battle commences there."

"He was so anxious to engage them. I'm frightened for both of you."

Jed sighed, then said, "Frannie, I have a favor to ask. I need to move on at daybreak but Tildie needs a few days rest. Can you tie her to your carriage and have her follow you home when you go?"

"Of course."

Jed rose and placed his hands on his sister's shoulders. "Then I should be going. I need to head to the livery to make arrangements for Tildie and requisition another mount. Remember your promise, Frannie. I need to know that you are safe."

"Yes . . . yes." She hugged him tightly before they headed for the door. "We've had no time to discuss how you've been or whether you've heard from Hannah."

Jed's expression clearly indicated the pain of the topic. "There have been a few cryptic notes, but no return address. We know she never arrived at her destination."

"Oh, Jed . . . What will you do?"

Closing his eyes, he wrapped his arms around his sister. "I'll continue making inquiries in every town I pass through and then I'll head to Tunbridge. But I must go now. I love you, Frannie. Please, let me at least know that you are safe. Please promise to do as we've discussed."

From that point on, Jed changed mounts frequently, driving himself to the point of exhaustion each day as he slogged through blizzardlike weather on his push north along the Atlantic coast. He made stops in New Jersey, New York, Connecticut, and then moved on to Massachusetts, hearing horror stories about the typhoid epidemic that was ravaging the region. It was March tenth when he entered Fort Winthrop along the Boston harbor, so cold from battling the frigid weather that he actually feared he had frostbite. His finger joints ached and swelled until he could barely hold the reins, and after meeting with the fort's commander and making plans for the second courier, the officer called a local physician in to attend to him. The venerable older man was so worried about Jed's condition that he frightened him into stopping for a day's rest at a local inn. After a hearty supper, Jed turned in and slept until the afternoon of the next day. It was the first time his body had felt rested since his deployment, but his mind raced with worries—about his assignment, about Frannie, Markus, the Willows, and of course, Hannah.

After discovering the devastating consequences jealousy had caused to befall his grandfather's love, Jed was determined not to repeat the tragedy. He was prepared to suffer the loss of Hannah if her happiness lay elsewhere, but first, he had to find her. He had made inquiries about the two women at every stop along his way, but no one had any certain information to offer, and so he planned to continue his errand, searching as he went.

Around three, Jed answered a knock at the door and found Dr. Halloran standing there, holding a kettle of steaming water. "I thought I'd check in on you today," the physician said, setting his bag down. After examining each of Jed's hands, he scowled. "Where did you say you're headed?"

"On to Lake Ontario."

The doctor shook his head. "Not with these hands."

Jed began to protest, but the doctor closed his eyes and shook his head again. "You don't have frostbite yet—but you will if you head back out there with these hands in this state. Besides, your joints are so swollen you'll never be able to steady yourself on your mount. I've never seen anything quite like it in one so young. Have you injured these before?"

Jed remembered the merciless beating he had received in Baltimore when, after his run-in with Hannah, he had gotten himself sopping drunk, falling prey to a pair of thieves. They had stomped on his hands, leaving them battered and broken. "Yes . . . about two years ago."

"Well, unless you want to lose the use of them, you'll sit tight here for a few days and let me continue to treat them. You've got a runner to head north for you. You can just as easily get another one to head west. They'll make better time than you anyway."

While Jed pondered the notion, the doctor swathed his hands in hot rags to soothe the stiffness. "From Baltimore to here is a hard run in twenty-seven winter days. You'll need a few more days rest if you don't want to get run-down and catch the fever, leaving some sweet lady to mourn over you. These dear women . . . I've seen plenty of them suffering over men they love. I recently had a patient who was in a hurry to get to Vermont to try and free her husband from a British prison. The poor thing was so ill with morning sickness she had to be carried off her ship, but still she begged me to give her a tonic so she could proceed. I wonder how she's faring."

Jed's head snapped up at hearing the story of the woman seeking her husband who was being held in a British prison. "Where did you say she was from?"

"I didn't, but it seems to me she was from Baltimore, same as you."

Jed jerked away so fast the doctor nearly fell over. "Might her name have been Mrs. Snowden, and did she have a sister? A sister named Hannah Stansbury?

The doctor tilted his head back toward the ceiling as he tried to remember. "I can't say that I recall the name Stansbury, but I'm sure my patient's name was Mrs. Snowden—"

Before he finished, Jed was on his feet. "How long ago was that?" He saw the man's face cloud and he added. "Two months? Three months ago?"

The doctor scratched his head. "Mr. Castlebury was housing them . . . he sent for me. I believe it was November."

November! "Did you say the ill woman was . . . was expecting?"

Dr. Halloran's head shot up. "Forgive me. I should never have mentioned her condition."

Beatrice Snowden is expecting—the cause of their secrecy and delay! "The other woman, Dr. Halloran," Jed asked excitedly. "The sister . . . was she well? I won't press you further, but please tell me. Was she all right?"

The physician offered a small nod. "I'd be pleased to get you feeling as well as she."

In five minutes Jed was racing down Queen Street to the Castleburys' home where Hannah and Beatrice had stayed. The older couple hadn't heard any more from the two sisters, but knowing the probable cause of their delay brought Jed great comfort, and hearing others speak of Hannah caused a flood of emotions he thought he had managed to suppress. Therein lay the real truth—he now knew he could never walk away from her merely for the sake of pretentious honor.

Bolstered by his informational triumph, Jed met with the two couriers who would help him fulfill his responsibility. He sent the first courier, named Burke, north with the duplicate packet and handed his own materials off to the second with orders to make up time by hurrying west, straight through to the distant forts along Lake Ontario, ordering them in turn to send the information on to the frontier. As soon as his hands healed, he would complete the route to the nearer forts along Lake Champlain.

Four days later, Jed set out, reaching Fort Pickering in New Hampshire on the ninth day. He met quickly with the captain in charge and was ready to depart for the final stop on his journey when he heard his name being hailed across the parade grounds. When he turned he saw Samuel Renfro in the company of another civilian.

"Samuel!" he cheered. "What miracle brings you here?"

After a hearty embrace, Samuel explained, "My colleague Dr. Tyler and I are treating typhoid patients. But more importantly, what are *you* doing here, so far from Fort McHenry?"

"Captain Robertson sent me north to deliver military dispatches, and I've been searching for Hannah along the way. Have you seen her, Samuel?"

His smile dimmed. "I have . . . and I can allay your concerns somewhat. She is well."

"You chose your words far too carefully, friend. Though I have no cause to expect more, but has she at least spoken of me? Do I have any hope of reconciling things with her?"

"Come with us out of the cold, Jed. We have much to discuss."

As the trio began to exit the fort, an exhausted courier pounded his mount through the gates. "Let me in! Let me in! I have critical information for your commander. The British have blocked the Delaware Bay!" the rider yelled as he pulled up beside the threesome.

"They've done it," groaned Jed. "First they dammed up the Chesapeake and now the Delaware. They've beaten our navy."

"You know about the Chesapeake blockade?" the courier asked.

"Yes, I carried that dispatch from Baltimore."

"Then you must be Lieutenant Pearson!" The young corporal offered Jed his hand. "Colonel Davis from Lewes Battery told me to be sure to thank you if I met up with you. He said to tell you that he's ready if the British make the mistake of firing on his town."

The young man gave Jed's hand a powerful squeeze, causing Jed to wince. "I'm sorry," he cried apologetically as he withdrew. "I forgot about your hands. They told me about them at Fort Winthrop—how you rode through that terrible weather. Have you finished your route?"

Jed worked his fingers to ease the pain. "Not yet. I still need to reach Lake Champlain."

The young courier's eyes suddenly widened. "That's where I'm headed next! I've got the information from your dispatch along with Colonel Davis's warning about the Delaware. Let me deliver both. There's no need for both of us to go, Lieutenant."

Samuel whispered under his breath, "He makes good sense, Jed."

Jed's expression reflected his dilemma. He desperately wanted to reach Hannah. He could finally find her and mend things between them, but his duty tore at his peace. He turned to the young courier. "You're headed straight to Lake Champlain?"

"Yes, sir. Sure am," he confirmed.

Thirty minutes later, Jed watched confidently as the young private thundered out of Fort Pickering on a fresh horse.

"It's hard to be both a private man and a good citizen during times as these," remarked Samuel. "I forget that your time is not your own anymore."

Jed's brow furrowed. "Perhaps . . . but . . . what day is this?"

Dr. Tyler, who had remained a fascinated onlooker throughout the exchange, piped in. "It's Monday . . . March 22."

"March 22, you say?" Jed did some calculations on his fingers, then sighed. "Then this session of my militia duty is completed. I would have carried on until I reached Lake Champlain, but as that responsibility is already filled, my time is now my own again, and there is but one thing on my mind at present."

Samuel Renfro beamed at his friend. "Then, as I said, we have much to discuss."

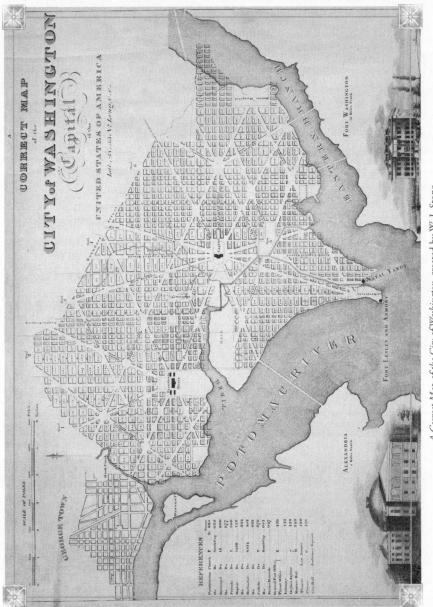

A Correct Map of the City of Washington, created by W. I. Stone.
Courtesy of New York Public Library. Original in Library of Congress.

CHAPTER 18

March 1, 1813
Washington City

Francis Pearson was slightly disappointed in the federal city's appearance as she stepped from her carriage onto Pennsylvania Avenue in Washington City. Barely more than a week earlier, the cast of *Le Jardin* had sung at Philadelphia's elegant birthday celebration for the illustrious patriot General George Washington. Beautiful banners festooned with sprigs of laurel had adorned the pristine City of Brotherly Love, while precision bands had played marching tunes to herald the day. With an inauguration only three days away, it appeared the fledgling city of Washington would produce poor efforts to laud Mr. Madison's reelection, efforts that would pale in comparison.

However, she did notice the cheery tones of a march being rehearsed off in the distance, and the smells of baking delicacies permeated the air. Wagons filled with bolts of bunting, merchant goods, and foodstuffs were moving along the wide streets that flowed with carriages and hacks ferrying people and luggage into the city for the inaugural. Most importantly, Timothy Shepard soon came into view with his arms spread wide.

"Timothy," she cooed from within his embrace. "It's so good to see you again."

"I'm sorry I wasn't here to meet your carriage. Forgive me?" He held her away from him and smiled admiringly. "I believe you may be guilty of a federal offense."

Frannie threw her hands to her hips and smiled coyly. "How so?"

"I believe you could be cited for upstaging the president's own fashionable wife."

Frannie chuckled, causing the green plume on her black velvet hat to dance. After Timothy made arrangements with the driver to deliver her bags, he offered Frannie his arm and led out. "Your employer, Mr. DeMourdaunt, is obviously quite well connected here in the city. Your hostess—a Mrs. Whitlock—is hosting a ball the night before the inauguration, but her primary delight is that the flowers of *Le Jardin* are her personal house guests."

"Henri's father was L'Enfant's chef or something or other. His father's old friends asked Henri if we could provide some entertainment at some of the events."

"Are you tightly scheduled? I made arrangements to be free to show you the city today."

"You mean if Mrs. Madison can manage without you for a few hours," she taunted.

"Francis," he scolded. "She is the loveliest of people. Her husband may well owe his second term to her incredible popularity. You know, the Federalists began calling themselves 'the Peace Party,' as if Mr. Madison went to war trivially, but Mrs. Madison charmed his friends and enemies alike. She is masterful at a dinner party. While most people think she is simply engaging in pleasant conversation, she is actually strategically steering topics to assess the positions of her husband's adversaries—or building alliances with their spouses." He sighed and chuckled.

"I've heard that some call her the Presidentress," said Frannie, who found herself surprisingly jealous over Timothy's admiration of the president's accomplished wife.

Timothy bristled at the comment. "She deserves the greatest respect. She is the president's greatest confidante and advisor, having come into the role with considerable experience. President Madison's public life threw her into powerful circles early on, and President Jefferson, being a widower, relied on his best friend's wife to serve as the hostess during his own administration, so Mrs. Madison is as versed in politics as anyone in this city."

Frannie sensed the changes Timothy's government service had wrought in him. Still playful and gentle at times, he was nonetheless passionate about this city and his new associates, and she felt a new unfamiliarity with him. "I didn't mean to offend. I was simply making small talk."

His voice calmed and softened. "I'm sorry. I've become quite close to Mrs. Madison. She is an amazing woman. You, Frannie, of all women, should appreciate her energy and vision. She is as fine a hostess as any president's wife, but she expects more of her opportunity. She believes she is as much a servant of the people as her husband, and she has great plans to ease the suffering of women and children in the city. In many ways, she reminds me of you."

Finding herself chastened by the comment, Frannie replied, "Seeing how highly you esteem her, I'm greatly flattered."

"Would you like to meet her?" Timothy asked excitedly as he led her up the walk to the president's house and to the door. He knocked soundly, and a butler quickly opened the door.

"Hello, Mr. Shepard," greeted the formally dressed Negro gentleman. Even Frannie was surprised at his meticulous diction.

"Good day, Christopher. Is Mrs. Madison in?"

Christopher whispered with a smile, "Yes, sir. She is in the drawing room planning her next 'dove party' with the Congressmen's wives. Shall I announce you, sir?"

"No, thank you. I'll just surprise her," Timothy snickered back, leaving Frannie feeling as if she were outside the joke.

Timothy took her elbow gently in his hand and escorted her into the elegant foyer with its resplendent chandelier and ornate, plastered ceiling. They headed down the splendid hall past beautifully wallpapered rooms until Frannie's mouth hung agape as the wonder of where she was and who she was about to meet finally hit her. "It's so beautiful," Frannie gushed.

"Like Mrs. Madison herself, her tastes in decorating and entertaining achieve a perfect marriage between simplicity and sophisticated elegance, suitably impressive enough to earn our president the respect of foreign visitors and political adversaries alike, while reflecting the simplicity of our nation's ideals." Timothy motioned for Frannie to wait while he turned into the room on the left. Moments later he exited with a tall, fortyish woman in his company. Her dark hair was gathered atop her head and streaked with strands of gray, but her beautiful blue eyes showed no trace of being dimmed by age. Timothy beamed at Frannie and said proudly, "Miss Francis Pearson, please allow me the great privilege of introducing you to Mrs. James Madison."

"Really, Mr. Shepard," the woman chastened him sweetly as she reached for Frannie's hand. "Lovely to meet you, Frannie. And please, call me Dolley."

* * *

An hour later, Dolley Madison was as beloved by Frannie as she was by Timothy. "She's wondrous," Frannie exclaimed once they were back on Pennsylvania Avenue. "I can see why you love working with her. Her wit is as sharp as Samuel's, and even Jed could appreciate her business sense. What did she say? She is hosting her 'dove party' and inviting only the wives of congressmen whose husbands oppose the president's policies?"

"Yes," Timothy laughed out loud. "And I can assure you, by the time those congressmen go to bed the night following her party, they will either capitulate to Mr. Madison's views or suffer the consequences of their wives' wrath for crossing their new best friend."

The pair laughed as they walked toward the docks at the edge of the Potomac. "Are you sure you can't spare another hour or so? I've so much more to show you."

Frannie squeezed Timothy's hands and looked across the water at Arlington, Virginia, casting her eyes south toward Alexandria. "I should catch this ferry and hurry to Mrs. Whitlock's. The rest of the company has probably arrived, and Henri will expect us to rehearse all evening."

"Very well, then. When can I see you again? Meetings will tie me up the majority of the day, but what about tomorrow night? Could you be available for an early supper?"

"Hmmm . . ." Frannie teased. "I think I could rearrange a few things."

"Splendid! I'll send a courier by in the afternoon to reconfirm." He helped her onto the boat and placed a gracious kiss on her hand before departing.

Rehearsals for the show the *Le Jardin* company was to perform on the eve of the inaugural devoured most of the following day as well. When Timothy came by to pick Frannie up for supper, Mrs. Whitlock begged the pair remain and join her and the rest of the troupe, but Timothy held firm to his plan. They rode the ferry to a Washington restaurant for oysters and rockfish on the waterfront. As soon as supper was finished, Timothy quickly whisked her away in a hack up a long, grassy meadow to the hill upon which the Capitol sat majestically overlooking the city. "Each of those two sandstone wings houses a portion of the Congress," explained Timothy as he pointed. "The southern wing accommodates the House, and the Senate occupies the northern wing. Beneath the Senate lies the Supreme Court's chambers."

Frannie noted that the building resembled a large, ornate box. Each of the two sandstone wings were three stories high and capped with short, round domes. They flanked the Capitol's center section, which was little more than a rectangular passageway between the wings.

"It's not finished, is it?" Frannie asked curiously.

"Well . . . no . . . but the war has drained the funds for its construction," Timothy explained defensively. "Benjamin Latrobe, the current architect, built a temporary walkway to join the wings before leaving town to pursue other work until the budget is sufficient to hire him back. You'll see. Eventually, the large center section will be taller, and its dome will be more pronounced, creating a grand rotunda inside. This Capitol will be a magnificent building, the very emblem of our democracy, like a light upon a hill. What a fine emblem she'll soon be."

"I've no doubt," replied Frannie, noting the change that came over him each time he spoke of the city and his new associations.

Candlelight could already be detected in several of the windows when Timothy led Frannie by the hand and through the entrance. Unfinished though it was on the outside, the inside was breathtaking. "Come with me," he whispered solemnly as he led her down a corridor. "This is the Senate Chamber."

The floor of the main hall was entirely covered with a Turkish rug, and the chairs were of mahogany with woven horse-hair cushions of crimson, set in three sweeping arcs before large mahogany tables that faced the Speaker's podium. A grand balcony overhung the room, providing a gallery for guests and visitors, and crimson drapes framed the windows.

"It's magnificent," Frannie conceded with her own measure of awe.

"I wish I could show you the Congressional Library. Mrs. Madison coerced the Congress to grant me access, but I dare not press the privilege. They are quite territorial about it. But what would you like to see next? I work so many hours I hardly allow myself time to enjoy the city. It's coming along quite nicely, don't you agree . . . not the swamp it once was a few years back."

"It's a wonderful city, Timothy, and you are helping to make it a wonderful capital."

"Thank you. I hope so," he said. "I believe my future lies here."

Frannie slipped her arm into his, and he laid his hand on top and patted it.

"There's a concert at the garrison—marching music, I believe," he added. "There's also a café on New York Avenue where they feature poetry readings. You do like poetry, don't you?"

"Yes, but . . . there was a time when you didn't feel a need to entertain me."

He smiled dimly and nodded. "I'm trying too hard to make you love the city. I apologize. I haven't even asked you about Jed. I saw him at Christmas, you know. He was a gracious host but a most miserable soul."

"He's on assignment right now, carrying dispatches to the forts along the coast and northern lines. He's received little word from Hannah since she left Baltimore."

"I know. I admire him for carrying on when his heart is so heavy, but hopefully this inaugural will boost troop morale and reaffirm that Washington is a world-class capital."

"I just want this conflict over so I can go home. Jed insists I'd be safer in Upper Marlboro with one of my father's old friends, a Dr. Beanes."

"Dr. Beanes? Why, he's a friend of Mr. Francis Scott Key—who gave the eulogy at General Lingan's funeral after the Baltimore riot. I've found Mr. Key to be quite a sociable host. Perhaps we'll find ourselves at the same parties . . . oh, but . . . I forgot. You abhor gentry parties, don't you?" Desiring to quickly change the subject, he saw a sign swinging from a storefront. "Ice cream?"

"Fine. Ice cream would be lovely," she conceded, becoming increasingly discomfited by the distance Timothy's new experiences was creating between them.

When they finished eating their frozen confections, she patted her mouth, feigning fatigue. "I think I should be getting back, Timothy."

"Are you sure? We could take a ride around the river. It's lovely to see the lamplights along the harbor. It will remind you of our rides along the Schuylkill that Philadelphia summer."

"Do you still think on those simple times, Timothy?"

His expression registered surprise and then hurt. "I'm sorry, Frannie. I've upset you with all my rambling about this city and its future."

"No," she offered regretfully. "It is I who should apologize. I suppose I'm fatigued. Perhaps we could take a ride another night. For now a quick ferry ride across the Potomac would be most appreciated."

Little was said on the ride back. Timothy stared off into the water, lost in his thoughts as he held her hand tenderly, but the incongruence rattled Frannie's senses.

* * *

March 3 flew by with last minute fittings and rehearsals. The stars of *Le Jardin* performed twice at the garrison, which had been fully transformed into inaugural splendor with laurel wreaths and garlands hung over every doorway and draped from every chandelier. After the final performance, Timothy came back to invite Frannie to a party in the city, but she declined, instead entreating him to join her at Mrs. Whitlock's for a quiet evening of backgammon and singing around the piano. She had hoped the old Timothy would reemerge in such a casual setting—the Timothy who preferred a simple evening at the Murdock School, singing old hymns together over attendance at a formal concert, or the Timothy who relished a private picnic by the river to fancy Washington dinners. Perhaps the nature of her employment had more than satiated her desire for such public entertainment, but after watching Timothy check and recheck the mantel clock, signaling his boredom, Frannie again used her fatigue as an excuse to end the evening early.

On March 4, the actual inaugural day, Mrs. Whitlock arranged ferry passage and hacks to transport the *Le Jardin* company along the parade route and to the Capitol. Before they left Alexandria they could hear the federal salute resounding from Fort Warburton and a similar tribute pounding out from the naval yards. Vehicles and persons of every description overran Pennsylvania Avenue, scrambling for a spot from which to see the presidential procession. Frannie and her friends watched as regiments from the militia, cavalry, and infantry passed by in full uniform and armament. Bands played spirited marches between each of the companies, and then carriages carrying the Cabinet members and assorted elected officials streamed by, but a grand hurrah spread as soon as the carriage carrying the Madisons came into the citizenry's view.

The street was a sea of humanity, all making haste to the Capitol. Those who had tickets or were fortunate enough to have arrived the earliest entered the building. As wide and spacious as were the passages, lobbies, galleries, chambers, and hall of the south wing of the Capitol, immense numbers of attendees were forced to remain outside and await word of the events.

By eleven o'clock, members of Congress, the foreign ministers, and the judges of the Supreme Court were taking their places. It was nearly noon when Mr. Madison entered, supported by an entourage of secretaries of various departments as well as the Attorney General and a senatorial committee. A brief introductory program ensued, including a prayer, and then Mr. Madison rose to deliver his inaugural address, after which Chief Justice Marshall administered the oath of office.

Two rounds of minute guns were fired after the ceremony concluded, and as Mr. Madison withdrew from the Capitol, nearly a dozen companies of infantry stood in full dress uniform awaiting their president's review. He then withdrew to his residence under the cavalry's escort.

Timothy waited near the president's house gate for the approach of Frannie's carriage. "Would you care to attend the president's luncheon? I should have mentioned it sooner." Timothy dropped his head in embarrassment. "You're welcome to come as my guest."

"You forgot to mention the *president's* luncheon to me?"

"I . . . I hadn't completely made up my own mind about attending," he lifted his head and smiled sheepishly, "but I'd be inclined if you were on my arm."

Dumbfounded but willing, she shrugged to her employer and waved to her friends as Timothy helped her down from Mrs. Whitlock's carriage. He squeezed her arm like a giddy child, conducting her from group to group as he introduced her to the prestigious assembly of guests, many of them members of Maryland's stifling gentry who were anxious to compliment her on her previous night's performance. This was a curiosity that merrily astounded her, since some of her current admirers were the selfsame accusers who had labeled her a tart and held her in scorn when she'd performed at *Le Jardin* in Philadelphia. *Such is the influence of Washington!*

When the bell for lunch rang, and everyone began heading into the dining room, Frannie noticed a particular young woman attached to a man she didn't know. Her entire countenance and bearing seemed female perfection, her body moving with fluid grace as if defying the very gravity that so often was Frannie's nemesis, yet Frannie could not dislike her, for the woman's every smile, every look, was at once both humble and confident, conveying goodness and kindness with every stroke of a lash and dip of her head. "Timothy? Who is that woman?" she asked, but apparently to no avail. When she looked up to make a second inquiry, she found her escort completely transfixed upon the same being, and suddenly many things made sense to her.

After lunch, all the guests began departing to make preparations for the evening's galas. When alone in Timothy's carriage, Frannie broached the obviously difficult subject.

"How long have you loved Miss Bainbridge?" she asked matter-of-factly.

Timothy's eyes closed immediately as a rush of air escaped him. He turned to face her, and his own expression changed from hurt to guilt. "There's nothing between us, Frannie. She's engaged to an infantry captain in New York. They are to be wed as soon as the war is over."

"Yet it's clear you love her," Frannie declared as nonchalantly as she could muster.

"I'm sorry if it appears so to you. I truly think if you and I were here together, that . . ."

Frannie reached for his hand and squeezed it gently. "We love whom we love, Timothy. And far be it from me to undercut the interests of a soldier, but you are here and he is not, and there is still time. You and I are the dearest of friends, but neither of us can say if more will ever exist between us. Why squander a chance at true love over a friendship that is already secure?"

"I assure you, I should be ever content to enjoy your company if that is all I am to have."

"Go to her, Timothy. If not today, then soon. Promise me."

When they reached the dock, he helped her down and lingered before leading her onto the ferry. His eyes were moist as he took her hands in his. Frannie stared into his face for several seconds, knowing that whether or not she held the premier spot of affection in his heart, her spot was true and everlasting, and surprisingly, it was enough for her. "Listen to me, Timothy. We each know what we are to one another, and we also know what we want from this life. If neither of us is to have more, perhaps we will explore what a life together might bring us. But while we are young, let neither of us settle for less than we *may* have."

He tipped her chin up and examined her face for several minutes, but Frannie was unable to decipher his expression. A sad smiled warmed his face as he leaned forward and placed a soft kiss on her lips. He held her chin for several seconds more, rubbing his thumb in its gentle cleft before asking, "Write me?"

"Of course," she replied as she stepped on board the ferry. As the boat set off, increasing the distance between her and Timothy, she waved and then sat staring off at the river, setting her thoughts on the one thing that made her secure—home.

CHAPTER 19

March 22, 1813
London, England

Trevor McGowan stood on the bridge and fidgeted nervously as he watched the expensive carriage draw near. It was their regular Wednesday routine, and though a part of him cringed as the moment arrived, another part of him breathed easier as he anticipated the fall of the coins.

When he climbed into the carriage, Ramsey sneered at him. "Are you following my instructions with exactness?" he demanded.

"Yes sir. To the letter. Me brothers 'ave been workin' the day shift at that warehouse and then they keep a secret watch on the earl at night, just like you requested."

"And you?" Ramsey barked impatiently.

"I'm on the night shift, and when I'm doing my surveillin', I keep meself hid."

"Good. I want the earl to believe the siege is over. Now tell me your report!"

"'Tis much the same as last week. They're still at Whittington Castle, and the viscount never leaves the house wifout the earl now. And two guards attend 'em as well."

"And the dog?"

"As you said. Ars'nic pressed into a hunk of lamb took 'im to 'is grave." It was a slight lie. He couldn't see wasting that pound of lamb to kill a dog. The beast had no sooner cracked the chicken bone before the poison took effect, and his children had had mutton stew that night.

"Good . . . good . . ." Ramsey growled. "Is that it?"

McGowan knew less information yielded fewer coins, and so, each week he was constrained to dramatize his observations. This week, however, he had drama aplenty to report. "Somefin's changed. I've seen that pup o' yours there nearly every day this week."

Ramsey's head shot up. "Arthur? I thought he had left for the war."

"Ev'dently not. 'E carried a mount'n o' gifts out o' the earl's place last Saturday."

Ramsey knew the reason immediately. "It was his birthday . . ." he moaned.

"'E's a reg'lar member o' the fam'ly, 'e is. Goes to church wif 'em as well."

"I haven't seen them at St. Paul's." A darkness filled Ramsey's eyes that only arose when Arthur's name was linked to the earl's, and McGowan noted it this time with interest.

"They don't go there no more. They go to a small parish church on the west side now." McGowan watched Ramsey's response carefully as a new strategy came to him. If he could raise the ante he could make himself indispensable and perhaps secure a bonus. It was a dangerous gamble, but one he believed was worth the risk; so he drove his point into Ramsey's heart. "I figger your son did that so 'e don't 'ave to see you." He watched to see if he'd hit his mark.

"Son? I have no son," Ramsey growled. He stared blankly into space as the words sank in. "What are you owed for your services?" His question carried an insinuation.

McGowan twisted the hat and cleared his throat. "Eight pounds," he answered. "Two each fer me brothers and me fer the surveillance, an extra two fer poisonin' the earl's dog."

Ramsey's eyes narrowed, and his jaw tightened as he snarled, "How would you like to earn a hundred pounds?"

McGowan cocked his head sideways at Ramsey as he attempted to hide his want. "That kind o' money don't come easy. What would we 'ave to do?"

"Get me the boy."

Shivers ran up McGowan's neck, replacing his smug smile. "Wait a minute, Mr. Ramsey. Frightnin' folks is one thing, but kidnappin' an earl's son?" He saw a strange mania in Ramsey's eyes, and the distance between his own situation and Ramsey's suddenly narrowed. When Ramsey had first searched the Barbados prison for a "suitable employee," McGowan had watched as Dupree's exploitable skills had rendered him worthy of being rescued, while McGowan had lingered there for two more years. Events had brought Ramsey back to the prison, and McGowan quickly made his loyalty an attractive asset, sweetening the pot by offering his two similarly-minded brothers as unexpected bonuses. But he was not quite as desperate now, and circumstances had stiffened Trevor McGowan's spine. He leaned back, sized the man up, and laughed. "Risk hangin' for a hundred pounds, eh? No thanks."

"Then I'll pay you a thousand."

The image of a table laden with hams and turkeys and the wide eyes of his children, clean and dressed in new clothes and shoes, made McGowan pause for a moment, but in the end he saw the gallows and the hopelessness of his children's futures and he declined again.

Ramsey was taken aback. "So . . . you won't be purchased cheaply. Name your price."

McGowan felt the blood rush from his head. "Why do you want the earl's boy?"

"I want him to know what it feels like to lose a son. I want him to spend the rest of his life feeling that ache, of caring little about his life's work because he has no heir to give it to."

"Do you mean to harm the boy?"

"I have no desire to injure the child, just to hide him from his father."

So that's it, eh? Still, McGowan knew the price would have to be enough to care for his family forever in case he was caught and sentenced to death. *Death?* He imagined what price he could ask Ramsey to pay in exchange for risking everything, including his very soul if harm came to the boy. *All I'd be guilty of is snatching the lad,* he rationalized.

Closing his eyes as if working out his price, he quickly focused on the faces of his loved ones. He saw the look of fear and disappointment on his wife's face and the hollow cheeks of his two sons, Michael and baby Hank, shivering as the winter wind rushed through the slats of their ragged shanty. He saw that scene over and over, wincing with each replay. *Some things hurt more'n dyin'* he thought to himself as he clenched his fist. "I'd want more'n money for such a job as that . . . and I'd want to do it separate from me brothers. Jest me."

"Agreed . . . and the price?"

"I'd 'ave to get some security fer me wife and me two boys. A guarantee that no matter what, they'd be fine."

"Simply name your price."

McGowan leaned close. "You say you have no heir?"

Ramsey's brow furrowed in consternation.

"Pay me the thousand pounds up front, and if I get caught . . . make my sons your heirs."

Ramsey leaned back and smiled wryly. "And why would I want to do that? So I can end up with a McGowan knife in my back when your little nits grow a bit?"

"Don't trust the fam'ly McGowan, eh? Fair 'nough. Then write somethin' in the will that nulls the agreement if your death comes by foul play . . . and jest to be fair, make my boys partial heirs . . . say twenty percent, if your own pup ever comes home."

Ramsey looked askance at McGowan. "That's a very steep price."

"Retribution don't come cheap, gov'ner."

Ramsey heard the sneer in McGowan's voice. "Very well. I'll draw up the papers."

"You do that . . . and I'll be needin' some o' that advance money tonight."

Ramsey glared at the man and then smiled weakly as he put his hand in his breast pocket, withdrawing his leather wallet. "Eight pounds even, did you say?"

McGowan shook his head and his finger simultaneously. "That were a lifetime ago. I'll be 'avin' a portion o' that thousand pounds now." He wriggled his fingers at Ramsey. "And don't go thinking' you can pull the wool over me eyes wif that will. A man of means, as I 'ave recently become, can afford to 'ave 'is own lawyer present at the signin'."

Ramsey emptied his wallet into McGowan's hand saying, "I want the job done soon, before they replace the guard dog."

Resolution replaced the smile McGowan wore as he riffled the bills near his head. "Tomorrow night, then. I'd like this one night to prepare things."

"Very well. Meet me here tomorrow at the same time, and we'll sign the papers." Ramsey called for the driver to pull over, dropping McGowan off exactly where he'd found him.

For a second after the carriage pulled away, McGowan considered running after it and calling the arrangement off, but as he slipped his hand over the roll of bills, he dared imagine he could pull it *all* off— kidnap the lad, deliver him to Ramsey, and flee with his family back into his father's native Scotland. Once he had adopted that mindset, he relaxed, determined to enjoy the feeling of wealth for whatever time it lasted. He strolled to a shop, purchased candies for Michael, a rattle for Hank, and a shawl for his wife, and rather than buying food for cooking, he decided to take them all to dinner to make it a night his wife would remember.

* * *

As always, the bells tolled five the next evening, but this time they sounded hollow to McGowan, like funeral bells predicting his future. He looked at his lawyer, an inebriated miscreant who defended petty criminals who were lucky enough to have slightly more money than brains and morals.

"Six pounds . . . up front," the man slurred with his hand outstretched.

After McGowan counted the money out, McGowan pulled the man up straight by his lapels, growling, "You'd best protect me interests!"

Before the man recovered from the manhandling, Ramsey's carriage arrived and the threesome took a short ride while the lawyer perused the documents.

"Jest tell me if it's all legal and bindin'," McGowan grumbled to the man.

"Never knew you to be a man of such benevolence, Mr. Ramsey," the lawyer said sarcastically. "It's a strange document, but its intent is clear, McGowan. *In the spirit of an act performed by Lord Ensor and the Mitchell family of the House of Commons, when they provided the means for an indigent child from Liverpool named Jonathan Edward Pearson to go to school and secure employment, Mr. Ramsey desires to follow their example. Therefore, upon the occasion of his natural death and the death of his employee, Trevor McGowan, Mr. Ramsey bequeaths his entire estate to the children of Trevor McGowan: Hank and Michael McGowan.*" The lawyer paused, interested. Then he summarized the rest. "*This will is contingent on his failure to reconcile with his own son, Arthur. However, if he and his son do reconcile, your boys will still divvy up a twenty percent share in the estate.* That's the gist of it."

McGowan nodded and watched as Ramsey signed the two documents. "Now, Mr. Ramsey, hand both copies to me lawyer so he can file one and deliver the other to me wife."

Ramsey refused. "I've met your terms . . . now it's time for you to meet mine."

"And have you tear it up once I leave this carriage? Oh no, sir. Now give him the will."

"I'll do no such thing!" Ramsey said as he opened the carriage door and stepped out, demanding that McGowan join him.

"You have no choice," McGowan declared. "We each 'ave too much on the line now. I know too much about *your* business and you know too much about me an' me brothers."

Ramsey's jaw worked side to side as he contemplated the situation. "Tonight then?"

McGowan nodded, "Aye. As soon as we part company, I'll begin."

"Very well," Ramsey agreed as he handed the copies to the lawyer. He then handed McGowan a card with an address, saying "Meet me here at ten tonight," and with that he rode off.

McGowan glared into the lawyer's eyes, issuing a warning to him as well. "And don't think about double-crossing me by sellin' that will back to Ramsey, 'cause if you do, you'll 'ave me two brothers to answer to."

* * *

"One more game!" Daniel pleaded with Clarissa as his father glanced at the clock.

"It's far past your bedtime already," the earl argued. "Clarissa's had a long day. She needs some time to relax without having to entertain you every minute."

Daniel looked wide-eyed at Clarissa as he addressed his father. "She doesn't mind playing with me, do you Clarissa?"

Clarissa looked apologetically at the earl as she clasped the lad's hand. "I love spending time with you, but you must obey your father. How could I help you rise to your post as Viscount Whittington if I encourage you to disobey him?"

With a shrug of his narrow shoulders and a reluctant smile, Daniel bravely agreed.

"That's my boy," the earl said lovingly to his son. "Now, say good night to Clarissa and then it's off to bed with you. I'll be up in a few minutes to say prayers."

"Yes, Father," Daniel replied, adding a well-rehearsed bow of respect. He turned to Clarissa next, employing the same show of manly deference. "Good night, Clarissa."

Her hand touched her mouth to still its mirthful quivering. "Good night, Viscount Whittington."

The strain of effort required to maintain this newly required level of decorum showed in Daniel's eyes. When the boy glanced at his father, the earl immediately understood the problem. Feigning annoyance, a smile of fatherly pleasure tugged at his lips until he nodded the desired permission. In a flash, Daniel sped back to Clarissa, falling into her ready embrace. "I love you, Clarissa."

"Good night, sweet boy," she cried softly. "Ohhh, I do love you too, Daniel."

Content with his hug, Daniel bowed again and retreated upstairs as Clarissa rose from her chair and went to the window, dabbing at her eyes with each step. "Forgive me, Lord Everett. Some fine nanny I am, coddling the viscount that way."

The earl came up behind her, seemingly to share her view from the window. "You're so much more than a nanny to him, Clarissa. He loves you like a mother."

Their eyes met in the reflection in the glass, causing Clarissa to shiver noticeably. She stood there transfixed, tiny goose bumps marring the perfection of her luminescent skin. The earl watched as a warm, crimson blush washed over her, revealing her emotions, and she turned abruptly, rubbing her arms as she walked a few paces away.

"I wish he could remain eleven forever," she uttered nervously, "though I know we must prepare him in case you are forced to send him away."

The earl caught the gentle scent of rose water that wafted in his direction as she passed. His burdened heart pounded, torn between the possibilities the moment provided and the dreaded reality regarding Daniel. "I just pray circumstances won't require it for a long time."

"As do I . . ." she said as she abruptly turned to face the earl. "I would hate to think the scoundrels could ever force you to send Daniel away for his protection. Of course . . . I just assumed you'd send me along with Daniel and his tutor . . . to ease Daniel's separation."

The thought was unbearable on both counts. The earl bit his lip and ran his left hand over his mouth in thought as his right hand gestured toward the red velvet divan. "Would you . . . sit for a moment, Clarissa?"

"As hard as it would be to leave," she began, lowering herself into the plush cushion, "wherever it is you've a mind to send him, I would go and guard him with my very life."

"Of that I have no doubt," Lord Everett sighed as he sat beside her. He leaned forward, staring blankly at his shoes, then, as the silent moments ticked by, he turned toward her to search her blue eyes, hoping to find more there than merely the love of a nanny for her charge.

Clarissa fumbled with her hands, becoming noticeably discomfited during the silence. "Are you reluctant to answer because you are hesitant to entrust Daniel to my care, sir?"

Sir? The return of her stiff mode of address bit into his heart. "Are you content to be a nanny and nothing more?" Lines of frustration marred his tanned brow, growing deeper as he admired the endearing way her lips quivered to fight her emotions. He slid closer, covering her busy hands with his own. When he spoke, he heard the waver in his own voice. "Don't you hunger for the things all women desire? A husband? A home? A family of your own?"

The young woman dipped her head and shuddered as the impact of the inquiry clearly hit its mark. "I . . . I . . ." She halted, bending forward until her body was nearly parallel to her lap.

The earl felt her hands clutch fiercely around his right one and his left dropped to her shoulder to turn her torso back toward him. "Speak to me, Clarissa . . . please."

She refused to look at him until his unrelenting entreaties rendered her unable to deny his petition. The earl saw the wetness of her face, yet she bore no mark of embarrassment over her show of emotion. Instead, she leaned close to him, imploring him with her eyes and the timbre of her voice. "All that you mentioned? I would gladly forfeit all of it, and more yet, simply to keep what I now enjoy . . . to have a hand in raising Daniel and to enjoy your company . . . and yet I know that by that very admission I have likely undone it all."

The earl cupped her face in his hands and smiled reassuringly at her. "No, no . . ." he assuaged encouragingly. "You have made it all wonderful!"

She peeled his hands away and stood, moving away from him. "How can you say that? It can never be the same again! I have no right to dream of such things let alone to mention them, but I let my guard down when you invited me to call you by your Christian name!"

Coming behind her, he gently took her shoulders. "You only dreamed of what I have hoped for as well," he whispered in her ear. "I love you, Clarissa."

Taken aback by his admission, she spun to face him. "How can that be? Me being what I am, and you being what you are?"

"What you are is a woman, Clarissa . . . a beautiful, kind, good woman. And I am merely a man who has fallen in love with a lady as fine as any at court."

"Do you mean that?" she whispered quietly.

"With all my heart . . . with every corner of my once-locked heart." He felt her slump against him, burying her face in the crook of his neck as their arms tightened around one another.

"Could this be true?" she asked as his warm breath brushed over her neck.

He delighted at the innocent way she reacted to him, wondering if she knew that he was just as completely awash in her. As he brushed his lips against hers, her sighs made him weak. He thought he heard a sound upstairs, but after months of strained vigilance, his attentions were suddenly focused elsewhere, his mind dismissing the noise as yet another creak of the old wood that had so often sent him scrambling unnecessarily.

Clarissa's equally vigilant ears detected it as well. "What was that?"

The earl laid a finger alongside her jaw, drawing her attentions completely back to him. "Most likely it's the playful footsteps of a disobedient young viscount we both adore."

The pair soon heard another sound. "We should go up and check on him, Lord Everett," Clarissa urged sweetly, but before they took a step, the outside guard, Mason, entered the room.

"There's a blaze in the shire, Lord Whittington! Three houses are already gone and two more are on fire!"

Lord Whittington's face washed white. "A fire? What caused the blaze, Mason?"

"I dunno. Maybe a cook fire caught the wind."

The earl looked into the eyes of the woman to whom he had just professed his love and realized how that moment had suspended his vigilance. "I have a bad feeling about this," he confided to her. "First the dog chokes to death on a chicken bone and now this? It's too odd . . . too many coincidences. I'll check on Daniel first."

He began to move toward the stairs when Robert, the other guard, came rushing in. "There's chaos in the shire, Lord Whittington. They need you out there."

Lord Whittington's eyes bore the haunted look of one burdened by diverse responsibilities. He looked to Clarissa, and she offered him her assurance. "You go and tend to the shire's troubles. I'll stay right by Daniel's bedside until you get home."

Both were aware of the curious looks their exchange was eliciting from the two guards, but neither bothered to note it or explain it. With a squeeze of her shoulders and a nod of understanding, the earl hurried out the door with Mason, ordering Robert to stand guard as Clarissa began mounting the curved marble staircase.

A waft of cold air loosened a yellow tendril of her hair and she brushed it into place, accelerating her pace to Daniel's room. Pushing his door open she came upon a ghastly sight. Daniel was sitting upright in his bed, with his arms bound behind him and a gag tied across his mouth, while his eyes, filled with terror and pleading for salvation, turned her blood to ice. Before she could rush to his side she felt a thick, coal-oil-doused hand clamp over her mouth, binding her against her brawny assailant. Then she heard his free hand turn the key, locking the door. Once their exit was secured, the man began stuffing cotton between her gaping jaws. She struggled against her attacker, but her mind was focused on only one thought.

She stared at the child, flailing her arms toward the door, urging him to rise and run. With the child's heart pounding, his chest heaving, Clarissa knew he was hyperventilating from fear, but she battled her assailant with her hands and feet, deflecting the man's incoming blows, buying the child time. As if understanding that both their fates rested in his escape, Daniel slid from the bed on the attacker's blind side. Clarissa saw him inch along the wall until he was only feet from the door, waiting for the opportunity to reach the exit. She threw her body forward, forcing her assailant to clutch her more tightly, and then she willed her body to go completely limp, becoming a dead weight in his arms, throwing his own balance off. In that second, she saw Daniel bolt for the door and turn his back to the knob, attempting to work it with his bound hands. Doubling her assaults, Clarissa fully engaged the attention of the man while trying to catch of glimpse of Daniel—to know when he was finally safe. She saw a look of relief in his eyes as his fingers found the key, but as he bent right, presumably to unlock the door, the attacker swept his leg across the lad's, toppling the boy to the floor.

Aggravated and panicked, the assailant returned his brutal attentions to Clarissa. His strong hands wrapped around her throat, cutting off her scant oxygen. Thrashing and kicking with her last ounce of strength, she knocked the coat stand over against the top sash of the opened window with a loud crash.

* * *

As the beautiful woman's body went slack in his hands, McGowan felt at once nauseated and hell-bound. He recoiled from the repugnant form on the floor, wiping his hands against his shirt to clean the stink of murder from them. For a moment, he felt empathy for the earl's son, now nearly catatonic from the sight of the beloved woman lying dead and still before him. But the pounding that had begun at the locked door forced him to quickly gather his wits, his only remaining desire that of securing his children's futures, particularly if his own was to be a noose.

McGowan heard the guard curse at the ancient locked door and then retreat. Limp and nearly faint, the child was easily stuffed into the canvas sack and tied to McGowan's back. He picked up the end of the long rope he had previously secured to the boy's enormous four-poster bed by the windowsill. He positioned himself to slide down the wall of Whittington Castle when he heard four shots ring out off to the left wall. Hurrying with the awkward weight of the child on his back, the ground was finally in sight when he heard a throng of angry voices behind him, closing in fast. He turned his head and saw the citizens of Whittington running up the hill, rakes and scythes in tow, with the earl leading the charge.

McGowan dropped to the ground, pulled a knife from its sheath, and cut the rope that bound the boy to his back. He made a vain attempt at escape, but sensing the hopelessness of his situation and fearing that his tongue would slip and nullify the terms of his agreement with Ramsey, he drew the blade across his own throat, ending his life to secure his family's.

Lord Whittington scooped his son into his arms and the boy threw his arms around his father's neck, allowing only one word to escape his shocked and disoriented mind. "Clarissa—"

Handing Daniel off to Mason, the earl flew into the castle and bounded up the marble staircase, yelling Clarissa's name. Close on his heels was Robert, followed by a crowd of men from the shire. The earl's guard moved in front of his anguished employer and, using the tools which were being handed forward, bludgeoned a hole large enough for his hand to fit through. The guard turned the key and then worked the knob until the door gave. As soon as the earl saw the slightest movement in the heavy barricade, he burst through and, within seconds, sounded out a mournful cry that echoed throughout the empty chambers of the castle.

* * *

Lieutenant Arthur Ramsey was not prepared for what awaited him as he entered Daniel's room, finding Lord Whittington hunched on the edge of his son's bed, his heavy head resting in hands that clutched blue satin slippers and a sash—the evidences of Clarissa's final struggle.

It was all too much for the young cleric who, succumbing to his own disbelief, leaned heavily against the frame of the battered door, hardly able to bear his own grief let alone the agonizing image of the earl's ghostly vigil. "I . . . I came as soon as I heard," he uttered softly.

The earl barely acknowledged the voice, offering no reply, and in his discomfiture, Arthur attempted to fill the silence. "How . . . is . . . Daniel?" he asked tentatively.

"Broken in mind and spirit," came the flat, despondent response. "I tried to keep him away while Clarissa's family removed . . . her . . ." he struggled. "He's resting in my bed with my mother by his side. I doubt he'll ever be able to sleep in this room again."

Arthur nodded his understanding. "I'm . . . so . . . sorry . . ." Never before had he felt at such a loss—he who was trained to soothe grief and to offer words of comfort about death and heaven's hope. He felt unworthy to offer these treasures . . . not under these circumstances.

"How is it that you are here so quickly from London?" the earl inquired, raising his head.

Arthur coughed to clear the tightness from his throat, but the words still came out raspy. "An aide from Admiral Cochrane's office sent word to me." The news elicited an immediate and malicious change in the earl's countenance, a look that made Arthur's neck and arms prickle.

"Did he tell you that I implicated your father as a conspirator in last night's attacks?"

The deliberate coldness of the words caused Arthur to stall. "Yes, but he claimed my father was able to offer a plausible explanation for his ties to the man who killed Clarissa."

"Murdered . . ."

Arthur's face went slack as the correction was made. "Yes. Murdered. Of course."

Lord Whittington's eyes went to the spot on the floor where a ribbon from Clarissa's hair still lay. He remained oddly focused on the object, asking, "Do you believe your father's story?"

Arthur drew in a deep breath to settle his nerves. "It is plausible. I went to him and challenged him on this. He said he hired the McGowan brothers to watch my movements so he would know when I was deployed for the military. Because I spent so much time here, he understood why it may have appeared that the men were following you and Daniel instead." He thought he saw the slightest flicker of doubt crack the earl's resolve, and he rushed in with more details. "He testified that on the night of my birthday, the McGowan brothers saw me leave for the barracks with all my gifts. Father said they commented about my good fortune and your wealth, believing it may have been that night that their greed led them to plot last night's heinous deeds."

The earl closed his eyes, releasing a long melancholy sigh that sounded more like an agonized groan. "No, no, no, Arthur," he muttered as his hands covered his face, his fingers rubbing deeply into his eyes while the low groaning continued. Finally, his head shot up and he challenged the young man. "Did Cochrane's aide tell you he filed a will early this morning?"

Now Arthur's head hung. "Yes. Naming the murderer's sons as heirs."

"Before she's even laid to rest he begins his games," the earl snarled, looking askance.

"Lord Whittington," Arthur began weakly. "Isn't it . . . I mean . . . can't you conceive with the tiniest possibility that perhaps he did so in ignorant benevolence?"

"No Arthur," Lord Whittington said curtly with a resolute shake of his head. "Your father knew exactly what he was doing by the heirs he chose and the terms he set. The child your father referred to in his will . . . the one the Ensors and Mitchells aided long ago? It was Jonathan Edward Pearson, the man whose family and property your father has targeted for obliteration in America. You've heard the stories from your own mother's lips. Can't you see? Your father is not honoring the Ensors and Mitchells by naming the sons of a murderer as his heirs. He is mocking them . . . and he's mocking you too."

The gentle sadness had returned to Lord Whittington's voice, but the softer timbre did not prevent the words from devastating Arthur, who pulled his gaze away from the revered man. Then the earl rose and walked over to the chair by Daniel's bed, and he watched the veneration with which the earl picked up the worn copy of "Mother Goose's Melody" which lay atop a copy of "The History of Little Goody Two Shoes." Arthur knew from previous evenings spent in the castle that these were Daniel's favorites, the very books from which Clarissa routinely read to the boy. He watched the earl slowly lower himself into "her" chair and reverentially leaf through the pages. After a few were turned, he saw a smile tug at the earl's lips that both relieved and dismayed Arthur as the expression quickly degraded from melancholy to morose. Soon, silent tears wet Lord Whittington's face as the proud earl's shoulders became racked with shuddering. Unsure how to respond, and believing himself to be both a comfort and an irritant, Arthur stood frozen and unsure until the simple truth of the moment struck him. "Dear Lord Whittington . . . How could I have missed it? You fell in love with her, didn't you?"

The earl clutched the books to his breast, his tears now denied behind steeled, determined eyes. "Loving her wasn't enough. I had to own her, to make her mine, and now she's dead because I let passion overrule my head!" Arthur instinctively stepped forward to provide a gesture of comfort, but unwilling or unable to be consoled, the earl cut him off, stood, and stepped away. "Don't question things you do not understand. I know the truth." His voice was again filled with anger and pain. "The fiend who murdered her received access to her and my son because I faltered in my duty . . . because I forgot my responsibilities. Well, never again!"

Arthur shrank where he stood. "No! My attachment to you brought this on. Regardless of whether it is because my father hired these men to kidnap Daniel, or if in his obsession to make contact with me he unknowingly brought these men to your door, the stain is upon me."

The earl placed a hand on Arthur's shoulder, but his eyes remained cold. "Then we are at an impasse, my friend. Neither of us will find forgiveness or forgetting in the other's company."

The chill in the earl's voice and words went straight into Arthur's young heart. He looked curiously at the man he had come to love above all others. "Is there anything I can do?"

Lord Whittington turned his back to him and walked to the window that looked out over the shire's rolling hills. "Will you fulfill the favors previously discussed?"

Arthur walked toward him but the earl kept his back to him and raised a hand, bidding him to stop. "It pains me to think my son will miss the greening of these hills in the approaching weeks, but I will no longer allow my heart to rule my head."

The skin of Arthur's face prickled. "Sir?"

"I've been corresponding with your mother, Arthur. We both feel confident your father has no further interest in pursuing her, and she at last feels she is in a safe place."

"I don't understand."

"I've been living a lie, Arthur, deceiving myself. I retreated to the quiet of this shire, enjoying my selfish peace while greatly ignoring the impact these years of warring have had on our nation and people—allowing tyrants like your father to prosper, only to breed other wicked men like McGowan. I believed that in time things would again be as they were, but these past hours have shown me that we cannot preserve the gallantry of Britain by remaining selfish and passive in our defenses." The earl finally turned to face Arthur, and when he did he bore the look of the battle-weary generals Arthur had served over the past few months. "I have failed my family and my country, and I've delayed you as well. The time has come for us both to get on with our duties."

Arthur sensed the finality of his words. "Are you clearing my deployment to Maryland?"

"Soon. Very soon. But first, I must ask two favors of you." The earl stared into Arthur's brown eyes until his own began to shine. "I've arranged leave for you so you can escort Daniel to Ireland, Arthur. Your mother is willing to care for him until he can return home safely."

Arthur was incredulous. "You're sending your son away? Time and time again you've promised him you would never do this very thing! It's the one thing he fears above all, and after losing Clarissa, it will destroy his trust!"

"You've no idea what agony I have suffered in making this decision! There is no other way to keep him safe while allowing me to serve Britain as I must!"

"Does he know? Have you at least explained this to him?"

"He knows only that you are taking him on a trip, and that is all he can know for now. I want no one but you and your mother to know of my plans. I trust no one else at this point."

No amount of flattery could settle Arthur's frustration. "So I am to tell him? Is that what you are saying? Recall that I know the anguish of a father's betrayal. I can assure you that what you have planned for the safety of his flesh will only serve to break his fragile heart."

"You cannot compare me to your father, Arthur. In time, Daniel will understand."

"Pray he does, Lord Whittington, for a lost boy will seek out another to fill the void! I was fortunate enough to have found you. He may not be so blessed."

The earl dipped his head and muttered, "What is done is done. Mason will use the activity on the estate to secret you out the back hills to Cornwall. You will then take Daniel to Ireland to meet your mother. When you return, you'll report to Bermuda until Major General Ross is ready to begin his campaign in Maryland."

"I see." Arthur nodded heavily. "And the second favor? You said there were two."

"Your mother knows you so well, Arthur. She said no matter what your father did, you would never stop trying to redeem him. She was right. Despite the evidence, you still leapt to his defense just now, hoping to explain his connection to McGowan. I hate your father, and as you cannot, and should not, I cannot continue our association."

As the consuming loneliness sank in, Arthur felt as if the life was being squeezed from him. "Even weasels have fathers, yet I cannot find a worthy one willing to take the job."

"I wish there was another way, but I have vowed to devote my life to bringing your father to justice, and I would hate myself were you to watch me do it."

Swallowing hard, Arthur fought to regain enough composure to speak. "Retribution and justice are not one in the same, Lord Whittington. If this is what you must do to find *your* peace, then help me find mine as well. All our pain seems tied to my father's vendetta against Jonathan Pearson. You say he's focused the military's attention on the destruction of Pearson's innocent family for his own gain. If that's so, then delay my orders further to grant me the time I need to get to Maryland and see my father's enemy firsthand. Perhaps I cannot prevent what is already in motion, but if I find them deserving of the fate my father has consigned them to, perhaps then I will be able to make some peace with his actions."

* * *

Whispering words of promised adventure, the earl gathered his sleepy-eyed son in his trembling arms and placed him in the carriage. "I love you, Daniel," he groaned, then turning to Arthur he added, "Despite how things have turned out, always know that I love you as well."

Arthur reeled from the pain in the earl's voice, but so jagged and raw were his own emotions that he could not utter an immediate response, and then the earl departed. As the carriage rocked along the path, he finally gave voice to his thoughts. "What good can come from such love?"

Perhaps it was the sorrow of his tone or the words themselves, but Daniel suddenly became aware that this was not a joyful jaunt. He sat upright and grabbed Arthur's coat, panic evident in his eyes. "Where are you taking me, Arthur, and why didn't Papa come along?"

"You should rest, Daniel. We've a long ride ahead."

"I want Papa, Arthur. Take me home to Papa!"

The combined trauma sent Daniel into a frenzy. He clawed at the door, screaming for his father and causing the entire carriage to rock dangerously back and forth. Arthur clamped his arms around the child, shushing him softly as he racked his mind for a comforting truth to offer the child, but he could find none. At length the child exhausted himself and crawled into a tight ball with his head resting upon Arthur's lap. Over and over he muttered until his voice became hoarse, "You promised . . . you promised . . . you promised . . ."

Arthur ruffled his fingers through the child's tangled locks as he wondered how many more disappointments and betrayals they each would have to suffer. Before severing their ties, the earl had finally agreed to Arthur's request to delay his deployment to Bermuda by eight weeks. It was time enough to reconnoiter the Patuxent . . . time enough to determine once and for all if his father was a patriot or a pirate. . . . And to determine if he still had a father at all . . .

CHAPTER 20

March 22, 1813
The Prison Camp at Lachine, Quebec

Major Dudley Snowden picked up the stone in his shivering fingers and etched the line on his rudimentary calendar. Today marked the sixth day of his seventh month as a prisoner of war. Seventeen more of his men had died from various ailments in the past month, many counting themselves fortunate for an end to the deprivations the camp had inflicted upon them.

But Laura Peddicord had been their angel where possible. Books, socks, occasionally even blankets found their way to the men through Miss Peddicord's compassionate hands. The Americans knew the risk she took to bring them these treasures, cajoling the guards with treats and offers to mend and launder their clothes in exchange for allowing a few small tokens to pass across the fence, making each worn and torn item ever more precious. As desperate as all the men were to keep warm, it was the books that brought the greatest pleasure, drawing the soldiers into clusters to hear a reader share the stories and verses. The temporary looks of contentment on each of their faces suggested that this slice of gentility transported them back to sweeter days, eliciting fond memories, reminding them for what and for whom they were surviving.

The prisoners' letters were passed to the guards to be read and edited before posting, and some men had received replies, but Dudley had received nothing from Beatrice despite his many attempts to reach her in every location he could imagine. In early February he received a worrisome letter from Stephen Mack, posted, of all places, from Detroit, inquiring on Dudley's condition and informing him that Beatrice had sent word in late December announcing a delay in her arrival to Tunbridge. The letter went on to state that Beatrice had sent no further word.

Having heard about the fever, Dudley became frantic to find his wife. He considered taking out an advertisement offering a reward for information leading to her discovery, knowing that Stephen Mack would assist him, but first he had to get a letter with Beatrice's description past the guards. Unable to bear the indignity of having such an intimate errand scrutinized and mocked by his captors, he began to devise another plan. Noticing that the British guards riffled through the books Laura *brought,* checking for contraband, he wondered if they would also scrutinize it if one of the prized volumes was returned. On one of Laura's weekly visits, he handed a book of verses back to her, much to her surprise.

"I thought the men loved the books," Laura queried quizzically.

"I've marked a verse by a particular author. Could you find more of his work?" Dudley asked, his eyes boring knowingly into hers. She frowned, unsure of his intent as he continued under watchful eyes. "In either case we'd very much love to have the book returned."

She had walked away, her confusion apparent, but no check of the book had been conducted by the guard, and, as per his request, the next week the book of verses, plus another by the indicated author, was returned, checked, and given to the men. Using a variety of excuses, he had conducted the same experiment three more times with the same conclusion. On the fifth week, as he handed the book over the fence, he pressed a note to the cover just long enough for her to read it before he crumpled it into his hand and away from the guards' eyes. It read:

I've hidden a letter inside this book. Would you post it for me?

Laura Peddicord's expression remained unchanged but the color drained from her face as she stalled silently by the fence, presumably weighing the cost of honoring the request. But before she could answer, her choice was made for her.

"Hey! What's goin' on, you two?" the young guard barked in a cockney dialect, shoving Miss Peddicord aside as he raised the barrel of his gun at Dudley's face. "No fraternizin' or we'll be cuttin' off these lil' privileges. We don't want no Americans fawnin' over our women." He turned his lascivious attention to Miss Peddicord. "Nor should a loyal British subject want to be cavortin' with the likes of them. Now, move along, lil' lady, before you get yourself into trouble."

Laura turned quickly and left in a near run, clutching the book tightly to her chest, her fear clearly imprinted upon her face. Dudley cursed himself for his selfishness and noted that she did not come the next week, but in the middle of the following week he felt his knees go weak as he saw her arrive at the fort in a military wagon in the company of an older officer. She stumbled from the wagon on visibly shaky legs, her face taut with terror as the older officer clamped his hand firmly on her arm, pressing her forward through the crowd of gawking soldiers. She refused to glance in the direction of the Americans, and Dudley began to shake with guilt and fear, terrified that his secret letter had been discovered. He heard the muffled sounds of angry voices filter from the building, and then the young cockney guard was brought to the building and the volume of voices rose again.

But what riveted his attention next was the sight of two officers hovering near the whipping post, lashes in hand. Dudley ran to the edge of the fence, begging for information and prepared to offer himself in exchange for the young woman. He called out to the guards, risking the lash for that very act, until one of the soldiers, a captain named Quartermain, who was in an unusually conciliatory mood, ambled over, willing to share news regarding the upcoming event.

"I didn't think you had a stomach for British military justice, Major Snowden."

Dudley struggled to remain calm and detached. "*Military* justice, Captain Quartermain?"

"That's right, and you'll be particularly interested in today's actions, bein' that you Americans have such a fondness for Miss Peddicord."

He could scarcely draw enough breath to speak. "What has this to do with her?"

"She's fine. At least she is now." The officer looked back over his shoulder at his curious comrades. "I know you care for the woman. Well, the guard that always checks her parcels is Corporal Riggins. He's been sweet on her for some time, and he hated that she was kind to you. Seems he had too much to drink last night, and he ambled over to her place. When she refused him he shoved her around and might have done worse had her father not returned in time."

Dudley shut his eyes against the images flooding his mind. "Then why was she brought here by that officer?"

"That officer is her father—Captain Peddicord. He dragged her here to testify against Riggins and to see that her honor is upheld."

Weak from relief, Dudley slumped against a fence post. "So it's Riggins who's headed for the whipping post. Please don't tell me Miss Peddicord will be forced to watch."

"Her father insists. Says if she hadn't been spending so much time here, none of this would have happened. She's being sent to Yorktown to prevent a repeat of this sordid affair."

Dudley felt his eyes sting as he walked away from the guard and gathered the men together to explain the situation. They stood silently as five lashes were laid across Riggins' back, offering their strength and support to the woman who had been their angel. As her father escorted the weeping, distraught woman to her carriage, they offered her a salute to honor her for her kindness. Her eyes remained fixed on them until the carriage rolled out of sight, but the men remained at attention seconds longer, allowing the finality of her exit to settle in.

Once Riggins was carried to his barracks, Quartermain approached the compound's fence with a book in his hand, motioning for Dudley. "She wanted you to have this."

Dudley received the volume, a well-worn Bible, with grateful hands. Laura had delivered six or seven bibles previously, but when Dudley opened this book, he found Laura's name written in the cover, making the precious scripture all the more treasured. Below her name she had written a verse from Isaiah chapter forty, the thirty-first verse. The inscription read, *March 20, 1813,* and was followed by:

> *With fondest regards,*
> *Laura Peddicord*
>
> *But they that wait upon the LORD shall renew their strength;*
> *they shall mount up with wings as eagles; they shall run, and*
> *not be weary; and they shall walk, and not faint.*

Dudley knew the verse would forever remain his favorite. He also found a ribbon tucked into John, chapter eight. The thirty-sixth verse was underlined and Dudley read:

> *If the Son therefore shall make you free, ye shall be free indeed.*

Behind the ribbon was a slip of paper that read, *Psalms 12:1.* When Dudley turned to that verse he found it underlined. It read:

> *Help, Lord; for the godly man ceaseth; for the faithful fail*
> *from among the children of men.*

The word *fail* was circled and in the margin the words, "*I'm sorry. L.P.*" were written. He understood. His letter had not been sent.

Dudley looked again at the beautiful verses she had chosen and wept.

CHAPTER 21

Late March 1813
Hanover, New Hampshire

Dr. Zachary Butler swallowed hard, again running through his mind the possible reasons why Dr. Smith would have summoned him. Convinced that he knew no reason for censure, he knocked on the door marked, *Dr. Nathan Smith, Dean of Medicine.*

Three quick raps brought the authoritative voice of his professor. "Please, come in."

Opening the door, he attempted to hide his nervousness, asking, "You called for me, sir?"

"Dr. Butler? Yes. Please, take a seat."

"Is anything awry, Dr. Smith?"

"You tell me, Dr. Butler. I have received a very anxious inquiry from a Mr. Stephen Mack inquiring after two much-delayed female houseguests—a Mrs. Snowden and a Miss Stansbury. Mr. Mack claims to have posted inquiries in the hospitals and in the local papers seeking information regarding the women. He is most distressed, and his inquiries have stirred no small amount of concern. It then came to my attention, Dr. Butler, that you ferried two sick women from the inn several weeks ago. Could these be Mr. Mack's missing guests?"

Noting the disappointed gaze Dr. Smith was giving him, Dr. Butler replied, "Yes, sir, but I moved them out of concern for Mrs. Snowden's unborn child."

"I find no fault in your moving them. My concern is that you did so without notifying their host or their families. Both have been rightly worried considering the epidemic in the area."

"I've urged them repeatedly, but the ladies insisted on handling matters their own way."

Dr. Smith leaned back in his chair. "Tell the women you have been ordered to answer these inquiries. Blame me if it will ease your conscience. Do we have an understanding?"

"Yes, sir." A contrite Dr. Butler rose to leave, but he had another concern on his mind that he could not miss the opportunity to raise. "Dr. Smith, may I consult with you on another case?"

The good doctor was instantly intrigued. "You are a fine physician and surgeon, Dr. Butler. Is there something special about this case?"

"The case is perhaps not as special as is the patient and his family, sir. They respect the gifts of science and medicine, but they are people of great faith in heaven's power as well."

Dr. Butler was unable to assess his mentor's response to such an unscientific observation, and so he rushed on. "You must understand, they've been fighting the disease for months. It ran though the entire family, nearly taking one of the daughters. The attending physician declared her dead, but the mother decried the declaration, believing she had been promised that the child would live. She rocked her child and prayed over her, and the girl did revive. Witnesses confirm it."

Dr. Smith leaned back and gazed at his protégé. "You asked to consult with me on a case. What has this story to do with your current patient?"

Dr. Butler swallowed. "My current patient is their young son, a boy barely seven years old. The fever settled into his armpit where one physician falsely diagnosed it as a sprain. Eventually, Dr. Stone was called in to lance the sore, but despite the removal of a quart of infected matter, the infection traveled into the lad's leg. Dr. Stone has made two more attempts, cutting down to the bone to clean the tissue, but as the lad seemed unimproved, our colleague requests a consultation. We all agreed that the bone seems to be feeding the infection, a situation that would normally warrant amputation to save the patient."

"And why do you hesitate if you have the confirming opinions of your colleagues?"

Dr. Butler wondered if his next statement would destroy his professor's confidence in him. "The mother insists she will not allow his leg to be removed because she believes there must be another alternative, and . . . sir? I am inclined to agree."

A furrow formed on Dr. Smith's brow. "The mother who prayed the child back to life?"

The very question made Dr. Butler cringe in embarrassment. "The same, sir."

Dr. Smith cupped his chin in the characteristic way he did when lost in thought. "When you speak of alternatives, are you referring to the experimental surgical procedure I diagrammed in lecture the other day?"

"I am, sir."

"You do realize that this procedure is still experimental? Most surgeons would prefer to sacrifice the limb rather than cause the patient to endure the painful surgery, especially since the procedure has the potential of failure, at which point the limb would eventually need to be amputated anyway."

"I understand all this, but I have become personally invested in this family, and I would like to avail them of every alternative."

Smith considered the request. "We must be men of science and allow rational thought, not emotion, to guide our decisions, Dr. Butler, but I believe a physician must also listen to his patient, or in this case, his patient's mother. Yes. I'll come and offer my opinion on this case."

* * *

It was dusk when Zachary Butler arrived at his grandfather's farm. Distraught, he entered the house with a heavy heart, pausing by the coat tree before engaging in conversation.

"You're stalling, Zachary. I take it you did not get the answer you desired."

With an exasperated groan, Zachary Butler shook his head and fell into the upholstered chair near his grandfather's. "Dr. Smith examined the Smith boy's leg, and he agrees that the limb should be removed. It was foolishness to expect him to say otherwise."

Emmett's weathered old hand reached to caress his grandson's. "Hope is not foolishness."

"No, hope is not, but in truth, I was not just hoping. I was expecting . . . I don't know . . ."

"A miracle?" his grandfather finished.

The very word made Zachary cringe. "I think so. I can't explain it. I just believed that this child was to be spared from losing his leg."

After a noticeable pause, Emmett rejoined the conversation. "Is the surgery scheduled?"

"Yes, for tomorrow. And were the day not distressing enough, Dr. Smith chastened me for withholding the women's whereabouts. Everyone is searching frantically to find them."

Emmett sighed, replying, "That's one burden I can lift from you. Beatrice says she is ready to move on. She sent word both to her sister and the Mack family announcing her estimated arrival. I think she hopes a change of environment will ease her grief over the loss of the baby."

"More discouraging news," he muttered. "And Hannah?"

"I cannot say." Emmett's tone became immediately somber. "She has reached some decisions of her own. We may soon lose the company of them both."

Before he finished his sentence, Hannah appeared. "Hello Zachary. Did you call for me?"

He gazed at her, soaking up the quiet beauty of her lean, flawless face. She was a study of peace at this moment, which he assumed came from the decisions his grandfather had referred to. "No," he replied. "Grandfather just mentioned that you and Beatrice are making plans."

An apologetic look disturbed her previous peace. "I was going to tell you myself . . . but . . . yes, Beatrice has posted a letter to the Macks, and they are expecting her."

Zachary nodded. "And you?"

Her expression remained soft while resolute. "No thanks are sufficient for all you two have done for us, but Beatrice and I have agreed that our silence has burdened our loved ones long enough, and we each must face our problems squarely now. Beatrice will head to the Macks' to begin her search for her husband, and I must go home."

Zachary's head dipped with the weight of her announcement. "Are you sure your future lies in Baltimore? I mean . . . you have been so beleaguered by the situation there."

"It was as much my doing as theirs."

His eyes closed against the finality of the situation. "I truly want you to find your happiness, Hannah, but if it's not in Baltimore, please come back to Hanover. We'd welcome you warmly. Wouldn't we Grandfather?"

In a voice heavy with emotion, Emmett replied, "She knows there will always be a place for her here."

* * *

The next day, Dr. Butler and Dr. Stone rode into the village of West Lebanon and up to the Smith family's small white-frame house. Accompanied by Drs. Smith and Perkins, with a cadre of other Dartmouth medical persons in tow, they were received by Mrs. Smith, a small, protective woman whose arms cradled a baby with the same tender concern reflected in the deep worry lines surrounding her eyes—lines that testified to the toll the previous five month's illnesses had taken on her.

Dr. Stone initiated the dreaded conversation. "Mrs. Smith, I'm sure you recognize my colleagues, including Dr. Nathan Smith."

"Gentlemen," she challenged, "what can you do to save my boy's leg?"

"We regret that we can do nothing, madam."

Handing her babe off to her daughter, Mrs. Smith called for a small son named Samuel to fetch his father. She took hold of Dr. Stone's coat sleeve and, petitioning him in earnest, beseeched, "Dr. Stone, can you not make another trial? Can you not, by cutting around the bone, take out the diseased part? Then perhaps that which is sound will heal over, and by this means you will save his leg? You will not, must not, take off Joseph's leg until you try once more. I will not consent to let you enter his room until you make me this promise."

Scowling, Dr. Smith immediately pulled Dr. Butler aside. "Did you hear the request she just made? Have you two already made promises to this woman?"

Butler's expression indicated that he was equally awed by the woman's question. "No, sir. We have never mentioned this surgical process."

"How can that be? She just outlined my technique!"

Dr. Butler visibly shivered. "It is as I told you, sir. They are no strangers to miracles."

Dr. Stone looked to Dr. Smith, entreating him in behalf of the mother. "What do you say to the mother's petition, Dr. Smith?"

Eyeing the boy's mother intently, Dr. Smith forewarned her, "The alternative procedure is grueling, madam, and if it fails, we shall still have to take the leg, having then put the child through twice the agony." Seeing that the mother was unmoved, Dr. Smith nodded and said, "But if you are sure, we will try."

As the esteemed surgeon and the remainder of the team approached young Joseph's bedside, Dr. Butler saw Dr. Smith nod respectfully to an older boy who was clearly the child's brother. The elder child remained protectively by Joseph's side.

Then the mood changed, and Dr. Butler tensed as Dr. Smith looked into Joseph's trusting eyes to prepare the lad. "My poor boy. We have come again."

Eyes wide and wary, Joseph asked, "You've not come to take off my leg, have you, sir?"

Dr. Smith glanced briefly into the expectant eyes of the boy's mother. "No. It is your mother's request that we make one more effort, and that is what we have now come for."

The relief in the room was momentary as the gentle surgeon detailed the particulars of the traumatic procedure. "Do you understand, son?" he asked the patient.

Joseph's attention was drawn to the large, anxious figure filling the doorway. His father came and knelt by his boy, peering into his pain-filled eyes. Imbued with courage, Joseph wrapped his thin arms around his father's strong ones and nodded to the doctor.

With a look of resignation, Dr. Smith placed a tender hand on Joseph's leg, nodded back, and began instructing his associates, "Bring me cords to bind the child to the bedstead."

Understandable alarm seized the lad. "No, no!" Joseph pleaded to Mr. Smith. Then grasping his father more tightly he implored, "Please . . . allow me my liberty."

Dr. Smith scowled at the notion. "Then, you must drink some brandy."

"No, sir," Joseph replied, looking up at his father for assurance.

"Wine then?" entreated the good doctor, attempting once more to reason with the child. "You must take something, son, or you can never endure the severe operation to which you must be subjected."

Two penetrating blue eyes searched his father's troubled face, then drawing nearer, Joseph whispered his wishes in Mr. Smith's ear before turning around to face the men of science, serene and resolute of countenance.

Mr. Smith clutched Joseph close and stilled his own lips' trembling before voicing his son's desires. "Joseph will bear the surgery much better if you'll allow me to sit on the bed and hold him in my arms. If you'll agree to this, he'll do what is necessary to have the bone removed."

Dr. Butler's eyes moved from Joseph to Dr. Smith, cautiously assessing how his mentor was responding to the child's request. But mere moments later, in full acceptance of the boy's terms, Dr. Smith left the room in the company of Dr. Perkins to prepare for the procedure. Butler marveled at Joseph, that despite his unwillingness to yield to any of Dr. Smith's points, his bearing demonstrated a quiet confidence devoid of false bravado or insolence, leading Zachary Butler to compare the odd scene—a small boy surrounded by a group of men representing some of the nation's premier medical minds—to the bible story about the boy Jesus teaching in the temple. As the verse echoed in his mind, a chill ran through him:

> *And it came to pass, that after three days they found him in the temple, sitting in the midst of the doctors, both hearing them, and asking them questions.*

Before the impact of that image had time to fade, another began as young Joseph gazed at his mother's grief-stricken face and again turned to whisper to his father.

"Lucy," Mr. Smith entreated in his son's behalf, "Joseph wants you to leave the room. He doesn't want you to have to bear his suffering as well."

Rapidly blinking back tears, Mrs. Smith began to protest, but Joseph pled to her, "Father can stand it, but you have carried me so much and watched over me so long, you are almost worn out. Promise me, Mother, that you will not stay. Will you? The Lord will help me and I shall get through it."

A sense of reverence and majesty filled Dr. Butler. He wondered if his companions were equally moved by the empathy and courage of the child, who again reminded him of another son—the Son on the cross—who too had placed His concern for His mother above that for Himself.

A lump formed in Zachary's throat as he viewed the mother's own dilemma. Hesitant to surrender her post, Mrs. Smith shared a few final tender moments with her boy, then after bringing several folded sheets and tucking them under her son's swollen leg, she offered parting words of love and hurried away past the window to a remote corner of the property.

* * *

"It was very thoughtful of you to think of this, Hannah," Emmett replied as he slapped the reins, urging the team down the lane and over the bridge. "I'm sure that boy's dear mother won't have the time or the presence of mind to cook today, poor dear."

"Whether one is mourning a lost child or a child's lost limb, grief is still exhausting."

"Yes it is," agreed Emmett. "All the more reason I wish Beatrice had come along."

"I think she was pleased for the solitude. She wanted to be alone and to spend some time near the baby's grave since she is leaving tomorrow."

"How do you feel about her decision? It's all happening so quickly."

"I'm relieved, Em. She won't make peace over little Bernard's death until she shares her sorrow with Dudley. But of equal importance, we can finally speak truthfully to our family. What meager information we gave our sister we vowed her to secrecy on, and I can only imagine what hardships she's borne as a result. The truth will free us all."

"And you think you can manage the team well enough to get to Tunbridge alone?"

Hannah chuckled good-naturedly and wrapped her arm over Emmett's. "If a blind man can find his way back and forth to Hanover, a sighted woman should be able to find Tunbridge."

The warm sun teased Hannah until she removed her bonnet and lifted her face, allowing the light to wash over her pale skin. It was a beautiful day, a fitting tribute to the optimism flowering in her heart, but at the first sign of the West Lebanon marker she was reminded that though her burdens were beginning to lift, the Smith family's were bearing down upon them.

That reminder became ever so clear when the home was yet fifty yards away. They heard a scream of pain above the sound of the horses' hooves, and then they saw a woman dash across a field and into the house. Another cry sounded through the widely flung door—the agonizing groan of a woman—and then a sorrowful plea echoed through the open doorway.

"Oh, mother . . . go back, go back. I do not want you to come in," the young voice cried loud enough for Hannah to hear. "I will try to tough it out, if you will but go away."

As the rig pulled to a halt beside the house, Hannah saw the woman stumble to the porch, bracing herself against the doorframe until another scream escaped the house, sending her inside again. Hannah suddenly regretted her intrusion upon the intensely painful scene, but unable to tear her eyes from the Smith house, she soon saw Zachary and another man dressed in blood-stained coverings lead the woman into the yard near their rig. She saw Mrs. Smith bury her face in her hands crying, "The blood! He was covered in blood!"

Zachary's arm drew more tightly around the anguished mother as he tried to explain. "The blood loss, though shocking to you, was not unexpected, Mrs. Smith. The surgeons reopened the incision and bored holes into both sides of Joseph's leg bone so they could break off the pieces of infected bone. They absolutely needed to remove them in order to save the leg. The worst will soon be over, and once they've dressed his wound and cleaned him up, you'll be able to see him."

Hannah grabbed Emmett's arm to get his attention. "Did you hear that, Em? Zachary just said they're trying to save the boy's leg! Isn't it wonderful? They didn't amputate after all!"

As if on cue, Zachary excused himself from his colleague and Mrs. Smith and headed for the rig. "Why are you here? Is everything all right?" he asked worriedly.

"Forgive us for intruding, but Hannah made a pot of soup for them for their supper."

"Thank you, Hannah." Zachary sighed, relieved. "They'll greatly appreciate the thought."

Hannah stepped to the back and began unwrapping the kettle. "You'll think us dreadful for listening, but did you say that Dr. Smith has consented to try to save the boy's leg?"

Before Zachary could answer, another cry sounded from the house, and he turned to check on Mrs. Smith's reaction to it. "That poor woman," he muttered, then returning to Hannah's question he replied, "Yes, at least there's a chance. At the mother's insistence, Dr. Smith agreed to have our team bore into the bone. What they found there convinced him that the chance of success was worth the risk, so he continued to guide the team through his experimental procedure. The surety of saving the leg won't be known for a few weeks," he added with rising emotion, "but I believe it will be a success. I've learned something more about the Smith family. Circumstances have pressed them to move several times, eventually delivering them here. Knowing that, and after what I've witnessed of them, I cannot accept that mere coincidence delivered them here just prior to their boy taking sick. Do you realize that had they lived anywhere else . . . *anywhere else* . . . young Joseph would have become a cripple this day?"

Hannah cocked her head curiously at Zachary and asked, "Are you saying you believe the Smiths have been given a second miracle?"

Zachary Butler was quiet as he weighed his response. Seconds later, he responded with conviction. "At the very least, the Lord's eye appears to be on this family."

CHAPTER 22

April 1, 1813
Hampton, Virginia

"Those little scamps are still awake, Drusilla," said Lyra Harkin, chuckling.

"They're so worked up with all this war talk. I'll tend to 'em in a minute."

"No. You just nurse the baby. I'll deal with Martin and Sean." She tiptoed in, and their giggles soon silenced. "And what are you doin' up? Your da is due home any minute and he'll tan ya both, he will." Lovingly tucking the quilts in around them, her hand brushed a hard stick protruding up alongside Sean. She pulled it out, declaring, "No wonder ya can't sleep."

"It's my musket!" Sean declared.

"Muskets . . ." sputtered Lyra under her breath. "Books and tops are what little boys need. Not guns. Martin, hand yours over as well." Amid groans and complaints, another "musket" appeared. "Now mind me. Not another word this night. Your mum is tired as will your da be, so let 'em have a moment's rest and you two sleep and dream about somethin' besides fightin'."

She closed the door, hiding the sticks in the fold of her skirt as she entered the kitchen.

Drusilla sighed. "War . . . it's all they hear from the men. Now they want to follow suit."

"Well, these two fine guns are going ta keep us warm!" She tossed them into the fire, pulled her ivory shawl over her shoulders, and opened the door to listen. "I hear a gaggle of men's voices comin' up from the dock. What's that Garland Haas so fired up about?"

Drusilla laid the baby down and came to stand beside Lyra. "That's Gino Antonelli who's whoopin' so loudly," noted Drusilla. "Oh, dearie, what've they gotten themselves into now?"

Lyra didn't wait to ask. Stepping into the path with her arms folded across her chest, she called out, "Markus O'Malley? Are you by chance among this pack of hooligans? We heard the boys carryin' on and Ryan hushin' the lot of ya, so what malarkey have you men been up to?"

The silence of Markus's reaction unnerved her, and a moment later she felt him shift to her side and whisper sharply in her ear. "I'll not debate my business in public, Lyra."

The flush of embarrassment reddened her cheeks, but undeterred, she ordered, "Go home, boys," then turned up the walkway to sit on the porch with Drusilla. The nervous tapping of her foot was soon joined by Ryan's and Markus's pacing and the sound of Patrick and Drusilla dropping onto the bench.

It was Ryan who began. "Don't expect us to apologize for feelin' like men again for the first time since the British blocked us in!"

Drusilla opened her mouth, but Ryan cut her off to continue. "We've barely been able to provide for our families, what with them blastin' every merchant vessel or stealin' the goods for themselves. They're chokin' our republic and cuttin' our nation in half since they captured the Chesapeake! But now we've got a chance to fight back. For this small window of time, half their fleet has sailed up to the Delaware Bay leavin' their forces thin here—though some merchants claim more British ships are in Bermuda. If these vessels are comin' to replace those that went north, we've only a brief opportunity to act. Our Point Comfort is well-manned, so British ships'd have a hard time sailing past her to reach us, and Colonel Armistead has fortified Craney Island, plus, with our military, the island's surrounded by shallow waters, which is to our benefit. We all know our Fort Norfolk is well armed, plus she's further protected by Tarbelle's flotilla of gunboats."

"We *women* would just like to be told what you're preparin' to do!" Drusilla finally interjected.

Patrick knelt in front of his wife and explained, "We've got good military support now."

"Support for what?" asked Lyra warily.

Markus sat beside her and took her hands in his, rubbing them tenderly before answering her question. "We want to sail the *Irish Lass* through the British line."

Both women gasped, but Markus hurried on.

"They don't know there's a vessel like the *Irish Lass* back here because we've done such a fine job of keeping her hid. She'll be seaworthy in a few weeks. If we're successful we can help free up the *Constellation* and open the mouth of the Chesapeake."

Lyra squeezed Markus's hand tightly. "But what good will a few cannons on a merchant ship do against half a fleet of British warships, Markus?"

"We're not plannin' on takin' them on *alone,* Lyra! We'll lure them into followin' us north into the guns of Point Comfort or south where Norfolk's guns can hit them."

A soft groan escaped Drusilla, who stood abruptly and headed for the house.

"Where're you goin', love?" called Patrick after her, her only response being the sound of her starting to sob. Patrick shrugged at his father and stared at the floor. "It all sounded a might more glorious an hour ago," he muttered as he turned and followed Drusilla into the house.

Ryan's compassion-filled eyes grew large. "Well then . . . let's call it a night, lads."

He shuffled away with his hands in his pockets, leaving Lyra and Markus alone on the porch. After several silent seconds, Markus stood and began to pace. From time to time he looked back at Lyra, and what he saw there broke his heart.

"I wouldn't give this a second thought if I didn't think it could work!" he argued. "The fate of the entire republic could hinge on opening the Chesapeake up!" He stared at Lyra, but her face remained frozen, twisted in grief, and he paced and argued on. "They'll take the Capital! They'll sail right up and lay waste to her, and then they'll take the Patuxent and Baltimore!"

He slumped by her knees and pressed his head to her lap. "Can't you see, Lyra girl? They'll destroy everything I love . . . all my hopes for our future . . . for our children's future. I fear it will all end if we don't do something bold."

She lifted her hands and set them on his shoulders, drawing small circles on his shirt. Unable to resist his closeness, she bent over him, laying her arms across his back, placing kisses there and upon his head. "All right. All right," she whispered. "Go and make your preparations and then promise to set this aside for as long as possible. Gather the lads together and ask them to help you build me that house you promised so we can move the weddin' date up."

Markus slowly untangled himself from Lyra's arms and kissed her softly on both of her cheeks, hovering above her lips as he said, "I love you, Lyra girl," before kissing her soundly.

She sighed as a solitary tear slid down her cheek. "If only lovin' were enough, Markus."

CHAPTER 23

April 3, 1813
Hanover, New Hampshire

Emmett's face was drawn as he addressed the women in his mild German accent. "Are you sure you have all your things, Mrs. Snowden?"

Placing her cheek alongside Emmett's, Beatrice whispered, "I'll never be able to repay you for the kindness you've shown me." Her hand then clasped Zachary's, squeezing it softly. "Dr. Butler, you saved my life, and you, Em, you saved my faith. That's why I can leave now."

Two embroidered linen handkerchiefs were pulled from her purse. Her eyes moistened as she handed one to each of the men. "I made these from one of the baby's nightgowns . . . so you will remember us." With that, she quickly stepped into the rig.

Zachary turned away as he reverently folded the gift, placing it inside his breast pocket, but Emmett pressed his to his trembling lips. Hannah quickly responded to his emotion with an embrace, as Emmett pulled an older, plain handkerchief from his pocket and dabbed at his eyes, tucking the new one away.

He cupped Hannah's hand in both of his and gave it a resolute shake. "Zachary is riding along until you reach the Smiths'. You and the team will have come to an understanding by then," he said, indicating the horses. "When should we expect you back, Hannah?"

"I'll stay in Tunbridge until Beatrice settles in, then I'll head back for a final visit before I set off for Baltimore. I'll send word a week ahead, all right?"

Emmett offered a strained nod. "You two be safe then. The weather's turning. I can feel it. And Mrs. Snowden, never you worry about your little one. I'll keep a watch over him."

By the time Hannah slapped the reins against the horses' backs, neither woman could see the road clearly for the stinging in their eyes. Hannah prayed continually to arrive safely at the Smiths' lane, grateful that Zachary would be leaving them on his way to the Smiths' and that the final good-bye of the day would be past. Upon arriving, Hannah slowed the carriage to a halt, and Beatrice took the lead.

"Thank you again, Dr. Butler. How blessed we were that you came to the inn that day."

"Mrs. Snowden, sometimes medicine is mere science, but other times, as in your case, it is a noble thing. I thank you . . . both of you . . ."—he allowed his gaze to slip to Hannah, and then he turned back to Beatrice— "for all you have taught me."

Beatrice blushed and stared back in confusion. "What had we to teach you, sir?"

"To be a man deserving of such devotion as you two have shown for those you love."

He guided the horse into a tight circle, breaking the tension of the moment, and Hannah dipped her head and offered her farewell. "I'll return in a few days, Zachary."

He offered a knowing smile, adding, "The Hannah Stansbury I have had the pleasure of knowing will not." He cocked his head and became sadly whimsical. "Something new has come over you recently . . . changed you somehow, and I believe it is for the better."

"The same could also be said of you. This week has changed us both."

"So it has," Zachary agreed as he cast a glance over his shoulder to the Smith house.

The hair rose on the back of Hannah's neck as her eyes followed his.

"I've spent hours with them—observing them, listening to them. They draw faith from the Bible and from their family members' marvelous dreams and visions, and oddly, I am not at all affronted by what many would consider strange, perhaps blasphemous, concepts. I accept that God can, and does, speak to some people this way, though His purposes for doing so are still unclear to me. You are one of those people, Hannah. I trust He will lead you to your purpose."

He set his horse prancing and pawing again. "Good day, ladies, and Godspeed."

As he headed up to the Smiths' house, Hannah set her eyes for Tunbridge and urged her team on. A few edgy moments passed as the sisters settled into their journey, but soon the rightness of their decisions buoyed them up and filled them with peace.

Beatrice began detailing her plans and arrangements. "I've sent Myrna a letter explaining these past seven months, taking full responsibility for every choice made. She may be cross with you for having supported my decisions, but she'll have no cause to charge you for them."

"Thank you, Beatrice, but I'm not afraid to deal with Myrna anymore."

Beatrice smiled at her sister. "No . . . you're not, are you? You'll be nineteen in a few weeks . . . a woman by every measure, but in truth, you've borne a woman's burdens for quite some time. It's high time you enjoy some of the privileges to which those burdens entitle you."

"Like tangling with Myrna?" Hannah laughed good-naturedly.

"Among others!" Beatrice laughed in return. "Now, I've also made a list of financial details that require tending. The bank manager will attend to getting my home repaired and sold, but my poor staff . . ." She fretted as she considered the members of her Negro staff who had been carted to her parents' Coolfont Plantation. "Who knows what trials Mother has subjected them to!"

"Recall that when Mama released Selma as my nanny and sent her out to labor in the fields, Father reassigned her to the kitchen to spare her. I'm sure he's done something similar for your staff. In either case, I promise I will attend to everything when I return to Baltimore."

"Thank you, Hannah. I was sure I would never smile again, but I'm excited to get to Tunbridge. I know I'll find Dudley, and somehow everything between us will be right again."

"Of course it will. You heard what Zachary said. What man could deny such devotion? You love each other, Beatrice. Two people who love each other so deeply must be together."

Hannah noticed that Beatrice sobered as she always did when the divine right of lovers to be united was raised. Hannah squeezed her hand, saying, "Trust me on this. You two will be fine."

Beatrice returned the affectionate gesture. "I believe that too. It's not that."

"Then what?" asked Hannah as she guided the team along the soft, rutted road.

"Hannah? Say something were to happen . . . to separate us, one from another. You're so strong and confident now. You know you would carry on fine, don't you?"

Hannah's eyes left the road to stare at her sister. "Are you not well, Beatrice?"

"No . . . I mean, yes I am and no, that's not what I was implying."

"Then why would you pose such a dreadful question? Mother and Father have hardly been parents to me. Selma safely steered my childhood, but once Mother took her from me, it was you, Beatrice, who nurtured and loved me like a mother. I do not mean to discount Myrna's influence, but it is you and Jed that I credit for who I am. And I want no more talk of such things as separations, nor do I want to hear what you were implying!"

"Then understand that I want the very same type of love for you that I feel for Dudley. When you get to Baltimore I want you to pursue the man you want. I don't care if it's Andrew or Jed or . . . or the man in the moon." She laid her hands on Hannah's. "Promise me you won't let the opinions of others direct your heart's course. Choose your own life, Hannah. Promise me!"

Beatrice's fervor astounded Hannah so greatly that it drew her full attention to her sister's face where it remained as the impact and rallying power of her words lifted Hannah's already determined heart. Only the alarming lurch of the buggy drew her attention elsewhere, and as she finally reacted to the unexpected tilt and sway of the rig, it was too late.

They had come upon a washout in the heavily traveled, sloping road, and with no clear direction from their driver, the horses had meandered to the right where erosion had created a bog of winter melt and mud that had been clearly marked by previous travelers. With no firm footing and axles mired in muck, they found themselves stopped and hopelessly stranded.

"Oh, dear!" reacted Beatrice with alarm. "And the skies are clouding as Em predicted."

"Of course they are," countered Hannah sarcastically. "How humiliating."

"I have had more adventures on this journey with you than in my entire lifetime." Beatrice chuckled. "But what will we do?"

Hannah stood to assess their situation. "I think one of us will have to take the reins while the other leads the horses from the front."

Beatrice looked down at the quagmire surrounding them and glanced humorously at Hannah. "Shall we cast lots for it?"

Hannah rolled her eyes as she climbed down, groaning as her first foot sank deep into the mire. "What was that you said about regret?" she teased as she slogged through the muck, grabbing the lead horse's bridle and pulling. After she and the horses made seven failed attempts to advance, Hannah slumped against the gelding and sighed. "We'll have to wait for help."

Looking back to survey the road, Beatrice cried, "A Conestoga wagon is coming!"

Both women began waving their arms and shouting for help as the wagon lumbered near. Six oxen were struggling to pull the freight-filled carrier laden with goods. The driver's English was impeded by his thick accent through which he called out some sort of directions to the pleading woman as he passed by on the high ground and pulled twenty feet in front.

"We're stuck!" shouted Hannah.

The man surveyed the situation, then gestured boldly, pointing to his oxen and waving his timepiece in the air while chattering in his strange European tongue.

In utter confusion, Hannah turned to Beatrice. "Do you understand a word he's saying?"

Beatrice raised her eyebrows and shrugged. "Something about 'driechs' and a 'brae,' and then I caught the words 'glaur' and 'besoms,' but I have no idea what any of it means."

"I don't understand you!" Hannah responded, receiving for her efforts a more irritated repeat of the man's earlier assessment of the situation.

Completely unaware that two riders had approached, she was startled by a male voice from behind that explained, "He's quite derogatory about the way you've handled your team."

As cold as she was, buried calf-deep in chilly, oozing mud, the voice that reached Hannah's ears sent a different kind of chill coursing through her. She was afraid to turn, afraid it was an illusion, that the face might not match the familiar voice from her dreams, and equally afraid that even if it did, the encounter might not be a pleasant one. She finally turned, fixing her gaze upon the riveting stare of the man who stood behind her. He eyed her curiously, as if regarding her from a distance though she was barely three feet away, and then his expression became melancholy. The expression took Hannah back to the idyllic day at the last Stansbury barbecue. "Jed . . ." she whispered.

Her arms lifted involuntarily in his direction in response to the unspoken invitation she believed was written in his eyes. She fully expected him to swoop down and carry her out of the mire in his arms . . . but he did not. He bowed politely, leaned his tall frame to her, offered her his hand, and gently pulled her to dry ground. "Hello, Hannah," he returned softly as he removed his overcoat, placing its musky-scented woolen warmth around her. He gently squeezed her shoulders, lingering there until her breathing turned to soft, nervous shudders. Then, in an instant, he stepped away, turning his attentions to Beatrice and leaving Hannah longing for his return.

"Lieutenant Pearson . . ." Beatrice uttered. "You always seem to arrive in the very moment you are most needed. How is that?" she queried. Then, noticing Samuel Renfro for the first time, she added, "Dr. Renfro, you led him to us, didn't you? Bless you for that."

Hannah heard the ensuing conversation detailing their stop at Emmett's farm, but her eyes never left Jed, noting the many times his own eyes darted back to hers. She surveyed the weathered appearance of his chapped cheeks and his unusually long locks of dark, wavy hair. She noted other curiosities, consequences of his enlistment she assumed, such as the new confidence he now radiated, showing no trace of the self-deprecation that had previously haunted him on occasion. But the change that most captivated her was the way he commanded the space around him, as if he finally accepted himself to be the man she always knew he would become.

Jed and Renfro helped the Scotsman hitch a yoke of oxen to the women's rig, then as the Scot cajoled his team, Samuel grabbed the lead horse's bridle to encourage him while Jed stepped into the muck with his knee-high boots, using his shoulders to push while tucking his hands protectively against his body. Worried as she was about Jed, Hannah also began worrying about the increasing wind and the darkening sky. Pulling Jed's coat more tightly around her to fight the effects of the chill settling in from her wet feet and legs, she watched as the men, after several unsuccessful tries, eventually freed the buggy from its muddy tethers.

Once it rolled onto firm ground, Hannah's attentions were focused back on Jed. Every letter they had exchanged, every moment they had shared, and, most painful of all, every moment they had lost, washed over her like a flood. Longing to join him, she nevertheless remained frozen in place, admiring him from a distance. Cursing herself for the choices she'd made, she wondered how her neglect had affected the frail understanding they'd begun to rebuild at their last meeting when, despite their obstacles, each had expressed their love for the other.

She caught Beatrice gazing at her, and when the sisters' gazes locked, a womanly understanding passed between the pair. Hannah next watched her sister steal several anxious glances at Jed. Then Beatrice called out, "Lieutenant Pearson!" Hannah's eyes followed Jed as he moved toward the buggy where Beatrice still remained.

"Yes, Mrs. Snowden? Is there something you need?"

Fretting over her sister's intentions, Hannah stared as Beatrice extended her gloved hand to Jed, who received it graciously. She strained to listen in on their ensuing conversation.

"Lieutenant, I must reach the Macks' by this evening, but I cannot ask Hannah to travel on as cold and wet as she is, and so I must make a great request of you. Could you do me the favor of asking whether the wagon driver could ferry me and my things on to Tunbridge . . ."

Hannah felt her throat tighten as Beatrice covered Jed's hand with her free one, boring her eyes into his, emphasizing her next request with slow, measured speech. "And would you do me the favor of escorting Hannah to a reputable inn where she can get into dry clothes and be warmed by a fire?"

Nearly faint with disbelief, Hannah breathed rapidly as Jed cocked his head and paused, asking, "Do I understand you correctly, madam?"

To which Beatrice replied, "I believe you do, sir."

Hannah's mood quickly shifted from irritation to anger at being bandied about like an aged milk cow. Her ire rose further but was abruptly cooled at Jed's handling of the request, for, before leaving to speak to the Scotsman, he bowed to Beatrice, then turned to Hannah replying, "I'll make the inquiry, Mrs. Snowden, but only if it is agreeable to Hannah."

Hannah had begun trembling as soon as Beatrice's suggestion had been uttered, and now she was unable to verbalize her response. She merely nodded, and Jed began negotiations with the Scot. After a few minutes, Jed returned to Beatrice. "It is all arranged, Mrs. Snowden."

Glancing at Hannah before replying, Beatrice spoke in a voice too low for her sister to hear. "Thank you, Mr. Pearson. In all our dealings, you've never been anything but kind to me. If I may prevail upon you once more . . . it would comfort me greatly if I could be accompanied by someone familiar. Might Dr. Renfro . . ."

Jed stalled before leaning close to answer in a voice equally soft. "Perhaps I was presumptuous, but believing that I understood the whole intent of your request, I made that arrangement as well, madam."

Nodding, Beatrice closed her eyes and sighed. "Then, if things have indeed been put right, it's time for me to take my leave."

Jed kissed Beatrice's hand, pledging, "Mrs. Snowden, I pledge to you on my sacred honor that I will see to Hannah's every safety and care."

Beatrice's eyes appeared moist as she replied, "Of that I have no doubt, Lieutenant. Now, I have one more matter to attend to. I must have a moment to speak with my sister."

Jed glanced over his shoulder, meeting Hannah's wary eyes, offering her an anxious smile. "Then Samuel and I will attend to your things," he said to Beatrice.

As often as Hannah had dreamed of such an opportunity, the moment raised unbearable anxiety in her. "Beatrice!" Hannah entreated as her sister approached. "What are you doing?"

"What I should have done long ago."

"I don't understand."

"No . . . you really don't, but it's high time you did. There's something I must tell you. It's a terrible thing actually, and once it's said you may never want to speak to me again."

Hannah shuddered as her mouth fell agape. "What could . . . Oh, no! Don't say it . . ."

"It's true, dearest. That letter you wrote to Jed nearly two years ago? It was Myrna and I who delayed Jed's receipt of it. We did it in order to find a suitor who could win your heart *and* Mother's approval. Regrettably, it soon became evident that we had no right to interfere. Dudley showed me that. In fact, it was his distress over this very issue that caused the rift between us and led to his consequent request for a transfer to Detroit. So you see," her voice became soft and contrite, "though you may never forgive us, Providence has returned your lost opportunity. Make of this moment what you will, Hannah. As for us, Myrna refuses to acknowledge our error, fearing she will lose your love forever. Neither of us could bear such a loss, for you are as dear to us as a sister can ever be, but consider that I have already paid a greater penance than any you could require of me. I know it's a little too late, but right things with Jed if that is what you desire. At some point we must each take responsibility for our own future. For you, that moment has arrived."

Without waiting for Hannah's response, Beatrice turned and headed back to Jed, muttering something briefly to him. With a final look back at Hannah, she took Samuel's hand and climbed up into the wagon, leaving Hannah and Jed standing awkward and alone on the road.

CHAPTER 24

April 3, 1813
Near Sharon, Vermont

Jed tentatively raised his eyes and softly called to Hannah. "Samuel mentioned a fine inn less than a mile up the road. We'll head there for the night and get you warm."

He extended his gloved hand, all the while entreating Hannah with his eyes. Numb and confused, she plodded toward him, lightly grasping his hand and stalling there as she brought her moist eyes to meet his. He laid his palm alongside her cheek, his fingers reaching behind her neck, drawing her face to his chest to kiss the top of her head. Pulling back, she lifted her gaze to his and opened her mouth to speak, but he stalled the inevitable conversation. As he placed his hands around her waist to help her into the buggy, she made a second attempt, but touching a finger to her lips he said, "Getting you to that inn is the only thing that matters right now."

Once mounted, Hannah pulled a quilt from one of her trunks and wrapped it around her, handing Jed's coat back to him. He slid into the coat, and once he slapped the reins and urged the team ahead, Hannah pressed him a third time. "I need you to be honest with me."

Jed's eyes remained fixed on the road ahead as he considered where to begin. "Everything I told you last August was true."

"Except that my family betrayed us."

"I had already spent months being tortured by that fact. Once I made peace with it, I saw no reason to subject you to the same."

"Had I not the right to know why or how my sisters attempted this deceit? How long have you known? And how did you uncover the truth?"

"I found your letter in January, soon after I buried my parents. It had been sent to my father, bundled amongst a miscellany of advertisements and handbills. I'm sure Myrna thought he'd discard the entire lot, but to my good fortune, he set the carton aside before he died."

"January?" she groaned. "That was well after our meeting in Baltimore. Why did you protect my sisters? Why didn't you come to me?"

"Oh . . ." he laughed sadly. "I did, sweetness. I most assuredly did. In fact, I ran to the Snowdens' the second I read the words *'Please do not delay, Jed,'* but I was too late. You were already at Coolfont with your parents, announcing your engagement to Lieutenant Robertson."

Hannah gasped softly. "I suppose Beatrice took great pleasure in her plan's success."

Jed reached a hand out to comfort her. "Trust me. She did not."

"When I didn't hear from you . . . I . . . I just assumed . . ." She turned her head away from Jed and muttered, "If I had known . . . I would have . . ."

"What? Crossed your family? Jilted Robertson? Regardless of what you or I may have *wanted,* can you truly say for sure what you would have done in those circumstances?"

"I tried once . . . in a moment of anger. Remember . . . on the trail from York Town last summer. You accused me of not knowing what I wanted, and—"

". . . You said we wouldn't be in our situation if what you wanted had mattered at all."

And when I questioned your meaning you told me to—"

"To go ask your happy family," he replied with regret. "Your words wounded me deeply, but as I stormed away from you I knew I had cast suspicion upon your sisters, taking your one security away from you. In a selfish flash of anger I caused you the greater injury."

"And yet on our last morning together you labored to restore my trust in them."

As the team rounded a forested bend in the road, the inn came into view. "We're here," Jed gratefully announced moments later as a stablehand took the team's reins.

"Help me understand, Jed," Hannah pled again as Jed offered her his hand.

"The answers cannot be had in a minute, Hannah, and I will not debate the past while allowing you to catch your death. We'll have plenty of time to bemoan our situation."

Chancing no further discussion, Jed helped Hannah down and led her into the elegantly appointed inn. Once inside, he signed for two rooms, two baths, and board for the rig and team. "And two meals, please. Have the lady's delivered to her room."

* * *

As anxious as Hannah was to have her answers, she was grateful for the time alone, time to allow the enormity of Beatrice's confession to sink in. As she slipped into the warm bath, she felt her emotions release along with the chill. Sadly, Myrna's involvement in the conspiracy hadn't surprised her, but she could barely bring Beatrice's face to mind, so deep was her hurt and confusion at the incongruity between her oldest sister's love and her actions. And as she struggled to measure what fragments remained of her fragile world, the tears began in earnest.

After Hannah was dressed and composed, the maid knocked at her door. "The gentleman says he's not hungry at present, but he asked me to see if you'd like your tray brought up."

Hannah leaned her head against the doorframe. "I believe I'll wait as well, thank you."

She walked to the top of the stairwell where she could see the entire first floor. It was barely two in the afternoon, and few people were there, making it easy for her to locate Jed in the sparse room. But as soon as she set her eyes upon his broad-shouldered frame, she knew she could have spotted him just as easily in a room filled with a thousand men, and she also knew with unfailing certainty that for her all men fell easily into two categories—Jed Pearson, and everyone else. His very presence anchored her, but quick on the heels of that surety came the plague of doubt as to what damage her five-month silence had caused.

She searched his face from the secrecy of her stair-top perch, her heart warmed at the way his uncombed hair fell into unruly waves along his brow, requiring him to absentmindedly brush an annoying strand from his eyes from time to time. It was a boyish gesture, one of the few remaining signs of youth apparent in the otherwise burdened man.

His collar was unbuttoned, falling loosely open around his throat, exaggerating the shadow of beard covering his face and neck. He leaned forward to stare into the fire, then abruptly slumped back to gaze at the ceiling, rubbing his fingers deeply into his eyes. Witnessing this wrestle he was having, Hannah hungered to know where the day's end would find them. Steeling herself, she descended the stairs, calling out to him, and as she supposed he would, Jed quickly brightened and smiled at her, coming toward her with his hands reaching for hers.

"Feeling better?" he asked, his concern evident.

"Much, thank you. In fact, I'd enjoy a walk in the snow."

Jed's brow furrowed. "The idea in coming here was to get you warm."

"I know." She smiled. "I'm not ill, mind you, and the snow looks so inviting . . ."

"And you want to talk," Jed added, bringing her hands to his lips and holding her gaze.

"Yes. Where we won't be disturbed."

He nodded and asked for her key. In a moment he returned with their coats and a scarf and muff for Hannah, then extended his elbow, Hannah slipping her arm inside it. The ground was covered in a thick white dust that stuck to their boots and marked their trail behind them as they walked. Allowing the solitude to wash over them, Jed led Hannah toward a wood-pile and set two large logs on end. He brushed them clean, setting Hannah on one, then taking the other to face her.

"You asked me why I didn't tell you about your sisters' betrayal. It wasn't chivalry that silenced my tongue. Had the immediate opportunity presented itself, I would have gladly risked turning you against every person who had kept us apart in order to keep you all for myself. But I thank heaven I was not afforded such an opportunity until I'd had time to think. However deplorable their actions were, I can now accept that your sisters acted out of love for you."

Hannah stood abruptly and fumbled with her hands. "So that's it? You forgive them because they professed to care for me? Well, you're a better person than I, Jed Pearson."

"Neither of us has known so much love in this life that we dare lightly cast any away."

"But . . . were you not at least . . . a little angry that opportunities were denied us?"

The very question seemed to draw the vitality from Jed. "Was I angry?" he repeated sullenly. "I had no idea what rage and despair resided in my heart until that day, but I also know that choices made in such a state are at best foolish and at worst devastating. Yes . . . I was angry over their interference, but Beatrice has paid dearly, and in truth, the lost opportunities I most bemoan are those *we* squandered. We are as responsible for our fates as anyone, Hannah. Not just Myrna and Beatrice. And not God. And unless we admit that, unless we pursue the opportunity before us and let go of the ones already lost, we have no right to expect more."

Hannah hung her head and turned away from Jed. Soon she felt his hands on her shoulders and felt his warm breath by her ear. "I didn't write," she whispered to him. "I'm sorry for that," she cried softly, shaking her head in shame. "I just . . ."

Jed turned her to face him and looked into her shining green eyes.

"It is I who should apologize to you, Hannah. I pressed you into promising me something when you were in distress. It was wrong of me."

"But I want to explain. I need you to understand."

"All right, but only if the telling of it will comfort you. For me, all that matters is here and now. I have choked on my anger and the taste of self-pity is bitter to me. I want to let go of past errors . . . to begin anew. I cannot be a soldier, claiming to fight for liberty and self-determination while I blame others for my circumstances and remain a slave to my excuses."

"Even you are subject to the human passions and foibles of men, Jed."

He pulled her to him until their foreheads touched. "I don't see how we can hope to govern a free land until we can govern ourselves. I don't want secrets separating us. Tell me what you need to, and I promise to answer all your questions. In return I ask you for one favor."

"Anything."

He pulled back, his eyes locked penetratingly on Hannah's. "Listen carefully to what I am about to say. I love you, Hannah. I have *always* loved you, and I will *ever* love you. I know that you love me as well, but you have suffered much these past months, and such trials can redefine one's feelings. So hear me on this. No matter what decisions you make regarding your future, and no matter to whom you pledge yourself, I will always love you and watch over you. Do you understand? When you choose a husband, I want you to choose for love and love only, secure that, no matter what, you will never lose my friendship and devotion."

Hannah was speechless. She wrapped her arms more tightly around him, and blinking against the emotion welling within her, she pulled to his side and tucked herself beneath his arm as they began walking silently through the falling snow.

"So what answers do you need from me?" Jed asked softly.

Hannah pressed her head against his shoulder. "Nothing. For now, this is enough."

* * *

They walked for an hour until the wet snowfall began to chill Hannah again, then they sat by the fire in the now-bustling parlor where Jed removed her sopping boots and set her feet on a stool to warm them. He watched the way the firelight glowed in the soft curves of her face until the nearness of her pained him. "They'll be calling for supper soon. Perhaps I should run and fetch your slippers."

His head was swimming, and as he returned he gave thanks for the peal of the dinner bell. When he extended his arm to escort her, Hannah curtsied flirtatiously, and he prayed—for the sake of his already frazzled nerves—that fatigue would overtake her immediately following dinner and end the day, or that she would offer him the mercy of announcing the decision of her heart.

Their dining seats were on opposite sides of the table, placing Hannah directly across from Jed. He marveled that for the first time in their nineteen-year association, they were not just picnicking but actually dining together, allowing him a firsthand view of the elegant and gracious woman she had become. The other men were acutely aware of her as well, and Jed exhausted himself trying to hedge off every conversation one of the men attempted with Hannah. After twenty minutes of making an absolute buffoon of himself, he finally settled down, at which point the ladies began to seek his opinions on everything from the war to tobacco, allowing him to enjoy the way the attention seemed to equally disconcert Hannah.

Following supper, the guests were invited into the parlor to dance, another pleasure he and Hannah had never shared. As the violin tuned to the pianoforte, Jed felt at once both nervous and emboldened with anticipation at the idea of holding Hannah in his arms. She was the woman he loved, the only woman he had ever loved, and suddenly the very purpose of all the noble principles he sought to ensure seemed embodied in the expectation of the moment.

A gentle waltz began and the pair fumbled like awkward children as they struggled to manage the vast array of emotions the music unleashed. But once Hannah's fingers intertwined with his, all uncertainty was erased. His shoulders squared, and his eyes held her complete attention as he commanded her around the floor, gently squeezing her waist while enjoying the realization that her eyes closed in a perfectly timed response to his teasing touch.

When a reel commenced with the required change of partners, both Hannah and Jed constantly glanced over their shoulders, searching for one another. And when the next waltz started up, a judge and his wife, tired of one another's company, monopolized the pair for the next two numbers. Before they could monopolize yet another dance, Jed grabbed Hannah's hand and led her away. When they were halfway across the room, an enamored dinner guest approached Hannah for a dance.

"The lady is fatigued," Jed announced without stopping as he pulled her away.

"I owe my life to you again," Hannah teased, bringing her hands to his chest and blushing when her touch revealed the pounding of his heart. "And what reward do you desire?" she asked.

Discomfited by the feelings she was harrowing, he did not reply.

"I am not a woman of great means, but surely there is some reward I could offer you."

"We are not children anymore, Hannah," he cautioned. "Kindly stop this game."

"There must be some gesture of gratitude you'd accept," she persisted.

Aware that she was enjoying his momentary loss of composure, Jed decided to turn the tables on her. He leaned close, making no attempt to tame his eyes. "There is one reward I seek."

"As my champion, you may name your prize."

Surprised that she had not been cowed by him, he carried on. "Then offer me a kiss."

Encouraged by the return of their former playfulness, she said, "*A* kiss? Only one?"

"Flaunt your prize and I *will* make you pay your debt!"

"But what of chivalry, Mr. Pearson?"

His hands reached behind her neck, pulling her near him. "What of chivalry?" posed Jed as he gazed into her expectant eyes. "What indeed!" he muttered as he pressed his lips to hers. He told himself to quickly end the game, but as the seconds passed he wanted to simply surrender to the yearning. Though he felt he could ignore the passing of time forever, honor bade him pull away.

"I should walk you to your room," he announced abruptly.

"Jed . . ." She reached a hand up and wrapped it around his wrist. "Jed . . ."

Looking away from her, he replied, "Come, Hannah. You've had a long and tiring day."

She stood and scolded him with her eyes. "A wonderful, perfect day."

For one second he allowed his gaze to drift back to her face, struggling not to fall into the green of her eyes or to seek the soft return of her lips. "Please, Hannah," he pleaded.

"All right," she tittered playfully. "Admit it, Jed Pearson. I drive you mad."

* * *

Hannah lay on her bed for an hour, pinching herself to be sure she had not dreamed the evening. She listened intently for the sound of Jed's boots in the hall, but his footsteps never came. Hearing the final chords of reverie from below, she descended the stairs to see what was still holding his interest. After a fruitless search of the parlor she headed into the dining room where the last of the coffee was being cleared by the maids. A lump formed in her throat, evidence of her fear that she had playfully pressed Jed too far without a confession of her own love, and that he was gone from her once and for all. She saw the judge and his wife pouring from a decanter of sherry. "My friend . . . Mr. Pearson! Have you seen him?" she asked.

"I saw him head outside some time ago, dearie," the woman answered. "Is everything all right?" But before she had her answer, Hannah was racing out the door into the snow. She had barely stepped off the porch when she saw him, a tall shadow framed against the blue of the snow, lit by the half-moon's light. "Oh, Jed!" she cried as she ran toward him. "I found you!"

"Please," Jed pleaded as he stepped away, "I cannot bear to stay and endure your folly, and I will not leave you alone here in this company."

"Oh . . ." Hannah taunted as she called playfully from her spot. "You cannot stay here with me, and you will not leave me here. There are so many things you will *not* do for me, Jed. Is there not one last thing you *will* do for me?"

Jed groaned as he hung his head in frustration. Pressing his fingers into his eye sockets, he grumbled, "What would you have me do now, Hannah?"

She clasped her hands nervously before her and tilted her head shyly to the side. "Marry me?"

"What?" he snapped as his head shot up.

Hannah approached him, her hands reaching toward him. "I've been trying to get you to ask me all evening."

"Hannah . . ." he warned cautiously.

Her eyes became glossy as she innocently repeated her request. "Would you marry me?"

The return of her shy manner took Jed back three long years to the day he'd hidden behind a tree at the Stansbury's barbecue watching her from afar. Dressed in a girlish frock too young for her years, she'd played with the children as she scanned the arriving guests, waiting expectantly for someone. When she finally caught sight of him and ran into his arms, his heart burst at the realization that he was the someone for whom she had waited.

"Marry you?" he uttered. "Are you sure you know what you are asking, because I cannot survive such a game."

"Oh . . . I'm very sure. I know who I want in my life. I love *you*, Jed . . . only you."

His mouth fell agape, and he struggled to draw enough breath to keep his mind clear. "I . . . I've been carrying this box since I left Baltimore," he stammered as he slid one hand into the pocket of his military jacket. "I've been . . . trying to decide what to do . . . about this."

He withdrew his hand from his pocket, and a small velvet sack lay in his open palm. "Open it."

Hannah's fingers trembled so badly they could scarcely unite the ribbons, but when she had finally opened the drawstring and lifted the bag, a beautiful emerald ring fell into Jed's palm.

"I was trying to decide whether to wait until you made your decision, or whether I should just knock on your door tonight," he confessed as Hannah covered her mouth with her hand.

"You *were* going to propose! I've ruined everything!"

Scooping her into his arms, Jed kissed her forehead and both her cheeks, then hovering over her mouth he said, "No. You've made it absolutely perfect. I promise I'll make you happy, Hannah." Then he brushed his lips over hers.

She pulled back, framing his face in her hands. "We'll make each other happy."

He kissed her softly, then, as the seconds ticked by, he kissed her again and again, nuzzling into the ebony softness of her hair. The old familial barriers came into his mind, but this time they posed no threat to him. "I have something to tell you, Hannah. I can never prove it to your mother's satisfaction, but I have proven it to myself."

"It doesn't matter anymore, Jed."

"But I need you to know that I cleared my family name. I know what happened to your grandmother. It was all a terrible waste, but no blame can be laid to my grandfather."

"I'm glad for you to have your peace. Now we can bury the gossip with the dead."

Jed nodded and enfolded her back into his embrace. "I can't wait to be wed, Hannah."

"Let's not wait. Think of it. No one but Beatrice will come from my family, and you have only Frannie. Would either of them delay our happiness just so they could attend our wedding?"

The light of hope beamed in his eyes and then died back again. "What of your parents . . . and what of the captain?"

"I'd rather tell them after we're married so no one can try to dissuade us. The judge and his wife are still up. We could be man and wife before the clock strikes midnight."

* * *

As soon as the judge heard their request, he bellowed his enthusiastic consent so loudly the parlor filled up again with the evening's revelers. Hannah wore a simple pink dress as she stood beside her uniformed groom to exchange vows. After a toast, the innkeeper brought out a tray of petits fours and cheese, but the newlyweds stole away while their guests feted their marriage in absentia.

Jed pulled the pins from Hannah's hair, releasing the twists that had previously crowned her head. "I can't believe you're mine," he moaned as his lips brushed along her shoulder. "I would have waited forever and still counted myself the luckiest of men to have this moment."

Hannah stepped into his musky-scented warmth and buried her head in his chest. Alone in the dim lamplight, every disappointment and obstacle became meaningless as their painful memories, along with their nervousness, faded into marital bliss. Jed awoke several times in the middle of the night just to stare down at her, to assure himself that it was true. He traced the curve of her arm and fingered the ringlets of her hair, all the while gazing at the beautiful serenity of her face. A sense of protectiveness rose in his chest, choking him and bringing him to tears. This, he knew, was the reason men fought. This, he now understood, was the treasure they defended. As much as he thought he understood before, his clarity had suddenly become precise on the matter. It was not for principles or land alone. It was for those whose lives were affected by those principles, and for the generations yet unborn who would work and play upon the land.

The darkness of the coming battles stifled him, frightening him for a moment, but he pulled Hannah so near that he dared even a shaft of light to separate them. He pitied all men who weren't him this night, men who carelessly forfeited married love for transient pleasure, men who might never know that in the gentleness of a wife's touch, a man could become more than anything he could previously comprehend. The magic had transformed him. In a moment he had become a husband, and, God willing, he would someday become a father, and he knew no king or kingdom would vanquish the power such noble callings instilled in him.

A tear of happiness dropped from his eyes onto Hannah's shoulder. Her arms raised, drawing his mouth to hers. "Happy?" she asked sleepily.

"A thousand miles beyond happy," he replied. "With you by my side, I can do anything God requires of me." He sat up and pulled her into his arms, nuzzling her neck as he spoke. "I've given a great deal of thought to God lately, Hannah. I vowed that if we were blessed to finally marry, I'd want God's influence in our home. I want not only to be your husband, but your partner in every way, including in spiritual matters."

"Oh, Jed," she muttered. "You'd be so ashamed of me if you knew why I didn't write. It wasn't because I was unsure of my feelings. It was because I was angry with God." She turned to face him with sorrow-filled eyes. "I foolishly believed that if He loved me enough to speak to me in my dreams, and if I followed His promptings, He would also finish the task by settling things with Andrew and bringing us together. When He didn't, and when I received no more answers in my dreams, I stopped reading the Bible and failed to pray. I was faithless."

"Yet here we are." Jed tipped her chin and looked into her eyes.

"Because Em helped me find my way back to Him."

Jed pulled her to him. "Samuel told me about your premonition regarding Beatrice. You very well may have saved her life by heeding that prompting."

"Oh, Jed, I can't describe it, the feeling of relief that washed over me once that crisis was over. I knew He still loved me. I never want to lose that again."

Jed brought her hands to his mouth and kissed them. "We must thank Reverend Schultz."

"Oh, yes! I need to send him word of our wedding. And I want you to meet the Smiths, relatives of the Macks. They too believe God communicates with His children in dreams."

"I want to meet all of your new friends, Hannah."

"How long do we have before you have to return to the militia?"

He held her tighter and kissed her head. "We volunteers rotate in and out to tend to crops and our homes. Some men have only themselves to manage their property, and face losing all if they aren't there to plant and harvest, so normally I contend that those of us who are most blessed should bear the greater burden. But we are, after all, on our honeymoon, and we have weeks before I am ordered to return, so we can enjoy a long tour of New England if you'd like."

Hannah flopped back humorously and stared through the darkness at the ceiling. "So, are you saying the wealthy owner of the Willows is prepared to spoil his wife?"

Jed joined her in chuckling. "Let's see what treasures I bring to this marriage: there are four fields of tobacco being readied—if they are on schedule, mind you—and a good assortment of cantankerous livestock—"

"We are rich!" Hannah teased.

"You may change your tune when you hear that the three barns are sorely in need of repair, and the house, though sturdy and tight, is a sight for wanting paint. We have only half a mill, as it is still under construction—but we've built a church right there on the Willows."

He propped himself against the headboard, and Hannah lay back into his chest as he said, "What I am most proud of cannot be counted as a financial advancement, but I think it is the thing that will most please you. I am freeing the slaves, Hannah. Bitty has a family now, and they were the first nine—" he thought about the new baby soon to arrive, "—make that ten, to be freed. The papers are drawn freeing the others. I just await the proper climate to ensure their safety and the Willows survival, and you will be a part of that happy day."

Hannah turned and kissed him. "Oh, Jed! That is the very best of wedding gifts."

"I plan to give land to every individual, so we will be left with eight hundred acres or so when everyone is free, but we'll manage."

"I am so proud of you! I know how much you love your farm, and I will love it equally. I'll help paint the house and barns. It will make me feel a part of the Willows." Jed tightened his embrace and Hannah suddenly noticed his scarred and knotted hands. "What happened to you?"

He held one up and examined it himself. "Remember the way we parted at the Lord Baltimore Hotel two summers ago? When I heard you were intended to the lieutenant I wanted to die. I wandered down to the wharf and got myself sopping drunk. It was a stupid thing to do. Some thugs took me outside, beat me senseless, and then robbed me. They broke some ribs and crushed both my hands, then left me for dead. Beatrice never told you?"

Hannah's eyes began to fill with tears. "Oh, Jed! How could she not have told me such a thing?"

Jed heard the anger in Hannah's voice, and he quickly leapt in to answer her concerns. "Dudley found me and took me to the hospital. He's a good man, Hannah, and Beatrice is a good woman. Months later, when I finally confronted her about the letter, the rift between them was apparent, and they told me that these events were the cause of their marital problems. She has paid a high penance, and tonight is proof that she has fully atoned for her mistakes."

"Oh, Jed! How can you still love me after all we've put you through?" she cried.

Jed swung her around until she fell across his chest and into his arms. "Three times you were meant to be mine and three times I lost you. Nothing could ever pull you from me now."

CHAPTER 25

April 8, 1813
Liverpool, England

"Blood money." Juan Arroyo Corvas scowled as he stared at his reflection, recalling how he had walked into the haberdashery with a purse filled with money. "My life . . . my blood."

"Is it not enough that you sold yourself to that man?" asked Ferdinand, his cousin and first mate. "Must you also take his whip and beat yourself every day? I'm raising the anchor and leaving this harbor for a few hours. The smell of the sea will calm you before your meeting."

Twenty minutes later, Ferdinand joined Juan on the bow, staring off at the gray water. "Why do you stay with me, Ferdinand? You're free to return to Cadiz with no penalty."

"What joy is there in sailing the Mediterranean without your company? Besides, had the offer of this exquisite ship—and a lifetime of well-paid employment serving as the man's personal transport—been extended to me, I would have signed also, and I have no doubt that you would have stayed by my side. No one could have known that his terms required you to leave Spain forever and claim England as your permanent port."

"I should have learned from the suffering of my father that the creditor's terms are never just! Greed ensnared Papa and now it owns me as well. Look at me! I'm not a sea captain . . . not a sailor . . . not even a man. I'm a dog on a diamond leash, housed in an extravagant cage—sailing only at my master's pleasure. I've lost the woman I love and I may never sail beyond England's horizon again, spending my life constrained by the creditor's beck and call."

"It is not your *creditor* that enslaves you, Juan. It is your *honor.* There is no shame in being a man who sacrifices all to keep his word. But he must make peace with the life his choices afford him."

Juan closed his eyes and drew in a long breath of the river's stale air. "You're right," he agreed, nodding soberly. Straightening his shoulders, he took his place at the helm. "To the point and back, then return her to port. I've business to attend to."

* * *

It was a more confident Juan Corvas who walked into the Boar's Head Inn to meet his creditor's representative. The man with the ram's head umbrella was seated at a table in the back of the dimly lit room facing the door. As soon the men's eyes met, Juan hastened to the table and took a seat, disarming Stephen Ramsey with his calm assurance.

Ramsey leaned back and surveyed his guest's fine appearance. Attempting to unsettle the man, he said, "I see that you are enjoying the terms of your agreement."

"Why was I summoned?" Juan asked curtly.

"Do not forget that you serve at the discretion of your benefactor!" snarled Ramsey.

"I am well aware of my legal obligation, señor. Simply tell me what I am to do."

A full minute passed as Ramsey took long slow sips from his ale while fingering an article tucked in the inside pocket of his coat. He eventually pulled the item, a miniature portrait, from his coat, and laid it on the table. "The creditor wants you to find this man . . ."

Juan studied the photo carefully, wondering why the face seemed so familiar.

"His name is . . . Arthur Ramsey."

Something in the man's uneasiness told Juan a secret had been disclosed. Playing on this advantage, Juan considered the request and then abruptly slid the portrait back across the table. "I am contracted to *move* men and documents. No mention was made of the *seeking* of men."

Ramsey's temper quickly flared and then he controlled his anger as well as his volume. Sliding the portrait back across the table, he demanded, "Consider *this* your document! You are to carry this portrait from port to port, making inquiries of every ship's captain you encounter."

Juan avoided the painting. "This is not part of my contract, but I will do this as a *favor.*"

"A favor!" Ramsey sputtered angrily.

"Yes, you remember. '*Favors for favors*'? Finding this man seems to be very important to my creditor." Juan carefully scrutinized the man's response to his assertion, and then his eyes fell upon the animal-sculpted umbrella head. Smiling inwardly, he picked up the portrait and compared the face to that of the man. "Is this because the missing man is his son, perhaps?"

"All you need know is that he sailed within the last three weeks, and there may have been a young boy in his care. I want . . . I mean . . . the *creditor* wants you to find him."

Juan leaned forward and smiled at his creditor. "Let us speak plainly, señor. I have incurred a hideous debt, but I think we must now negotiate a few changes to our agreement."

"There will be no negotiations."

"I think there will be. You see, *Mr. Ramsey . . .*" he drew the name out dramatically and deliberately, "I now know that you, sir, are my creditor, and the man you seek is your son. While that changes nothing legally, it does ease my mind to know exactly who it is that enslaves me."

Ramsey glowered at Juan over the edge of his glass as he drew a long sip of his ale. "Then nothing has changed between us, has it Mr. Corvas?"

"Oh . . . it has for me, señor. My creditor was a faceless devil to whom I had sold my soul. But you, Mr. Ramsey, are just a man—a man beset by his own terrible demons, a man who needs a favor from me—and knowing that frees me somewhat. So I will help you find your son, but not because I fear you. I do it because honoring my word pleases my Lord. And then we will discuss the favor I desire in return."

* * *

Juan left the inn and sniffed the air, the scent of the sea transcending Liverpool's crowded stench. He was finally able to recall the old sailing stories his father used to tell him that had long been repressed by guilt and shame. They were stories from his grandfather's days, and from his grandfathers before him, clear back to Enso Corvas, the ancestor who had sailed with Cristóbal Colón, known to his new British companions as Christopher Columbus—the man who discovered America.

Enthralled by the glory of the man's successful expedition to the New World, Enso appealed personally to Admiral Colón, the "Admiral of the Ocean Sea," for a position on his crew while Enso was still a young man in Cadiz, Spain. His sailing journal meticulously recorded Columbus's recounted tales of the answered prayers and spiritual whisperings that had guided him on his great expedition, a quest to heed the cry of the ancient prophets, to find and bring salvation to those of God's scattered children who had not yet heard of the Christ.

Passed down through generations, Juan had grown up with the accounts of Columbus's testimony embedded in his heart. Before his slavery to Ramsey, they had transformed sailing the world into more than a vocation for him. It became a sacred calling, uniting cultures and peoples, allowing him to share the good news of Christ and to hear the testimonies of the faithful uttered in diverse tongues.

Settling his father's debt with Ramsey had involved Juan in deeds that had robbed him of those feelings, and his own situation had further deadened his soul. But today was a new day, for Juan recalled that even Columbus, the inspired explorer, had once fallen from grace. He too had lost his way for a time, fearing man more than God, involving himself in deeds that landed him in chains in an ignominious return to Spain. But he too had paid the price for his sin, testifying boldly of God through his writings, his book of prophecies— *Libro de las Profecias.*

And didn't God hear him? Did he not record a final vision, one of atonement? And did he not record that the voice comforted him with the words, "Fear not, but have faith"?

Yes, he did! Columbus was now revered by men and favored of God, the explorer whose travels brought Christianity to America, the land of freedom and hope, whose capital city bore both the names of its discoverer and its defender—Washington City in the District of Columbia!

Freedom and hope . . . The words that had long mocked his oppression resonated sweetly in Juan's mind this day. *Yes, Columbus served Spain, and so will I serve Ramsey . . . until my debt is paid.* Confessing his errors to God, he thought he heard a voice whisper to him. *"Fear not, but have faith."* He glanced at the portrait in his hand and drew in another breath of sea air.

"It is as Ferdinand said. Honor binds me . . . not fear."

CHAPTER 26

April 20, 1813
The Willows

Spring was bursting so beautifully along the Patuxent that Frannie tried to ignore reports of British attacks along the waterways where homes and businesses had been menaced and plundered. Their ground forces had not yet arrived, but knowing it was just a matter of time before the real havoc commenced, she intended to enjoy her respite at the Willows.

Discovering Markus's old work clothes in the barn, she donned his overalls and hat and saddled Jed's precious Tildie to give the old mare a good, restorative run. Then, allowing a shard of common sense to bridle her enthusiasm, she slid a rifle into its sling before setting off.

She waved to Abel, Jerome, and Jack as she rode past the mill site. Jack chased after her on foot, hollering at her like a worried uncle, but she waved and urged Tildie on, racing under the willow trees, laughing each time a miscalculated branch smacked her cheeks or slapped against Markus's hat. Turning at the White Oak boundary, she galloped hard between the fence and the sweetened tobacco fields. Then, as she approached the huge Wye oak tree, she thought she caught a flash of color in its low boughs. A nervous chill raced through her as she conjured frightened thoughts of spies and soldiers lurking about. Unwilling to be cowed by her fears though, she slowed Tildie down and turned the animal back toward the tree.

She identified the red object as a weathered bandana whose aged knot did not release easily. Inside, Frannie found a pearl button strung on a ribbon, and a wooden flute from which extended a rolled piece of parchment. Gingerly pulling and twisting, she retrieved the tightly rolled scroll which she anxiously opened, revealing the sender and the message. As soon as her eyes recognized the handwriting she began to shake, and the further she read, the worse her trembling became, traveling up her arms and into her torso until she could no longer stand. Guttural moans tore from her throat as Abel and Jack rode up with Jerome close behind.

Jack ran to her first and sank to his knees beside her. She looked up into his face, and her fear stole the light from his eyes as well. "What is it, Miss Frannie?" he begged.

She raised her cupped and quaking hands to Jack, who stared at the objects cradled there. Gingerly, he picked up the two objects. "This here is Priscilla's pearl necklace, made from a button off her weddin' dress . . . and this is her boy's flute . . ."

Slowly, the reality of the signs bore down upon him, rounding his shoulders like a stone. His face went slack and his brown eyes teared. "No . . . no . . ." he repeated as he slumped to the ground.

Frannie wrapped her arms around his neck while Abel lifted the parchment from the grass and began reading aloud:

> *Dear Frannie,*
> *In order to get word to your people of a tragedy that has befallen Bitty's family, I took the chance that you might still ride past this old tree. Priscilla's son was identified as the spy who warned you about Dupree. For that deed my father and Dupree saw that he and his parents have paid the ultimate penalty. Please tell Bitty that I saw to having them buried and managed to slip these items to you as proof of my words.*
> *I would have come in person, but my wife and I are as imprisoned as the slaves.*
>
> *Forgive us,*
> *Frederick*

"I'm so sorry, Jack," muttered Jerome, placing a hand on Jack's shoulder. "So sorry . . ."

Abel clasped his hands atop his worried head. "What are we going to tell Bitty? You know how she asks if there's word from her sister every time one of us walks through that door."

Jack stood, let out a groan, and wiped an arm across his eyes as he stuffed the items into his shirt pocket. Handing Frannie a handkerchief, he helped her to her feet. Laboring to settle his voice, he softly asked her, "You all right?"

She nodded, but her eyes told the real tale. "Is this how it will be, then? They'll just kill anyone who dares to cross them . . . even women and children?"

Jerome shook his head absently. "Our concern now must be Bitty. She's not doing well."

Abel's eyes grew wide. "What do you mean? She's fine."

Jerome hung his head. "No, she's not, son. This baby's taking a terrible toll on its mother. There are signs in her eyes and in the lines of her face and legs. She's swelling too, not just in her ankles like most women do. It's everywhere. This news could make matters worse."

"The toll of not knowin' will kill her just the same," agreed Jack. "We have to tell her."

* * *

Bitty rose heavily from her seat on the front porch as soon as she saw the group of riders coming in. Lumbering over to the railing, she called out, "Soup'll be ready soon enough. By the way, did any White Oak wagons roll past while you were working on the mill today?"

Her round face—the face all but Jerome had assumed was plump from the fatness of motherhood—now drew looks of worry from her loved ones as the riders dismounted. Frannie and Jerome gathered up all the horses' reins while Jack and Abel approached her soberly.

"What's the matter with you two?" Bitty scolded nervously as anxiety began to dim her smile. She began backing up like a fearful child as she waved the pair away. "Don't say it! Don't say it!" she repeated with increasing volume. Abel rushed to her side, and she collapsed in his arms while poor Jack knelt beside her, squeezing her hands as he delivered the tragic report.

"No! No! No!" she screamed as she flailed at the men.

"Please, Bitty!" cried Abel. "You'll hurt yourself and the baby."

"Why bear a babe into such a world!" she wailed wildly, then, just as suddenly as it began, her mournful tirade ended. Jack and Abel held on tightly, expecting another wave of flailing, unaware that her calmness had been accompanied by her eyes rolling back into her head.

Jerome saw it, and in an instant he was there, crouching beside her. "Lay her down!"

In a flash the men responded, and Jerome turned his attentions to Frannie. "I need sweet basil! Lots of it! And head down to the river by the mill! Bitty has a patch of evening primrose planted there. Pull it up and bring it all here! Everything . . . even all the roots, but especially the seed pods. Scour the ground and see if any from last season survived the winter!"

Frannie jumped on Tildie and flew first to Bitty's herb patch. After gathering bunches of sweet basil, she raced down to the river and made two frantic circles of the mill trying to identify the evening primrose plants from amongst the leaves and tree litter. After identifying them, she dropped to her knees and began yanking at the young stems, trying to pull the roots free, but the effort proved fruitless. To her extreme relief, she found Jed's set of eating utensils in his saddlebag. Rushing back, she dug ferociously with the spoon until she had a sizeable pile of roots, and then she turned her attention to collecting seed pods when a rustle of brush sounded behind her. With her nerves already nearly spent, she crouched low and froze until the sound of approaching motion sent her crawling toward Tildie. Positioning herself on the far side of the animal, she drew her gun and rested it along the horse's haunches as she sighted a brown-haired intruder coming through the trees, leading a black horse.

He carried no apparent weapon, but the images of a pearl button neck-lace and a boy's whistle haunted her frazzled nerves. *Not one more step,* she warned silently as the man moved to within twenty yards of her position. Fingering the trigger, she set the sight upon the man's shoulder, and as he cleared a willow branch from before him, Frannie squeezed back and fired.

He cried out and dropped to the ground, scrambling for cover while pressing a hand over the spot from where blood now oozed. Frannie stepped forward with her rifle ready.

"You shot me!" he yelled accusatorily. "You nearly killed me!"

"Shut up or I'll shoot you again!" she warned. "Who are you? Are you alone?"

"Yes, I'm alone, and I'm clearly not going anywhere!" He moved to take a look at his wound, and Frannie jerked the rifle to his face and cocked the trigger.

"I'll say when you can move. Who are you?"

"Are you a barbarian? Would you have me bleed to death?"

Frannie noted his accent and the European cut of his clothes. "Don't tempt me. One less British spy won't be missed."

"Spy?" he argued. "Look at me! I've no weapon, no uniform . . ."

He leaned his head back against a tree, closed his eyes, and groaned. Frannie, initially unmoved by his performance, felt a wave of sympathy as his color faded and his head began to wobble. Keeping her gun raised, she drew close to him and knelt down to look at his wound. He turned his pallid face to meet hers, and she found herself oddly moved by the soft brown of his eyes and gentle lines of his face, though the closer she neared him the more puzzled he appeared.

"You're a woman!" he cried in astonishment. "But . . . I thought you were a . . ."

Insulted, Frannie scowled. "And you're a coward. The bullet missed the bone entirely."

"Well, excuse me for not knowing the proper etiquette after being shot!"

"You really aren't a soldier, are you?" Frannie agreed as she stood, staring at her prize. Offering the man her hand, she ordered, "Get up while I figure out what to do with you."

The man stalled warily. "*Do* with me? I've done nothing wrong! I was just searching for the Pearson plantation, so you needn't *do* anything with me.*"

"Get on your horse," she barked. "I've a pressing errand to attend to. I don't trust you enough to let you go, but I can't leave you here for the animals to eat," she explained as she tied his hands to the pommel. Gathering up the primrose pieces, she leapt onto Tildie and guided the two horses into the tobacco barn. After settling her prisoner on the barn floor, she called to Abel's oldest son, eleven-year-old Caleb, as she reloaded. "Do you remember how to fire this gun?"

"Yes, ma'am," he answered shakily.

"Then point it at this man, and if he tries to escape, shoot him in the leg. Understand?"

With wide eyes, Caleb asked, "Miss Frannie, is Bitty Momma going to be all right?"

An immediate softness overtook her. Framing his face in her hands, she replied reassuringly, "Your grandfather is as good as any doctor around, and we're all praying for her, aren't we?" After prying a tiny nod from the boy, Frannie raced into the house while calling Jerome's name and bounding up the stairs toward his reply. "How is she?" she asked nervously.

Jerome handed her a mortar and pestle. "Crush those seed pods, then squeeze the mash through linen and catch the oil in that little bowl. Jack, you grind up the primrose leaves. And Abel, grind this basil, then steep it with the primrose leaves to make a tea. You need to spoon as much of it as you can into Bitty."

As Frannie ground the seeds, she noted how Abel struggled to steady his large, shaking hands so he could spoon the green fluid between his wife's stilled lips. Once the oil was extracted from the evening primrose seeds, Jerome asked Frannie and Jack to leave the room.

"I'd rather stay," begged Frannie. "Isn't there anything else we can do, Jerome?"

"The herbs and primrose leaves ease the heart, and the oil should bring on her labor. We need to bring that baby along, so just wait . . . and pray," he answered before closing the door.

"Oh, Jack," Frannie cried as she fell against him. "She can't die. She just can't."

"No, she can't, Miss Frannie. She's all I've got left in this world."

"That's not true, Jack. No matter what, that would never be true." But Frannie also felt the gnawing fear that Bitty was slipping away. "How long before we'll know anything?"

"It's hard to say. In either case, we should go and tell the others."

Frannie recalled the man she had left tied in the barn. "I . . . I need to tend to something first. Ring the bell if you receive any news."

* * *

The British gentleman studied the face of the child for an hour, recalling the complete change in the woman's voice and manner as she spoke to him. "So Caleb," he began, "what did you call the lady? Frannie, was it?"

"Yes, sir . . . Miss Frannie Pearson."

"Frannie *Pearson*?" He smiled appreciatively at Frannie's nerve. "And you called her *Miss* Frannie. Do you mean to say she's not Mr. Pearson's wife?"

"No sir!" laughed the boy. "She's Mr. Jed's sister. Mr. Jed owns the Winding Willows." He studied the man's face, then inquired, "You seem nice. Why did Miss Frannie arrest you?"

The man raised his bound wrists and flinched. "It appears that trespassing on the Willows is a serious offense."

The young guard chuckled, delighting the man. "Caleb's a good biblical name," he ventured.

"I read about Caleb from the Bible. He was Joshua's friend."

The man looked curiously at him. "You can read?"

The boy immediately recoiled, and his darting eyes began to fill as he realized what he had disclosed. The British man leaned forward. "Don't be afraid, Caleb. It's all right. I'm delighted you can read. Truly delighted."

"We're not allowed to tell anyone. Mr. Jed said it would cause us trouble."

"So . . . are you saying that Mr. Pearson *let* you learn to read?"

"Yes, sir. So long as we don't tell anyone. Will you keep our secret?"

"I will. I promise." He watched the boy's face relax, adding, "So, you like your master?"

"Oh, Mr. Jed isn't my master no . . . *any*more. He made us free . . . me and my family. He's going to make the others free, too . . . as soon as it's safe."

"Really?" The man leaned back. "Tell me more about Mr. Jed."

"He brought my family here from White Oak to save us from Mr. Stringham's whip. Bitty Momma said God gave Mr. Jed so much heart that it pushed itself right out of his chest and clear onto his shoulder."

This comment drew the man in close. "What do you mean by that, Caleb?"

Caleb pulled his own shirt collar down to illustrate his point. "Right here on Mr. Jed's shoulder is a purple birthmark shaped like a heart. It's just like the one his granddaddy had, so they say, and they also say that's why Mr. Jed got the Willows."

"Is that so?" the man mused.

"It sure is. I've seen it myself!" Caleb testified as Frannie entered the barn.

"What have you seen, Caleb?" she asked sternly as she took up the gun from the barn floor where the lad had absentmindedly lain it. She aimed its barrel to the chest of the stranger. "Has he tried to trick you, Caleb?"

"No, ma'am! He is a fine man, Miss Frannie. Miss Frannie? Is Bitty Momma well now?"

The boy's query again brought an immediate softness to Frannie. "Your grandfather is taking real good care of her, Caleb. In the meantime, why don't you run along and find your brothers and your sister, all right? And tell no one about this man. It's our secret, understand?"

In a flash the boy nodded and flew out the door, leaving Frannie and the man alone. He raised his bound hands in her direction and asked, "Will you untie me now? Surely you realize that I could have easily escaped during Caleb's amiable watch."

Grunting her reply, she pulled a knife from her boot and moved toward her apprehensive prisoner. "I need to clean that wound, anyway." She sighed as she cut his tethers.

He stared curiously at her until she could no longer avoid his gaze. "You intrigue me, miss," he admitted. "Would you mind removing your hat so I can fully see my captor?"

Tentative and wary, Frannie lifted her hat, sending her long hair tumbling down in a cascade of auburn mayhem.

"You're very lovely."

She stood abruptly. "Unbutton your shirt. I'll get some alcohol and cotton."

The man began to comply and then stopped short, choosing instead to rip the sleeve off. When Frannie returned with the supplies, she knelt a mere few inches from his inquisitive gaze, quickly becoming as unnerved as a schoolgirl. "What's . . . your name?" she asked awkwardly as she applied an alcohol-soaked swab to the wound.

"Arthur," he groaned as the sting hit him.

Feigning indifference, she asked, "You say you're not a spy. Then what are you?"

Frannie began to roll the torn shirt back away from his wound to clean further up his shoulder, but Arthur grimaced and pulled away. "What am I?" he snickered self-deprecatingly. "What am I, indeed?" He leaned his head back and pressed his hand over his shoulder as he studied the woman seated beside him. "I studied Divinity at Cambridge University."

"A reverend?" She surveyed him under this new light. "You're not what I expected."

Arthur smiled sadly. "I tricked Caleb into telling me who you were. You're not what I expected either, Miss Pearson. The truth is, you're the reason I am here in Maryland. I came to find you . . . you and your brother . . . and the Willows."

"So you *are* a spy." Her disappointment was palpable as she moved away from him.

Arthur took her hand and bore his eyes into hers. "I heard reports of a dangerous man who plans to use the war to wreak havoc on a family of traitors. I sailed here to determine if I would serve mankind best by allowing two deserving predators to destroy one another, or if by my silence I would be permitting harm to come to unsuspecting innocents."

Frannie rubbed her hand over her prickling arm. "And?" she challenged.

Falling back, Arthur diverted his eyes and sighed. "The very fact that I remained Caleb's willing prisoner should give you your answer."

The heavy sadness in his voice both confused and wounded Frannie. "Then why do you seem disappointed to find that we are not the barbarians you supposed?"

Again he moved to her, pleading, "It's not that. What I've discovered here profoundly affects my future as well." Her face became a palette of confusion, and he rushed to explain. "How could you possibly understand? I hope the time will come when I can say more, but hear me on this. The name of the devil who has set his sights on the Willows is—"

"Sebastian Dupree."

Arthur fell back and shrank in the futility of his timing. "So you already know . . ."

"He's already here," she replied sullenly, suddenly remembering the alcohol soaked cloth in her hand. She began to tear the shirt higher, up to his shoulder, but Arthur's hand quickly clamped over hers, offering her a gentle squeeze while his anxious eyes searched hers.

"What are you doing to prepare?"

Frannie stared him down, challenging him. "Your question implies a level of trust we have not achieved, nor shall we until I know how you've come to be acquainted with Dupree."

"We've never met, but his reputation precedes him. He is not a man to be trifled with."

"Neither are you, perhaps."

Disappointment clouded his face as he watched Frannie methodically fold a wad of sterile cloth and press it over his wound. "What can I do to prove my integrity to you?"

She began wrapping long cotton strips across his chest and over his shoulder to hold the bandage in place. Once she was confident the wound was properly attended to, she backed away from him and leaned against a tobacco table. "You can start by telling me your full name."

Arthur hesitated before replying. "Benson . . . Arthur . . . Benson."

"Then time will tell the truth of your story, Mr. Benson."

"You plan to hold me prisoner?" he exclaimed.

Frannie bolted up and pointed the gun barrel back at his chest. "As I see it, you have two options. I could turn you over to the men right now and let them decide if they feel safe letting you go, but inasmuch as they just received word that three members of their family were murdered by Dupree's accomplice, I think you'll prefer option two."

"Which is?" Arthur asked warily.

"We have a hunting cabin about an hour's ride upriver. I'll take you there and leave you with provisions. No horse, but food and supplies. In the meantime I'll verify your story and see if any more 'angels of mercy' arrive to 'warn' us."

* * *

Frannie knocked on the door and heard Bitty tearfully castigating herself for the things she had said about the baby earlier, while Jerome warned her of the necessity of remaining calm.

"Try to make her understand, Miss Frannie," Abel pled at the doorway.

"I will," Frannie pledged, wringing her hands with worry as she entered the room.

As soon as Bitty saw her, she raised her arms to Frannie and wailed all the louder. "I didn't mean what I said. I love this baby. I don't want anythin' bad to happen to it."

"Of course you don't," Frannie assured as she sat at her beside. "You were just in shock. The news about Priscilla and her family was horrible, and I'm so sorry, Bitty. I'm so sorry."

Frannie had never seen Bitty broken this way, and the very sight of it caused her own tears to flow. Interestingly, as soon as Bitty saw Frannie's distress, she settled and drew Frannie to her bosom. "There, there, child . . . We'll get through this . . . We'll get through it."

The men watched in awe at the power each woman possessed over the other. Mere minutes after worrying that Bitty's frenzied state would bring her demise, they heard the woman begin to hum and then sing a sweet, familiar lullaby. Seconds later, Frannie joined in, and as they rocked and sang the tunes of motherhood, Bitty's own tears stopped, and a smile of maternal love spread across her face. Sleep finally overtook her, permitting Frannie to withdraw. Abel quickly filled the void, taking Bitty's hands in his own and leaning his large head on top of them.

"What do you think, Jerome?" asked Frannie as she witnessed the tender scene.

Pressing a brown hand to his brow, he said, "It could be hours before we know anything."

Frannie nodded and walked to where Jack was silently sitting. "There's something that I need to attend to, Jack. I'll be gone for a few hours," she whispered.

Jack's head popped up immediately. "Is somethin' wrong?"

"Nothing I can't handle," she replied glibly. "I'll be back by nightfall."

"Trouble finds you every time you get it in your mind to go off on your own."

His warning sounded in her ears as she walked away, heading for the larder. She grabbed a flour sack and tossed in the standard provisions she would have packed for herself, then heading for the smokehouse, she grabbed a slab of bacon and a salted rabbit as well. She tied the bundle up and cautiously stole away to the barn where Mr. Benson was fast asleep against a stack of burlap bags. Staring at him from the doorway—his brown curls framing his face, softening his square jaw, matched by long, brown lashes that gave him an innocent appearance—she found it easy to picture him as a child, and her fear was dispelled. Still, his torso twitched, becoming rigid, and his face occasionally contorted in response to whatever dream was besetting his peace. She heard him mutter, and then his mutterings became cries as he pled, "No! No! No!"

She approached slowly, calling out, "Mr. Benson . . ." But he didn't respond until she dropped beside him on her knees and shook him gently saying, "Arthur! Arthur!"

He responded with a startled jerk. "What are you . . . ?" he cried out in alarm.

"I'm sorry. You were having a nightmare," she quickly explained as she stood and offered her hand to lift him up. "We need to move you. Gather your things."

Frannie tethered his black gelding to Tildie's saddle, and the pair moved quietly from the barn into the meadow toward the trees. From there they made their way diagonally up the rise to the craggy cliff walls that overhung the river's edge below. Looking back, Frannie saw her guest smiling broadly. "What's so humorous?" she inquired with forced irritation.

"Are you really as fearsome as you pretend, Miss Pearson?"

"I'd advise you not to risk finding out."

"We both know that won't be necessary. Obviously, the more isolated we become, the more relaxed you appear. I doubt you'd feel that way if you feared I was a dangerous man."

Frannie raised one eyebrow and smiled. "Let's see . . . *my* horse, *my* gun, *my* land . . . Hmmm. You tell me. Am *I* a dangerous *woman?*"

He smiled as he studied her, then closing his eyes, he chuckled. "Of that, I have no doubt!"

The old hunting cabin sat on the highest rise of the Pearsons' woodlands. Frannie dismounted and untied the sacks, her skin prickling with delight as she entered the old place. She quickly saw that Mr. Benson was not nearly as taken with the rustic old cabin. She tossed the sacks onto the roughly hewn table and pulled two bearskins from a wooden chest and laid them out on the floor near the huge stone fireplace. "You'll be plenty warm between these and the fireplace. There's a freshwater spring behind the cabin, and utensils and pots on the shelf on the wall. I'll return as soon as I've verified your story. Otherwise, you've enough provisions for a week in case circumstances delay my return." As she turned to leave, she caught Arthur peering apprehensively into the sack of food. "There are eggs and two meats, a tin each of coffee, sugar, and tobacco, a jar of molasses, a loaf of bread, and a sack of beans."

"Yes . . . right you are," Arthur conceded unconvincingly.

"You *can* cook, can't you?"

"Just a little . . . out of practice, but . . . not to worry . . ." he answered sheepishly.

Simultaneously exasperated and amused, Frannie took off her coat and walked him through his first meal. As she again turned to leave, she noticed the fatigue in his face, and she moved to him, instinctively placing a hand on his shoulder. "How are you?"

Inches from him, she found him studying her again, searching her eyes and canvassing the shape of her face. "Not to worry," he assured her warmly, moving his hand over hers.

She attempted to deflect the spark of attraction they'd momentarily shared. "You need to eat and then rest. There are some books in that chest. They'll provide you some entertainment."

He sat awkwardly on the table end and nodded, still restraining her hand, his concern apparent. "I can't bear the thought of you riding back through those woods alone. Take me back with you. I'll throw myself on the mercy of your workers."

"I'll be fine." She blushed as she slid her hand free. "I'll see you soon."

* * *

It was nearly dusk when she returned to the Willows. Before she tied the two horses up, Caleb and Eli rushed up with the news. "We got a sister, Miss Frannie!"

Frannie bounded up the stairs to the sweet sound of an infant's cries, meeting Jack at the door. Relief, then disappointment, altered his countenance at his first sight of her.

"You had us worried sick, miss. You had no cause to do that, especially today."

"I'm . . . sorry, Jack. I've got a lot to tell you, but first, where's Jerome?"

"He was so exhausted after the baby finally arrived that Sarah made him lie down and rest. She's comin' back to stay the night with Bitty so Abel and I can keep the watch."

"Let me visit with Bitty, and then we'll talk, all right?" She slipped past Jack to where the elated parents sat admiring their new daughter. "She's beautiful, Bitty, but how are you?"

"Just fine. Come and meet our baby girl. We're naming her Priscilla, after my sister," she said, her eyes tearing.

Frannie spent an hour fussing over the baby until Sarah shooed them all out. Jack and Abel waited by the door for Frannie. "Do we have more trouble?" Jack asked.

"I'm not sure. I shot a stranger on the Willows property today. I need to go to Calverton tomorrow and make some inquiries. Will you go with me?"

Jack scrutinized her face. "You *shot* someone and you're not sure *if* we have trouble?"

"He's fine. At least he will be. I just want to verify his story. Will you go with me, Jack?"

Jack sighed and rolled his eyes. "I s'pose so. I know it won't do me any good to try and change your mind. Right now you'd best change out of Markus's clothes."

* * *

"His story checks out, Miss Frannie. The captain of the Sunfish admits to dropping off one British-soundin' man here in Calverton yesterday. He remembers him clearly because he kept wonderin' if he should shoot him in case he was one of Cockburn's men."

"That's why I tend to believe him, Jack. I do believe he came alone. He's either an idiot or an innocent. Besides, no one I spoke to has seen any other strangers lurking around.

"Take me and Abel to him, Miss Frannie. We'll find out for sure."

Cringing at the thought of a meeting between the gentle Mr. Benson and Abel, Frannie slipped away with the horses early the next morning, avoiding any further discussion of Arthur's interrogation. Before she arrived at the cabin she heard a hymn wafting through the trees. Watching secretly through the foliage, she found Arthur sitting on the front porch steps, leaning his back against a railing with his face turned skyward, eyes closed. She basked in the peace shining in his countenance, unable to deny the feelings of trust he stirred in her cynical heart, and as she remained through two more little hymns, neither could she deny her attraction to the man.

The horses' whinnies forced her from her hideaway. As she dismounted and tied Tildie alongside Arthur's black gelding, she watched Arthur carefully, monitoring his strange reaction to her—as if he were seeing her for the first time. He remained frozen in place at first, and then he smiled admiringly at her, rising to reach for her hand to place a long, soft kiss on her knuckles.

He retained her hand and complimented her. "You are an absolute vision, Miss Pearson."

"Oh? Then I should invite you to Philadelphia to see me in one of my stage costumes."

Arthur tipped his head and gazed dubiously at her. "You're . . . an entertainer?"

"Yes," she replied defensively. "I'm not always in overalls, Mr. Benson. I'm also a singer . . . and I play the piano—in a lovely little establishment called *Le Jardin.*"

"*Le Jardin,*" he repeated slowly in a French dialect more lovely than Henri's. "The Garden . . . what other marvels don't I know about you?"

"What do you want to know?" she found herself whispering as his eyes drew her in.

Melancholy tainted his smile as he answered, "Absolutely everything." A flush of color tinted Arthur's cheeks, and he dropped his head as he led her to the porch bench to sit.

"You've quite a lovely voice, too. I heard you singing as I arrived," Frannie ventured.

He scanned the tree line thoughtfully. "I feel the Spirit of God here. I haven't felt that for a long time, I'm sad to say. I was afraid I had lost it forever." A comfortable silence ensued until Arthur said, "My mind was racing long after you left, so I pulled items from the chest and read by firelight—copies of *Poor Richard's Almanac* and some of Jefferson's writings. Just fascinating!"

"They must have been my grandfather's."

"Your grandfather was born in Liverpool, England, was he not?"

Frannie noted a forced nonchalance in his voice. "How could you have known that?"

"It was inscribed on the title page of one of the books. I'd love to know more about him. What kind of man must he have been to have come so far and to have built the Willows?"

"Why does it matter to you?" Frannie asked carefully, her suspicions rising once more.

"I'm intrigued by what inspired British men like him to leave Britain for the colonies."

"My grandfather's family was very poor. His mother was the maid for a government official named Mitchell, and as a favor to her, Mitchell paid for Grandfather's education."

"Remarkable . . . Do you know anything else about her . . . or her husband?"

"His mother, Adelaide Pearson, was nearly fifty when Grandfather was born, so I suppose it's also a miracle that any of us are even here. We've no information about his father."

Arthur was contemplative and didn't respond immediately. "And aside from being poor, you've no idea why your grandfather left England and came to America?"

Frannie cocked her head and became wary again. "This is more than mere curiosity."

"Please trust me, Frannie. I'm trying understand why your family has been targeted."

"Jed came upon one of Grandfather's letters just last winter. There was a mention of his having been spurned in his youth. Soon afterwards, someone named Lord Ensor arranged for his indenture to the States. But if he came to America to run from a broken heart, he found more of the same here. The poor dear married and buried four wives while fathering eleven children."

"Eleven children? You must have cousins you've never even met."

"Jed and I have only one another now. We hardly see the family anymore."

"I'm an only child, though I was raised close to a cousin who is as dear to me as a sister. My mother prays we'll wed." He cast a sideways glance at Frannie. "Tell me, has your brother hand selected some far-off cousin for you, or do your tastes run more to Philadelphians?"

Frannie stood with deliberateness and dusted the back of her long, split skirt. "My tastes, Mr. Benson, run to men who do not ask me so many questions. Now let's examine you."

After Arthur scrambled to his own feet, Frannie placed a hand on his forehead, and he closed his eyes in response to her touch. "No fever," she declared weakly. "Now sit back down and let me examine your wound." She stooped to pull some supplies from her satchel, and when she stood, she found him looking down into her brown eyes, which nearly buckled her knees. She reached a cotton-filled hand to his shoulder and nudged him. "Come and sit . . ."

Taking her hand, Arthur kissed her knuckles. Turning her hand over, he peeled the cotton away and kissed her palm, lightly brushing the cloth against her scented wrist. "You must go, Frannie," he whispered. "Just leave the supplies, and I'll clean the wound before I leave."

"Before you leave?"

"You and I both know you verified my story. If you hadn't gotten your answers you wouldn't have come alone with my horse in tow and smelling of fine French perfume." Frannie blushed, and in embarrassment she tried to move away, but Arthur wrapped a gentle arm around her waist, requesting she remain. "I've never met anyone like you before. I barely know anything about you, have barely spent any time with you, and yet . . ." He closed his eyes and moved from her. "I can't remain here while wolves surround you. I must get away and try to stop Dupree."

"What do you know that will help you stop Dupree?" she challenged, her guard raised again.

Arthur's eyes begged her to trust him. "I know who sent him."

The idea of a connection between the pair made her body go slack.

"Dupree is a mercenary, Frannie, a hired assassin who won favor with Admiral Cockburn because of his familiarity with your waterways. Now he has two powerful men pulling his strings like a marionette—one wants to destroy your family and claim the Willows, and one will allow any depredation to befall the region as long as he gets his military victory."

"I know all that already. Tell me why they hate us! Tell me who marked my brother!"

Arthur hung his head and groaned. "Ironically, your grandfather did."

"What?" Frannie asked incredulously.

"Your brother's birthmark . . . the heart. Caleb told me about it. The very sign that blessed your brother is most likely what marked him as well."

"But . . . but why? It doesn't make any sense."

"I can't waste time explaining my suspicions to you." He framed her face with his hands and gazed intently into her eyes. "I must go now, Frannie, and I need you to trust me."

Frannie felt limp and powerless. "Two men have returned my trust with betrayal. I sought the love of one and the help of the other. Both turned on me. Dupree was one of those men, Mr. Benson, so consider carefully that you are asking me to offer you what is most precious to me."

Arthur's eyes were moist as he pulled her brow to his. "I'm an imperfect man beset by my own devils, Frannie. I came here seeking redemption and forgiveness, so I cannot promise that I will never disappoint you, but I can promise that I am dedicated to your protection."

"Can't you tell me where you are going or whom are you seeking?"

Arthur looked away from her. "Those are among the very answers that would disappoint you. If my suspicions prove true, this situation has sprung from a simple misunderstanding. If so, I may be able to reason with the parties and settle the matter without bloodshed."

"Blood has already been shed, Arthur."

"It will have been but a speck compared to what is planned," he groaned.

"All the more reason to answer my questions. I'll trust you, but you must trust me. I'm not one to defer my own safety into another's hands while I sit and fret. I need something, Arthur—at least a name I can listen for and against which my family can defend itself!"

"Of course you do," he conceded heavily. He groaned and rubbed a hand across his tense brow. "The man behind Dupree is named . . ." He closed his eyes and swallowed hard, the painfulness of his disclosure evident. "His name is Stephen Ramsey."

Frannie placed her hands on either side of his face and pressed her cheek to his. "Thank you, Arthur. Thank you." As she pulled away, sadness filled his eyes. "Will I see you again?" she asked.

"Just go now, Frannie." She began to protest, but he closed his eyes and pled with her, "Please, Frannie. Just go." His emotions were too raw to allow the moment to linger, but he found it equally agonizing to watch her depart, knowing that he might never see her again.

He sat heavily upon the steps to attend to his aching shoulder. A melancholy smile broke across his lips at the sight of the medical kit Frannie had left for him. He brought the strip of cotton to his nose and smiled freely now at the trick he had unwittingly played with her, brushing it against her wrist, purloining the essence of her perfume onto the fabric which he now savored. He tucked the scented fabric into his pocket and unbuttoned the shirt until he could easily slide the fabric away, baring his shoulder. He examined the bandage, and pleased that it showed no trace of discoloration, he rotated his shoulder joint to ease its stiffness. Before replacing his shirt, he craned his neck to see the back side of his shoulder, anticipating the ache the action would cause. The physical discomfort was measurable, but the ache in his heart was far worse. Gingerly and regretfully, he traced the outline of his own heart-shaped birthmark.

* * *

Arthur arrived in Calverton before dusk and checked into a rooming house, pacing back and forth across the floor as he tried to make sense of the situation. When no reasonable answer came to him he knew his only option was to confront his father, so he calculated and recalculated the dates. He was to report to duty in Bermuda on the eighteenth day of May, giving him ample time to return to England, but not enough to also sail to Bermuda to meet his date of deployment. Seeing his limited options, he sat at the desk to write a letter.

> *April 23, 1813*
> *Maryland, United States of America*
>
> *Dear Father,*
> *As you can see, I have come to the very axis of our dispute. I have met Jonathan Pearson's granddaughter and observed firsthand not only their fine farm but also the nature and character of this family. They are outstanding people, and I implore you with the strength of my every faculty to call off Dupree and discontinue your retributive plans, for they are unwarranted and evil.*

Tell me, Father, what is truly at the crux of your enmity for these people? You claim that but for your mother's poor judgment and a twist of luck, what the Pearsons have might have fallen to your family. I say that in very deed it did, for I believe these people are your family, Father, for they too bear the same mark of birth you passed down to me. How is this possible?

Stop Dupree, Father, and quickly answer my questions. I believe I am owed these things.

Arthur

CHAPTER 27

May 5, 1813
The Prison Camp at Lachine, Quebec

Dudley sensed a change in the attitude of the guards. They'd never been gregarious with the prisoners, nevertheless, there had been a few, like Captain Quartermain, who had made a point to be courteous and who tried whenever possible to offer more palatable rations, but something had changed. The coldness of their captors was the first sign, and then the prisoners' meager rations deteriorated. Not a scrap of meat had been seen for days, not so much as a shred in the broth which was served with moldy bread and wormy beans. Fearing starvation, the Americans ate what was offered, and soon the entire lot of them were suffering with diarrhea while their officers, Dudley in particular, pled with the British—in the name of humanity—for some decent bread.

"My men are sick . . . some are near death from dehydration!" Dudley had explained.

"Far as I'm concerned, one dead American is one less to feed!" came the guard's retort.

"In the name of heaven, sir!" pled Dudley to the guard, who in response angrily swung the empty pot around, clipping Dudley along his cheek. His head jerked sideways as a sharp pain radiated along his neck and shoulder. Stumbling weakly in a long, drunken spiral, his legs failed him and he sank to the frosty ground in a pool of mud and blood. When he came to, he was lying on a cot near a coal stove. Captain Quartermain was leaning over him, examining the gash in his head.

"I think you'll be all right," the British officer reported brusquely.

Dudley tried to sit up, but the effort nauseated him, and he fell back again.

"As soon as you're able, get back to your men. All things considered, I think it wise."

"Has something happened, Captain? I recognize that we are enemies of war, but I . . . I thought that as men we had . . ."

Captain Quartermain's face remained grave. "Something *has* happened, Major. The American forces sacked our capital at York. They laid torches to nearly everything, sparing only a few buildings that would otherwise have left widows and their children homeless and without any means. They killed good men there, too, many of whom were citizens only and very dear to the soldiers here at Fort Lachine. So now you understand why our mood is dour. And if the food is not to your liking, know that this assault has interrupted *our* supplies as well."

Dudley closed his eyes, his pounding head barely able to process the news, but the word *York* caught his immediate attention, bringing him up fast. "York? Wasn't that where—"

"Where Miss Peddicord and her father were sent? Yes. It was."

The blood drained from Dudley's face as two scenes came to his mind. In both, Laura Peddicord looked frightened and alone, and both times—the moment when he informed her about the secret letter in the book, and after she had been informed she was being exiled to York—he had been at the crux of her troubles. "Have you any word regarding her? Is she safe?"

Quartermain's face softened with compassion. "No. I have no information at this time."

Urgency filled Dudley's eyes as he searched for a bucket. Quartermain tossed him a towel, and Dudley vomited and dry heaved as the officer turned to go. He paused and looked back at his prisoner. "You were right, Major Snowden. In another place . . . another situation, I believe we could have been friends, but this assault has changed everything. I'm afraid it will have dire repercussions for all sides. Britain will not allow such an assault to go unpunished, and the retribution will likely be grave indeed."

Dudley wiped his mouth clean and swung his legs around, determined to stand. "Will you tell me, sir, if you hear anything regarding Miss Peddicord?"

The officer diverted his eyes before looking at Dudley. "You will not be here long, Major. A prisoner exchange is planned. Because of your rank, you'll be one of those bartered for our men. Those not exchanged will be sent to Melville Island Prison in Halifax, Nova Scotia."

The news of his intended release brought no peace to his guilty heart. "I decline release, Captain. Send another soldier home to his family in my stead. Allow me to write one letter, and then I'll go to Halifax."

CHAPTER 28

May 7, 1813
Burlington, Vermont

Hannah smiled and stretched under the covers, immediately reaching for her husband, whose muscled warmth she had already become so accustomed to, but empty coldness was all she found. She sat up curiously and scanned the room for him, finding him perched on the window seat with a comforter loosely draped across his bare shoulders as he stared blankly out the window. The first light of morning broke across the green meadows of New York state, and Hannah guessed such was what had drawn his attention.

"Good morning, Mr. Pearson," Hannah greeted happily as she took the remaining comforter and draped it likewise. "Couldn't you sleep?"

Jed pulled himself from his troubled musings and spread his arms wide to welcome her into the expanse of his embrace, replying deeply, "Good morning, Mrs. Pearson."

She melted against him and snuggled into the crook of his neck. "Had I known marriage was going to be this lovely, I would have allowed you to catch me sooner."

"Ha!" Jed chortled as he nuzzled her ear. "Mark those words so when my behavior warrants censure you'll remember to forgive me—before sending me out to sleep with the dogs."

"Would *I* ever do that?" she teased.

"*You,* my love, are apt to do anything!" He picked her up and playfully tossed her onto the bed, then reached for her hands in a more contemplative mood that Hannah quickly noted.

"The Willows is on your mind, isn't it? You're concerned about Dupree."

A guilty frown crossed his face. "I'm sorry. I guess I'm more worried about what's going on back there than I've admitted."

"Then we should head home, Jed. I've loved our honeymoon trip and I love this little inn, but I'll wake up to a waterfront view every day for the rest of my life."

Jed stood and attempted to divert the conversation away from talk of their return to Maryland. "So you wouldn't be terribly upset if we turned back for Tunbridge today?"

"I'm ready to return to Maryland, Jed."

"You need to resolve things with Beatrice first, Hannah."

"Very well. And I would like to see Em before I head south as well."

Hannah dressed while Jed arranged for breakfast. When she arrived downstairs she found him settling their bill with the innkeeper. They headed off at a trot past tidy residences following the south road back toward Tunbridge as it wound along the curve of Lake Champlain. Midmorning, they ate meat sandwiches and mincemeat pie packed by the inn's cook, washing the meal down with a jug of sweet tea. Jed stretched out against a rock to get a quick nap, and Hannah stared at him, admiring her husband's swarthy appearance. He wore his heavy, blue trousers and a green flannel shirt that brought out a handsome ruddiness to his complexion. He hadn't shaved that morning, nor had his dark hair been trimmed in weeks, and she wondered if she should admit how much she favored this burly look.

"Are you flirting with me, Mrs. Pearson?" Jed asked with playful innocence, enjoying her perusal of his physique.

"I most certainly am, Mr. Pearson," she teased back, continuing on more seriously. "Do you realize that during all our years growing up, you always came to the barbecues in your finery? I rather like you dressed all rugged and manly."

"So, you think this attire is rugged and manly, do you?"

"I most certainly do." She swooned comically.

"Well," chuckled Jed, "you'll soon see how truly manly a farmer can be!"

Hannah snuggled close beside him, filling him with contentment as he soaked up every detail of her face. He ran his finger along her cheek, sweeping her dark hair aside as he did. "I can't wait until this war is over so I can wake up every morning knowing you're by my side."

"Neither can I. And I'll love the Willows people, too, especially Bitty, because she's been as much a mother to you as Selma was to me. And now, after all these years, to have a husband and stepchildren to love, not to mention a child of her own! She must be elated."

Jed's face grew melancholy. "The baby may already be here by now. And Sarah and Jerome—I miss them all. You'll love them . . . and when they finally get to meet you, they'll adore you."

* * *

They stopped in Montpelier, choosing to get an early night's rest, but Jed's sleep was plagued by the same recurring images of Dupree leading a band of Redcoats down from White Oak with their cannons and guns raining fire and lead upon everything he loved. He bolted upright, and unable to return to sleep, pulled on his clothes and headed downstairs, where voices still drifted up from the dining room. An Indian boy, about ten years of age, was wiping tables and sweeping the floors as Jed entered the sparsely filled room. He stopped by the bar and gave the barkeep his order, then carried his drink, a hunk of bread, and some cheese to a table in the back corner. After a few minutes of watching the boy, Jed noticed that he wore a necklace similar to the one Charles Kittamoqund had worn the night he'd visited Jed at the Willows.

"Are you Algonquian, son?" Jed asked as he sliced a piece of cheese from the block.

The boy became apprehensive at Jed's inquiry and offered a weak nod.

"Do you know Chief Four Eagles or his son Charles Kittamoqund?"

The boy's eyes narrowed, and he become stone-faced and unwilling to answer.

"It's all right," said Jed. "My grandfather and Chief Four Eagles were friends."

Ever so slowly, the boy accepted Jed's words as true, and as he did so a smile appeared on his otherwise emotionless face. Still, when the barkeep came out from the back, he became alarmed by the sight of Jed speaking to the boy,

"Go tidy up the back room, Johnnie," he instructed the lad, who immediately obeyed. Several of the bar's patrons had turned to stare at them. The barkeep turned to Jed. "He's a good boy, mister . . . an orphan. He isn't looking for any trouble."

"Nor am I," Jed replied emphatically. "I was just admiring his necklace."

As the barkeep walked away, the other patrons' interest returned to their drinks and cards. A few minutes later a sergeant dressed in a ragged uniform came stumbling in, tripping over tables, and landed in a stool at the bar. The young boy peeked out of the curtain to see the cause of the racket, and when he did, the soldier leapt over the bar and yanked the youth out into the room by his hair, deftly withdrawing his knife from its sheath and pressing it under the boy's throat.

The frightened barkeep came out with his hands raised in the air. "If you've got a problem with Indians you can just take your business down the street, mister."

Wild-eyed and frantic, the soldier began backing up with the boy. "Where are the others hiding? In there?" he hollered, pointing to an adjacent room. "Up there?" he asked as he began backing the boy up toward the first step.

Jed slowly rose from his chair, noticing the deathly fatigue in the soldier's eyes. "He's just a boy, Sergeant, and he's all alone. We're all Americans here, so you can drop the knife."

The knife-wielding soldier jerked the boy's head up and back even further and took another step up the stairs. "Are you trying to tell me that this one's an American too? More likely he's one of Tecumseh's spies," he growled near the lad's ear. "Didn't your people get their fill of white men's blood when you scalped and tomahawked all those poor people along the River Raisin? Are you disappointed Fort Meigs didn't surrender like Frenchtown—open its gates so you could fly a flag of truce and slaughter them as well?"

Lieutenant Robertson had told Jed the unspeakable tales about Frenchtown, where a division of one thousand soldiers, most of them Kentuckians, were cut down or taken captive by a dishonorable British commander named Proctor who used his Shawnee allies to commit the worst savagery imaginable by men, even burning wounded soldiers alive in their sickbeds. "Just put your knife down there, Sergeant," Jed pled as he slowly moved toward the soldier. "That Indian never rode with Tecumseh. Look at him. He's Algonquian."

The soldier took two more steps up, and his hand began to shake as emotion overcame him. "There were so many! Different tribes . . . different dress . . . all cryin' for blood." With each recollection he retreated another step up the stairs toward Jed and Hannah's room.

Jed fingered the cheese knife, balancing it in his hand as he continued to try to negotiate. "If you want to cut your teeth on someone, save it for Proctor."

Awakened by the ruckus, Hannah suddenly appeared on the balcony. The dim light obscured her face while her long dark hair drew the man's attention. "Butchering squaw!" he hollered as he released the boy, ascending the steps with his knife poised to be thrown.

"Hannah!" Jed screamed. Unable to reach her before the man did, Jed fingered the knife in his hand and sent the blade sailing through the air. It hit the soldier in the shoulder, sending him reeling for a moment. Then, in a newly fomented rage, the man lunged for Hannah again.

Jed heard Hannah's scream, only slightly aware of a motion behind him followed by the crack of a musket, and in the next moment the raging soldier slumped to the steps in a heap. Jed ran to Hannah, then turned to survey her rescuers. Another soldier—a captain—and a frontiersman dressed in buckskin, had come through the door as Jed had flung his knife. When Jed's attempt failed, they had raised their guns against their friend, and now he was lying still.

"Thank you," Jed uttered solemnly as he clung to Hannah. "He came in here like a maniac. First he went after the Indian boy, and then he turned on my wife."

The captain's jaw drew tight, and he wiped a hand across his eyes. "Sergeant Edwards was one of the few who survived the River Raisin massacre . . . He heard the men's cries as they were burned alive. Kentucky honored those men as heroes, but Edwards said he could never go home and be honored for being the one who lived. He's never been the same."

The frontiersman removed his hat and knelt beside his friend. "He's bleeding bad, but he'll make it. Let's get him over to the doctor."

After the men carried the sergeant's body from the tavern, Jed and Hannah returned to their room. Still shaken, she lay in Jed's arms for nearly an hour before she finally fell asleep. Jed kept a protective vigil over her until her breathing became steady and deep, but no sweet peace of sleep would come to him, so he slipped back out of the room and downstairs where he found the frontiersman sitting alone at a table, lost in thought.

Jed approached him with his hand outstretched. "Sir, I'm Jed Pearson. I wanted to thank you again for saving my wife. I'm . . . sorry things turned out as they did for your friend."

"Simon Liston," he replied, returning Jed's handshake and pointing to an empty chair. "The sergeant will live, but I don't suppose a man can see what he's seen and ever be all right."

Jed understood that. Scenes from the riot in Baltimore still plagued him, images of the pillars of the community wreaking savage acts upon their neighbors. He recalled the mournful cries of those who had been mutilated, stabbed, and burned, some begging for mercy and some begging for the sweet release of death. *No, you can't ever get those images from your mind,* he silently agreed.

"Was it Tecumseh who led the massacre at the Raisin?" Jed inquired.

"No," Simon answered strongly. "Tecumseh would never sanction such a disgrace. I've sat in council with him many times. He's not what most Americans think. He's a brilliant man and an eloquent, persuasive speaker, both in native tongues and in English. He can read and write English proficiently too, and he's very fond of Hamlet." Simon chuckled. "He's even studied the Bible. I don't know many whites who are as spiritual as he."

Jed's eyebrows rose at that thought. "But . . ."

Simon raised a hand to hold Jed's question off. "He wanted to be the white man's friend. He admires and respects aspects of our culture, particularly our ability to record and print our history. Interestingly, his nation's oral history includes tales similar to the story of the children of Israel's exodus from Egypt and the miracle of Moses parting the Red Sea."

Jed shook his head in wonder. "Then how could such a man kill in cold blood?"

"In return, he asks us how the people could crucify their God."

Jed had no answer. "But are the British not as white and as flawed as we?"

"They've done a better job of keeping their promises, but we keep redrawing boundaries in violation of our treaties. In short, he doesn't trust us anymore. Oh, he knows there are honorable Americans too. In fact, he fell in love with an American girl named Rebecca Galloway and asked her to marry him, but she wanted him to adopt the white man's lifestyle. It pained him greatly to lose her, but he couldn't dishonor himself and his people by rejecting his own ways." Simon shook his head. "Defeating the British may be the easiest part of this war. It's what we do next, how we settle things with the Indians that I worry about. There are new troubles brewing in the south. Have you heard about the Creek War?"

"Not much."

"Neither have many people north of the Carolinas, but I'm afraid that might soon change. You see, the Creeks have been divided over the incursion of white man's culture into theirs. Those that chose the old ways took the name of Red Sticks and they sided with the British. Back in February, a group of Red Sticks massacred two families of white settlers along the Ohio when they were returning home to Alabama from Detroit. When the Indian agent demanded that the old chiefs hand the six warriors over to federal agents, the chiefs decided to handle the problem internally—the agent ordered their execution. That decision set the entire Creek nation off. Right now they're mostly fighting amongst themselves, but word is that the Spanish governor of Florida is getting involved. If that's the case, it'll just be a matter of time before we're drawn in."

The thought so sickened Jed that he didn't hear the barkeep approach. The proprietor began dousing the kerosene lamps, calling out, "It's midnight, gentlemen."

As the pair rose, Simon asked Jed, "Where are you headed?"

"To Tunbridge and then home to Maryland."

"Maryland?" Simon repeated with concern. "As I hear it, the British are setting the Chesapeake shores aflame. Cockburn brought several warships up into the northern part of the Bay to run raids all along the coast. He even menaced Baltimore, I'm told. The city still stands, but it appears he's flexing his muscles in the hopes that Maryland will surrender to him."

Jed physically lurched from the news. "I've got to get home . . ." he groaned.

Simon drew the last swallow and banged the glass on the table as he grabbed his hat. "Let's be done with this war so we can all get back home."

Jed's heart was whirling with thoughts of future Indian wars while he feared what Dupree and Cockburn were already doing. He opened the door and found Hannah sitting up in the bed, her long, dark waves spilling along her flannel-covered shoulders. Unprepared to speak about his concerns, he smiled and went to the window to stare out at the moonlit yard as he lowered his suspenders. His wife was soon standing behind him, fully in tune with his mood. She leaned across his back and softly whispered in his ear. "Don't worry, my sweet. I'm fine."

He was inconsolable. "What if they hadn't arrived when they did, Hannah? I can't get that question out of my mind. I couldn't protect you. I tried, but I failed. What if . . ."

"I'm fine, Jed. Regardless by whose hand, I was protected. That's what matters."

He sat on the window seat with Hannah beside him, leaning his head to the side in futility until it rested upon hers. "Can I tell you a secret?" he whispered softly.

Hannah kissed his neck and whispered back, "Anything."

"I'm afraid sometimes. There are moments when this life seems too much for me to manage, and I feel powerless, as if I'm more child than man, casting stones at laughing giants."

She wrapped her arms around his neck, pressing her cheek to his. "Must I fear that if our children fall or if harm comes to them in any way, you will love me less or mistrust me?"

He turned to face her and combed her dark locks away from her face. "Of course not!"

"Then don't berate yourself or count my love any more fickle." She grabbed the cleft of his chin and squeezed it playfully. "We are young, Jed, and we must allow that we are still learning. Courage we have, and wisdom will come a lesson at a time, my darling husband, but let us not squander this pleasant season of youth to be so very old today."

He pulled her close and kissed her cheek. "I feel as if I were born an old, old man. It is only with you that I feel that weight lift. That's why I can't ever let anything happen to you."

* * *

They arrived in Tunbridge the following day as the first streaks of sunset kissed the freshly harrowed fields. Their first inquiry provided directions to the residence of Stephen Mack, who was a celebrity of sorts in the community for being a veteran of two wars and a highly successful entrepreneur. They passed the schoolhouse and the Universalist Association building.

"The Universalists . . ." mused Jed. "There are so many churches and religions. We'll soon need to align ourselves with one or another, I suppose. Which would you prefer?"

"Can't we just study the Bible for now?"

"That's fine with me, but don't we need a clergyman to officiate at baptisms and such?"

"Well . . . yes, but let's visit several churches before making up our minds. I would like to find a religion whose teachings bless its members as much as scold them."

"We will," Jed assured her as they rolled into the village of Tunbridge proper. They passed frame homes and merchant shops. "We just passed the village store," said Jed.

"Then we're very close." A few minutes later she pointed. "I think that's it."

An inviting residence surrounded by finely appointed barns and outbuildings sat beside a stream spanned by a small bridge. Jed set the wagon brake, and as he helped Hannah down, a young lady of about eight years came to the door to survey the family's guests.

"Momma! We have company!"

A maid came to the door, scolding the child. "Almira Mack! Is that any way for the captain's daughter to behave? Now go tell your momma in a proper fashion!" She turned to Hannah, saying, "And it's clear to see that you must be Mrs. Snowden's sister! Please, come in."

"Are either Mrs. Mack or Mrs. Snowden in?" inquired Hannah.

Her answer came as both women entered the foyer. "Hannah!" Beatrice called out, her eyes shifting curiously between a beaming Jed and Hannah, who remained cool and polite. When Beatrice took her hands and noticed the emerald ring on her sister's left hand, she fought back tears. "So you're married. I assumed as much when so much time had passed." She leaned in to embrace Hannah, but her sister remained detached, prompting a hurried release.

Visibly embarrassed by the stilted moment, Beatrice blushed, and Jed rushed in with a warm hug and joyful greeting. "Hello, Mrs. Snowden. It's wonderful to see you again."

Beatrice wiped at her eyes and suddenly remembered her hostess. "We're family now. You must call me Beatrice," she gushed. "And where are my manners?" She took Temperance Mack's arm and led her forward. "Please allow me to introduce Mrs. Stephen Mack. Temperance, this is my youngest sister, Hannah, and her new husband, Lieutenant Jonathan Pearson."

Temperance Mack was a woman in her mid-forties with slight streaks of gray in her hair. Elegantly dressed, though modest and subdued in her demeanor, she offered her gentle hand and Jed bowed and kissed it. "Mrs. Mack, lovely to meet you. You have an exquisite home."

"Thank you, Mr. Pearson . . . the blessing of marrying a merchant." She laughed.

"Indeed, but I hear he is far more than a mere merchant."

"Yes, far more. This place is a veritable museum of Stephen's adventures and travels. Perhaps you would allow me to give you a tour of the house while your wife and Mrs. Snowden chat."

Jed crooked his arm to the woman, raising a cautioning eyebrow to Hannah, entreating her to be courteous. Hoping for the best, he allowed Mrs. Mack to lead him into the formal parlor. With its imported Wilton woolen rug and its upholstered mahogany furnishings, this room was clearly a space set aside less for living than for viewing. Mrs. Mack led the way, guiding Jed to a large, framed portrait of a handsome man in military garb. "This is Stephen before he left for Detroit." She then lifted a smaller portrait of a tall, rail-thin boy in his teens wearing a gun belt and hoisting a musket across his shoulders. "And this was Stephen as a privateer during the Revolutionary War," she added affectionately. "He served with his father and brother Jason."

"He was just a boy . . ." muttered Jed.

"Seventeen. By then he had already been engaged in many battles on both land and sea. He looks even younger than his years because he nearly starved to death on some campaigns. He tells a story about how during one occasion, when their ship's rigging was cut away, he and the cabin boys escaped to shore to a house where a woman was frying sweet cakes in the skillet. The cannon fire followed them up to the house, and the woman chose to retire into the cellar, inviting the boys to eat the cakes if they were of a mind to. The lads were so hungry they stood amidst the deadly barrage, frying and eating the cakes until they'd had their fill."

Jed chuckled with incredulity. "I hold such men in the highest regard, madam."

She nodded. "Stephen sacrifices the society of his family, laboring to open up the wilderness in order to allow us to remain here enjoying the comforts of town life and our family associations. He absolutely insists the children receive the finest education possible. Our son, Stephen Jr., is currently in school in Boston, though I assume once he graduates and his father returns from the war, he will head west to help my husband manage all his business ventures."

The comment confused Jed. "I'm sorry. Isn't Captain Mack here? I was under the impression he and the militia were pardoned after Detroit fell."

"They were, but Stephen was promoted to major and ordered to Frenchtown to handle the exchange of the American prisoners who survived the massacre at the River Raisin."

"The River Raisin massacre?" he gasped. "I've heard reports but . . . I can't imagine . . ."

"Stephen has spared us the details to protect us. I know he's anxious for the assignment to end so he can build his planned city in Michigan where we'll be together. Family duties make us capable of many hard things, Mr. Pearson, as you well know. When I think of what Mrs. Snowden has done for love, and that Miss Stansbury abandoned all to accompany her . . . And you, Mr. Pearson, I know you are a good man. Beatrice had hoped to hear that you two were wed."

Jed dipped his head graciously. "We are so grateful for your kindness to Mrs. Snowden."

"It's been my delight. She's an admirable woman, and her company is most welcome." Jed shifted feet, and Mrs. Mack noticed the worry on his face. "Is something amiss, sir?"

"I wondered if I might impose further upon you, Mrs. Mack."

Mrs. Mack pointed to a velvet-covered chair near the piano. "Please sit and let us chat."

* * *

The women made idle small talk while the maid puttered around setting up tea. When she left, Beatrice invited Hannah to sit, but the younger sibling politely declined.

"Air your complaints so we can determine what is left between us," directed Beatrice.

Hannah scarcely knew how to proceed. "Your meddling altered my life, Beatrice!"

"I have already admitted to being indefensible on that point," Beatrice replied contritely. "My thinking was entirely twisted . . . to try to mold your life to meet Mother's wishes to secure her approval for you and to earn all of us her love, as destructive as it is. I also confess that were I to return to Maryland, I would likely fall back under her spell. That is why I am selling the Baltimore home as soon as it's repaired and am buying a home here in Tunbridge."

"Beatrice!" Hannah wailed, her anger now completely diluted in the news. "You're much stronger now. If you do this we'll never see one another, and how will Dudley find you?"

"Dudley is being moved to a prison in Nova Scotia, and though Captain Mack remains in Michigan, Dudley still thinks we should make a fresh start here when he is finally free."

Hannah crumpled by her sister's chair, laying her head upon her lap. "Please don't do this, Beatrice. I love you and I fully forgive you. Please come home with us."

"No, you have Jed now, and you are able to stand up to Myrna. If you desire it, you can establish a new bond with her. Despite her rigidness, she adores you and she will adjust to your marriage in time. And no amount of distance can alter our love. That will never change."

Beatrice saw Jed and Mrs. Mack appear in the doorway. "And now that you are the wife of the wealthy Mr. Pearson, I believe you can convince him to bring you north for regular visits."

Hannah looked to her husband and saw a hard set to his jaw. "What's wrong, Jed?"

He brightened with feigned happiness and cleared his throat. "Nothing is wrong. Everything is wonderful. It pleases me to see you and Beatrice together again. In fact, I'm . . . willing to share you with your sister . . . and . . . Mrs. Mack is delighted to have you as well."

Something in his voice made Hannah dubious about his motives. "And you?"

His features looked drawn and his eyes pled with her. "I need to get back to Maryland."

Hannah faced him squarely and set her jaw. "Then we'd best be on our way," she announced as she rose and headed for the door.

Jed took her arm to implore her. "No, Hannah. I want you to remain here where you're safe." However, with one sharp spin, Hannah broke free. Jed gawked from Hannah to Beatrice and back to Hannah as his wife said her good-byes, hurried through the door, and got into the buggy. "You're being foolish, Hannah, and you're risking what matters most to me."

"I could say the same. Are you not what matters most to me? Beatrice and Myrna tried to choose what was best for me. Don't you be guilty of doing the same, Mr. Pearson!"

Jed groaned as he snapped the reins. "Very well, Mrs. Pearson."

It was a quiet fifteen-mile trip to Hanover. Hannah noticed how tightly Jed was gripping the reins, and each time she dared glance at him, she saw the lines deepen along his brow. She began to regret her stubbornness, but as soon as she laid a hand on her husband's knee, he shifted the reins to one hand, covered hers with his own, and the tension released between them.

In West Lebanon they rounded a bend near the Smith home and Hannah saw Emmett sitting in his buggy out in front. She turned to Jed. "Could I have just a minute . . ."

"Of course. Who knows how soon you'll be back again."

He set the brake and helped Hannah down.

Grabbing his hand, she led him to Reverend Schultz's wagon. "Em!" she squealed as she climbed onto the wagon seat to hug the man.

"Hannah? Or should I say, 'Mrs. Pearson'? I hear the happiness in your voice."

"Hello again, sir," said Jed. "Thank you for helping me find her."

"Mr. Pearson! As soon as I met you, I knew you and Hannah were meant to be together."

"Thank you, sir," Jed offered. "I'll leave you two old friends to visit."

Once Jed left, Hannah asked Emmett, "How is Zachary? Is he still The Smith boy's physician?"

"I've never seen him more satisfied in his work and as a man. This child, Joseph, has captured his heart. And though he is still lame, it appears the surgery will be a success. Bless his poor mother. She carries him about, and when she does not, his brothers and father ferry him to and fro. Zachary says it will be months, perhaps even years, before he will be able to walk unassisted. Bone fragments—remnants of the surgery—are still surfacing, breaking through the wound and delaying healing, but he remains cheerful. Zachary is amazed by him."

"And how is Mrs. Smith? Jed and I cannot stay long, but I did want to see her."

"She's in the woods, I believe. She goes there to pray. She says that in a household as busy as hers, it is her only chance to find solitude. Now what of Beatrice? Is she well?"

"She is doing as well as possible under her circumstances."

Emmett nodded his understanding. "We've shared a lot in our little time together, Hannah. I've heard about the troubles in Maryland. I assume that's why you're hurrying home?"

"Yes. Jed wants me to stay here where he thinks I'll be safer, but . . ."

"But you can't bear to be parted again. I understand these feelings. Go with faith, Hannah. I'll make your regrets to Zachary and the Smiths. The Lord has need of you, and He will keep you safe until your work is accomplished, but if you can bear some uninvited advice . . . remain in touch with this family. They have many spiritual insights that greatly intrigue me and my grandson. I . . . I think they can help answer many of your questions as well."

"I will, Em. I surely will." Hannah kissed Emmett on the cheek and climbed into the buggy with her husband when he returned, unsure when or if she would ever see her friends again.

CHAPTER 29

May 19, 1813
London, England

> *I have met Jonathan Pearson's granddaughter . . .*

Stephen Ramsey read his son's letter for the third time to fully comprehend it. The news had instantly incensed him, that in an effort to thwart his father's plans, Arthur had placed himself in harm's way where Dupree's sights were set. But no amount of displeasure could detach Stephen Ramsey's heart from his son. He knew that without question.

Something else in the letter tore at him even more as he reread it.

> *I believe these people are your family, Father, for they too bear*
> *the same mark of birth you passed down to me. How is this*
> *possible?*

"The heart?" he muttered in wonderment.

He had never known his mother's people, so the only key to his miserable fate had been Grandma Ramsey's tales of how her simple boy had won the hand of Bridget Lane, the woman who spurned Jonathan Pearson, her neighbor's educated son. Curiously, the source of his grandmother's joy had been the source of Stephen's anguish, for after rebuffing the Pearson's prodigy, his mother chose Stephen's father—the Ramsey's uneducated and equally uninspired offspring.

> *Why? Though she was a housemaid she was lovely . . . she was*
> *intelligent . . .*

He remembered how she would gather her six babies together to read to them from the great literary masters in a tongue that was eloquent and poised. She embellished their austere world by helping them pretend that the heart-shaped birthmark he and his mother shared was a noble's crest. The tender memory pained him. *What she could have been . . . What we could have been . . .*

Accepting his fate had been unthinkable; so in his childhood, as a dock rat running wild along the wharf, he'd internalized the game, dreaming that his mother was a duchess secretly hidden in Liverpool for safety, and that one day a nobleman would sail into the harbor on an exquisite ship to claim his daughter and her poor children and carry them away to his castle to live.

He knew it was likely the desperation with which he had clung to these childish notions that made him so bitter when, at age eight, his father had indentured him on a filthy merchant ship, and then again at age sixteen when he finally learned what Jonathan Pearson had become.

Why had his sainted mother spurned the prince for the pauper? As a young man coming into his own, he could imagine only one answer—perhaps Pearson was a rake and a libertine!

With such a simplistic analysis, he'd attained the moral upper hand. The Pearson devil had prospered, requiring biblical justice, and he, sixteen-year-old Stephen Ramsey, imagined himself as Pearson's judge, a boy archangel merely answering the demands of the law, allowing Providence to restore to him what had been denied. On the day he reached this conclusion, his childhood dreaming ended and the space those sweet imaginings once filled was replaced by machinations to recover his losses. He knew how crazed it sounded when each thought was explicitly detailed, but he couldn't deny how ingrained those notions had become in him.

> *. . . these people . . . bear the same mark of birth you passed down to me . . .*

Stephen Ramsey remembered the bedtime tales his mother told about the noble House of Ensor. She knew every noble and all their exploits back six generations. *How?* he asked himself as a curious image came to mind. He pulled the stack of payment notes from his desk drawer, leafing through them, paying special attention to the family crest pressed into the wax on each. When he came to Lord Ensor's note he felt a curious chill run down his spine. Why had he not noticed it before? The Ensor crest included an oddly shaped heart—a shape very similarly to the mark found on his shoulder and on Arthur's . . . and on his mother's!

While he was desperately trying to make sense of it all, the new maid knocked on the door.

"Forgive me, sir," she begged respectfully. "There's a Mr. Corvas here to see you."

Stephen Ramsey scowled at the interruption caused by the new maid, Mrs. McGowan, the widow of the criminal, Trevor McGowan. Originally, he had brought the woman and her two young sons to his estate simply to monitor those who would someday represent his legacy, but their arrival had brought him unexpected consolation—except for contemplative moments such as this, when their very presence reminded him of the estrangement he suffered with his own son. "Very well, Mrs. McGowan. Show him in."

After directing Juan in, she resumed polishing the parquet floor of the grand foyer.

"I have the information you requested about your son," Juan began as soon as he entered.

"You're too late! I already know that my son is in America," Ramsey barked. "So there'll be no *favors* paid you today, Mr. Corvas!"

Juan did not flinch, knowing how desperately he needed this favor. "And the boy?"

Ramsey sighed. Knowledge of the earl's son might yet prove helpful in the future. "Your terms?"

"To achieve the dream you employed to lure me . . . to have a wife and a home and a family. I want to return to Cadiz for one month to bring the woman I love back to England."

Ramsey had no reason to deny the man. "Very well. Now tell me about the boy."

"Your son and the boy sailed to Dublin, then three days later a woman and the boy drove Arthur to the dock from which he sailed to America. Your son called the woman 'Mother.'"

"Mother?" Ramsey sputtered. "My wife, Felicity? Of course . . ." He dropped his head into his hands. *He turned to his mother to protect the boy from me.* That very confession drove a blow deep into Ramsey's heart. *What have I done?*

His son's condemnation weighed heavily on his heart as his eyes drifted back to Juan. "I have another errand for you, Mr. Corvas. Come here tomorrow, and I will have documents for you to deliver. When you return from your trip, you'll be free to travel to Cadiz."

As Juan prepared to exit, he heard the scuffle of feet hurrying away beyond the door.

"What was that?" barked Ramsey. "See if someone's been skulking about."

As Juan opened the door, he met the pleading eyes of the maid who begged his silence before quickly hastening beyond his view. Casting a glance back at Ramsey, he smirked, replying, "There's no one here."

* * *

Stephen Ramsey dispatched Mr. Corvas to Maryland with two notes—one for Dupree, canceling the plans to take the Willows, and a note to Arthur, assuring him that he had complied with his son's request. What had Arthur called his plans? *Unwarranted and evil?* He cringed as he reread the phrase, knowing his son would require a greater atonement than the miniscule efforts he had thus made. And now, the astounding revelation about the birthmark raised new questions, new breaches of trust he could not mend without paying a visit to the House of Ensor.

"Mrs. McGowan!" called Stephen. "I need my carriage readied! Mrs. McGowan!"

The maid arrived, head dipped, voice flat, avoiding his gaze. "I've sent word, sir."

Her bleak manner stung him. This day of all days he needed the cheery presence she and her sons had brought into his dreary existence. "Are you angry with me for being abrupt earlier, Mrs. McGowan?"

Raising her downcast eyes, she replied, "I appreciate the steady work here and the li'l cottage you've provided me and the boys. You know that me sons have taken to you, Mr. Ramsey. You've been real sweet with them, and they've formed an attachment to you now."

Ramsey knew he was vulnerable on this subject since, in his abject loneliness, he had allowed himself to become attached to the two little imps. Each day before leaving for their cottage, their mother would bring them by to recite a few words of gratitude for his benevolence or to sing a little ditty. In truth, he was equally intrigued by the woman—the abused wife of a miscreant, yet so devoted to her sons and her husband's memory. It was another painful topic, reminding him that Felicity had shown him no such loyalty, while stirring raw memories of his own mother's love. In angst he turned away to stare out the window before asking, "Your point, Mrs. McGowan?"

"Life 'ere is the best we've ever 'ad, sir, but I can't forget what price me 'usband paid for these comforts. I know reconcilin' with your Arthur would adversely impact my boys' futures. Still, I've no desire to begrudge you the company of your own son, but that bein' the case . . ."

Ramsey's heart skipped a beat, fearing she would take her boys and leave . . .

". . . I was wonderin' if there could be some allowance for an education for me boys."

The relief Ramsey felt was physical, yet he struggled to bridle his joy. "I'll see to the hiring of a tutor, and if they show promise, we'll discuss boarding schools for the future . . ." Needing to secure his position, he dared make a request of his own. "But in return I'll want a hand in the rearing of these boys, since they'll someday represent a portion of my legacy."

"You'll respect that I'm their mother and not try to take them away from me?"

"No, madam," he replied, careful not to frighten the woman.

* * *

After mailing his letters, Arthur had boarded a ship for Bermuda, praying each moment that his father would stay Dupree's hand and spare the Willows until he could meet with Major Ross and explain the situation to the very man who would coordinate the Chesapeake ground assault. On May 19, upon his first view of Bermuda with her white sandy shores and iridescent waters, he thought he was in paradise, but as soon as he landed and headed for the fort entrance, he passed a regiment of dark-skinned soldiers, freed slaves he supposed, and he felt the intensity of war preparations all around him. He presented his orders and made inquiries regarding Major General Ross, and the response turned his comfort to concern as the guard directed him to report to Admiral Warren, the commander of all naval operations against America.

A young ensign escorted him to the junior officers' barracks where he found his belongings set under a cot. "These arrived several weeks ago, sir. After you're dressed I'll escort you to Admiral Warren's office."

Arthur dressed quickly. Once inside the admiral's office, he shot to attention, snapping his hand to his head in a salute. "Second Lieutenant Arthur Ramsey reporting for duty, sir."

"At ease, Lieutenant," directed the aged admiral as he read through the lieutenant's orders. "Lord Whittington afforded you the highest of recommendations, and you come at a time when your services are most needed. I understand you speak French?"

"Spanish and Portuguese also, sir."

"I'm only interested in your ability to speak French. I understand you were a student of Divinity, yet you did not pursue the clergy. Do you not still consider yourself a man of God?"

"I do still strive to live by the example Christ set, if that is what you are asking me, sir."

"It is, Lieutenant. You see, I am at a very difficult crossroads. We're spread too far in too many conflicts, causing us to resort to some unorthodox tactics. You may have heard that we are forming regiments of freed slaves. In return for their service we offer land here or in Trinidad." The admiral stood and strode to a large map of the Chesapeake Bay. "We are also about to deploy two regiments of the Chasseurs Britannique, pulled from Dartmoor Prison."

Arthur paled at this mention of using French military prisoners as soldiers for Britain.

"I see you've already heard about the French solders' reputation for brutality in Spain. Though we have nothing but their desire not to return to prison to keep them in line, they will be serving under Sir Sydney Beckwith's command commencing in a battle at Craney Island." He pointed to a spot in the Virginia waters of the Chesapeake Bay, then returned to his seat.

"The Admiralty thinks I have been too lenient with the Americans, and I've now been ordered to make an example of the Chesapeake forces to repay their burning of York. Unlike Admiral Cockburn, I take no pleasure in terrorizing the citizenry, but it will be hard to control these Frenchmen. That's why I'm bringing you along. Your command of French, your sense of honor . . . I need you on the ground, reporting to me and recording the events so that I may have an honest appraisal of the military value of using these French prisoners."

Arthur saw his ability to stop Dupree thwarted. "I'm to be assigned to Major Ross, sir . . . to the Maryland campaign."

"And so you shall," Admiral Warren replied curtly. "The major is still recuperating from his injuries and will join us later in the upper Chesapeake when those engagements occur. We will transfer you back to his command when that time comes."

Beads of sweat formed on Arthur's brow. "And when do you think that might be, sir?"

Admiral Warren scowled at Arthur. "I know you're not a regular soldier, Lieutenant . . . that you're a man of letters rather than combat, but allow me to explain a few things to you. We are working with certain Americans—peace men they call themselves—who want to help us. Primarily prevalent in New England, they want an end to this war so they can again engage in free trade, and to that end they have helped us identify American merchants and ship owners willing to circumvent the law by providing food and goods to British forces. They've supplied critical tactical information regarding General Smith's Baltimore defenses and the militia buildup in the city and in Fort McHenry. That's why we've stalled our assault there, but in so doing, Cockburn turned his rapacious attentions to plundering small towns, and now these peace men and their Peace Party have grown noticeably silent. At the very best, they are being cautious, and at the very worst, we fear their sympathies are changing. We need a decisive victory in Virginia, but we need to do it honorably, so in answer to your question, we sail tomorrow for the lower Chesapeake, but when the campaign against the upper Chesapeake begins will depend greatly on our success in the south. I can offer you no timetable other than that."

CHAPTER 30

June 1, 1813
Hampton, Virginia

"Ahhh!" cooed Drusilla O'Malley. "Lyra Harkin, you're an absolute vision. Markus won't be able to get through eatin' the gander at the wedding feast for wantin' to take you in his arms on the spot."

Lyra blushed and touched her hair. "You're sure now? You'd not pull the leg of a blind woman on her weddin' day just to make her feel good, would ya?"

Drusilla hugged her. "Because I love ya so much, I might. But it clearly isn't needed."

"Now tell me why it is that you fine Irish ladies roast a gander for the groom the afternoon of the weddin," asked Patrick. "Is it a sign that his own goose is actually cooked?"

"Oh, you! Now hurry and change your shirt. Markus and your da will be here soon!"

Lyra heard a sound outside and rose quickly to her feet, fumbling nervously with her hands. "He's here, Drusilla! He's here!"

"Be calm!" Drusilla screeched, linking her arm in Lyra's for support. "Now breathe," she directed as the simultaneous creak of the door met the gush of approval from Markus.

He walked to his bride and stood inches from her, delicately tracing her face as if reassuring himself that she was real. "You're beautiful," he said breathlessly, placing a soft kiss on her lips.

Again, Lyra blushed and dipped her head humbly. "It's my Irish mother's weddin' dress. I'm very grateful for the Harkins, but today I feel as though my Irish parents are also with me."

"Well, we'd best get to eatin'," Drusilla said as she sniffled. "We've got a weddin' in two hours!"

The traditional goose-eating supper was long and lavish and filled with happy banter. Despite the revelry, Patrick noticed the conspicuous quietness of his father.

"Aren't you well, Da? You've barely said a word throughout the meal."

Ryan's eyes began to shine. "Can't a man be touched?" he argued unconvincingly as he popped up from his seat. Anyway, isn't it time for we men to be goin'? Let us give you a hand with these dishes, Drusilla, and then I'll scurry the groom and his attendant off to the church."

Though the uncharacteristic offer now raised Drusilla's curiosity, she was too preoccupied with last-minute details to pursue it. As the men set the dishes to soak, Drusilla tended to the food. "Take those pies and that big bowl of puddin' with you. Now, you boys remember that you're the lantern bearers tonight."

Once the men were gone, final preparations were made for the bride. "Let's check and see if we have everythin'. First of all, good weather's a very good omen. And we've sewn two bells on the sleeves of your dress for good luck, and here's your white handkerchief that we'll turn into a bonnet for you're first bairn."

"And my horseshoe wristlet. It's on the pie stand."

Drusilla retrieved the starched piece of linen. Shaped like a horseshoe and strung on a ribbon, she tied it on Lyra's wrist and reported, "I believe you've got enough lucky charms, my dear." She then set the veil, which was held in place by a wreath of flowers, over Lyra's porcelain face. "Here's your bouquet," she said, placing it in Lyra's trembling hands. "Are you ready?"

Lyra took a deep breath and smiled. "So much more than ready."

Drusilla picked up the baby and signaled to the boys. "Martin? Sean? Get your lamps!"

As they headed out the door, Lyra began counting the steps to ease her nerves. "Twenty-three steps down the walk, then make a left," she rehearsed aloud as they walked. A few seconds later she added, "Forty-two steps and a left turn takes me to my new little cottage." She beamed as the two boys giggled. "But straight another sixty-three steps and a turn to the left puts me on the path to the *Irish Lass,* across from Little England farm. But if I just keep goin' straight . . ."

She stopped in her tracks as the first strains of music began lilting from the church. "Oh, squeeze my hand, Drusilla! We can't be there already, can we? Are we at the church?"

"Yes we are, Lyra darlin'." Drusilla laughed.

"Oh . . . describe it for me . . . Tell me everything."

Drusilla's eyes began to sting as she laid out in beautiful detail the images for the blind bride. "There are lanterns stretched along the walk for you, Lyra, and flowers strewn in the center. The chapel doors are flung wide open, and all the people are turned in their pews just beamin' at ya. Ryan has his elbow crooked to walk you down the aisle, and candles are blazin' along the walls. And there, in front, is Markus with Patrick by his side."

"Does Markus see me yet?"

Drusilla wiped another tear away. "Aye, he does. Twice Patrick's had to hold him back. He has tears in his eyes, Lyra. If ever a man loved a woman, Markus does indeed love you."

* * *

Father O'Halloran spoke sweetly about the couple and delivered the service with Markus's hand protectively clinging to Lyra's. After the vows were exchanged a final prayer was offered, then the priest declared them man and wife. Markus carefully peeled the veil back and framed Lyra's face as he drew her near him. "Here's an Irish vow, just for thy ears, my love: By the power that Christ brought from heaven, mayst thou love me. As the sun follows its course, mayst thou follow me. As light to the eye, as bread to the hungry, as joy to the heart, may thy presence be with me, oh, one that I love, 'til death comes to part us asunder. I'll love you every day of my life . . . 'til the day I die," he whispered to her.

"Oh, much longer than that, Markus O'Malley. After all, what is heaven if not this?"

"Indeed, Mrs. O'Malley. Indeed." And then he drew her to him and kissed his wife.

The guests rang bells as they followed the couple out of the church and into the grove. Someone handed Lyra an old shoe for good luck, and the crowd cheered as she tossed it over her shoulder. Despite the revelry, Patrick noticed his father hanging back, and he confronted him.

"Weddings are happy occasions. So why do you look like you've see the grim reaper?"

Ryan pulled his son aside. "The British are regrouping in the mouth of the bay."

"What do you mean? New ships too?"

"Shhh . . . Twelve frigates and eight warships are joinin' all their other vessels."

"Then we need to warn the others!"

"They already know. Weren't you curious about the sudden outbreak of the grippe?"

"And what do we tell Markus?"

Ryan eyes teared again. "Let's give the poor dears their weddin' night at least, shall we?"

Lanterns and torches lit the wedding party as Father O'Halloran blessed the food and offered a toast to the happy couple. As the music began, Markus bent to carry Lyra away, but she protested. "Fairies love to collect brides. If you lift me off the ground they can spirit me away!"

"Not my Irish sprite." Calling to Ryan he asked, "How many brides have you seen carried away by fairies?" Markus finally noticed the gloom permeating his uncle's countenance, and then he looked to Patrick and saw the same. He began mentally listing the missing men's faces and, fearful of the news that would explain it all, he held Lyra even closer.

Lyra stopped to speak with Drusilla, and Markus headed for the men, barking, "Out with it!"

Ryan shook his head in defeat and came up scowling. "Name it, and it's worse than that. There're twenty frigates and warships plus a grand assortment of others all congregatin' at the mouth of the bay. Gosport Naval Yard is ready to protect Norfolk, and Captain Tarbell and the *Constellation* are protectin' the Elizabeth River, plus some of her sailors are goin' to defend Craney Island. Between Craney's shallow waters and the blockade by Lambert's Point, no big vessels will be able to sail in there. Now Hampton and the James River are altogether different. All we have to protect us is a few hundred bayonets on Point Comfort and the militia batteries at Little England Farm. The battery has seven guns—four sixes, two twelves, and an eighteen pounder. They'll have to sail through shallow waters, so if they come, it'll be in low-draft vessels."

"Then we'd best go and reinforce Little England's battery!" said Markus. "We can sight the approach of ships up the James and blast the devils if they make a run on Hampton."

"Clear your mind of this for tonight," counseled Ryan, "and give Lyra a proper weddin' night. This trouble's goin' to be here for a while."

After a pause and a somber nod, Markus agreed, though it was with a heavy heart that he returned to his bride. "You're awfully quiet tonight," she observed teasingly. "I wouldn't have taken you for a nervous groom."

Markus responded with a blush and a chuckle. "Will you always be this open with every thought that crosses your mind? I didn't think we'd be discussin' the matter beforehand."

"Who says it's beforehand?"

He smiled an ornery little smile. "Are you sayin' you're ready to leave the festivities?"

"Oh no," she replied seriously. "Just the party."

Markus pressed his lips close to her ear and asked, "Is there any danger of fairies croppin' up if I pick my wife up and carry her away now?"

"None to which I'm aware," Lyra answered soberly, eventually releasing a wide smile.

Markus scooped her up in his arms and brought her lips to his in a long, passionate kiss that set the guests off in another loud cheer. "We'll be takin' our leave now," he announced.

He set her down when they crossed the threshold of their cottage and closed the door. Then, gently lifting the floral wreath from her head, he released her hair from the pins that bound it, running his fingers through her long tresses as her eyes closed in delight. Wrapping his fingers behind her neck, he drew her close and pressed his lips to hers again. Suddenly, out in the yard, a riotous noise erupted. Pots banged, bells chimed, and voices hooted and sang as loud as possible.

With their lips still pressed, they both began to laugh until the passion faded into humor.

"So how long do shivarees generally last around here?" asked Markus, chuckling.

"It all depends on the guests. Sometimes they stop quickly if you go out and show them that they've succeeded in interruptin' things," Lyra whispered through their kiss.

Markus shook his head and embraced her more tightly as he reveled in the joyful noise of their loving celebrants, knowing that soon the British would be the source of dreadful clamor.

CHAPTER 31

Early June 1813
Baltimore County, Maryland

Jed wanted to head straight south and shoot for home, but laden with Hannah's trunks and Hannah herself, his progress had been agonizingly slow. She had offered to travel separately and be ferried home by boat, but since the entire eastern coast was now under blockade as of May 26, Jed wouldn't risk her being captured by British pirates, and so they proceeded on. One morning he had awakened and found Hannah and her trunks missing. Heart pounding, fear coursing through his veins, he charged through dressing and raced barefoot down the hall to the front desk clerk. "My wife!" he demanded. "Have you seen her this morning?"

The intimidated clerk had pointed out the front window. There, dressed in a riding outfit, stood Hannah, handing money to a man upon whose wagon her trunks were loaded. Jed sprinted out the door pleading, "Hannah! Where are you going? Don't leave me!"

Sorrow had washed over her face as she hurried to reassure him. "Oh, no, darling. I've hired this man to haul my things, and the livery man will trade our rig for two good mounts and saddles, plus we'll make a little on the trade. My things are the burden slowing us down."

Jed groaned and drew her to him. "Please forgive me, Hannah. Having you with me is never a burden. But you should have spoken with me. Riding horseback for hundreds of miles is grueling, and there's no protection from the weather. I can't agree to this."

But Hannah's eyes had begged him. "Please let me try, Jed. I made you bring me along. Now let me show you that I can be your partner. If it doesn't work out we can get another rig."

And so they had begun their great adventure. They raced through small towns, resting in inns when they were able, but more enjoyably, they spent some nights under the twilight canopy of the evening sky, nestled together under blankets and listening to the sounds of the night. They discovered how little they required for happiness and, as if writing a new chapter in their life together, they established a bond of trust that surpassed anything either had known.

"What are you thinking?" Hannah asked one night while enfolded in Jed's arms.

"I wondered if the pain of our past would remain between us, limiting our ability to know the closeness we once shared, but I can't even remember the hurts. They are gone from me."

"You feel it too." She sighed, snuggling more tightly against him.

Jed kissed her mouth, clasping his hand over hers and raising their combined fist. "This is how we are together, Hannah. Not two, not just man and wife, but a more perfect whole."

* * *

That closeness was tested after they crossed the Susquehanna River near Havre de Grace. The once graceful river city appeared like a scene from Armageddon, charred and battered, the earth churned to receive its dead. The horror etched on Hannah's face assured Jed that the British behemoth's capacity to destroy his world was no longer merely a nightmare. It was reality.

Without a word he changed their course and headed west.

"Why are you heading to Coolfont?" Hannah challenged. "We won't be welcome there!"

"*You* will be. You're still their daughter, Hannah. They'll keep you safe."

Hannah urged her horse ahead and blocked Jed's way. "I ran off with Beatrice and neglected to write to them for nine months. When I return—married—I doubt they will welcome me."

Jed bit his lip to control his churning emotions. "Then I'll take you to Myrna's."

"A few nights ago you told me we were better together, Jed. Let me remain with you!"

He looked at her, and his eyes began to tear. "Not after seeing Havre de Grace, Hannah. I can't take you home to the Willows until I know what we're facing. Please don't ask that of me."

The magnitude of his concern drained the fight from her, and she conceded.

So they rode down the once stately lane which lacked for care, as did the house. The stableman, named Mobey, recognized Hannah from far off and ran toward her, calling her name.

"It sure is good to see you, Miss Hannah. We'll sure be glad to have you back."

She offered him what cheer she could. "Hello, Mobey. How are Mother and Father?"

"Yo father is fine, but yo mama . . . well, she done po'ly since you left. Miss Myrna . . . I mean, Mrs. Baumgardner, is here fo' a visit. She'll be pleased to see you."

Hannah gave Jed a last petition, but he was unchanging as he assisted her to the ground.

"I don't know if I can do this," she pleaded again. "Come with me."

He held her close and promised her, "We both know what will happen if I walk in there, but you can do this, Hannah. You're not the same person, and I'll be here if the worst happens."

Jed kissed her and brushed her hair from her face. As she headed for the front entrance she noticed the erratic opening and closing of her parents' bedroom curtain. Without seeing the face, she knew it was her mother, and all her childhood insecurities returned. She looked back at Jed to be sure the past nine months had not merely been a dream which was now depositing her back in her nightmare. The butler answered her knock at the door and then left to bring her father, but before he returned she heard her mother caterwauling from upstairs.

"So the little tramp is back, is she? I saw her with the Pearson trash . . . kissing him, letting him touch her! Ruined, she is! Just a ruined trollop. I want her out. Out I say!"

Hannah's haggard father, Bernard Stansbury, arrived, his face gaunt and showing a mix of delight and dread. He opened his arms to his baby girl and quickly sent a maid to administer a dose of medicine to his wife, Susannah, while he escorted Hannah to his study.

"Your mother is considerably worse, concluding that you and Beatrice were dying or dead." Hannah began to explain, but her father quickly jumped back in. "Oh, I know Myrna heard from you from time to time, but you can imagine the drama she brought with each letter."

Hannah's shoulders slumped. "I'm sorry, Papa. Beatrice became ill, and I did the best I could to care for her. We didn't want you and Mama to worry."

Her father meandered to the window. "You learned too well from my example. Ignore the situation and accept as little help as possible. Well, what should I expect?" he muttered.

"I'm married, Papa . . . to Jed Pearson. He can prove to you that his grandfather was not responsible for Grandmother's death. There's no reason to snub him or his family any longer."

Susannah Stansbury wailed again.

"Your mother will never accept him. You know that."

"But the truth . . ."

Bernard closed his eyes. "We heard the truth from your grandfather's own lips, but it did not alter your mother's perception, and that is why I prayed this day would not come."

"You knew? All this time? You could have told me and given me your blessing!"

"There was no blessing to give! Your mother will be tormented by your marriage, and since Coolfont is her sanctuary, you will never be welcome here again. Who is blessed by this?"

His words resounded like a pronouncement of death. "So that's that? You could turn your back on me simply because I married the man I love?"

Bernard took her in his arms for the last time. "I'll always love you," he said quietly, the emotion showing in his voice. "And if you love him enough to marry him against our advisement, that love will fill the void."

As he began walking away, it was all Hannah could do to remain on her feet, quaking as she was from heartbreak and shock. "May I ask a final favor, Papa? You told me when I was small that I could always have Selma. May I borrow a carriage and take Selma today?"

Bernard halted. "She's not well. Go see her, and I'll sign her papers over to you."

Hannah found the round, aged slave who had mothered her through her miserable childhood. She was bent over, sitting on a stool peeling potatoes and singing to herself. As soon as their eyes met, the old woman began to cry, "I knew my girl'd come back. I always knew it!"

Hannah rushed to her. "I'm taking you away, Selma, and you'll be free," she promised.

The woman clapped her hands together. "Free?" Then raising her voice heavenward, she cried out, "Thank you, sweet Jesus! At last I'm gonna be free!"

* * *

Jed began to be hopeful about Hannah's meeting until he saw Mobey leading the Stansbury's carriage. "Miss Hannah'll be out presently," he uttered. "Here's Selma's papers."

Jed opened the form and read the transfer of ownership of one slave named Selma from Bernard Stansbury to his daughter, Hannah Pearson, and wondered what had passed through the man's mind as he'd penned her married name one minute and turned her out the next. He helped Selma into the carriage, and, despite his wife's red-rimmed eyes, she offered him a brave smile.

"Father always knew the truth about Grandmother. We'll never be welcome here."

Jed was helping Hannah in when Myrna came around the corner in an obvious snit. "Father told me about your marriage; Mother is beside herself. Didn't I warn you?"

Hannah took one angry step in Myrna's direction and the woman immediately shrank back. "I know what you did, Myrna," Hannah explained calmly. "Beatrice told me everything, and *I* will now tell *you* how things will proceed. From today on, I have no family other than my husband and those who welcome us both. You choose what course our sisterhood shall follow, for unless your opinion changes, I will not contact you again." She abruptly turned for the carriage where Jed stood beaming proudly at her. He took her hand and placed an appreciative kiss upon it, then helped her into the carriage beside Selma and took his place up front.

Hannah tucked Selma's shawl more tightly around the old woman and grabbed her corpulent hand. "We're going home now, Selma. And now you're finally free." She hugged her old nanny and called to her husband, "I'm ready now, Jed." Astounded, she watched starched-and-proper Myrna running up alongside the moving rig, waving and calling out to her.

"The gentry will expect a party to toast your marriage. As your sister, I suppose . . ."

Hannah didn't acknowledge the offer. Instead, she repeated her desire to leave, and as the whip cracked, the carriage lurched and the distance from Coolfont increased. It was clear to Jed that it was not merely Selma who felt she had finally been set free. From time to time, he would look back over his shoulder at the scene. For the first few minutes, Hannah had nestled close to the woman who had been her childhood emblem of security, but as they moved onto the main Baltimore road, she sat erect and became the comforter rather than the comforted, and when Jed's eyes met hers, he saw a woman, the mistress of the Willows, smiling back at him.

Nonetheless, the scene from Havre de Grace still continued to haunt him, and he needed to assess what dangers lay ahead for them. "Hannah?" he broached carefully. "I want to stop by Fort McHenry and get a report on the Patuxent. I need to know what we'll face before I ride in there with you."

Hannah's eyes grew wide. "Are you going to speak to Andrew? About us?"

He stopped the carriage and swung around to assess Hannah's mood. "Now that Myrna knows, he'll soon hear, and I think it would be better coming from us than from someone else."

Hannah nodded her agreement. "Would you agree to let me tell him, Jed . . . alone?"

"If . . . that's what you think is best," he replied hesitantly.

Jed's unease was assuaged when they discovered that Captain Robertson and his superior had been reassigned to shore up the defenses along the Potomac. In their place, a Major Armistead was being assigned to defend Baltimore after distinguishing himself during the capture of Fort George.

"Now what do we do?" Hannah softly posed to Jed. "I just want this all settled."

"And it will be, just not today. Why don't you wait with Selma while I get a report on the area, and then we'll decide whether it's safe to head home to the Willows."

Jed left the women and got the reports of how the British had the entire state in turmoil, conducting pinprick raids on civilian targets that left the victimized areas scorched and desolate while their purloined treasuries made Cockburn as wealthy a pirate as Blackbeard had ever been. The only good news was that the British had yet to attempt to navigate the treacherous oyster beds of the Patuxent, and that meant that the Willows had been unmolested.

Unless Dupree has come through . . .

Invigorated by the familiar scents and smells of home, Jed coaxed the team on through the night. He dreaded the mile-long stretch of riverfront that bordered the White Oaks property, and with his rifle at the ready, he slowed the team to a walk, cautioning the women to lie low in the seat for safety. Nothing was as sweet to him as the sight of the fence line that marked the Willows boundary. Stopping at the end of the tree-lined lane, he announced, "We're home, Hannah. Welcome to the Willows. As I said . . . she needs work," he added apologetically.

Hannah poked her head and shoulders through the front window and stared at the Willows set in summer's moonlit beauty. "No, it's beautiful," she replied breathlessly. "It's the home I've dreamed of since I was a child when my family attended a summer party here. I even drew sketches of it to remember every detail," she admitted with a chuckle.

Jed's eyes shined as he took Hannah's hand. "You dreamed of my home and my world?"

Her own eyes now glistened. "My dreams of this place were my refuge, Jed. When Mother would punish me, I came here in my mind, where I knew you were. That's how I survived—with that little game and my Selma. Now I have everything I've ever hoped for."

Jed swallowed hard and kissed her hand through the carriage window. "Maybe your grandmother was calling you here. Her grave is over there . . . by the mill site."

"So that's where your grandfather buried her. They're both here . . . together after all. I hope this marriage makes them happy. Perhaps it will eventually bring that peace to our families that Charles Kittamoqund mentioned. Can we go there tomorrow in the daylight?"

"We can come and see it every day, Hannah. You're home now. We're all home, ladies."

He urged the horses on, but barely seven rods in, four armed figures popped from the thicket. Jed was about to run over the assailants until he noticed that the smallest attacker was barefoot and had a slingshot dangling from his hip pocket. "Caleb?" he called out.

"Mr. Jed!" he hollered back, and soon Abel, Royal, and Royal's oldest son moved into view.

"Sorry, Mr. Jed," called Royal. "We heard horses and we worried it was that Dupree."

Jed looked at Abel. "Has he been here, Abel? Has he tried anything?"

Abel shook his head. "There have been some strange occurrences that have rattled everyone's nerves, so we've got bells hung everywhere. We'll explain it to you in the morning."

Jed tensed until the carriage door opened and Hannah appeared. He jumped down to take her hand and introduce her to everyone, beaming and grinning like a schoolboy as he led her forward. "Mrs. Hannah Pearson, allow me to introduce you to some of the Willows family."

Hannah stepped forward, beaming, and stalled before the first child's face, placing her hands on his shoulders. "So you're Caleb. Well, I think we're going to be good friends, Caleb."

"Yes ma'am," he agreed wholeheartedly as she hugged him. "She's pretty, Mr. Jed!"

"Thank you, Caleb," Jed agreed with a chuckle as Hannah wriggled Caleb's chin.

Hannah moved before the largest man and said, "You must be Abel, the miller who married Bitty. Am I right?"

"Yes ma'am," he replied, removing his hat. "Pleased to meet you, Mrs. Pearson."

"Please, call me Hannah. Has your baby been born yet?" she asked with genuine interest.

Abel's smile radiated across his entire face. "Yes, ma'am!" he answered proudly. He looked at Jed and announced, "A baby girl named Priscilla, nearly two months ago."

Jed's face fell at the passage of time. "Everyone is well?" he inquired worriedly.

Abel gave him an assuring smile. "Yes. The baby is thriving, and Bitty is as happy as I've ever seen her, except for you, Jed. She's missed you terribly."

Jed's smile quivered. "I can't wait to see her." Before the last word fell from his lips the glow of lanterns began appearing from every corner of the yard and house as people gathered to see the cause of the ruckus in the yard. First it was Jack, bleary-eyed from having just finished his shift at guard duty, and following him came the rest of the Willows workers in the company of Jerome and Sarah. Jed caught Sarah and Jerome in a warm embrace as they arrived, then he hugged Jack, thumping his old friend's back. "How have things been while I've been away?"

"There's been some bad happenin's at White Oak, but we're doin' fine. There's things we should discuss, and you'll want to sit down and talk to Miss Frannie about a visitor she had."

"Frannie is still here?" Jed asked incredulously.

Jack rolled his eyes and smiled. "I believe all this news will have to keep for now. It appears there's someone new for you to meet." He looked toward the house.

Standing on the home's porch, backlit by the glow from inside the house, stood the other two women in his life. Jed grabbed Hannah's hand and started moving toward them, but as they came his way, Hannah released her hand from his, nodding for him to go alone. He did, breaking into a run.

Frannie met him first, leaping into his arms as he swung her around and around, laughing and scolding her at the same time. "You agreed to go to Dr. Beanes!" he said as he set her down.

"And if something happened, I fully intended to, but now that you've brought Hannah here . . . Well . . . if she's staying, then so am I."

Jed shot her an exasperated glance and strode to the diminutive woman with a babe in her arms. "Bitty . . ." he cried softly as she presented her infant daughter. He bent down and kissed his surrogate mother. "I hear she's named after your sister. Priscilla must be so proud."

Tears filled Bitty's eyes, and Jed remembered Jack's mention of trouble at White Oak. "No . . ." he moaned as the reason for her tears hit him.

Bitty nodded and busied herself by tucking the blanket more tightly around her babe. "Not tonight. We'll discuss it later. Now's a time for celebrating. Where's Miss Hannah?"

Still holding the baby in one arm, Jed walked over to Hannah and cradled her in the other. "Frannie . . . Bitty . . . say hello to my wife."

Frannie rushed over to Hannah and embraced her old friend. "It's about time," she joked. "I'd about given up on you two, but what's right is right. I'm delighted to finally have a sister."

The two young women chattered, and then Hannah turned to Bitty. "Hello, Miss Bitty."

"*Miss* Bitty?" Bitty grinned. "No one ever called me that before. Jest Bitty is fine, child."

Hannah embraced her, towering over the tiny woman. "I know how dear you and Jed are to one another." Reaching for Selma's hand, she explained, "You see, Bitty. I too have a woman as dear to me as a mother. Her name is Selma, and I hope you two will grow to be close friends. We are both grateful to be here at the Willows."

Bitty teared up. "I know all about your life, Miss Hannah. My Jed cried his heart out to me many a time over you. You're home now, child. You and your Selma are home now."

Bitty led Hannah toward the house, leaving her baby in Jed's tentative care. Passing the child off to Frannie with a kiss, he said, "I have something I must attend to. He ran up behind Hannah and scooped her up into his arms, then he raced to the front porch steps, ascending them two at a time. At the top of the porch he paused, silhouetted against the house, and kissed his bride, eliciting a loud cheer and applause from the Willows crowd.

As he set Hannah down, he called for old Jerome to join them, and as the old man ambled up, Jed spoke. "I've been away for a long time. I hear it's been a frightening time, but I feel happy tonight . . . and hopeful. Good things are on the horizon for all of us. Can you feel it too?"

A loud cheer went up from the Willows crowd, who were in need of a little hope.

As Jerome mounted the steps, Jed asked, "Can you pray for us, Jerome? Pray a blessing on this house and our marriage, and bless the Willows tonight?"

Jerome smiled and nodded and removed his hat. He took Hannah's hand and squeezed it, then he took Jed's and placed it on top with a loving pat that made Jed blink to clear his eyes. When Jerome bowed his head, a hush came over the crowd, who then followed their spiritual leader, bowing theirs as well. Then, in a resonant tone that testified of his confidence in the divine, he asked the Lord to bless Jed and Hannah, to bless their home and their family, and to bless their Willows family as well. When the amens sounded throughout the crowd, Jed shook Jerome's withered hand, and Hannah embraced him. Then picking his wife up again, Jed kissed her long and sweetly. "I love you all," he called out across the lawn. "Good night."

He carried Hannah toward the threshold, but she protested softly, asking to check on Selma.

"Don't you worry about Selma," Bitty assured her. "I'll settle her in."

"Thank you, Bitty. Good night," Jed called out again.

"Good night, puddin'," Bitty replied, eliciting a smile from the child she had raised.

"Good night, Selma," Hannah called out as she disappeared into the house and up the winding staircase that led to Jed's room.

Bitty linked her arm in Selma's and led the older woman toward the house. "No matter how big they get, they are always your babies, aren't they?"

"Ain't it grand?" Selma replied. "Ain't it jest grand."

CHAPTER 32

June 18, 1813
Hampton, Virginia

The signal had been prearranged. Ryan O'Malley encouraged Markus to enjoy his newfound marital bliss, promising to keep him apprised of the British navy's movements by leaving bottles on his doorstep. A full bottle meant he had time to settle in to married life. As the days passed, Markus dared hope Cockburn and the armada would again depart, but the bottle was empty when he arose the morning of Friday the eighteenth.

* * *

Lyra noted her husband's inordinately long absence with a heavy heart. His dedication to her over the two weeks following their wedding had been complete—tenderly loving her, working by her side to settle into their new home, and then guiding her until she had mastered the whereabouts of everything in their little cottage. He'd also patiently counted steps in tandem with his wife until she could independently navigate into the bustling village of Hampton again.

She worried over his urgency to restore her sense of independence after their move, remembering Markus's passion about mounting an offensive against the British and fearing that his efforts to restore her confidence were partly to prepare her in the event of his absence.

As soon as she heard his rapid footsteps on the walk, her heart fluttered, somehow knowing he was coming to her with bad news. He took her in his arms and pressed his cheek to hers, but all she could do was cry. Tightening his embrace he said, "Don't fret Lyra darlin', my magical little sprite. We've got a wee bit of trouble that needs tendin', and I don't want you to be alone while I'm away, so gather a few things and I'll take you to Drusilla's, all right?"

She pulled back and challenged his assessment. "You slip into that thick Irish accent when you're sweet-talkin' me. Tell me the truth. We've got a tad more than a 'wee bit of trouble.'"

He let his hands slide down her arms until they met her hands. "All right. Three British frigates are breakin' off and headin' up the James toward us. They've got a fair wind and they're comin' slow and easy, but we need to get down to the battery to try an' hold them off."

Lyra nodded bravely as she began to gather a few items. "Should I pack a nightgown?"

"That might be wise."

"And what of some knittin' and sewin'?"

"Anything you think will help you pass the time."

"Should I pack a black dress and a widow's veil as well . . . just in case?" she quipped sarcastically, breaking into tears again. When she finally had herself under control, she stoically sent her husband off with a hug, insisting that she could get herself to Drusilla's alone.

For the first time in his life, the fight in Markus seemed dimmed by love, but as soon as he looked through a spyglass and saw the Union Jack bearing down on the mouth of the James, thoughts of protecting Lyra spurred him on passionately. He joined Ryan, Patrick, and fifty-three other Hampton men who were making their way across the bridge to the batteries when a barrage of cannon fire erupted and billows of smoke began to rise above the James's shore. Markus broke into a full run past the batteries toward the river with the others close on his heels. The crackle of fire could be heard, and pungent black smoke was visible just beyond the trees near the water's edge. Sure enough, several small fishing boats that had been outfitted with guns were aflame in the water.

"How'd they get past the battery? They had to sail right past her!" Patrick shouted.

"If only we'd gotten the *Lass* outfitted sooner we'd be chasin' them devils."

Suddenly, Markus groaned and broke into a run toward the shore, drawing the attention of the other men who now noticed small craft launching from the frigates. They bore British landing parties armed with bayonets, and were nearing Murphy's and Celey's plantations.

"Wait, Markus! Think!" cautioned Patrick as he yanked his cousin back. "We've got nothing but a few muskets between us. If we go runnin' in there empty-handed, all we'll accomplish is to leave our wives widowed. Wait for the militia at Little England to arrive."

Markus looked over the land. A few sprawling plantations like Celey's—the farm where he had asked Lyra to marry him—and Murphy's, were situated along the James River while the bulk of the local population lived along the gentle harbors of Hampton Creek. To Markus, that seemed a more chilling prize. "What if they also send a boat up the creek to Hampton, Patrick?"

Beads of sweat formed on both men's worried brows. Markus was breathing so hard he had to clamp a hand over his mouth to silence himself. He turned to his cousin. "I'm not goin' to chance it. I'm goin' back to hide the women and children in your root cellar."

"Aye," agreed Patrick as the pair broke off from the group. They found the area quiet and unmolested, and torn between guarding their families and fighting for their neighbors, they chose the former and sat nervously awaiting the outcome along the James.

Ryan returned a few hours later with the disturbing report. "They burned every vessel moored along the James and then they just tramped through the homes taking what they wanted—gold, food, even family heirlooms! Lucky we had the *Lass* tied up on the creek."

"Aye," agreed Markus angrily, "but next time those pirates come I'll want more than to keep her hidden. I want her outfitted and ready to fight!"

* * *

Lieutenant Ramsey stood on the deck of Admiral Warren's personal barge, the elegant and ostentatious green-painted *Centipede,* as he and the commander observed the return of the party who'd raided the James. The three frigates sailed into protected Lynnhaven Bay near the mouth of the Chesapeake where the flotilla was anchored to Cockburn's flagship, hoisting their booty into the air while sounding victorious cries to their sneering commander.

Admiral Warren peered through his spyglass, shaking his head in disgust. He looked away, and Arthur couldn't miss the opportunity to question the disparity of the situation. "You clearly don't approve of Cockburn's tactics, sir. Why submit to *his* rule of war rather than insist on having them follow your more noble leadership?"

Admiral Warren dropped heavily into his chair. "The Admiralty has sternly censured me for being too lenient with the Chesapeake. They want a swift end to this conflict, and they are willing to tolerate men like Cockburn and his unscrupulous deeds to get it. Look at the composition of Beckwith's forces. Freed slaves, freed French Chasseurs . . . Do you think any of them care about Britain's sacred honor? Vengeance and plunder! That's what they're here to win. The slaves at least think they're fighting for a new life of freedom in the Indies, but I've heard rumors that some of the freed slaves Cockburn sent to the islands were actually resold into slavery on sugar cane plantations."

Arthur gasped. "Cockburn resold some of the men he freed? He is profiting from this?"

Admiral Warren shrugged. "I have no proof, but so I'm told. No wonder he is so willing to free the American captives. He will leave this war a very rich—though very despised—man."

"Yet no one will chasten him," charged Arthur.

"The Admiralty will not, and I am the instrument of the Admiralty. My orders are clear: I am to do what must be done to break America. As long as I remain the commander in chief of the North American station I shall fulfill their Lordships' directions. That's why I need you, Lieutenant. I want the actions of these men documented. Someday we will have to account for what will be done here in the next few days, and Britain must have a clear record."

A sweep of nausea cramped Arthur as he thought of Frannie and the Willows lying further north in waters the Crown also intended to subdue. Feeling powerless to do anything to protect her, he also doubted his father's ability to rein in Cockburn's darling spy. Wondering what atrocities he would be tainted with by nature of the uniform he now wore, Arthur momentarily considered jumping ship and fleeing north to Frannie, but knowing that his father had placed personal gain before the interests of Britain, how could he become a traitor and also betray Mother England?

* * *

Markus took Lyra home, calming his wife by holding her in his arms until she fell asleep. Sleep would not come to him, however, as he wrestled with the day's unnerving events. He heard a light tapping on the door, and a knot formed in his stomach as he hurried to answer it.

"Want to have a little fun?" teased Patrick. "The wind has died down and stranded the British ship *Junon*—about three miles away from her consorts. She's all alone, and Commodore Cassin has ordered Captain Tarbell ta take her down in answer ta what those pirates did today. Do you want to take the *Lass* out for a sail and watch?"

Markus looked back over his shoulder in the direction of the room where Lyra lay asleep. "I'll not be leavin' and causin' her worry just for my entertainment."

Shame crossed Patrick's face. "Aye . . . you're right. But it sure would be nice to wake up tomorrow and find out that we blackened their eye for a change."

About four A.M. Markus's restless slumber was disturbed by the sound of distant cannon fire, which lasted for nearly an hour. The next morning, as he was leaving Sunday services with Lyra, an exultant whoop sounded from the dock. The three O'Malley men sauntered over to the shore where a sailor was standing on a barrel describing the events of the night's raid.

"So what do you make of it?" asked Patrick of his father.

"Doesn't seem as if they accomplished much other than to splinter a few British boats and scurry home without gettin' themselves killed."

"But surely there's merit in showin' them Brits we're not afraid ta stand up ta them."

"Fight the dog, if you must . . . but taunt the dog?" Ryan asked dubiously.

Markus just shook his head. As he left to find his wife, Patrick hurried to catch up with him, saying, "I'm glad you talked me out of goin' last night."

Markus didn't comment as they walked on. "Where's your father?" He finally spoke up.

"He's practically livin' at the battery now. Hey, I was thinkin'—why don't we pack up the families and have a picnic today? Goodness knows the women could use a little pleasure."

An hour later, Patrick's family had barely arrived at Markus and Lyra's cottage when cannon fire began to the south, coming from the direction of Norfolk. The men immediately scurried their families back to Patrick's house, warning them to go into the root cellar under the house at the first sign of trouble. Leaving crying children clinging to fearful wives, Markus and Patrick grabbed their guns and headed to the batteries with the rest of the men.

Ryan was on top of a barrel, searching the horizon through his spyglass. "The British are mounting a full-scale attack on Norfolk, but they've got to get past Craney Island first."

Every muscle in Markus's body was tense. "What can we do?"

Ryan pointed to a uniformed soldier. "Major Crutchfield is sendin' volunteers to Wise's Creek. It appears the British plan to attack the rear of the island by land and the front by sea. If they conquer Craney, Norfolk'll be next, and then they'll be comin' here, lads."

So Markus, Patrick, and a group of volunteers joined a detachment of regulars and sailed across the James, hugging the opposite shore past Hoffleur's Creek, stealthily moving through the brush until they neared Wise's Creek where they spied the British landing spot. In the distance they could hear the long roll of the drum, punctuating the arrival of boat-loads of over two thousand British sailors. Feeling helpless against the endless gleam of British bayonets and swords, the highly outnumbered Americans held their position until they saw a more discouraging sight. Another wave of fifty or so barges was crossing from the British line toward Craney Island, each of them carrying a full load of additional soldiers. Worse yet, another detachment remained at the landing point, setting off an explosive barrage of rocket fire to cover their comrades' advance at Wise's Creek. The rocket concussions threw the Americans to the ground in shock and fear where they lay watching the fiery path of the weapons as they fell in incendiary blasts along Craney Island, disrupting the American defenses.

"What in the name of heaven or hell is that?" shuddered a local.

"Those blasts are traveling nearly two miles!" shouted Markus. "The island's cannons can't defend against so remote an attack."

"We've heard tell of a new weapon the Brits have called Congreve rockets," explained a militiaman who was sheltered behind a tree stump. "They're not very accurate, but they'll devastate whatever they hit and burn everything near where they land."

Another blast sent the men scrambling to cover their ears as fires began to ignite trees, docks, and buildings, covering the British line's advancement toward Craney. Looking through his telescope, Markus spotted the mammoth British fleet situated north, midway between Craney and Hampton. Within easy reach of Hampton, he was relieved that their atten-tions were fully focused on moving southward toward the true prizes—Norfolk, the *Constellation,* and the navy yard. The lowly American squadron of sloops and schooners sat in a defiant blockading curve spread from Craney to Lambert's Point, a few miles north of Norfolk.

"What do you see now?" asked Patrick.

While scanning the approaching British troops, Markus remained grim, and then he released a loud whoop. "They can't ford Wise's Creek! Those rockets are meant to cover their advance, but the creek's too high for them to cross!"

Markus's optimism was short-lived. "Oh no!" he cried out. "Another flood of barges is rowing toward Craney. If the island doesn't soon mount a defense they'll land and overrun her," he grumbled as he squinted and refocused the glass. "There's a dandy of a barge in the mix. Bright green with a brass cannon on the bow."

The militiaman seemed excited by the development. "Does it have about twenty sets of oars sticking out on each side?"

"Yes," replied Markus.

"That's the *Centipede,* Admiral Warren's personal transport. If we could take her out we might have a chance of ending this successfully."

Markus began keeping an eye on the *Centipede* as well as monitoring the advance of the British troops who were nearing the bridge to Craney Island. Finally, Craney's big guns opened up with precise rapid fire, spitting grapeshot into the enemy's lines until they began to retreat.

"We're returning fire!" hollered Markus as the men rose to cheer the British troops' retreat. "They're opening up on them with everything they've got on the island!" He returned his attention to the *Centipede,* whose bow was riddled and splintered from the assault. "Someone's down on the *Centipede!*" Markus shouted with a cheer. "She's sinking and so are three others!"

"And look there!" shouted Patrick as he pointed to a line of boats that had drawn within one hundred yards of the shoreline. "Providence is surely shinin' on us, lads! They're trying to drop off soldiers near the shore, but they're gettin' stuck in the mud. They can't reach Craney!"

"Ha!" gloated Markus. "They're climbin' back in their boats and rowin' away to save their crews!"

As the British engaged in a full retreat, Markus and his squad hurried across the James in case the British turned their rapacious attentions on Hampton, but their fears were unrealized. Within a few hours, Admiral Warren's assault on Craney had proven to be a complete tactical failure, but Major Crutchfield did not allow his American forces to celebrate their victory. He told them the British would come again with even greater ferocity.

That evening when Markus and Lyra were alone again, he could see the toll the events were taking on his normally resilient wife. Her blindness had become more of a hindrance, rendering her fretful when in the house and too timid to venture out. Lyra leaned back against Markus in the porch swing Ryan had made them for a wedding present. Stroking his finger along the curve of her neck, Markus asked, "Do you want to leave Hampton, Lyra? Say the word and we'll pack our things and go."

He could see by her silence that the idea intrigued her for a moment. She drew his arms more tightly around her, asking, "Where would we go? North to the Willows?"

Just the mention of the name of the farm made Markus miss the old place and the people. "No." He sighed. "Leastwise not soon. It's just more of the same there. We could go west . . . say . . . to Kentucky or Tennessee . . . get away from the coast until things settle down."

"But what would you do? You're a seaman."

"And a tobacco farmer. I've learned a lot from Jed these past few years."

Lyra nestled into his chest. "Did you write to him about our marriage?"

"I sent word, but there's no tellin' when he'll get it. He's likely on militia duty. I've heard Cockburn hit the upper Chesapeake pretty hard. There's no tellin' how the Willows is or if . . ."

Lyra sat still as moments of silence passed. She suddenly turned toward him, pressing her cheek against his. "Oh, forgive me, Markus. I've been a selfish wife, worryin' about myself, never thinking for a moment that you've got those you love up north in the fray."

His big hands framed her face, and he kissed both her eyes before placing a soft kiss on her mouth. "Your eyes may not see as others' do, but you've a gift to peer right into my heart, Lyra. I am worried about my friends, but you're anything but selfish. We'll get north soon enough. For now I only want to enjoy the treasure I have right here, just bein' with you."

"I promise I'm goin' to try not to whine or fret any more time away, Markus. I don't want to squander another moment."

He suddenly longed for her to see him—to have her know his face, to see the pride shining in his eyes, and hold his image in her mind forever, so that no matter what befell them, he would be engraved in her memory always. But all they had was sound and touch and smells to instill memories of their time together. He suddenly wanted to tell her he loved her so many times that she would hear the echo of his words ringing forever in her mind. He wanted her to remember the scent of his store-bought cologne and the smells of wood and tar from his work shirt. He wanted her to remember the gentleness of his touch when he stroked her neck and the burn of his lips on hers. He wanted to be such a part of her that whenever they were apart, and when they were finally parted in some far-off day, she would never doubt that she was loved and who it was that made her feel so. His eyes became moist with the unexplained urgency he felt, and he was just as suddenly grateful for the darkness that obscured his fears from her.

"I'm goin' inside to get ready for bed," she uttered softly. "Will ya be long?"

He kissed her palm and shook his head, carefully muttering a choked "no." As the door closed, he dropped to his knees, importuning heaven to dispel the dread settling over him.

* * *

"I have a question before I complete my report of the battle, sir," stated Lieutenant Arthur Ramsey as he approached his commander. "Some of the men are charging atrocities against the Americans, saying that one of our barges became locked on a shoal and that instead of taking the men as prisoners, the Americans murdered them in their boat. Is this true?"

Admiral Warren sighed, replying, "Unsubstantiated. Tell me the final figures."

"Six dead, twenty-four wounded, and one hundred fourteen missing. Best estimates are that forty of the missing are either prisoners or deserters."

"And Beckwith promised his men they'd be breakfasting on Craney in the morning. Some of the pompous idiots carried their shaving apparatus and dogs along in the barges."

Arthur felt anger broiling within him. "Will there be anything else, sir?" he asked curtly.

Admiral Warren's eyes closed as if they were too heavy to remain open. "Would you please . . . pray with me, Lieutenant? The men who lead this venture are nobles and sons of nobles. I have no doubt Sir Sydney Beckwith will now do all that is within his power to avenge today's loss in order to restore what he falsely believes is their honor. Sadly, the force he employs to obtain this prize will likely cost him the very thing he seeks."

"Sir, can you not dismiss the Admiralty's chastisement of your previous handling of the region and command these men in a virtuous path?"

"I can no longer clearly see my duty, Arthur. This is why I ask you to pray with me."

Arthur felt diverse feelings course through his veins. Pride, honor, fear, repugnance. He dropped to his knees beside the greatly esteemed commander and was momentarily at a loss for words. When they finally came, neither could *he* clearly see his duty.

* * *

Four days passed, and while the British line sat in the mouth of the bay, an uneasy lull settled over the region. The O'Malleys began gathering at every meal to ease the tension with sociality, but the women could feel the anxiety of the men increase each day. At supper on the third day, Wednesday, June 22, the women raised the topic.

"We have a proposition for you," began Lyra heavily. "Drusilla and I have given this considerable thought and . . . we've decided we'd like to leave the village."

Patrick and Markus both looked at their wives. Neither man seemed unduly surprised by the announcement, but Patrick responded first. "Where would you like to go?"

Drusilla chimed in. "Just up to the Kirbys' mansion, not far from Celey's and Murphy's places. Grandpa Kirby is doin' poorly. Greer said she and her grandmother could use the help."

"The British already went through there last week and took what they wanted from those farms, so they're more likely to raid and pillage Hampton next," reasoned Lyra.

The two husbands looked to Ryan, who shrugged and supported the women's thinking.

"What's this about?" posed Markus. "You think you'd feel safer away from the town?"

"We need a break from the tension. You men are as nervous as cats while you're in the house . . . which is every wakin' moment now," explained Lyra. "We just think you'd be more relaxed if you knew we were somewhere safe. Besides, any ships that sail up the James will have to pass by the point, and you've got more watchmen looking out for them now."

"So when do you want to leave?" asked Patrick sadly as he fingered his son's russet hair.

"We'd like to head up in the mornin' with the children," Drusilla replied. "You're welcome to come and stay as well . . . whenever you've a mind. Greer said so."

Markus stood and paced the floor, irritated. "Don't you believe I can protect you, Lyra?"

"Of course I do, Markus. And perhaps we'll return in a day or two, but we all need some peace. After all, it's only two miles away. I'll probably still hear you snorin' from that distance."

Markus smiled at her attempt at humor, fully aware of the nervousness it was intended to disguise.

* * *

On Thursday, the men packed up the wagon and their families and carted them up to the Kirbys' off Celey's Road. Greer Kirby, a thirty-year-old maid, welcomed them wholeheartedly.

"Where's all the stock, Greer?" asked Ryan O'Malley.

"The British drove it all off. I spent days gathering a few chickens and a milk cow back home, but we'll be fine. The larder's full of salted fish and pork, and the garden is still in tact."

As the adults talked, it was clear the children saw the move as a grand adventure, but Patrick's heart was rent as he said his good-byes, and Markus lingered by Lyra's side, checking and rechecking with Drusilla, making sure she'd get his blind wife oriented quickly.

"Now kiss me and then off with ya, my darlin'," Lyra teased. "This could be a merry idea. After all, they do say that absence makes the heart grow fonder."

He intertwined his fingers with hers so that when he moved away she was forced to follow. "Lyra O'Malley!" he teased, pulling her to him. "Do you want me to leave or not?" Again he played the silly game, stepping away and drawing her to him, then rebuking her playfully with kisses. "Let me go, woman! Do ya see how she cannot bear to let Uncle Markus go?" he hollered to the children who squealed with delight at the scene. When the game played itself out, he ran his fingers through her fiery hair and pressed his brow to hers. "You're the love of my life, Lyra. What will I do without my Irish sprite to keep me warm tonight?"

Lyra's voice grew husky as she replied, "You'll forgive me, won't you, Markus? Times are, women just need the company of women. This is one of those. And all I ever need is a single thought of you to make my heart burn. That'll hold me until we're back together again."

He laid his hand along her cheek and brushed his thumb over her jaw, then with one final kiss, he let her fingers slip through his and the men departed.

* * *

Late on the evening of Friday, June 24, twenty-five hundred of Beckwith's British soldiers, including the unruly French Chasseurs Britanniques, moved stealthily up the James River so far from shore that the sliver of moon did not disclose their approach. Before dawn, Beckwith's forces were in concealed positions in the woods behind the Murphy home while Cockburn's flotilla anchored off Blackbeard's Point within shelling distance of Little England and the battery.

That night, Markus couldn't sleep. His body now felt foreign in the bed without Lyra lying near, and after wrestling with his loneliness for hours, he dressed and headed to Little England to harass his Uncle Ryan. As he crossed the footbridge over Hampton Creek, the clouds cleared and a beam of light fell upon an object in the water. He peered carefully until his knees went weak. Running to the bell, he sounded the alarm and immediately, men rushed from tents and across the bridge from Hampton. As soon as Major Crutchfield saw Cockburn's flotilla off the shore, his American resistance went into readiness, loading guns and moving into battle formation.

Patrick was among the throng of men careening toward the point when another breathless messenger rode into the camp yelling, "The British have landed!"

Two men pulled him from his horse to inquire further, and on quivering legs he pointed west and explained, "There's so many of them! Hundreds— maybe thousands—making their way toward town along Celey's Road. The woods are scarlet from the number of British marching through, and the field is emerald with uniforms of green . . . like a swarm of locusts!"

"Green uniforms?" a man prodded further.

"The French Chasseurs," groaned Major Crutchfield. He immediately dispatched Captain Servant and his rifle company to check the enemy's progress and ordered the battery to prepare a vigorous assault on Cockburn as soon as his ships came into range.

By now, many of the volunteers who had heard the report were breaking ranks to cross the bridge and secrete their families away before the marauders' arrival. Patrick and Markus grabbed two guns and haversacks of cartridges and sped toward the woods on the shortcut to Celey's Road.

* * *

"Lyra! Wake up! The neighbors are passing word that there's an army marching this way through the woods!" Disoriented, Lyra panicked and flailed her arms until Drusilla's stern voice brought her back to her senses. "Greer refuses to leave her grandparents, but we've got to take the children and run! Do you remember your way to the front entrance? Six steps to the staircase, twelve steps down, then four to the door." Drusilla placed the baby in Lyra's arms, the need for vigilance clearly steeling Lyra's rattled nerves. "I'll get the boys, and you wait on the porch. Now hurry!"

Lyra felt along the floor for the edge of the carpet and began to count, cradling the baby against her thundering heart. She heard the fear in Greer's voice, undermining her words, "I can't leave my grandma and da. The last time the soldiers came through they robbed us blind but they never abused us . . . so we should be fine. We'll be fine . . . Now you four go!"

"Listen outside," Drusilla tapped Lyra's talents. "Do we have time to hitch the wagon?"

"No. They're very close. I don't think we even have time to saddle the horses."

As they rushed to the barn, Drusilla said, "Let's follow the woods as far as we can and get to the Hopes' place. That should keep us out of the fray." Lyra mounted one horse, and Drusilla placed a sleepy-eyed Sean behind her. "Hold on tight to Aunt Lyra, darlin'. We're goin' ta have a little ride." Drusilla then lifted Martin up and placed the baby in his ready arms. "That's my little man," she cooed, trying to hide her fear. Once she mounted in front of him, she took the baby in one arm, holding tight to the horse's mane with the other. "Wrap your arms tight around Mommy, Martin. Are you ready, Lyra? We'll just walk slow and easy through the woods. These two horses have been yoked together most of their lives. They should follow one another along."

* * *

Tearfully closing the door, Greer went inside where her grandmother met her. "Why didn't you go with them, Greer? Go child!" cried her grandmother. "Run quickly and maybe you can catch up with them. We've lived our lives, so if the worst happens, we're prepared, but if anything were to happen to you . . . Now run, Greer. Run!"

Out the door she ran, tripping over her nightgown. As she scrambled to her feet, a shot rang out beside her. "Arrête!" the voices ordered as twelve black boots surrounded her. When she looked up, she saw green-jacketed soldiers pulling her to her feet and smiling lasciviously. The men laughed as they fingered her hair, turning her around admiringly. "Une dissidente!" they jeered as they covertly dragged her into the barn and closed the door behind them.

The scarlet-uniformed leader of the company finally arrived, unaware of the missing Frenchmen. He pounded on the door, and when Mrs. Kirby answered, he and a dozen others began rifling through the home's remaining contents, all but emptying out the larder. An ugly stray dog barked and leapt at the salted pork in a soldier's arms. Irritated, he kicked at it and chased the dog into the house. A few minutes later several shots rang out, and a woman's scream silenced the troops. The officer in charge ordered the men from the house immediately and regrouped in the yard. "Where are the six French Chasseurs?" he demanded. Minutes later the six lechers exited the barn with chickens and a milk cow in tow. "Leave the animals and prepare to march!" the officer barked. "Now!"

As the company reformed, a captain arrived in the company of Lieutenant Ramsey. "Did you meet any resistance?" the captain asked of his subordinate.

"We did have a civilian casualty," the officer noted. "An old man . . ."

"Regrettable, but the Americans murdered twelve good men stranded in their barge."

Arthur stood in shock at the callousness of the conversation and war in general. He strode to the door of the home and opened it, finding the old woman crying over the body of her dead husband. He helped the man to the floor and laid a blanket over him. "You need a doctor," he said to the trembling old woman.

"My granddaughter, Greer! The men in the green coats stopped her near the barn."

Livid, Arthur stood on the porch and scanned the area as the troops filed out to meet up with the sea of uniforms streaming through the open fields. The captain looked back at him, and warned, "Document what you choose, but I will not hold up these men for your scribbling."

"There was a younger woman here," Arthur barked. "Did your men report seeing her?"

Disinterested, the captain shrugged and marched on while Arthur headed for the barn from which he heard soft sobs emerging. When he opened the door, the disheveled woman screamed and scrambled into a corner like a wild cat. He approached slowly, speaking soothingly to her as he noted the torn gown, the scratch marks on her arms and legs, and the swollen cheek and bloody mouth that testified to her treatment. Slumping heavily against a stall, he offered her his hand, but she was heaving so rapidly she finally succumbed and fainted. Picking her up in his arms, he carried her into the house to the mournful cries of her grandmother and laid her down beside her grandfather. "I'm . . . sorry," he pled to the old woman. "I'm so very sorry."

* * *

Markus and Patrick neared Celey's Road where the full measure of the massive British forces came into view. Knowing the British had already passed the Kirby mansion filled them with dread, but the enemy spread so far and so deep they could not get around the troops' flank. Forced to hide in a thicket until the army passed, they noticed an American sergeant named Parker with a few men and an artillery piece set at the junction of Celey's Road and the highway to Yorktown, Virginia. As the enemy column advanced, three British officers led out with a company of green-coated French Chasseurs. As a barrage of precise fire broke loose, Markus and Patrick joined in the unexpected attack, dropping several British officers in rapid succession. Parker fired his cannon and the British ranks became disoriented and confused, but within seconds the marines regrouped and returned fire, continuing their advance and driving the American sharp-shooters back.

Forced to take cover behind a tree, Markus and Patrick prayed for support from the battery. "Surely Major Crutchfield will send more troops," Markus grumbled.

Patrick scanned the scene and pointed to a break in the tree line. "We must be engagin' them to the south. See how the British line is pullin' back?" The sound of British cannon fire broke where Patrick had been pointing. "Oh, no," Patrick muttered. "That's grapeshot."

Soon, American fighters were scrambling away from the attacking red-coated enemy.

"Our line just broke," growled Markus as he sighted his musket again. "And Parker's cannon isn't firing. Something's wrong and the British know it. They're movin' in on them!"

Working in tandem, the two men fired and loaded, laying down cover fire while Parker and another soldier hid in the brush. As the British approached the presumably dead gun, the younger cannoneer leapt from the thicket and touched the fiery brand to the fuse, sending a barrage of fire into the enemy ranks. As panic ensued, Markus and Patrick knew the time had come to make their move.

They skirted beyond the right flank of the British line and crossed behind them to the Kirbys' farm. All seemed fine until they opened the door where they were met by unmeasurable suffering. Their sympathies and terrors aroused, they attempted to succor the women and determine the fates of their own wives, but the only information they could secure was the news that their families had fled on horseback before the British had arrived. Armed with that small shred of hope, the two men set off in defense of all they loved.

* * *

Arthur watched as the American troops retreated from their pursuers. When the British had them backed against New Bridge Creek, Major Crutchfield surrendered rather than see his men picked off in the water. Any hope Arthur had for an honorable victory was dashed as the senior British officer addressed his triumphant troops.

"Colonel Beckwith will be most pleased with your performance today. As for Admiral Cockburn, I think he has made his sentiments regarding your reward for victory quite clear!"

A victory whoop sang out from the British ranks that made Arthur wary, but the senior officer's next command made Arthur tremble.

"Subdue the citizenry while we establish a base of operations."

And with that, the British forces were set loose upon the village of Hampton. The Hope family's farm caught the attention of a small detachment of French Chasseurs and Britons. They burst through the door and found an elderly man of sixty-five years whom they treated brusquely as they went from room to room, seizing what they desired with no effort made on his part to resist. One soldier reentered the parlor with a woman's nightcap in his hand. "Où est la femme?" the soldier asked, inquiring about the missing female owner.

"She is away," answered Mr. Hope nervously, trying to protect the women and children who had sought his help.

The French soldier smirked and nodded to his compatriots who shoved the old man against the wall at bayonet point. "Où est la femme?" he asked more deliberately.

"I am the only one here!" Mr. Hope explained. "You've searched the house."

"These Frenchmen have ways to break the bravest men, so why don't you just tell them what they want to know?" sneered a British regular. "They've either been in prison or on a ship for the last four years. That's a long time to want for feminine company, so I'd just tell them."

From the root cellar hidden below the parlor floorboards, Drusilla and Lyra crouched with the children, listening to the horrors transpiring above. They tried to cover the children's ears and mouths to silence their responses to Mr. Hope's agonized groans until a loud scream escaped the old man, followed by a chorus of laughter mixed with Mr. Hope's pleas for mercy. They could tell by the conversation that his abusers had stripped him and were repeatedly piercing his body with their bayonets. Each of the women knew it was only a matter of time before one of the children's muffled screams escaped, revealing their position, so Drusilla did not attempt to dissuade Lyra when she exited the cellar with the old Dragoon pistol Mr. Hope had handed them before hiding them away.

She made it to the obscured outside exit near the summer kitchen. Safely traversing the short distance to the hedge row, she crawled until she reached the edge of the porch and scooted underneath where Mr. Hope's dog was known to lay. Orienting herself, she aimed the gun toward the house and fired through the porch's floorboards, shattering the front window. She heard the soldiers scrambling before exploding from the house with their guns at the ready, streaming down the porch to determine the shooter's location. Then she heard silence. She thought her plan to scare them on to another place had worked, but soon she heard the return of boots on the porch above her, then snickers of laughter broke loose from the men's lips as a finger pointed to the hole in the porch floor. Two pairs of boots descended the steps again—one pair breaking to the right while another broke to the left.

She cowered against the center of the foundation, pressing her body against the cold stone as she strained to listen. Soon she heard snickers on the one side and she began to scramble to the other. As soon as she cleared the porch she leapt to her feet and began to feel her way back along the wall, and then she heard laughter surrounding her. She spun around to swing at the sounds then began to run in the opposite direction.

"She's blind!" the Briton declared. "Look, she can't see a thing."

"Très belle," leered a Frenchman as he grabbed her and laid his mouth over hers.

Lyra bit his face, and in his anger he slapped her hard, sending her to the ground. Squealing, she scrambled to her feet as the men formed a ring around her. One by one they taunted her, drawing close and chasing her into the arms of another until she was so disoriented she had no notion of her surroundings. She lowered her frame and bolted hard past the arms of one man who received a scurrilous taunting from his mates. Blindly running, mad with fear, she tripped and fell, gashing her forehead, but again she picked herself up and ran on, fleeing from the voices pursuing her. She heard the sound of water and raced for it, running smack into the corner of a dock support. The blow wrenched her right shoulder so severely the searing burn of pain nearly stole her consciousness. Her right arm was useless now, dangling limply by her side, but her pursuers no longer enjoyed the game that had damaged their prize. As she reached the edge of the dock at New Bridge Creek, she heard the voices closing in on her, and then the crack of musket fire and a sound like Markus's voice calling her name. She was well past the point of reason, too far to discern between reality and mere illusion, and trusting her fate to God and the water, she jumped in and tried to cross the creek.

She heard two more shots and her name being screamed again, then a third shot and she knew it truly was Markus who was calling for her. She tried to force her right arm to work, to will it to usefulness, but it would not obey. As the current took hold of her, she heard Markus scream one last time, then his voice went suddenly silent.

She remembered her wedding day and the tender words she and Markus had shared in secret at the altar:

"I'll love you every day of my life . . . 'til the day I die," he had whispered to her.

"Oh, much longer than that, Markus O'Malley. After all, what is heaven if not this?"

She smiled and closed her eyes as the current carried her away.

CHAPTER 33

June 26, 1813
Hampton, Virginia

> *Murder . . . rape . . . and every other atrocity which can be*
> *perpetrated upon men or women was committed by men*
> *serving under the flag of His Majesty's forces.*

Admiral Warren recoiled as he reread Lieutenant Ramsey's horrifying report regarding the atrocities committed at Hampton. He was still unable to accept that His Majesty's warriors were capable of such monstrous actions, and despite the testimonies of his officers, which almost universally ascribed the worst and most heinous acts of violence committed against the women to the Chasseurs and to the freed slaves, Warren found little solace in such reports, knowing that the responsibility for a soldier's actions rested squarely upon the shoulders of their leaders.

Sir Charles Napier's confession still burned in his thoughts:

> *Every horror was perpetrated with impunity—rape, murder,*
> *pillage . . . Strong is my dislike to what is, perhaps, a necessary*
> *part of our job, viz., plundering and ruining the peasantry.*
> *We drive all their cattle, and of course ruin them. My hands*
> *are clean; but it is hateful to see the poor Yankees robbed, and*
> *to be the robber.*

With trembling hands, he picked up the formal protest by American General Taylor, including a fervent denial of the atrocity charged to the Americans regarding the deaths of the barge load of British sailors. One section in particular resounded in Warren's mind:

*I am prepared for any species of warfare which you are
disposed to prosecute. It is for the sake of humanity that I enter
this protest.*

He couldn't help but wonder what venom and resolve his men's action
would unleash in a nation they had so nearly subdued. They had conquered
the city, but they had forfeited the moral high ground, and Parliament—at
least certain members of it—would not look kindly on it.

* * *

As Arthur escorted Admiral Warren through the conquered village, they
looked into the hollow faces of those pillaged and those mourning their
dead. These expressions of shock and anger were familiar to him—they were
the expressions of defeat, and as a conqueror, he had become steeled against
them. But there was another face of war in Hampton—the hollow countenance of women from whom the divinely endowed gift of virtue had been
rent.

And the fury . . . It was as if Beelzebub himself trod in their shoes. Such
was the way the people looked at them. One by one, Ramsey took the
admiral to the houses where the greatest atrocities had been perpetrated.
The town had been subdued, but Arthur knew as clearly as he knew
anything that these people would now die before uniting with Britain. But
he did notice that the Americans were pleasantly disposed to him. As they
passed the church, he recognized the O'Malley family, and the good lieutenant's eyes became moist as he passed by. The husband nodded respectfully while Mrs. O'Malley ran to him and pressed a flower in his hand.
Arthur stepped from the line to receive the gift and inquire after the family.

"Thank you. We'd've all been dead if you hadn't come along when you
did." Drusilla O'Malley began to softly cry. "When I heard Markus's voice I
thought we were safe and I brought my babies out of hidin'. Then once
Markus and Patrick started shootin' at those barbarians that were chasin'
Lyra, I knew they were dead men. And I knew we'd be too, but you stopped
the devils from killin' us, and I can't ever thank you enough for that."

"The man . . . Markus . . . did he live?"

"It took nearly an hour to bring him around after being hit with the
butt end of that Frenchman's gun stock. He cried like a babe when he woke
up and found out about Lyra. He believed if he'd had a moment more, he
could've gotten to her and saved her. She was found down the creek, washed
up on a shoal. They carried her to the house, and she had a few lucid

moments . . . time enough to say good-bye." Mrs. O'Malley wiped at a tear and continued as she pointed to two fresh mounds of earth. "We buried two today—Lyra and our dear father, Ryan O'Malley, who was cut down when Cockburn's men stormed the battery."

Arthur couldn't bear the weight of guilt that pressed upon him as he witnessed the suffering of these people. "Please tell Mr. O'Malley how sorry I am for his loss."

"He's gone. As soon as the amen was sounded at the funeral, he rode away, back north to the Willows farm where he's employed, I suppose. I doubt he'll ever return to Hampton."

Ramsey countered the woman. "Do you mean the Willows farm on the Patuxent?"

Mrs. O'Malley drew back, and the mood instantly chilled. "How do you know of the Willows farm? Don't tell me you and yours are headed there next! Is there to be no end to the sufferin'?" She retreated as if her civility had been exhausted by his mere recognition of the Willows farm. Arthur couldn't tell her why the place was also familiar to him, or that the place that both he and Markus dreamed of was indeed destined to be in Cockburn's crosshairs.

As if summoned by the very thought of him, Admiral Cockburn suddenly emerged, making an imperial entrance. His bearing was cold and smug, and he moved with deliberateness, showcasing his cocked hat and his epaulets as if they were royal adornments. He strutted, square-shouldered and tall, commanding the very air around him, and Arthur Ramsey realized why Admiral Warren could not rein the man in. Clearly, Cockburn knew upon whose shoulders the Admiralty's confidence lay, and though Warren was still commander in chief of the North American station in name, it was apparent Cockburn overran his superior. A single glance at Warren's countenance, diminished in Cockburn's presence, told the young lieutenant that change was on the horizon. *If not Warren, then who? And what would this new commander's entrance mean for Cockburn and the Chesapeake?*

* * *

Arthur was relieved when the morning of the twenty-seventh arrived and he heard the return of the barges ferrying the troops back off the Virginia coast. The fleet was moving north, and a ship was sailing for England to carry the report of the sordid Hampton campaign back to the Admiralty. He felt inspired to write several letters home.

Home . . . Having seen what he had of war, and having seen the toll warring could have upon men, even good men, he no longer thought his father to be as diabolical and unredeemable as he once had, and he hoped they could sit down as men when he returned after the war to see if they could right things.

Paramount to his mere desire for reconciliation was his need to secure certain promises from his father—promises regarding Daniel Whittington's safety and promises regarding his father's attitude toward the Pearsons. He felt some progress on the latter, knowing as he now did how very small and insignificant a role his father actually played in whatever events befell the Willows. He was, however, becoming increasingly troubled over his family's impact on the lives of Lord Whittington and his son.

His mother had written him regularly, penning loving notes that were becoming increasingly filled with references to Daniel, until he could feel her attachment changing from that of a temporary guardian of the boy to that of a mother. He asked himself on numerous occasions if his apprehension over this increasingly tender relationship was prompted by his concern over the hurt both parties would experience when Lord Whittington arrived to carry Daniel home, or whether it was prompted purely by jealousy. Assuring himself that it was the former, he further worried that his mother's doting could make it impossible for the earl to ever win back the love of his angry son and to prepare him to assume his rightful place in Parliament some day. He shared these concerns with her in a letter.

He felt inclined to write two others—one to Daniel, and one to Lord Whittington. In Daniel's letter he began by recounting past shared times and then ventured into what stories he felt he could share regarding his military service. Finally, he segued into the real reason for writing:

> *. . . I watched a family mourn two lost loved ones this week, Daniel, and my heart was rent over how desperately they yearned to reclaim their family members, to enjoy again the sweet association that others so casually squander, and worse yet, decline.*
>
> *Let us not be guilty of such crimes, Daniel. Love and forgiveness are gifts we each possess, and their giving will provide treasures far beyond those which moth and rust doth corrupt, or those which thieves desire. Love of God and love of family—these are heaven's treasures.*

Forgive your father, Daniel. Write to him and ease his mind . . .

Fondly,

Arthur

In his letter to the earl, Arthur felt it urgent to chronicle the current military situation, but in closing he essentially afforded him the same counsel he had given to his son:

I have witnessed the aftermath of the utmost cruelty of which man is capable, meted out to the oldest, the frailest, and the fairest of God's children. Some of those men called to lead our forces are morally blind, and others seem to have temporarily lost their way. Who is now at Britain's helm? Where is that noble North Star which ever guided her path? Can you still see it? For I cannot. Or has bitterness clouded your vision as well?

I watched a family mourn two lost loved ones this week, my friend, and I was sickened by it—for they so desperately yearned to reclaim their family members while we have squandered opportunities to enjoy association with our own.

As Britain's families go, so goes Britain, they say. If that is so, then let us not be guilty of contributing to the decline of our dear England, Lord Whittington. Love of God and love of family—these are heaven's treasures. I pray you will go to Daniel and beg his forgiveness. Reclaim your son whilst you still may, and having restored your house, I pray you will shore up Britain's.

Ever your fond servant,

Arthur

CHAPTER 34

July 2, 1813
The Willows

News of the barbarism at Hampton had traveled north and south, anchoring the previously vacillating resolve of many Americans. Jed Pearson's worry for Markus and Markus's new bride cast the only pall over his own otherwise perfect happiness. His life on the Willows was as a dream. He had Hannah by his side, and all the people he loved were safe and as enamored about his choice of a wife as she was of them. His old feelings about the estate had returned in full measure, and despite the uneasy mood in the region, he was optimistic about the future. Hannah called his optimism "faith," since he based his hopefulness on his confidence that God had guided him this far and that He would continue to do so.

The morning broke on July 2, with the sun kissing Jed's and Hannah's faces to awaken them from a peaceful slumber. Jed rose, pulled the heavy drapes shut, and attempted to cajole his wife into remaining in bed a while longer by pinning her under the covers.

"I need to help get breakfast!" She giggled. "It's time I started acting like a wife!"

"Bitty and Selma aren't missing you as much as I will if you leave."

Hannah rolled her eyes at his pitiful expression and acquiesced, snuggling into the crook of his arm. "All right," she relented. "But tomorrow, *I'm* going to make your breakfast."

They kissed and cuddled until the enticing smells from the kitchen beguiled the pair from their roost. When they appeared in the bustling kitchen, smiles and elbow prodding passed between the two kitchen matriarchs, Selma and Bitty. Frannie was busy playing with the baby, while Jack, Jerome, and Abel looked on and ate.

"You two just sit on down." Bitty chuckled as she loaded food onto their plates.

"Jed?" Jerome spoke softly. "We're ready to set the waterwheel and grindstones on the mill today. It'll take all the men to do it, so we should head down as soon as you've eaten."

"I'm amazed! You three have gotten us well ahead of schedule."

Jack beamed with delight. "It was all of us. Every man, woman, and child helped."

"Every rock we added to the mill somehow made us feel we were defying Stringham and Dupree," remarked Jerome.

Jed stood and absently looked out the window. "It's believed there are many traitors and British loyalists burrowed amongst us besides Stringham. Since Dupree passes through White Oak arbitrarily, a raid on the farm would likely accomplish nothing, and since the Stringhams are now his prisoners as well, it was wise to focus your efforts on strengthening the Willows."

Jed continued to stare out the window as a cloud of worry passed over his face. Abel sidled up beside him under the pretense of getting more eggs. "Is something else on your mind?"

Jed's eyes met Hannah's, and understanding passed between them. "When Hannah and I came home we passed through Havre de Grace. The British torched much of the city, and what they didn't burn by hand their rockets set afire. We need an underground shelter—big enough for everyone—stocked with supplies and ventilated so we can stay down there for some time if need be."

Jerome nodded as Abel began sketching on the table with his finger. "That would only take us a few weeks to build," the big man noted with optimism.

"Good," said Jed. "Let's scout a site as soon as we set the wheel."

Bitty jumped in. "We need to store up all the food we can gather. Who knows if we'll even be able to plant next year?"

"All right, Bitty. You're in charge of storing food." He looked over at Hannah and realized he had completely sidestepped her. "Oh, Hannah . . . What do you think we should . . . ?"

"I can make jam," she offered timidly. "Selma did teach me a few things when I was little."

Jed swallowed hard. "Excuse us for a moment, please?" Jed asked as he led Hannah out of the room and away from the others. His gentle hands moved to her shoulders. "I'm sorry for neglecting you back there. This is all a little awkward, isn't it?" he probed carefully.

Hannah's expression confirmed his concerns. "I don't quite know where I fit in, that's all. I'm capable, and I'm not afraid to work. Bitty doesn't need to pamper me. She can rely on me."

Jed hadn't foreseen how difficult the transition might be, bringing a new mistress to the Willows when Bitty was so firmly entrenched at its helm. "What can I do?"

"Perhaps all we need is a little time to get to know one another. Things will likely work their way out."

He wrapped his arms around her and kissed her. "I love you, Mrs. Pearson. More than anything on earth. You do know that, don't you?"

"I do. That's why I want this to go smoothly. So you go now, my dear husband, and trust me on this. Everything will work out fine."

The worry picked at his concentration even as they attended to the dangerous task of setting the great mill wheel. He noted how nervous Abel was as he stood on the mill's roof, looking down into the water as he pulled on the ropes to place the waterwheel. "Ever since I saw my father slip beneath that wheel, nearly drowning in the current, water terrifies me. What is it for you, Jed? What sets your knees weak?"

Jed looked at the barn where he saw Hannah and Frannie departing on a berry hunt. "I'm just a worrier in general," he scoffed as he turned his attentions back to the task at hand.

By noon the waterwheel was turning, and the grindstones were set. As the big stones began to turn, a victorious whoop broke loose from the men, and Jerome beamed proudly. "It'll take a while to polish the stones, but she's going to be a fine mill, Jed!"

"This mill will set the Willows' future. And Abel, as miller, you're going to be a big part of that. Our neighbors will bring their grains here too, and that income will make it possible to free everyone else. Right now, I'm ready for lunch! How about you men?"

Jack pulled Jed aside. "After lunch, should we go scoutin' a spot for the shelter?"

Jed looked at his old friend and nodded. "I want to get started on that right away."

During lunch they heard a rider thundering up the lane. Jed leapt out the back door to find Frederick Stringham on his property.

"I came to tell you Captain Blunt is ordering the militia to Fort Warburton immediately."

"How do I know Dupree didn't send you to remove the men from the region so he can plunder the area unhindered?" Jed asked warily.

"You can trust me. I risked my life to send you people news of Bitty's family's death!"

"You mean their murder!"

"Yes! Their murder, but my hands are clean on the matter! I am only able to come here today because I know Dupree and his men are elsewhere right now. That's the reason for the alarm. Cockburn and his fleet have been sighted in the Potomac!"

Jed paled at the thought that the British might be heading for the capital. "If it had been any other rider, Frederick, but I need proof before I'll abandon my family on a word from you."

Frederick's mouth tensed, and he dropped his head. "I also came to ask a favor of you, Jed. Perhaps when you hear it you'll trust my word."

Jed cocked his head. "I'm listening."

"I was wondering if Penney could find refuge here at the Willows if need be. I want to keep her safe, and the Willows is the last place Dupree or my father would think to look for her. Thus I would have an added incentive to keep you warned of Dupree's movements."

Jed looked over his shoulder where Bitty and Jack stood. "It's up to them."

Brother and sister conferred. "If havin' his wife here keeps all of us safer, let her come."

"Tell your wife she's welcome," said Jed. "How will we know when to expect her?"

"I'll post a message the same way I did before, by hanging a bandana in the oak tree.

An icy chill ran through Jed's body "Is this it, Frederick? Are they attacking the Capital?"

"I wish I had something more to tell you. I live my life as a ghost, seeing no one and hearing nothing . . . until today. Godspeed to you, and thank you, Jed. Thank you all."

Frederick galloped away as Jed looked into the worried faces behind him.

"We'll see to the building of the shelter, Jed. Don't worry 'bout that," assured Jack.

Jed nodded silently as he scanned the trees for any sign of Hannah and Frannie. "I can't leave like this," he confessed with choked words. "I need to see them before I go."

"I'll find them whilst you pack," offered Jack. "I'll fetch them on home."

An hour later he was coming down the steps with a bag in his hands and his saddlebag and haversack slung over his shoulder, the joyous mood of the morning seeming like a faded memory. As soon as Hannah flung the door open and saw him dressed in his uniform she stalled on the landing and her eyes began to water. Jed lumbered down the last few steps, his eyes reddened as he moved toward his bride.

"Cockburn's in the Potomac," he began. "I've been called to report to Washington."

"So soon?" she asked with quivering lips. "You're leaving right now?"

Jed's mouth hung agape as he nodded his reply. "I'm sorry. I know . . ."

Hannah pressed her fingers to his lips. "Please . . . just return to me, Jed."

He swept her into his arms, trying to remember the scent of her and the feel of her soft warmth there. He saw Frannie tearing up from afar, and he opened his arms to draw her in. "We never talked about your visitor," he muttered with regret as he kissed her head.

"We will. We'll have plenty of time when you get home," she cried. "And you will!"

"You two ladies take care of each other. Promise me," he said as he tore himself free. Jed found Jack holding Tildie when he hurried through the door. "Get that shelter built quickly," he implored both Jack and Abel, then he set off for Fort Warburton.

CHAPTER 35

July 20, 1813
London, England

Lord Whittington waited in his chambers at Parliament for the report of Commissioners Thomas Griffin and Robert Lively, the men appointed to investigate the atrocities charged in the campaign against Hampton. When they entered his office their faces were drawn and somber.

"Have a seat, gentlemen," offered Lord Whittington. "Thank you for giving me a preliminary report on your findings before announcing them to the whole of Parliament. I take it the information I supplied you corroborates the reports of the other officers in the campaign."

"It would appear that your Lieutenant Ramsey's assessment was accurate. Several other officers' reports concur with his, though Admiral Warren and Colonel Beckwith attribute the grossest crimes directly to the use of the French, a practice we are immediately suspending."

The earl closed his eyes and groaned. "And Cockburn? Is no blame to be laid at his feet?"

The two commissioners looked at one another before Thomas Griffin spoke up. "We cannot prove anything, your Lordship. There are references in several of the accounts to certain innuendoes made by the Admiral . . . promises of pleasure and plunder upon the successful sacking of the town, but no one directly quotes him ordering the men to commit such crimes."

"What of the claims regarding many of the slaves that were freed along the Chesapeake—that he sold them back into slavery in the Indies?"

"We have heard those same rumors, but without proof . . ."

"Without proof?" charged Whittington. "Check his bank deposits! I hear he has become very wealthy while serving the interests of the Crown, as has his puppet, this Sebastian Dupree of whom I've spoken. Is there any mention of *his* presence in the Hampton melee?"

"None in Hampton, though his services in other Chesapeake campaigns have been applauded by members of the Admiralty who are growing increasingly desperate for a decisive and quick end to this conflict," Lively explained. "You must understand, Lord Whittington, while the noose is tightening around Napoleon, this conflict with the French has cost us dearly in men and money, and now that we can no longer use the Chasseurs, the Admiralty is more determined than ever to end this as soon as possible. Some are calling for peace negotiations while others simply want our victory assured. To that end they are counting heavily on General Ross's planned diversion near Washington to aid the battles for upper and lower Canada."

"Which side will bear sway . . . those calling for peace or for a continuation of the war?"

"With battle-tested soldiers returning from Europe? I believe those who press for victory will push our forces to make an attempt on Washington."

"So what will your statement on Hampton say? Does honor still matter, or will we sweep this affair under the carpet and accept that a victorious end justifies the most brutal of means?"

"I beg your pardon, Lord Whittington. We place the honor of this land above all things. Our official statement will include this," he said as he began to read the proclamation. "'From all the information we could procure, from sources too respectable to permit us to doubt, we are compelled to believe that acts of violence have been perpetrated which have disgraced the age in which we live. We confess that the sex hitherto guarded by the soldier's honor escaped not the rude assaults of superior force.'"

* * *

Lord Whittington read Mrs. Ramsey's letter, setting his eyes on the last two paragraphs.

> *I read your letter to Daniel since he was unwilling to open the note himself, but at the conclusion he assured me that were you to come and ferry him home, he would run away and return to me. It appears that your decision to send him away after Clarissa's death has so traumatized him that he has made me the substitute for his affections.*

Perhaps the more prudent course would be for you to allow him to remain here and continue with his tutor, Mr. Healy, with whom he has also formed an attachment, until he has coped with Clarissa's loss and desires to return to Whittington Castle . . .

The earl saw the unraveling of his relationship with his son and again he cursed Stephen Ramsey. *No amount of penance, no redemption, should be able to clear the beast of the agony he unleashed at McGowan's hands,* he thought to himself as he penned his reply to Ramsey's estranged wife, the woman, in hiding herself, into whose care he had entrusted his own son.

He felt as if his heart would break apart whenever he compared his current situation to that bliss he had known just a few months before when he enjoyed the delight of Daniel's love and sweet Clarissa's company as well. He castigated himself for Clarissa's death, believing that if he had been satisfied with their previous arrangement, he would not have been so easily distracted by passions that night and would have responded to the first sound of the intruder.

Swept up in the onerous depths of his own grief, he had ignored Arthur's caring counsel without considering how deeply the events of that evening had affected his gentle son. Daniel's physical safety had been the earl's primary concern, but he had erred in sending Daniel away. He saw that now, and he could not fail his son again. He penned these words:

Can Daniel truly be so angry with me that he would threaten to run away were I to bring him home? He is my only child, flesh of my flesh and my only heir. Aside from England, it is only Daniel that gives my life purpose. Tell him this for me, will you?

If he is unwilling to even speak to me, I will make plans for an extended visit to Dublin when circumstances permit my absence from Parliament. Arrangements are included to secure Mr. Healy's continued services as Daniel's tutor. In the meantime, please tell my son that I am pained by our separation, and that I love and miss him desperately . . .

* * *

Stephen Ramsey had been rebuffed by Lord Ensor's secretary, leaving him no option other than blackmail to obtain the man's ear. The terse, inflammatory note describing his birthmark had been mailed the previous week, evidently sending a shockwave through the House of Ensor that ended in a promise that a representative of the noble would be arriving shortly.

The day had finally come. An interesting giddiness swept over Stephen Ramsey as the carriage rolled up to his opulent London house. He felt like a child at Christmas, about to receive a great surprise . . . one for which he had dreamt and prayed a lifetime.

His butler met the guests on the stoop, and when they were escorted into Ramsey's study, it was not Lord Ensor who appeared, but an ancient, weathered, grand dame, wrapped in layers of gathered brown silk with a large bonnet festooned with more gathers and bows. She leaned heavily upon both a ruby-studded cane and her driver's arm while peering at Stephen over her spectacles, exclaiming, "So, you are Stephen Ramsey, I suppose."

"I . . . yes, I am, but . . . I was expecting Lord Ensor."

"Where shall I sit? Can you not see that I am an old woman?" she barked weakly, sending Stephen scrambling to point out the best chair in the room. "Who *I* am is of no consequence. I thought you were interested in knowing who *you* were."

The driver led the woman to her seat and then was dismissed with a cursory wave of her gnarled hand. She silently studied Ramsey for several seconds before she began. "It was not your threats that brought me here, Mr. Ramsey. They fell on unimpressed, disregarding ears. I am here because, having heard my family titter about your suppositions over supper one night, I felt inclined to come and tell you a story—one that will lay your questions to rest, but one that is just for your ears. I am the last living person who can corroborate it, and since it will soon follow me to my grave, once it is told I shall deny having ever spoken a word of it. Do you understand?"

"Do I have a choice?"

"You correctly identified the source of the Ensor crest—a heart-shaped birthmark that had appeared in one or two Ensor heirs every generation. The fifteenth Lord of Ensor had two children who bore the mark—a girl named Fiona and a son named William. In 1711, Fiona entered into a summer flirtation with Henry, the engaged son of Mr. Mitchell, a member of the House of Commons. A moment of indiscretion produced a son, born out of wedlock, that threatened the reputations of two families and the destruction of young Henry Mitchell's planned nuptials. To quiet the scandal, the Mitchells agreed to arrange for the baby's adoption, but unbeknownst to the Ensors, the Mitchells placed the infant with their childless household servant, Adelaide Pearson, so they could watch over the boy and provide assistance. The child was Jonathan Pearson."

Stephen Ramsey sank into his chair, already able to see where the story was heading.

"Fiona married and bore more children, Henry Mitchell married his betrothed, and the families' secret remained buried. But things became complicated with time. The Mitchells discovered that their secret heir was a gifted scholar, and they sent the boy to the same school where Robert, William Ensor's own son, attended. Unaware who Jonathan Pearson actually was, the Ensors invited him to their home, changing all our fates.

"On Pearson's last visit, Pearson jumped in the lake, and William recognized the birthmark. A single inquiry to the Mitchells confirmed his suspicions regarding Pearson's parentage, and the Mitchells agreed to separate the boys by sending Jonathan to America as an indentured tutor. What no one realized was that during those visits, Bridget Ensor—William's young daughter—who also bore the birthmark, had fallen in love with Jonathan. He was, after all, a dashing, young scholar of twenty-two, quite irresistible to a young woman of seventeen years, despite the fact that he was, by every public standard, beneath her station. He loved her as well, and so, at the first mention of being separated, the young pair began discussing marriage."

"What has this to do with *my* line?" argued Stephen, who felt his hoped-for connection to the Ensors slipping away. "I thought Pearson proposed to *my* mother, Bridget *Lane*."

The old woman raised a knowing eyebrow. "He did. Bridget Lane *was* Bridget Ensor. You see, her parents refused to entertain the union, knowing that the secret would come out, destroying Fiona's and Henry's families. Citing a difference in stations as the reason, they coerced Bridget into refusing him. Jonathan left for America, brokenhearted and alone, and Bridget ran away, rebelling against her noble ancestry."

Ramsey's eyes bore into the old noble woman's. "In truth, she was right all along, wasn't she? Regardless of the scandal, your family never would have sanctioned such a marriage."

The grand dame's head shook slowly. "It's irrelevant now. Perhaps it would have been better for everyone to have admitted their sins and allowed the child to know his heritage. So many lives were affected by denying the truth. Pearson had no reason to love England and her nobles since he believed that social status alone had kept him from having the woman he loved."

"And when did the family realize that Bridget married and had a family?" Stephen asked angrily. "If you felt such sympathy for Pearson, why was no effort made to embrace *us?*"

"Bridget adopted the name of Lane and eventually moved to Liverpool, hoping Jonathan's parents could help her locate him, but the Pearsons had passed away. We begged her to come to her senses and return home, but she declared that she'd marry a pauper before returning to us, and in complete fulfillment of that promise, she married your father."

Ramsey could hear the scorn in her voice. "A sin too great for the Ensors to forgive . . ."

"She did it for spite, not love."

Ramsey felt the old fury churn. "Yet you knew of us! Why not spare her children?"

The woman's voice showed its first sign of emotion. "We attempted to render acts of service through the years, but she would rarely accept our aid. We watched and waited to see what she would pass on to her children . . . if any of the nobility bred and instilled in her would make its way into her posterity. The first five scamps were too like their father, but we had high hopes for you until your choices demonstrated your darker nature. We saw great promise in your son, Arthur, but what will become of him now, once he faces your man, Dupree?"

Stephen shrank in shame. "You know about Dupree?"

"We know many things, Mr. Ramsey," she declared coldly, "and we've heard many others. We know the blood of Lord Whittington's nanny stains your hands."

The woman glared at him and then abruptly called for her driver, who entered and hurried to help her up. Ramsey could feel her disdain for him, and he railed against her condescending attitude. "I don't even know who you are! Why should I believe anything you've said?"

"Because I, Mr. Ramsey, was Bridget's mother."

He heard sorrow tinge her detached voice, and with a momentary hope, he cried out, "Then I am your grandson! I have a right to claim what is mine!" he threatened.

She looked pointedly back at him. "Do as you have always done . . . put your wants ahead of others, but realize that it is exactly that mindset that created this situation. You have no proof, and no one will believe you. I came here so you would know that the people you have set your sights to destroy in America are among your closest remaining kin. I felt you had a right to know that, but what you do with this information is now up to you."

CHAPTER 36

July 28, 1813
Fort Warburton
Seventeen miles south of Washington City

Matthew Copely, the portly Calverton gunsmith friend of Jed's grandfather, studied the structural improvements at Fort Warburton. "We're lucky those Brits got hung up on the Kettle Bottom shoals and couldn't make it upriver, Jed. It's hard to say how this ole girl would've faired if they'd a made it up the Potomac, even with all your militia company's work."

"Do you think they'll try again, Lieutenant Pearson?" asked a soldier named Dixon. "Secretary Armstrong says they don't want Washington bad enough to take another run at her."

Jed winced as he remembered Havre de Grace. "It was Cockburn's respect for the defenses at Annapolis and Baltimore that turned him away from them. We'd do best to have the Capital equally prepared. The British are in the Carolinas now, but sooner or later, whether by land or by water in shallow vessels, I'm afraid they'll be back."

"Shallow barges! That's how the devils sacked Hampton!" ranted Matthew.

Jed's stomach tightened as images of the reported atrocities committed there assaulted him. He had yet to hear from Markus, and the silence tore at his peace of mind. A small gathering of uniformed officers was moving in the men's direction, and Jed studied them for a moment before returning to the task of digging the mud from his boots.

"I wish they'd send us to shore up Alexandria," said Dixon. "Our mayor has begged for help. He's even gone to see Mr. Madison and Secretary of War Armstrong, but no one's done a thing so far. Now see that captain? He's supposed to be some expert at fortifications."

There was something familiar about the captain's bearing, and Jed felt his jaw tighten. At the same moment a corporal was running around the exterior of the fort calling out, "Is there a Lieutenant Pearson here? Has anyone seen a Lieutenant Pearson?"

Jed watched the officer hail the corporal while Dixon shot up, hollering, "Lieutenant Pearson's over here!" drawing the entourage's attention to Jed.

The captain crossed the distance in quick time, reaching him before the corporal had a chance, and Jed's suspicions were soon confirmed. "Captain Robertson." His unease was apparent as he offered a cursory salute. "Lieutenant Pearson. Might I have a word with you?"

Jed knew the hour of disclosure had come, and as he dragged his filthy body up to meet his defeated rival, he regretted not having planned more for this moment.

Robertson led off a few paces from the group, then turned to ask, "Did you find her?"

Momentary guilt prickled Jed's face at the fulfillment he enjoyed in being married to Hannah. "I did," he dodged. "She and Beatrice were on the last leg of their trip to Tunbridge."

Robertson's face twisted with worry. "In June? What was the cause of their delay?"

"The women contracted the typhoid, but both are fine now," he hurried to add. Seeing the corporal hovering ten feet back, Jed wanted to address his concern and send him away, but Robertson returned with yet another question.

"Why didn't she write and ask for help? Why didn't she at least send for her sister?"

Raising his hand to stall Robertson, Jed suggested, "Allow me to answer the corporal's question, and then I'll tell you everything."

Robertson blew out a rush of air before taking an irritated step back. Jed turned to the corporal with equal aggravation and asked, "Can I help you, Corporal?"

The young soldier sheepishly announced, "Mrs. Hannah Pearson is here to see you."

Robertson spun on Jed. "Mrs. Hannah *Pearson?!*" he snarled accusingly as he lunged for Jed. "I trusted your altruism—that concern for her well-being was your motivation for riding north! I might have known you'd exploit the opportunity to prey upon her!"

"It was *I* who proposed, Andrew." The approaching voice was compassionate but firm, and both men recognized it before Hannah moved between her husband and Captain Robertson. "We stopped by Fort

McHenry as soon as we returned to Maryland. We wanted to tell you ourselves, but you had already been reassigned. I'm sorry, Andrew, and I care deeply for you, but I discovered in New Hampshire that Jed and I had been kept apart by sisters who falsely interpreted what was best for me. It grieves me that you were also caught in this deception, but I cannot ignore an attack on my husband's honor when *I* am the one who asked *him* to marry *me*."

Robertson became aware that others' attentions were drawn to the scene. Straightening his shoulders, he led Hannah a few steps away, asking. "Have your parents accepted this?"

"No," she confessed. "But regardless, I am happy, Andrew . . . and I'm free. And now that Jed and I are finally together, you are free as well—free to set honor aside and pursue a woman who will love you as completely as you deserve. Then my perfect joy will be complete."

He swallowed hard, extending his arms to her, and she fell into his pained embrace. "Then . . . congratulations, Hannah . . ." he muttered as he extended a hand to Jed, ". . . to both of you."

Jed noticed Frannie standing nearby, but knowing how difficult the moment was for the proud officer, he kissed his wife and sent the women to the gate to wait for him while he turned back to Robertson. "I appreciate your civility. Your feelings have been her utmost concern."

"You never told her that it was I who convinced you to give her up? Why?"

"I didn't know with certainty who held her heart until an hour before our wedding, and afterwards . . . well, I saw no reason in undermining her trust or hurting her further."

Robertson studied Jed for a moment, then stoically rushed on.

"More than enough suffering has been doled out, and I have more to tell you. You've heard of the Hampton misery? Well, there are some strange ties between that place and your farm."

Jed took a step closer and tensed. "How so?"

"I believe you have a farm manager named Markus O'Malley?"

Jed felt his knees go weak as he struggled to reply, "He's also my friend."

"Members of his family were protected by a young British lieutenant named Arthur Ramsey, who later mentioned the Winding Willows farm. Major Crutchfield asked me to follow the lead to see how he became familiar with your property."

Jed's frustration erupted. "He must know Sebastian Dupree. Haven't you heard any of the reports I've filed about Dupree?"

Robertson tensed and nodded. "Cockburn's guide."

"Yes! He's been headquartered at the farm that borders my property. Someone has set this Dupree against me and the Willows for some reason. He's the man who ordered me shot!"

"He made arrangements with several different farms . . . not just White Oak and the Stringhams, and he moved between them invisibly, making it impossible to capture him. We believe he's shipboard again, conducting raids for Cockburn."

"And yet Stringham is still free."

"We tolerate Stringham for now in the hopes that he may yet prove useful," Robertson shot back.

Jed shook his head at the incredulity of the situation, irritating Robertson further.

"I'm not satisfied that Dupree is this Ramsey's connection to the Willows. I suggest you make inquiries when you get home, and I'll investigate as well. In the meantime, Commodore Joshua Barney has been commissioned to organize a water defense for this region. He's been combing the tidewater for sailors with skills in shallow water, and your friend was on his list until a sopping-drunk sailor was identified as this O'Malley. You can imagine the impression he left. If you care about this man, you might want to head to the waterfront to search for him. He's been in a bad way since Hampton, drinking himself into oblivion."

Jed noted the stiffness in Robertson's voice, and he replied respectfully. "I'll request leave so I can look into it."

"Save him if you can, Lieutenant. Commodore Barney's plan may be our best hope of manning a naval defense if the British come upriver."

As soon as Robertson left, Matthew sidled up beside Jed, who closed his eyes and sighed. "What do you think our chances are, Matthew?"

"We can't beat the British fighting *like* British. I kept tryin' to tell fellas like him. Harry tried too. I offered to train 'em to fight like we did in the French War, but they weren't interested."

"What did you propose?"

"See, we ain't got enough guns, or enough ships . . . not even enough men that know how to fight, so the ones we got'll have to be smart . . . Indian smart. They'll need to track like a hound, fight like a mountain cat, and be as alert as a deer to changes and danger."

"'Indian smart'?"

"They'll need to know where they can hide and where they can set up a trap, and more importantly, where their enemy will set his. They'll need to know where the wind's carryin' the snap of a twig and they'll need to be able to read the streams—where the enemy might cross, know what it looks like before a foot enters it, and what it looks like after. Most importantly of all, they've got to know their enemy—how he thinks and moves and fights. Your grandpa and your pa understood all this last time around. They knew we couldn't stand toe-to-toe with the British 'cause of their numbers. Pinprick attacks . . . that's what we need. Shoot and move into cover. Do that often enough, hittin' key people, and the bulk of the British line will scatter."

Jed's face grew increasingly interested. "Would you train me, Matthew?"

* * *

Jed's steps were heavy as he met up with Hannah and Frannie. He drew his wife into his arms and gently squeezed Frannie's shoulders. "Are you all right?" he asked her.

She nodded and smiled, her relief apparent. "I'm so relieved Andrew knows, Jed. The worst is behind us, now. I hope he quickly finds someone who will love him as he deserves."

Jed tightened his embrace as he weighed the day's twists of fate. "What brought you two here? I don't like you two traipsing about the countryside without an escort. It's too dangerous."

Frannie quickly piped up. "You received a letter from Markus's family, Jed. Considering everything that happened in Hampton, we thought it might be urgent."

The very sight of the letter made him nervous as he considered what his friend could have suffered that would have sent him back to Maryland alone, setting him off on a binge. He broke the seal and began to read. Tears welled and trickled down his cheeks past his lips, which he bit to still their trembling. "His bride and uncle were killed in the attack," he explained to the worried women. "His family asks us to watch for him and send them word if we find him."

"Oh, Jed . . ." muttered Frannie. "I can't believe it. We've got to find him."

Jed folded the letter and placed it in his pocket. "I know where to begin. We'll leave in the morning for the Willows, and once you two are safely home, I'll set out for Markus."

Hannah looked at Frannie and back to Jed. "Since the British are far south now, leave us here in the capital. Frannie's friend Mrs. Whitlock welcomes us, and your old college chum, Mr. Shepard, offers to be our escort. That will set you off two days earlier to find Markus."

* * *

Jed set off the next morning, making inquiries at every establishment along the western bank of the Patuxent, and every place seemed to have a sorrier tale than the last regarding Mr. O'Malley. He finally found his drunken old friend singing a sad little Irish ditty, repeating the words *shule agra* as he wept and drank from a bottle. Jed knelt before him, calling repeatedly to him, but it was as if only a shell of Markus O'Malley remained. Pulling him to his feet, Jed wrapped Markus's arm over his shoulders, led him into the pub, and ordered a pot of hot coffee.

"Let's see some money first. He don't got any. He done sold his horse for that pint," the barkeep stated.

Jed glared at the man. "Just send a pot of coffee over!"

He lugged Markus over to a table and eased him into a chair, his heart breaking with every mumbled, unintelligible word. When the coffee arrived he tried to force his unwilling friend to drink, but Markus flailed his arms, sending the hot liquid everywhere.

"Please, Markus. You can't go on like this."

"I don't want to wake up. Leave me go . . . I just want to die."

"I heard about Lyra, Markus," Jed confessed tenderly. "I'm so sorry . . ."

Markus's head dropped to the table, rolling back and forth. "Don't say it! Don't mention her name. Don't wake me from my dream! I'm twenty-six and I feel as if my life is over."

Wrapping his arms around Markus, Jed finally stilled Markus's quaking body. "It wasn't a dream, Markus," he whispered sadly in his ear. "It was real. Lyra loved you and you loved her, and nothing and no one can take that away from you."

Raising his head, Markus stared into Jed's compassion-filled face. "She did love me, Jed. For a short while I knew what it was to be loved . . . and I miss that. I miss the touch of her . . . the way she made me feel." He began to cry. "They took her away from me, Jed."

Jed turned his head away, all too aware of the tender new feelings marriage had also brought to him and the accompanying fear that underlay those feelings each time he thought about the dangerous times in which they lived. Renewed determination stirred in him—a determination not to let the British war machine roll on unhindered. He tightened his embrace around Markus and tried to rally his friend once more.

"Some batteries are using the name of Hampton as a rallying cry. What happened there and those who suffered won't be forgotten, but you have a chance to take your pain and use it to keep others safe. They're coming for

Washington and Baltimore, Markus. They'll soon come up the Patuxent to the Willows. If you help Commodore Barney build and arm his flotilla, you can make sure they don't do to anyone else what they did to Lyra in Hampton."

Markus stared straight ahead, his wobbly head shifting on his neck as his mind debated the idea. "We've got to stop 'em, Jed. We've at least got to try."

"Yes we do, Markus. Now drink up."

A few hours and three pots of black coffee later, Markus was on his feet again. Jed wondered if his wry Irish smile and wit would ever return, but that worry would wait for another day. Jed laid down cash and bought Markus's horse Donovan back, and the pair set off to find Commodore Barney still scouring sailors' haunts along the waterways. They found the decorated hero bent over a series of blueprints in the back room of an inn where he was quietly recruiting more hand-picked leaders to build his flotilla. When Markus walked through the doorway, Commodore Barney barely even recognized him.

"I hear you're lookin' for men that can captain a ship over the shoals of the Patuxent."

Barney stood up and surveyed him. "I need men I can rely on, Mr. O'Malley."

Jed started to step up and speak in his friend's behalf, but Markus held him back and shook him off, stepping forward to speak for himself. "I was there in Hampton, Commodore. I lost my bride and my uncle that day. I'm not making excuses for my behavior . . . I just want you to know that I know what we're up against, and I'm ready to make my stand."

Commodore Barney's jaw flexed as he considered the man. "I'm sorry for your loss, Mr. O'Malley. You've seen their tactics? Do you know the draw of their boats?"

"Aye. As I said, I know what we're up against."

"Do you, indeed? We've got scant funds and no navy to speak of, yet we're going to take on the greatest naval power on earth. We're going to design a fleet of shallow draft vessels that can carry heavy artillery and still float over the shoals. We'll make them so light and functional they could be transported over land if need be. It's a daring, some would say foolhardy, plan, but it's our last and only hope of stopping them from ravaging us by sea. Are you still ready to make your stand?"

* * *

An hour later Jed held Tildie's reins in his hand as Markus stood beside him on the ground. "So you're sure you want to stay with the commodore now? Don't you want to come home for a while and catch back up with these men after you've had a chance to rest?"

"I need to be busy, Jed. I can't go home to the Willows . . . at least not right now. I couldn't save Lyra, but maybe building this flotilla can help me understand why I survived."

"Then it's as we planned long ago. You'll fight on the water, and I'll fight on the shore."

Markus nodded and extended his hand to Jed. "Tell me . . . You found her, didn't you? Hannah, I mean. I recognize that new look in your eyes . . . that mixture of joy and anxiety a man feels when he has something precious to protect. I know that look . . . You don't need to apologize for your good fortune or hide your happiness from me. I'm glad for you. I truly am."

"Thank you, old friend. We may not see one another again until this conflict is over." Nodding with confidence, Jed ended the painful moment and turned his horse northwest. He crossed the Potomac by ferry and arrived in Alexandria in the afternoon. Then he headed Tildie along the cobblestone streets of the old town, enjoying the merry clip-clop of her hooves. People dressed in their city finery walked along, popping into restaurants and pubs while others, whole families, strolled the banks of the Potomac River, enjoying the view. As Jed approached Mrs. Whitlock's home, the pleasant sound of laughter drifted on the evening air along with the sweet scent of roses, and, for a moment, all was well in the land. As soon as she saw him, Hannah rushed down the stairs and into his arms, making his bliss complete.

"Did you find him?" Hannah questioned caringly.

He didn't want to speak . . . to break the moment with sad tales and war plans. He drew her to his breast and nodded, saying only, "I did."

Frannie stood on the porch between Mrs. Whitlock and Timothy. The hostess called for her maid to bring more refreshments while Timothy and Frannie remained afar, allowing the young couple a moment alone. Hannah eventually pulled back and laid a calming hand along Jed's cheek. "Come and sit for a while," she offered, to which he smiled and followed along quietly. The group chatted lightly for an hour about Washington gossip and the social opportunities the city offered, while Jed remained uncharacteristically taciturn and edgy.

"I need to report in at the fort," he interjected as he abruptly stood. "I just wanted to let you know I was back."

Hannah rose and addressed her hostess. "I'll walk Jed to the ferry, Mrs. Whitlock."

"I believe Timothy and I will join them," Frannie chimed in.

While the foursome strolled in silence, enjoying the cadence of Tildie's steps, Jed replayed the events of the past few days, steeling his determination to learn whatever skills Matthew was willing to teach him. He caressed Hannah's hand, enjoying the last moments of nearness to her, and caught his sister glancing worriedly at him. Noting the compassion registered on her face, he smiled at his wondrously brave sister. "Frannie, we never discussed your recent visitor to the Willows. Who was he?"

Her expression clouded at the mere mention of the man. "Why do you ask now?"

"It was a British lieutenant that saved Markus's surviving family members. Days later, when the family attempted to thank him, he made a reference to the Willows. It's raised some curiosity amongst the military, and they've asked me to investigate recent visitors to the farm."

She rubbed a hand over the prickled skin of her arm. "He was a British divinity student."

Jed's motion stopped abruptly as he spun on his sister. "What?"

"I know what you're thinking, Jed. I thought he was a spy too, at first. I shot him, as a matter of fact! But I confirmed his story . . . and he didn't at all seem like a spy or a soldier. He was gentle, Jed, and naïve. He didn't even know how to take care of himself at the cabin."

"You took him to the cabin? Why didn't you just give him a map of the estate and point out all its weaknesses so he could more fully exploit them!"

"I'm not a fool, Jed!" she snapped.

"No, but neither do you understand the nature of the people we are dealing with. *Naïve and gentle?* A *divinity student?* Please, Frannie! You've been duped by a master charlatan!"

"No! No!" she cried defensively. "He knew about Dupree! He came to warn us, Jed!"

"Of course he knew about Dupree. He's one of his spies!"

"I don't think so!"

"Why, Frannie? Because he was so gentle and innocent?"

As Hannah gripped his arm more tightly to calm him, Timothy interjected. "Hear her out, Jed. You're talking to the very person whose judgment you've valued most in the past."

Realizing the injury his sarcasm was causing Frannie, Jed broke loose of Hannah's grip, walked away a few paces and returned, running his nervous fingers through his long dark hair. "All right. I'm listening. Tell me what he said to make you believe he posed us no threat."

Frannie was at the brink of tears but stood boldly before her brother. "He knew about your birthmark, and that Grandfather had the same. He said the man who targeted you and the Willows did it because of something that had to do with Grandfather. He said he had come to see for himself if we were vile people deserving of Dupree's wrath."

"Frannie," Jed groaned as he placed his hands on her shoulders. "Anyone who has done the slightest research on our family could have said those things."

"But he gave me the name, Jed . . . the name of the man who sent Dupree!"

Jed's interest was clearly raised. "I'm listening."

"The villain's name is Stephen Ramsey. Arthur said he had only a brief opportunity to stop him. He was trying to help us, Jed. You weren't there. You didn't see his face!"

Jed's hands began to slide slowly down Frannie's shoulders, stopping at her arms when the name *Stephen Ramsey* was mentioned.

"That name means something to you, doesn't it?" she asked.

Jed looked at her and then back to Hannah. "The name of the young lieutenant who saved Markus's family was *Arthur Ramsey*." The crestfallen look on Frannie's face told him he had hit a nerve. "What was your visitor's name, Frannie?"

"No," she cried out. "It doesn't make sense."

"His name, Frannie . . . Tell me his name."

"Arthur Benson . . ."

Jed felt her body go limp beneath his touch.

"It could be a coincidence," offered Hannah timidly. "Perhaps they're two separate men."

"Not likely," Jed rebutted, "but the kindness he showed in Hampton bodes well for him."

"He lied," muttered Frannie. "I begged him not to betray my trust, and he lied to me."

Jed drew his arms around her. "Dupree sits safely in Admiral Cockburn's pocket. If this Stephen Ramsey controls *him,* then how powerful a man must *he* be?"

Timothy drew closer to add, "And how close must this Arthur be to Stephen if he has a chance of swaying a man of such prominence? His son, perhaps?"

"What do we do now, Jed?" Frannie asked.

"We wait . . . and we prepare. I am long delayed in my return to the fort. Timothy? You'll look over the women for me? See that they get safely home to the Willows?"

Timothy's arm instinctively went around Frannie as he answered, "Of course. I'll escort them myself." Jed led Hannah aside for a few minutes of privacy before departing, and Timothy turned Frannie to face him. "You fancied him, didn't you?" he inquired tenderly.

"I can't explain it. I'm not one to easily gush, but I felt such a kinship with him from the very first. I still can't accept that anyone could feign that measure of goodness. I just can't."

Timothy tipped her quivering chin up and gazed into her eyes. "Neither of us has had much success being led by our hearts. Look at the disaster I became over Miss Bainbridge."

Still reeling with hurt, Frannie left his comment hanging in the air, and Timothy filled in the silence. "I finally tired of only dreaming of happiness and I decided I should pursue something more real. My lot has been happier ever since."

"But you love her, Timothy. No one should walk away from love without a fight."

He gazed into Frannie's eyes again. "No . . . they shouldn't. But we must try and recognize all of love's opportunities. Stay in the city for a while, Frannie. If for no reason other than that we each could benefit from a dear friend and a chance to smile."

"It isn't in me now, Timothy. I am too numb . . ."

"A friend, Frannie. Let's be that and that alone. I could surely use one. Couldn't you?"

* * *

Hannah adjusted Jed's collar, gazing up at him with eyes that made leaving her all the more difficult. "You wounded Frannie, Jed. You need to mend things with her before you leave."

He closed his eyes and pressed his forehead to hers. "I know. I will, but first, let me just enjoy these last minutes with you. I can't say how long I'll be away beyond my militia rotation. I feel the necessity of accepting any additional training Matthew Copely can give me."

Hannah nodded as she blinked back tears. "By all means, you must go with Mr. Copely."

"I trust that Jack and Abel will build the shelter quickly. Then hurry to stock it, Hannah, and promise me that at the first sign of trouble, you'll herd everyone down there."

"I will, Jed. I promise."

"And please listen to your promptings, Hannah." He pulled her into his arms and closed his eyes. "Oh, dearest God, please keep my wife safe while I'm away."

Hannah pulled away to peer into his glossy eyes. "Did you just utter a prayer for me?"

"You were always right," he whispered. "God does have a plan, and I trust in it now."

"Yes, He does, Jed," she acknowledged gratefully. "And He will help us realize it."

"I believe His plan is both for us and for this land. In fact, I believe that he who distances himself from heaven will never fully comprehend God's purpose for America." He turned her in the direction of the capital and pulled her back against him. "I believe that America is more than a nation or a single people. I feel as if the hope of the world rests in what the Lord can do in such a place of freedom and hope. I don't know what He intends for this land, Hannah, but I know we cannot afford to fail her. We cannot let ours be the generation who squanders the sacrifice of our forefathers or who forfeits the privileges God intends for this place."

Hannah intertwined her fingers in Jed's and raised their coupled hands. "We'll each go and do what we must to prepare, and then we'll see what God will do with us."

HISTORIC FIGURES DISCUSSED OR WITH WHOM THE FICTIONAL CHARACTERS INTERACT

MAJOR GEORGE ARMISTEAD, American commander of Fort McHenry from June 27, 1813 until his death in 1818.

SECRETARY ARMSTRONG, U.S. secretary of war under President Madison.

COMMODORE JOSHUA BARNEY, captain of the American vessel *Rossie*, serving later as the commander of the Chesapeake Bay Flotilla.

DR. WILLIAM BEANES, a physician and friend of Francis Scott Key, who resided in Upper Marlboro, Maryland, who was taken prisoner by the British on their retreat from Washington.

GENERAL SIR SYDNEY BECKWITH, led the ground forces in the British attack on Hampton, Virginia.

BLACKBEARD (EDWARD TEACH), the infamous pirate who plundered the Atlantic during the early eighteenth century.

CAPTAIN JOHN CASSIN, American commandant of Gosport Naval Yard in 1813.

ADMIRAL SIR ALEXANDER COCHRANE, while a vice admiral he succeeded Admiral Warren, commanding the British forces during the final stages of the Chesapeake campaign, including the burning of Washington and the Battle of Baltimore.

ADMIRAL GEORGE COCKBURN, British second in command during the Chesapeake campaigns of the War of 1812, serving under Admiral Sir John Borlase Warren and then under Warren's successor, Admiral Sir Alexander Cochrane.

CHRISTOPHER COLUMBUS, primary explorer credited with discovering the Americas, whose desire to spread Christianity throughout the world drove his many voyages.

MAJOR STAPLETON CRUTCHFIELD, commander of 450 Virginia soldiers at Little England Battery, Hampton, Virginia.

DR. JOHN BEALE DAVIDGE, driving force behind the founding of the College of Medicine of Maryland in 1807.

COLONEL SAMUEL BOYER DAVIS, led American militia and local residents during a British attack on Lewes, Delaware in 1813.

REVEREND JONATHAN EDWARDS, American religious leader who in 1742 penned these words: ". . . the latter-day glory is probably to begin in America."

PRINCE REGENT, (later King George IV), who ruled Great Britain when King George III's health rendered him unable to fulfill his duties as monarch.

THOMAS GRIFFIN, British commissioner appointed to investigate the atrocities committed at Hampton.

ALEXANDER CONTEE HANSON, publisher of the *Federal Republican.* Hanson and his supporters were attacked by an angry mob in the Baltimore riot of 1812.

MR. HOPE, sixty-five-year-old resident of Hampton who was savagely tortured.

COMMODORE ISAAC HULL, nephew of General Hull and captain of the USS *Constitution,* which was nicknamed "Old Ironsides."

GENERAL WILLIAM HULL, commander who surrendered Fort Detroit to the British in 1812.

RED JACKET, CHIEF OF THE SENECA INDIANS who worked to persuade his people to change loyalties from the British to the Americans.

MAYOR EDWARD JOHNSON of Baltimore, mayor during the Baltimore riot of 1812.

LIEUTENANT JONES, American artilleryman at Hampton.

FRANCIS SCOTT KEY, an American lawyer and writer best noted for detention shipboard during the attack on Baltimore, during which he wrote the poem, *"In Defense of Fort McHenry,"* now known as *"The Star Spangled Banner."*

MR. KIRBY, resident of Hampton, Virginia, was slain in his home during British attack.

MRS. KIRBY, female resident of Hampton who was shot in her hip during British attack.

CAPTAIN JAMES LAWRENCE, American, commander of the USS *Chesapeake.*

LIGHT HORSE HARRY LEE, father of Robert E. Lee, was a Revolutionary War hero and friend of George Washington. He was tortured in the Baltimore riot of 1812.

ROBERT LIVELY, British commissioner appointed to investigate the atrocities committed at Hampton.

ALMIRA MACK, daughter of Captain Stephen Mack, cousin to Joseph Smith, Jr.

CAPTAIN STEPHEN MACK, served in Fort Detroit during Hull's surrender in 1812. Brother of Lucy Mack Smith and founder of Pontiac, Michigan.

TEMPERENCE MACK, wife of Captain Stephen Mack, aunt to Joseph Smith, Jr.

MRS. DOLLEY MADISON, wife of President Madison.

PRESIDENT JAMES MADISON, fourth United States president, in office during the War of 1812.

SIR CHARLES NAPIER, British lieutenant, second in command to General Beckwith.

CAPTAIN PARKER, American artilleryman at Hampton.

DR. CYRUS PERKINS, Dartmouth colleague of Dr. Nathan Smith, the surgeon credited with saving Joseph Smith, Jr.'s leg.

CAPTAIN PRYOR, American commander at Hampton.

SARAH ROGERS, disabled artist of Alexandria, Virginia, who painted during the early nineteenth century.

CAPTAIN SERVANT, American military leader whose rifle company met the British army's approach to Hampton.

HYRUM SMITH, brother of Joseph Smith, Jr.

JOSEPH SMITH, JR., prophet and founder of the Church of Jesus Christ of Latter-day Saints.

JOSEPH SMITH, SENIOR, father of Joseph Smith, Jr.

LUCY MACK SMITH, mother of Joseph Smith, Jr.

DR. NATHAN SMITH, professor and founder of Dartmouth Medical School and the surgeon accepted as performing the operation that saved Joseph Smith Jr.'s leg from osteomyelitis that resulted from typhus.

DR. STONE, the surgeon who arranged for the "council of surgeons" from Dartmouth which was led by Dr. Nathan Smith.

MASTER COMMANDANT JOHN TARBELL, American naval leader who assumed command of the *Constellation* following the British blockade that locked her within the Elizabeth River.

BRIGADIER GENERAL ROBERT B. TAYLOR, American commanding officer.

TECUMSEH, Shawnee leader who attempted to rally American Indian tribes to protect their lands. Rallying behind the British, he aided General Brock in the defeat of Fort Detroit in 1812.

ADMIRAL SIR JOHN BORLASE WARREN, British Commander-in-Chief of the North American Station through March 1814.

GEORGE WASHINGTON, first president of the United States.

TWILIGHT'S LAST GLEAMING
HISTORICAL NOTES AND SOURCES

My sweet husband and I spent a week in the Hampton area scouting the locations where the events in this book take place. It was sobering to look out over the landing point where the British began their conquest of Hampton, imagining the approach of vessels filled with enemy soldiers, knowing now what the consequences of defeat were for the men, women, and children of the village. We also spent half a day at Point Comfort. This little point where the lighthouse guided ships to safe harbor and where the first sightings of the British occurred became Fort Monroe, a stronghold intended to prevent any recurrence of the dreadful events of 1813.

I was awed as I walked through Fort Monroe's catacomb-like tunnels and as I climbed upon stone bastions that guarded the entrance to the Chesapeake. At that moment, the debt we children of technology owe to those who carved and chiseled fortresses with bare hands became personal to me. I considered what lazy patriots we can be, regarding our citizenship much as if it were a voucher for passage on a cruise ship called *Democracy*, expecting to be afforded a pleasant journey while being served and protected. Hopefully, current events will remind us that America is not a pleasure ship. She is a working vessel, and we are not her passengers but her crew, in whose hands lie the opportunity to improve her condition and steer her on her divinely intended course, and upon whose shoulders lies the accountability when—by silence or disregard—we neglect this sacred obligation. Allow me to share the sources that have helped me understand this privilege a little better.

Chapter Three
In 1812, fearing the atrocities Tecumseh and his followers might commit if Fort Detroit were to fall, American General William Hull surrendered the

facility to the British without a fight in exchange for promises of protection for the families. He was court-martialed and sentenced to be shot, but citing his courage in the Revolution and recognizing the War Department's failures to properly support Hull's campaign, his life was spared by a pardon from President Madison. Three days after Hull's ignominious surrender of Fort Detroit, his nephew, Captain Isaac Hull, became an American hero and rallying figure. His ship, the *Constitution,* so badly crippled the British frigate *Guerriere,* that her own crew set her on fire as they abandoned the ship, bolstering the hope of America in her egregiously undersized navy.

Chapter Four
The Baltimore riot detailed in book one of the series, *Dark Sky at Dawn,* and referred to in several places throughout this book, occurred in July of 1812. Several Revolutionary War heroes such as Light Horse Harry Lee and General James McCubbin Lingan, as well as other prominent members of Maryland and Washington society, were savagely tortured as a result of their defense of the *Federal Republican* newspaper's right to print antiwar and antigovernment editorials. General Lingan was murdered, and Harry Lee eventually died as a result of his treatment. The depositions of the abused can be found at http://memory.loc.gov/cgi-bin/query.

Chapter Five
The condition of the conquered American soldiers from Fort Detroit as they arrived in Montreal is well documented. Benson J. Lossing's book, *A Pictorial Field-Book of the War of 1812,* completed in 1869, is still considered the benchmark on this war. It can be accessed online at http://freepages.history.rootsweb.com/~wcarr1/Lossing2/Contents.html. Also, three stirring eye witness accounts of the American prisoners' march were given by Peter B. Porter, an American soldier from across the Niagara, and two young British lads whose accounts can be found at http://www.galafilm.com/1812/e/events/detroit_eyewit.html and http://www.galafilm.com/1812/e/people/finan.html. Read more about Red Jacket at http://www.danielnpaul.com/ChiefRedJacket.html.

At http://www.firstpeople.us/FP-Html-Legends/TheCreationStory-Iroquois.html (case sensitive), the beautiful Iroquois creation story is detailed, and at http://historymatters.gmu.edu/d/5790/, you can read Red Jacket's fascinating dialogue on religion.

Chapter Seven

The profligate life of the Prince Regent continued until his death and was summarized by this quote from *The Times* (London), 15 July 1830, quoted in Hibbert's, *George IV: Regent and King 1811–1830*, 342:

> There never was an individual less regretted by his fellow creatures than this deceased king. What eye has wept for him? What heart has heaved one throb of unmercenary sorrow? . . . If he ever had a friend—a devoted friend in any rank of life—we protest that the name of him or her never reached us.

Chapters Eight, Nine, and Eleven

The medical information from which the typhoid epidemic storyline was drawn came from a variety of sources including ER specialist, Doctor Jeffrey L. Fillmore; the student manual for the CES course from The Church of Jesus Christ of Latter-day Saints, *Church History in the Fulness of Times*, 23; the CDC's Web site on typhoid found at http://www.cdc.gov/ncidod/dbmd/diseaseinfo/typhoidfever_g.htm; and other sources noted in chapter fifteen, including the biography of Dr. Nathan Smith entitled, *Improve, Perfect & Perpetuate*, by Oliver S. Hayward and Constance E. Putnam, published by the University Press of New England/Hanover and London in 1998. This last source also provided insights into the highly esteemed Dr. Smith.

Chapter Thirteen

The words and the music for the Irish melody "Shule Agra" can be accessed at http://www.contemplator.com/ireland/shulagra.html.

Chapter Fourteen

Facts regarding the dress and service of dragoons can be found at http://www.mdld.org/.

The movement of the British troops is carefully documented in Lossing's *Pictorial Field-Book of the War of 1812*, noted above, as well as in *Tidewater Time Capsule*, by Donald G. Shomette, Tidewater Publishers, 1995, and *The Burning of Washington*, by Anthony Pitch, Naval Institute Press, 1998.

Chapter Fifteen

Wonderful insight into the art and history of the Gutenberg Bible can

be found at http://www.gutenbergdigital.de/gudi/start.htm. For the basics
on the Bible, including links to explore specific topics, see
http://en.wikipedia.org/wiki/Gutenberg_Bible.

Page five of *Joseph Smith's America,* by Chad M. Orton and William H.
Slaughter, published by Deseret Book in 2005, contains comments
regarding the Reverend Jonathan Edwards and the mindset of Americans of
the era who foresaw a divine purpose for America.

George Washington's Farewell Address, given September 19, 1796,
can be read in its entirety at http://www.access.gpo.gov/
congress/senate/farewell/sd106-21.pdf. In a speech given at Brigham
Young University on 28 March 1976, Ezra Taft Benson, United States
secretary of agriculture under President Eisenhower, and former president of the Church of Jesus Christ of Latter-day Saints, said this about
President Washington's Farewell Address:

> It would profit all of us as citizens to read again
> Washington's Farewell Address to his countrymen. The
> address is prophetic. I believe it ranks alongside the
> Declaration of Independence and the Constitution.

Chapter Sixteen
The story of Blackbeard was included to help put the stories about Joseph
Smith Jr.'s treasure-seeking into some historical context. http://www.ship-
wreckregistry.com/index10.htm, http://www.activemind.com/Mysterious/
Topics/OakIsland/ (case sensitive) and numerous other Web sites verify
tales of fortunes lost to shipwrecks along the Atlantic Coast and the
Caribbean.

Chapter Seventeen
While my tour of Fort McHenry provided me with the layout of the
fort and each of its buildings, Scott Sheads, curator of the site, provided the
majority of the historical background regarding the logistical arrangement
of the militia's camp and the militia's relationship with the regulars.

Information regarding Atlantic coast batteries and forts was found at
http://www.geocities.com/naforts/de.html and http://www.galafilm.com/
1812/e/catalogues/fort_index.html.

Chapter Eighteen
Notes on the 1813 appearance of the White House, the Capitol, and
Washington City came from several sources: Betty C. Monkman's *The White*

House, published in 2000 by the White House Historical Association and Abbeville Press; Mr. Pitch's book; *Spectacular Washington,* by Von Hardesty, published in 2000 by Beaux Arts; and the U.S. Capitol Historical Society site at http://uschscapitolhistory.uschs.org/history/uschs_history-00.htm.

A firsthand look at Washington City and Mr. Madison's inaugural came through the journal of Sarah Ridg [Schuyler], who documented her attendance at Madison's first inaugural and her impressions of the city and Capitol. Her entries can be read at http://memory.loc.gov/cgi-bin/query. The author used Miss Ridg's account of Madison's first inaugural to recreate Madison's second inaugural, finding it the most credible account available.

Biographical information on Dolley Madison came from the First Ladies link on the White House Web site found at http://www.whitehouse.gov/history/firstladies/dm4.html, as well as at http://www.firstladies.org/biographies/firstladies.aspx?biography=4

Chapter Twenty-One
Information on Joseph Smith's leg surgery has been accumulated from a wide variety of sources, beginning with the *History of Joseph Smith by His Mother,* Lucy Mack Smith, copyright 2004 by Covenant Communications; Mr. Putnam and Ms. Hayward's aforementioned volume on Dr. Smith (see notes on chapters eight, nine, and eleven); *Old Mormon Palmyra and New England,* by Richard Neitzel Holzapfel and T. Jeffery Cottle, published in 1991 by Fieldbrook publishers; *Joseph Smith—Rough Stone Rolling,* by Richard Lyman Bushman, published in 2005 by Knopf, a division of Random House; as well as several volumes mentioned above, such as *Joseph Smith's America.*

Dr. Jeffrey Fillmore adds this medical note: "Although germ theories were still decades away, the description of Joseph's illness and infection are comparable with what we know about typhoid fever today. In 1812, medical experts were able to describe the groupings of symptoms and signs that constituted individual disease entities. Some of them occurred as epidemics, such as typhoid fever, which spread from person to person with fever and, in some cases, suppurative (pus-forming) infections of bones or joints."

Chapter Twenty-Five
Juan Corvas's tales of Columbus come from *Christopher Columbus: A Latter-day Saint Perspective,* written by Arnold K. Garr, copyright 1992 by the Religious Studies Center, Brigham Young University.

Chapter Twenty-Seven

The American victory at York proved extremely costly. Though it contributed to the defeat of the British fleet on Lake Erie by cutting off its supplies, it was also the catalyst in a series of retaliatory atrocities, the culmination of which was the burning of the American Capital. Mr. Lossing's previously noted book discusses this in great detail, but for an abbreviated view on the engagement see http://www.galafilm.com/1812/e/events/york.html.

Brief descriptions of the Melville Island Prison and Deadman's Island, the prison's burial ground, can be found at http://www.udata.com/users/hsbaker/melville.htm.

Chapter Twenty-Eight

The character Simon Liston is loosely based on the true-life character of Simon Kenton from the historical account, *The Frontiersmen, A Narrative,* compiled by Allan W. Eckert, published by Little, Brown and Company in 1967. The amazing details of Tecumseh's life and character are also drawn from this historical narrative as are those leading up to and including the horrific massacre at Frenchtown on the River Raisin. Again, Benson Lossing's *Pictorial Field-Book of the War of 1812* provides another specific account.

Lucy Mack Smith's previously mentioned biography of her son Joseph gives many details about her brother Stephen Mack's life and military service, including his service at Fort Detroit at the time of its surrender. However, in the book *Emma and Lucy,* written by Gracia N. Jones, published by Covenant Communications, Inc. in 2005, there is a reference to Stephen Mack having been given the responsibility of handling the prisoner exchange for those souls who survived the battle at the River Raisin. Historical accounts from Mr. Lossing's book state that the Fort Detroit militiamen were pardoned and sent home, meaning they signed an agreement not to raise arms during the remainder of the conflict. Nevertheless, it appears that Stephen Mack was promoted from captain to major and reassigned to conduct this humanitarian mission.

Additional insights into the life of Stephen Mack are available at http://en.wikipedia.org/wiki/Stephen_Mack. His equally interesting son, who is also named Stephen, bears study as well. See http://www.geocities.com/old_lead/mack.htm and http://macktownlivinghistory.com/history.htm.

Chapter Twenty-Nine

The link http://links.jstor.org/sici?sici=0026-3931(196121)25%3A1%3C11%3AIFOCC%3E2.0.CO%3B2-S connects to a historical article which discusses the atrocious consequences of the use of the Chasseurs Britannique in Hampton.

Chapter Thirty

Irish wedding customs can be found at http://www.ireland-information.com/articles/irishweddingtraditions.htm.

One can research the history of the USS *Constellation* at http://en.wikipedia.org/wiki/USS_Constellation_(1797) and http://www.geocities.com/Athens/Oracle/3750/war1812.htm.

Chapter Thirty-One

At http://www.history.navy.mil/photos/events/war1812/atsea/ches-sn.htm, readers can find the details surrounding the USS *Chesapeake's* capture.

The ravaging of the Maryland city of Havre de Grace is described in detail at http://freepages.history.rootsweb.com/~wcarr1/Lossing2/Chap30.html, chapter thirty of Lossing's *Pictorial Field-Book of the War of 1812*.

Information regarding Major Armistead's role in preparing Fort McHenry for war can be found at http://www.nps.gov/history/history/online_books/hh/5/hh5toc.htm.

Chapter Thirty-Two

A map of the battle positions of the British and American forces involved in the Battle of Craney Island is available at http://members.cox.net/2varegiment/craneyisland/679-operationscraney.gif. In 2006, the Old Wythe Neighborhood Association compiled a book called *Hampton's Old Wythe,* which contains maps and descriptions of British movements during the defense of Craney Island and the retaliatory attack on Hampton. A description of the mechanics behind the deadly Congreve rocket is available at http://www.nps.gov/history/history/online_books/hh/5/hh5l.htm.

The events seen and experienced by fictional characters Lyra Harkin and Drusilla O'Malley are portrayals of actual events that occurred during the attack on the village of Hampton. The Kirbys and Mr. Hope were real victims of the atrocities described. Mr. Hope's salvation from his torture came as a result of the soldiers' discovering a woman who had taken refuge in Mr. Hope's home. They spared the gentleman, instead turning their rapacious attentions to her. Details of these atrocities and the resultant inquiry are included in chapter thirty of Mr. Lossing's *Pictorial Field-Book of the War of 1812.*

Chapter Thirty-Three

Under pressure from the Admiralty, Admiral Warren ordered the fleet to leave the mouth of the Chesapeake and set a course for the upper Chesapeake and the Potomac River that ran along Washington. After terrorizing small communities along the shore and on islands in the bay, the fleet was unable to traverse the Kettle Bottom Shoals and forced to postpone its attack on the capital. Admiral Warren was removed as British commander in chief of the North American Station six months later, and Admiral Cochrane replaced him.

Chapter Thirty-Four

Thomas Griffin and Robert Lively were the actual names of the two Britons appointed to investigate the atrocities charged in the campaign against Hampton. The statements provided to them by the British officers present in Hampton and their resultant conclusions, can be read in chapter thirty of Mr. Lossing's *Pictorial Field-Book of the War of 1812.*

Chapter Thirty-Five

Some insight into scouting and fighting tactics employed during the French and Indian Wars can be read in Mary Higgins Clark's book entitled *Mount Vernon Love Story,* republished in 2002 by the Mount Vernon Ladies' Association.

Detailed information on Commodore Joshua Barney and the Chesapeake Flotilla can be read in the aforementioned *Tidewater Time Capsule,* by Donald Shomette.

OTHER BOOKS USED:

The Bible

Bushman, Richard L., *Joseph Smith and the Beginnings of Mormonism.* Place: University of Illinois Press, 1984.

OTHER WEB SITES TO WHICH I REFERRED:

Medical
http://www.hpathy.com/diseases/typhoid-symptoms-treatment-cure.asp
http://world.std.com/~krahe/html2a.html

Map Of Craney Island
http://members.cox.net/2varegiment/craneyisland/679-operationscraney.gif

Musketry and Armaments
http://ccv.northwestcompany.com/musketry.htm
http://en.wikipedia.org/wiki/Breech-loading
http://www.longrifles-pr.com/harpersferry.shtml

Parliament and British Nobility
http://www.chinet.com/~laura/html/titles12.html

Images
http://teachpol.tcnj.edu/amer_pol_hist/thumbnail96.html (U.S. Capitol in 1800)
http://teachpol.tcnj.edu/amer_pol_hist/thumbnail109.html (Presidential election of 1812)
http://teachpol.tcnj.edu/amer_pol_hist/thumbnail110.html (Burning of Washington)
http://www.spartacus.schoolnet.co.uk/LONbuckingham.htm (Buckingham Palace, 1808)
http://www.pbs.org/wgbh/aia/part3/3h253b.html (Black people's prayer meeting)

ABOUT THE AUTHOR

Laurie (L.C.) Lewis was born and raised in the history-rich Baltimore-Washington area where she currently resides. While raising her family, she used her free time to write novels and plays, honing her research skills during a seven-year stint as a science-education facilitator in the Carroll County Public School System. As her children left home, she focused her energies on writing full time, releasing her first novel in 2004. Laurie loves traveling with her husband to research various locales and their colorful people, which she now employs in writing historical and family dramas.

Laurie loves to hear from her readers. She can be contacted through her Web site at www.laurielclewis.com, where other supporting historical information can be found. Laurie's other novels include *Unspoken* and *Dark Sky at Dawn*, volume one of the *Free Men and Dreamers Series*.